W9-BFZ-280

FINSTERWOLDE

SCIENCE CENTER

OIDEION

AUTO POOL

GREAT HALL

MENAGERIE

GONZAGO'S BOWER

GE RANTS PS

SNAKE PIT

THISTLE MAZE

SERVICE ENTRANCE

POISON GARDEN

BOOT HILL

PRIMROSE PATH

THE TANGLE

BAMBOO FOREST

WOMEN'S DORMITORY

HEADQUARTERS

LAUNDRY COTTAGE

RAVEN RAVINE

FOXGLOVE COTTAGE

MASTERTOWN

CASTLE GUY

AVID

READER

PRESS

THE McMASTERS GUIDE TO HOMICIDE

MURDER YOUR EMPLOYER

from the chronicles of **Dean Harbinger Harrow**

The McMasters Conservatory for the Applied Arts
Dean of Admissions and Confessions
Professor Emeritus, Department of Arts and Blackmail Letters
Senior Fellow, International Guild of Murderists

Edited by **RUPERT HOLMES**

Illustrations by **ANNA LOUIZOS**

Avid Reader Press
NEW YORK   LONDON   TORONTO
SYDNEY   NEW DELHI

Avid Reader Press
An Imprint of Simon & Schuster, Inc.
1230 Avenue of the Americas
New York, NY 10020

First Avid Reader Press hardcover edition February 2023

AVID READER PRESS and colophon are trademarks of Simon & Schuster, Inc.

For information about special discounts for bulk purchases, please contact Simon & Schuster Special Sales at 1-866-506-1949 or business@simonandschuster.com.

The Simon & Schuster Speakers Bureau can bring authors to your live event. For more information or to book an event contact the Simon & Schuster Speakers Bureau at 1-866-248-3049 or visit our website at www.simonspeakers.com.

Text design by Paul Dippolito

Manufactured in the United States of America

10 9 8 7 6 5 4 3 2 1

Library of Congress Cataloging-In-Publication Data is available.

ISBN 978-1-4516-4821-8
ISBN 978-1-4516-4823-2 (ebook)

To the Unknown Deletist

Long may you never receive
the credit you so richly deserve

Terms of the Applied Arts

DELETION Our preferred term for "murder" [*vulg*.], although some younger staff have lately adopted "omission" as less austere. Note that while "to delete" is our verb of choice, we do not use "to omit" as an alternative.

EXECUTIVE Preferred term for the individual whose deletion (as in "execution" [*vulg*.]) is due to your initiative. We believe the term "victim" is far too subjective and may not fairly take into account your history and motivation. Although scholars may occasionally use the word for the sake of clarity in a lecture or textbook (such as this), we discourage it in conversation, for if one's conversation has been recorded, the word "executive" sounds infinitely preferable to "victim" when played back in a court of law. Please note that **TARGET** is also acceptable.

EXECUTOR This means you, if all goes as intended. Please note that McMasters places the stress on the second syllable ("ex-ZEK-cu-tor"). Nothing betrays a novice on campus more than calling themselves an "ex-e-CU-ter." This is appropriate only if you hope to be a cowboy.

DELETIST A McMasters graduate whom the conservatory has deemed capable and worthy of performing their target's deletion, or who has already successfully done so.

HOMICIDALIST An unacknowledged executor of the past who managed to succeed in his or her deletion(s) despite the lack of a McMasters education. These noteworthy but regrettably unnoted amateurs have been given posthumous honorary degrees acknowledging their groundbreaking contributions. Distinguished names on this list include Mrs. Bess Weiss (Bess Houdini), Buffalo Bob Smith, first lady Lucretia Rudolph Garfield, Colonel Harland David Sanders, Her Majesty Queen Victoria of the United Kingdom and Empress of India, Dale Carnegie, and Joan Sutherland.

THE ENEMY This term is *never* used to refer to your target. Rather, it applies to those forces who conspire against the McMasters graduate. Under this heading we include police on the local and state level, the office of the district attorney, and scientists and technicians working in forensic laboratories other than our own. We do refrain from using this term in reference to the Federal Bureau of Investigation, as we count so many of their number as alumni.

Death is better than slavery.

—Harriet Ann Jacobs
Author and abolitionist

Agreed. But whose death?

—R. M. Tarrant
Dean of McMasters, 1937–41

It is simplicity itself to fire one's employer. All it takes is some kindling and a match.

—Guy McMaster
Founder

Foreword

So you've decided to commit a murder.

Congratulations. Simply by purchasing this volume, you've already taken the all-important first step toward a successful homicide of which you can be proud, one that would gain you the admiration of your peers, were they ever to learn of it.

This book will see to it that they don't.

Until now, the first-time deletist had few options beyond stumbling blindly in full view of the law. For the sincere and well-intended amateur, courses of study (not to mention the most basic of textbooks and tables) were unheard of. Ask any librarian for a book on criminal investigation and you will be cheerfully directed to 363.2, where sturdy volumes on forensic science and the analysis of evidence await. Ask the same librarian for a book on how to facilitate the demise of your CPA and you will be warily directed toward the exit—or more likely, a security guard will be directed toward you.

Considering the consequences of failure, the McMasters Conservatory for the Applied Arts has for years been the only sensible path for the aspiring expirer. Yet up through the present day the McMasters discipline has been out of reach for all but the well-to-do. After all, it's difficult to obtain a student loan for a school that not only denies its own existence but teaches its students how to deny other people theirs.

Lamentably, McMasters receives no underwriting from such often-generous sources as the United States government, despite so many of our alumni being highly placed there. Thus, McMasters is forced to go it alone, a necessity regrettably reflected in our tuition fees.

On the plus side, room and board at the conservatory has long maintained a coveted (if unpublished) three-star rating in *Le Guide Michelin*.

For years I have urged our trustees to allow me to share some of the basic tenets of McMasters with select members of the discerning public. Its existence in the form now before you represents a lifelong dream: that of placing in your hands, bluntly, an "instrument of peace" to facilitate a Rest in Peace for your intended target. It is my fervent hope that the lessons contained herein will take you beyond the realm of fairy-tale daydreams and help you achieve the true-life happy ending of a deserving someone.

— ♠ —

Everyone says "I could just kill so-and-so," and yet few do anything about it.

For those who consult this guide because you are not yet certain if murder is your best option, I would say that such a decision should never be made lightly. Homicide, after all, is a life-changing event, *not the least for your target*! Before moving forward, you should ask yourself what has come to be known at freshman orientation as the Four Enquiries.

#1: *Is this murder necessary?*

In short, is there no other remedy? How quickly some turn to what they believe is the easy solution without exploring alternate possibilities. Are you murdering your CEO without first attempting to woo his son or daughter? How foolish you would feel, having committed your "crime" with all its risks and travails, only to learn there'd been no need. This would surely be overkill, in the most literal sense of the word.

#2: *Have you given your target every last chance to redeem themselves?*

Search your mind. Have you offered your target the opportunity to change their ways and lead a new and improved life? You will sleep better the night after your murder if you know that, on the day before, you gave your target every chance to wake the next morning. If they refuse to reform, you can proceed with a clear conscience. After all, when the behavior of another person leaves you no choice but to kill them, their murder is simply involuntary suicide.

#3: *What innocent person might suffer by your actions?*

Do not ask for whom the bell tolls. Ask who would mourn in hearing it. If answer comes there none, then more power to you (especially if you are planning an electrocution). But conversely:

#4: *Will this deletion improve the life of others?*

At the end of the day, when our work is done, may every McMasters alumnus be able to say that the world has been left a better place because their adversary is no longer in it.

If you can answer Enquiries #1, #2, and #4 in the affirmative and #3 with "none," then I encourage you to read on with my full approval and the wish that our founder once voiced to me: "May the only justice you face be poetic."

After much discussion and reflection, we believe we can best steer you down the weedy garden path of the McMasters Way by allowing you to vicariously follow in the footprints of past students. **_Be advised_**: Not all those figuring in these narratives met with success, and under no circumstances should you embrace any approach without first learning the outcome of their missteps. Among the success stories of death over life that follow, we also seek to show you where mistakes led to failure, for which a McMasters student can pay as grim a price as they ever intended for their target.

Since the anonymity of our graduates and staff is always a foremost concern, we will where possible avoid using the real names (or adopted aliases) of our student body, even though in revisiting the mid-twentieth century—which many consider to be the halcyon days of dear old McM— most of those who might be at risk from such revelations are now well beyond the reach of the law. Where I am concerned, Fate has been unfathomably charitable, granting me health, time, and several bright-eyed assistants to help reconstruct the scene of so many crimes, with my own copious notes from the period bridging any gaps in my memory.

Bear in mind that hereafter I will be cloaking my normally ebullient personality within the guise of an anonymous third-person narrator (though I would be the first person to cry " 'Tis I!" given half the chance). On those occasions where my narrative may seem to stray into the omniscient, revealing the inner thoughts or private moments of others which I could scarcely have witnessed firsthand, rest assured I am most frequently drawing upon both the shared confidences of those directly involved (often in my role as their faculty advisor) and the incisive reports of the conservatory's recruiting and field agents. And where I write about those most odious to the McMasters *weltanschauung* (worldview), I will attempt to disguise my personal disdain by speaking in as academically detached a manner as I can sustain.

Some may argue that relating examples from the years following the Second World War does not properly prepare one to commit a contemporary homicide. To this I would answer that although the science of our enemy has advanced, the underlying principles of a McMasters deletion are as timeless as the haiku of Issa, the prison sketches of Piranesi, or Beethoven's last quartets. Indeed, opening the door to the Golden Era feels like a gust of fresh air has blown away the stale, cold-blooded calculations of current forensic science or, as we call it, "stuff and nonsense."

You should not be surprised if those who figure in this volume were previously unknown to you. We at McMasters take considerable pride in our lack of notoriety. Consider the legendary homicidalists of ages past: Nero, the Borgias, Dr. Crippen . . . even the unconvicted Lizzie Borden. Think for a moment. What do all these supposedly great killers have in common?

Answer: You've *heard* of them! Shame, and for shame!!! If you take away but one thought from this preamble, let it be that the successful deletist is the *unacknowledged* deletist! I cannot begin to tell you how many McMasters graduates at this very moment illuminate the worlds of entertainment, sports, and politics. I cannot begin to tell you because if I did, they would all be on trial for their lives. It is a frustrating but necessary tribulation for our conservatory that we may never boast of our plethora of successful alumni. A common saying on campus is, "Wherever a murder goes unsolved, there goes a McMasters graduate."

Not everyone is suited for this discipline. Some wish for glory and recognition. They crow of their crimes, write letters to the press, or leave behind any number of heavy-handed clues, simply begging to be caught. We shun and discard such applicants at McMasters! Should you yearn to be infamous or, masochistically, punished—despite all our best efforts on your behalf—then you should proceed no further.

In this volume we will explore a few delights of our labyrinthian grounds: the half-timber shops and dining spots nestled around the impressive Mead Mere Pond; our lyrical gardens of the decorative, culinary, and poisonous variety; our sparkling fountains and gleaming esplanades, sunny swimming lido, Thistle Maze, playing fields, quaint faculty homes, and the dense forest called the Finsterwolde. However, this tome is not intended to serve as a guide to the campus. (The popularly priced *Illustrated Guide* is always available at the Little Bookshop-off-the-Quadrangle, Mussel's Tuck Shop, and the Student Union, cost partially refundable upon the book's mandatory return at graduation.) Rather, it is my modest attempt to replicate the McMasters campus experience for those engaged in home study, via the experiences of past alumni as they came to first understand our methodology and perspective.

Let me close by stating with fervor (we do not like to use the word "conviction") that along with the many practical lessons to be learned at McMasters, there are rich philosophical insights to be gleaned as well, whether you spend your time with us on the conservatory grounds or here in this volume. During the course of your tutelage, I hope you will come to better understand and appreciate the remarkable frailty of all life . . . and that you will learn to live each day as if it might be your enemy's last.

Concerning the Focus of This Volume

In the billions of years during which Life—an indispensable ingredient to Homicide—has been teeming on this earth, from that momentous primordial dawn when one bold amoeba set foot on land with the intent of becoming either a chicken or an egg, it was understandable that the strong would have dominion over the weak. But in recent millennia, flying in the face of Darwinian precepts, we have evolved into a planet where the *un*-fittest not only survive but often flourish, holding sway over their betters in a social order where dim-witted, dim-watted employers all too often lord it over their considerably brighter subjects. We at McMasters call this perversion of nature's intent "the devaluation of the species," and no modern pestilence is more pernicious in our overview than the Sadistic Boss. It is with pride that McMasters offers a powerful helping hand (or leg up) to those under the thumb (or heel) of such oppressors.

Thus, although the majority of Earth's surface is covered in water, there are also a great number of shoe stores, many of which are staffed by one owner, one employee, and a person at the register named Jackie. Each night across the great globe, shoe-store employees return home to their mates and ruin each other's dinner and digestion as they ritually review the latest indignities inflicted by the reviled owner-boss, a despot who occupies more of the couple's conversation than Mr. Hitler occupied in the talks at Yalta.

Of course, repressed rage and seething resentment toward one's ostensible superior is by no means limited to shoe-store personnel. It is the stuff of naval mutinies, prison riots, and convent life.

When discussions grow heated even as the fire burns low in the paneled study of the Faculty Residence, we frequently compare case histories of past disasters, triumphs, and near-misses in search of a unifying theory for the McMasters Method. At such times, I often find myself voicing the sentiment that in all of perdition there is no more unpredictable force of nature than the sadistic employer.

To quote Kipling: *We know what Heaven or Hell may bring, but no man knoweth the mind of the King.* It is important to remember Kipling, if only because none of us are ever likely to meet anyone else named Rudyard. And nowhere in the McMasters syllabus is there a deletion that better embodies the concept of individual sacrifice for the greater good. Topple a despotic monarch in the days of feudalism and a hymn of thanks was sung by indentured servants across the farmland—from serf to turf, as it were. Such remains the case today.

In this volume, I have chosen three students from the same graduating class to lead you by example through the challenges and pitfalls of deleting an employer who lords it over you. Their names are Cliff Iverson from Baltimore, Maryland; Gemma Lindley from Haltwhistle, Northumberland, England; and a woman who for the moment we will refer to as Dulcie Mown, late of Hollywood, California.

We will commence with Mr. Iverson, since he was a sponsored student (his tuition being paid for by a patron) and as such, he was obliged to maintain an ongoing journal of his education so that his benefactor, unknown to him, could be kept aware of how Cliff's matriculation was proceeding (and his patron's investment was maturing). Because of this, we are luckily able to use entries from young Iverson's journal to share with you firsthand the experience of attending McMasters. We shall focus on Gemma's and Dulcie's unique experiences a bit further along in this volume. *A somber note:* Sadly, lessons taught by that cruel mentor Failure are often the most bitterly learned and vividly remembered. Therefore, I advise you in advance that *not all three students* exemplified here will meet with success in their respective missions!

I will add that one of these three arrived on campus with less knowledge of our conservatory than even you currently possess. For while you have displayed unerring judgment in selecting this volume, and clearly aspire to the McMasters discipline with premeditation and at least a modicum of malice aforethought, such was not the case for young Cliff Iverson, who began his studies here in a state of ignorance which I could hardly call bliss.

From the Journal of Cliff Iverson

Although I don't consider myself particularly vain (except perhaps for considering myself more often than I should), I was pleased to have conceived such an expert murder, especially since I'd never previously considered committing one.

My first year at Caltech I had initially pursued a dual major of aeronautic design and English literature, which was sort of like going to Juilliard to study piano and field hockey. As a man without a penny or parent to my name, I was quickly notified that the more-than-generous scholarship I'd been awarded was to develop my budding skills at design and not for any designs I had on deathless prose.

I imagine there are a lot of people out there like me who discover they have a skill at something they like rather than <u>love</u>. But most of us have to earn a living, which is probably why there are any number of accomplished urologists in the world. (And if my sponsor who is reading this journal happens to be an accomplished urologist, thanks for your kindness up until this last sentence and I'll start packing my things now.)

Eventually Caltech led me to MIT, which led me to aircraft manufacturer Woltan Industries, which led me to homicide. This was not entirely MIT's fault. I don't even blame Woltan that much, except for their choice of senior executives, one being my supervisor Merrill Fiedler, who needs to die.

Please understand that by nature I oppose all senseless killing . . . but in Fiedler's case, murder makes perfect sense.

I have no idea if you know me personally, dear sponsor. If you don't, let me simply say my looks have been described by some as studious and by my myopic aunt as handsome, but this matters little where this journal is concerned, for on the day my relationship with McMasters began, my face was concealed by an unfashionable fedora with its brim pulled low, a wig and false beard of straggly gray hair, and a pair of MacArthur-style sunglasses, at a subway station in Midtown Manhattan. My tall frame was cushioned like a department store Santa by a long vest of padding that amply filled a trench coat four sizes larger than my own.

I maneuvered my newly cumbersome form as daintily as Oliver Hardy doing a soft-shoe with Stan Laurel, passing through the gauntlet of a turnstile and down concrete steps onto the subway's uptown platform, and discovered with satisfaction that my target was standing exactly where I'd wanted him to be: Merrill Fiedler, a crisply groomed success story in his early fifties, in town on business for Woltan's Baltimore plant, where he'd been my supervisor. He was currently thumbing a magazine by a newsstand at the south end of the platform only a few yards away from me, precisely as I'd managed to contrive. I needed Fiedler positioned on the platform where uptown trains entered the station. At the far end, the train would already be braking to a halt and might not deliver an instantly lethal blow.

I know. I'm such a nice guy.

But it was the train that would kill Fiedler, I told myself for the hundredth time, knowing this to be the shabbiest of self-deceptions. I had all the intent of a killer but not the soul. Guns, knives, poisons . . . these were murder weapons, all of which I'm too inexpert or squeamish to wield with any guarantee of success. But I'd also ruled out poisons and all other arms-length methods that had sprung to mind, for they seemed too calculated and detached, requiring the meticulous planning of a certifiable psychopath. Then the notion of giving Fiedler one good, hard shove had come to me. Yes, I could probably manage that, particularly after having to restrain myself from doing so for the last three years, each time Fiedler savaged another helpless employee. A shove, a push, a jostle seemed very unlike an act of murder. It was simply what might happen at the beginning of a good old-fashioned barroom brawl, before someone in authority called out, "Now-now, boys, there'll be none of that here!" One justifiable shove for all the demeaning, degrading insults and condescending sneers Fiedler flayed and spewed in all directions each workday.

The telling difference would be that this particular shove would occur while Fiedler was standing at the edge of the platform as the IRT train bulleted into the station.

It was the train that would kill Fiedler.

I had also further reasoned that shoves don't have to be registered with the authorities. One can't test-fire a shove and trace it back to its origin, there's no entry wound revealing its angle, nor does it leave telltale residue. Yes, I might leave a bruise mark, but the oversized leather gloves I was wearing would conceal the size and shape of my hands, not to mention my fingerprints.

In its oafish way, it really was a pretty well-constructed murder method. To any witness on the platform, I was a bulky man in a trench coat at least fifty pounds heavier than my real weight, face obscured by my hat brim, dark glasses, false gray hair and beard. Sure, maybe I looked laughable, a man who might even be remembered by witnesses, but certainly not anyone who resembled myself. I peered over the top of my sunglasses, wondering who such witnesses might be. A few steps away a drab, slouch-hatted man with features and complexion as hard and dark as onyx was waging a duel of wits with a Chiclets vending machine. An elderly nun stood alongside the stairs I'd just descended. A short, muscular fellow directly to my left licked the tip of a pencil stub while laboring over a tabloid's crossword puzzle.

A piercing metallic squeal sounded from somewhere down the tunnel like a tin pig being dragged by a chain through a steel slaughterhouse. I could hear my heart now and feel it pulsing in my wrists and temples. From my research I already knew that this ear-splitting screech occurred eleven or twelve seconds before a train on the northbound track burst into the station. If I were really going to do this unthinkable thing, it had to be now. My target would never be more perfectly in place, thanks entirely to my own ingenuity.

How I wished at this moment I could whisper in Fiedler's ear the same words I'd spat at him on that last degrading afternoon in the Woltan employee parking lot. I'd approached my car to discover Fiedler standing at its rear, arms folded and security guards at his elbows. They'd clearly forced open the trunk and spread out for display the sober black-and-yellow-striped folders reserved for Woltan designs, whose removal from the premises was forbidden. Scattered atop them were a litter of American Communist Party pamphlets laid out for my peers to see, as if the parking lot was hosting a rummage sale. Fiedler had planted them, of course, and he informed me in his most officious voice that I was in breach of the Industrial Secrets clause in my contract, Jacek Horvath and I were no longer employed by Woltan, a report had already been telexed to New York and Munich, and I'd soon be thoroughly discredited and persona non grata in the industry.

I heard my voice but didn't recognize it. "The things you do to people, Fiedler . . ." I flailed. "One day you'll get what's due you." Yeah, that sure showed him.

"I <u>have</u> gotten what's due me," Fiedler answered evenly. "That's why they made me your boss. And sometimes those in charge have to do unpopular things. Surgeons cut people open. Generals order men to their death—"

"We're not patients or soldiers!" I yelled. "We just work here. And when we took our jobs nobody said, 'Incidentally, the real reason we're hiring you is because we have this one executive whose ego takes priority over the well-being of everyone else.' It isn't as if the company had been searching for a house bully and you came highly recommended. Someday I hope it gets knocked into you how you made decent people dread going to work." I looked at the other employees hovering by their cars; they all seemed to have taken a sudden interest in their shoes. At least Cora wasn't seeing this low point in my life . . . but of course, that was only because her own life was over.

"The results speak for themselves, and for me," Fiedler replied with maddening self-assurance. "We're number one in the region."

"Anything good we did on the job would have happened without you. The 1950s are going to be boom years for companies like Woltan, all you've achieved is making life harder for all of us!" I moved to square off with him but the security guards blocked my way. "Woltan's a good fit for you, but you'd be as happy running a prison or a hospital, you wouldn't care. You just need to be The Boss."

But now, on the subway platform, Fiedler had no security guards, and the train would soon be upon us or, more importantly, upon Fiedler. The curved rails leading from the subway tunnel into the station were beginning to glow where the long beam of the front car's headlight was hitting them. I was about to become a murderer.

Who'd have thought my life would have come to this? The only law I'd ever knowingly broken was white wine with steak . . . What would Cora think of me, in this ridiculous costume and about to do this unspeakable thing? I shook off second thoughts by picturing the horrified passengers on the W-10, that I'd designed, as its cabin suddenly went dead quiet, its electrical power as lost as every soul on board, its stabilizer locked and gently tipping the plane's nose toward the ground ten thousand feet below. If I hesitated now, surely I'd never have this chance to save them again.

My intended victim was looking down the tunnel, impatient for the arrival of the train that would kill him. I eased up behind him, my brain madly replaying images of the damage he'd already done or might do. Push him. For Cora, for my friend Jack Horvath found dead in a filthy city park, for every unlucky worker whose life Fiedler had ruined or spirit he'd smothered, for the children who might fly on a W-10 someday trusting their parents had known what they were doing when they'd purchased their tickets. Rage built in me until it was not now just about Fiedler but all that was wrong in the world, with the remedy requiring nothing more than ramming this pompous peacock as the train rocketed into the station.

No longer in control of what I was doing, I lowered my shoulder and drove my body into Fiedler's left side like a halfback making a crucial block. With that impact, I joined the ranks of those who have killed, from Cain to soldiers defending their homeland, from the guard pulling the switch at Auburn prison to children stepping on centipedes, some with society's blessing and monuments built in their name, others cursed by their species and deposited in unmarked graves.

The angle of my shove did not let me see Fiedler's face, and I ricocheted away like a carom shot in billiards as I heard cries of alarm. I felt strangely uninvolved in what had happened, my only thought now being to vacate the platform, rush up the stairs through the nearest turnstile and, as per my plan, head for the revolving door on the far side of the station into the understaffed bargain basement of Brandt's Department Store. Once inside, I threaded my way through a maze of haberdashery display tables and entered a portal leading to the men's changing rooms. Inside one of the tiny cubicles, I pulled the gloves from my hands, stripped off my coat, beard, wig, and padding, brazenly leaving them on the wooden bench beside me. In the unlikelihood that anyone would connect these clothes with the regrettable accident on the subway tracks, they surely couldn't be linked to me, as I'd purchased each item at different Army & Navy stores around the city only the day before. I allowed myself two seconds to straighten my hair and appraise my demeanor in the changing room's mirror. Not the face of a killer, I thought. No triumph in my expression, just the sadness of knowing my life would never be the same.

I left the changing room and feigned passing interest in a display of wool ties as if I had all the time in the world, then deftly stepped onto the escalator up to the ground floor. A breathless salesman sprayed me with a sample of cologne, but I shrugged him off with a breezy "Not today, thanks!" and allowed the store's ever-revolving door to scoot me out onto the sidewalk. Face down, I entered the thick of seething pedestrians, all with missions of their own but surely none like the one I'd just completed. I envied them their easier burden, my newly minted secret being a leaden knapsack I bore to the grandly outmoded Van Buren Hotel and Ballrooms where I was staying. Once in my room and more exhausted than I'd ever known, I fell upon the thin blanket on my undersized bed in what could best be called a swoon, and slept with the solace of knowing I'd committed a perfect murder.

A few minutes later, the phone in my room rang.

I reached for the receiver, reassuring myself that absolutely no one on earth knew I was registered at this hotel, so the call could not be personal. "Yes?"

"This is the front desk, Mr. Williams." (Williams had been the blandest name I could think of after Smith or Jones, easily forgettable unless one's first name was Ted.) "Some detectives from the police are on their way up to see you. They said not to tell you, but I'm doing so as a hotel courtesy. Should they ask, I didn't tell you."

I heard the rolling back of the elevator door down the hall and, before I could imagine a more innocuous reason why the police would wish to visit a stranger to New York only a few minutes after he'd murdered someone, I heard three not very polite pounds on the door, followed by "Police, Mr. Iverson! Let us in."

Jesus, I thought—I have my spiritual moments given the right circumstances—they know my real name! My mouth went instantly dry as if a cup of flour had been tossed down my throat. How, how could they possibly know who I was? The only other way out of the room was the fire escape to the street eight stories below, and with flight being evidence of guilt, I summoned all the bravado left in me and discovered there was none. I felt both corners of my forced smile twitching like a jumpy nerve as I opened the door. "Yes?" I asked, striving for the puzzled tone of a model citizen.

I found myself inspected by a charcoal-faced man in a slouch hat and gray suit. His cheap tie looked like an obligatory birthday gift from an unloving wife. He showed me a billfold designed solely for the purpose of displaying a badge bearing the seal of New York City. "Captain Dobson," he said, saving me some reading. "This is Sergeant Stedge."

Stedge was a short, muscular man inadequately contained by

the seams of his rayon suit. He sported an identical tie to the cap-tain's, indicating either that he was having an affair with Dobson's unloving wife or that they'd bought their ties at the same store from a display labeled "None Over a Quarter." The handle of a police revolver peeked from behind his left lapel where it nestled uneasily in an ill-fitting shoulder holster.

"Where were you the last hour or so?" Dobson asked without preamble.

Despair set a place for itself at the table. Was it always this easy to catch a murderer? One sentence in and we were already at the opportunity stage. "At the newsreel movie theater in Grand Central."

"What did you see?"

I pretended to search my mind. "Uh, Tom and Jerry cartoon, newsreel, travelogue about Morocco, Three Stooges, short subject on glassblowing."

"Anyone see you there?" asked the sergeant.

"No, I'm from out of—wait." Trying to sound spontaneous, I moved to the tiny dresser across from my single bed. "There," I said, pointing to my watch, wallet, and a fragment of thin red cardboard. "I still have my ticket stub."

Dobson had not taken his eyes off my face, but it seemed safe to assume he didn't have a schoolboy crush on me. "Were you plan-ning to ask why I want to know where you were?" he asked with genuine curiosity. "See, usually when I ask someone for an alibi, they want to know why."

"Well, I assume there's been some crime committed in the hotel and you're talking to all the guests," I said casually. "But yes, I would like to know what this is about."

Dobson picked up the ticket stub. "Someone pushed your boss into the path of an IRT subway train today."

"My God!" I reacted. It may not have been the very best read-ing anyone's done of that line.

"You must really have enjoyed the Three Stooges," he continued. "I don't know many people who save their ticket stubs as souvenirs. If you'd found it in your pants pocket with some lint attached to it,

I'd understand. But there it is, proudly sitting with your watch on the dresser when there's a wastebasket right next to it. Why would you hang on to it, unless you wanted proof of your alibi?"

"I don't know. Haven't you ever emptied your pocket, found an old gum wrapper, and didn't throw it away?"

"No, not really," said Dobson. "But maybe that's me. And maybe this is you." From his breast pocket he produced a larger translucent envelope containing a pair of MacArthur sunglasses identical to those I had bought the day before.

So I was sunk. If Dobson knew enough to show me those sunglasses, then he had me dead to rights. I wondered if they planned to arrest me here and now. I sure would have liked a last beer before going to prison. I doubted they had beer in the death house. Certainly not draft. Suddenly, life imprisonment and a job in the library sounded like a vacation in sunny Madrid.

My eyes went to the hotel room window.

"There's a man posted at the bottom of the fire escape," Dobson mentioned helpfully. "Now about these glasses. And your . . . disguise." His voice put the word in quotes. "See, a good disguise is shaving off a beard you've had for five years. Or if you're a nun, wearing lipstick and eye makeup. Even just looking ho-hum is pretty useful. If I ask someone for a description, and they say average, I have no idea what to do with that. But if they say a man wearing sunglasses on a subway platform, in a padded coat, fedora, and false whiskers . . . well, I may not know what you look like, but if I can find your disguise, I've got you."

"I have no idea what you're talking about."

"You bought a ticket at the newsreel theater early this morning, watched until the hour of short subjects repeated itself, got into your clever camouflage, somehow lured Fiedler onto the subway platform—I'll give you an A for that—then you did your nasty little deed and raced into the basement level of Brandt's to lose your disguise. Ever hear of shoplifters?"

Sergeant Stedge answered the question for me. "Brandt's has. People pinch something, step into a changing room to remove the price tags, and hide the goods on their person. So the store will post operatives posing as shoppers near the changing rooms, to watch for customers who exit a little larger than when they went in."

Dobson explained, "But a friend of mine, Dave Vlastnoff—retired cop, works for Sentry Security—saw a bulky, bearded man enter an otherwise empty changing room and a minute later the lone occupant departed clean shaven and a lot lighter. He followed you up the escalator and, pretty brilliantly, sprayed you with a new cologne that's available only at Brandt's."

I managed to bleat, "I'd like an attorney."

"So would my kid sister but she settled for a plumber," answered Dobson. "By the way, in your eagerness to remove your mystifying disguise, you must have taken your gloves off first, leaving a pristine print on the sunglasses' right lens. So: a man in a ridiculous disguise pushes your former employer into an oncoming train, your fingerprints are on the glasses and in the cubicle where you removed the clothes, a professional security guard followed you from the changing rooms to here, and by the way, we've had a police Labrador brought to the lobby who's decided he loves the cologne you were sprayed with and can't wait to meet you."

"The name is Wanderlust," Stedge offered helpfully. "The cologne, I mean. The Labrador's name is Roscoe."

I sat on the bed without realizing I'd done so. "I have nothing to say."

"I do," said Dobson. "You're under arrest for the attempted murder of Merrill Fiedler."

"Attempted?" I bolted to my feet. "He's not dead?"

Dobson and Stedge looked at each other with infinite pity as I realized the words "He's not dead?" could be used against me in a court of law. Despite the miraculously good news that I'd evaded the electric chair, the nearly-as-bad update was that I'd be going to prison for attempted murder while Fiedler was alive and free to be a menace to the world.

Dobson consulted his sidekick. "Coupled with the physical evidence and obvious premeditation, what would you figure he's got coming?"

Stedge's shrug threatened the stitching of his jacket. "Maybe twenty years, and if you ask me, it ought to be without parole. I mean, amateur killers are a danger to the public. Somebody could get hurt."

I decided I'd nothing to lose and, adopting a look of defeat, held out my wrists to Stedge, right atop the left. "Go ahead, cuff me," I said with what I hoped sounded like resignation. Stedge seemed to approve my wisdom and, as he reached for a pair of handcuffs in his pants pocket, I lunged forward and my already outstretched right hand yanked Stedge's .38 from the loose nest of his shoulder holster. "Okay, both of you freeze and I won't need to hurt you," I warned. "Now I'm backing out of this room with the gun pointed at the doorway, and you're staying here while I take the elevator to the lobby." Actually, I planned to take the fire stairs to the second-floor ballroom, which surely would require access to the hotel's kitchen, and from there to a service entrance onto the street. But there was no need to tell them that.

Stedge gently counseled, "Uh, the safety catch is on, Cliff."

I reflexively looked down at the gun as Dobson interjected, "No, the sergeant's pulling your leg. Revolvers don't have safety catches."

Stedge disagreed. "Smith and Wesson Model 40 does."

"That's a grip safety."

"It's still a safety," said the sergeant, adding, "Oh, and Cliff? The gun isn't loaded. But the captain's is."

I turned to see Dobson with an identical .38 trained on me. Dobson explained, "The sergeant likes to make his empty gun a tempting prospect. Trying to steal an officer's weapon is further evidence of guilt."

I pointed the gun toward the bathroom and pulled the trigger. Its click was humiliating.

"Give my sergeant back his weapon and we won't mention this awkward incident in our report," Dobson suggested.

I handed Stedge his gun. "I was never going to shoot either of you," I said, as if they might wish to understand me better. "There's only one person in the world I want to kill, and I thought if I could get away from you, I might have a second chance." I looked at their passive faces and mumbled, "You can't understand."

"Sure we can," said Dobson. "Fiedler's a thug who controls and manipulates everyone around him for pleasures sadistic or sexual, or for successes that boost his career. Sometimes he can pull a hat trick and score all three. He's robbed you not only of your promising career but also of a woman you had a thing for and a friend you genuinely liked. And he's covering up a major defect in a modification he made in your design that sooner or later could result in a terrible end for a lot of innocent people. What else could lead a decent guy like you to attempt murder?"

I was stunned. "How . . . could you learn all that just in the time since—"

"Oh, we've taken a personal interest in you for weeks. We were on the platform when you pushed Fiedler." He nodded toward Stedge. "The sergeant here was the heroic passerby who yanked Fiedler away from the tracks."

I looked at Stedge and said, bitterly, "I guess I should have tried to kill you first."

The two men apparently found this amusing, but then Dobson inquired in a more serious tone, "So tell me, Cliff: No regrets for what you did?"

I tried to retrieve a remnant of dignity from this fiasco. "Only that I didn't do it right."

Dobson's response was yet another surprise. He hit me between my shoulder blades with the flat of his hand, like a congratulatory slap on the back. "That's the right attitude!" he enthused. "You gotta get right back on, just like falling off a horse."

"Which is a great way to kill someone, incidentally," added the sergeant in a helpful manner.

They both looked almost pleased with me, as if I'd successfully completed some unholy hazing ritual. I sputtered, "What . . . what kind of policemen are you?"

"The best where you're concerned. Excommunicated."

"The badge you showed me is fake?"

"Real but expired. Eighty-Third Precinct out of Bushwick."

Stedge took a tiny gunmetal flask from his breast pocket. "A man we had in custody also expired, that's why we got defrocked," he explained. "He was a wealthy child molester who went free by paying off the right jurors. We were driving him back to his estate in Alpine, New Jersey, but he stopped in Edgewater, because that's where people stop when they fall off the Palisades cliffs." Stedge smiled as if this explained everything, stepped into the room's tiny bathroom, and took a tumbler from the sink.

"So . . . you're not going to arrest me?" I asked, feeling a multitude of angel feathers brushing my face as I rose from an abyss into radiant light. "What about Fiedler?"

"I showed him my shield and explained there's been a rash of subway shovings," said Dobson. "Told him we were hot on the heels of the perpetrator."

"Which we were," said Stedge, pouring the contents of the flask into the tumbler.

"Then I'm free to go?" I asked in disbelief.

Dobson's features became dour again, obviously their default position. "And try to strike again, just as ineptly? The hell with that. You're in desperate need of some schooling."

The sergeant produced a half-pint bottle of Early Times from his hip pocket and topped off the tumbler's unknown liquid with a generous slug of the bourbon. He stirred the contents with his pinky and handed me the murky bathroom glass. I stared at the tumbler and commented, "And so beautifully presented. How do I know it's not poison?"

"You don't. You just have to take our word," Dobson acknowledged.

"Shame on me for doubting you after all the minutes we've known each other!" I said, scolding myself. "Then again, if you'd handed me poison a moment earlier when I thought I was under arrest, I probably would have drunk it."

"It's a kinder version of a Mickey Finn," explained Dobson. "With our assistance, you'll just be able to make it through the lobby and into a cab. After that, you'll be leaving everything to us. Down the hatch."

Foremost in my mind was that Fiedler was still living, but also living in ignorance of my desire to kill him. If I refused to do what these ex-cops said, they could turn me in, and that would be the end of that. Better to give Dobson and Stedge the impression that I was cooperating, find a way to break free, and take a second stab at killing Fiedler, perhaps literally. I drank the potion with the abandon of a Dr. Jekyll who's just learned that a fortune has been bequeathed to any man named Hyde.

"Oh, and when you wake," added Dobson, "your head will be bandaged so you can't see where you are. Don't panic. When new students regain consciousness, they sometimes think they've gone blind, or worse."

What was he talking about? "Students . . . ?"

"All in good time," said Dobson. "You're getting a reprieve."

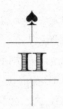

II

As young Cliff Iverson was both figuratively and literally in the dark during his journey to the conservatory, I shall briefly recount his initial arrival here at McMasters. Once he was able to view his surroundings, I will again let his journal speak for him. —HH

All first-time entrants to McMasters must stop dead at its palatial main gate, an outsider's sole entry point in the nine-foot-high wrought iron fence surrounding the twelve-hundred-acre estate. The fence's black iron pickets are spaced more closely than bars on a prison cell door, and each is crowned with a pointed, razor-sharp finial that resembles the ace of spades, this perhaps intended ironically, yet the barbs serve their purpose all the same.

Signs placed at intervals along the fence warn that it is electrified. Three squirrels and a large crow lying dead at the base of the fence lend the ring of truth to this admonition. (Needless to say, the animals were taxidermically treated after dying of natural causes; McMasters forbids cruelty to nonhumans or making them unknowing accomplices to our endeavours.)

The left side of the ornate gateway displays a distinctive coat of arms: an inverted Egyptian ankh symbol of life flanked by a solemn cat and owl. The right side bears a bronze plaque offering a terse explanation for the forbidding fence: MCMASTERS HOME FOR THE CRIMINALLY INSANE. This declaration, intended to both satisfy and deter the curious, is not without an element of truth as well as whimsy, for our students certainly have criminal intent and our faculty might be deemed unbalanced for assisting them. But while there may be madness in McMasters methodology, our curriculum has proven itself to be of sound mind and student body.

Were you yourself to attend McMasters in propria persona, it is unlikely you would ever view this gate from the outside. Candidates for admission travel from their part of the globe to the nearest city offering a harbour or private airport. From there, the candidate is escorted to the campus under sedation wearing a head bandage to prevent sight. All efforts are made to muddle perception of how long or by what route the journey to McMasters takes. Some living in close proximity may travel longer than those from the other side of the globe. Back in the late forties, one hapless student was launched on a four-day voyage by cargo freighter, then taken by chartered airplane on a three-hour flight that landed on the same airstrip from which it had departed, and concluded their journey by pony cart, this itinerary being even more remarkable because the student lived but sixteen miles south of the school.

Many undergraduates firmly believe they are in some part of the United Kingdom, and although we are international in terms of faculty, student body, and scope of studies, the atmosphere here *is* decidedly British. This is in no small part because a majority of the buildings both grand and humble that dot the realm of McMasters were veritably plucked from a far-ranging estate in Derbyshire named Oxbane, whose Victorian Gothic manor was a major expansion of a seventeenth-century mansion built on the gritstone remains of a Norman fortress.

How founder Guy McMaster came to acquire his family's estate is a chilling story best left untold here, one that he himself shared with me as a deathbed confession. (Precisely *whose* deathbed we were at when Guy made his boastful confession is a private matter.) But immediately upon procuring the family seat, Guy had its mansion disassembled, numbered, and transported to its current clandestine setting, along with its millhouse and wheel, gardener's cottage, stables, lodge, guesthouses, bungalows, chapel, Grecian Revival folly, and more. Guy rechristened the manor house and its wooded surroundings "Slippery Elms," and the estate stands today virtually identical to its original ground plan. Whilst hopscotching the globe to compound his family fortune, Guy would delight in bringing home some architectural folly that might otherwise have faced the wrecking ball and further ornamented the old estate as a millionaire might enrich and expand a lavish model train layout.

In the same way that the Bronck family farm gradually became "Bronck's Land," then "the Broncks" [*sic*], and at last the Bronx, so Guy McMaster's relocated estate quickly became known (to the few who were permitted to know it) as "McMasters," forever shedding its apostrophe. A series of obligatory accidents befell those who'd supervised the move, and soon the conservatory's whereabouts were a secret to all but a few trusted souls—though I readily concede we experience four distinct seasons, and those treading through snow to a hearty breakfast in the Great Hall will affirm we are probably not situated anywhere near Palm Springs.

The school's wood-panelled station wagon pulled up outside the main gate, steered by Captain Dobson, who preferred to drive. He turned to his sergeant. "Do the button-pushing, will you, Carl?" he requested. "I hate the rigmarole and I can't remember what my password is today."

"Sure thing, Captain," said Stedge. In the company of third parties, he always addressed him by his former rank, even though Jim Dobson had been stripped of the title years earlier.

"And watch not to brush the electrified fence," he reminded. "It packs a punch."

The sergeant stepped from the wagon, grateful to stretch his legs. Dobson looked back at the car's other passenger, whose head was swathed in medical gauze like the Invisible Man minus the eyeholes. "Almost there, Iverson."

"After the bandages come off, will I be beautiful, Doctor?" asked Cliff through the bandage. There was a hole in the gauze near Cliff's mouth to facilitate drinking through a straw, but it was not conducive to chatter.

A small green box was mounted on a waist-high pole just in front of the fence, and Stedge pushed a button on it marked "Talk."

Cliff's hearing, heightened by visual deprivation, discerned a metallic voice coming from the box. *"Yes?"*

"The Knocking at the Gate," was Stedge's reply.

"Here's a knocking indeed!" replied the tinny voice. *"State your name."*

"Thomas de Quincey."

"Hello, Sergeant. All clear?"

"Yes, Mr. Pashley."

"What have you got for us?"

"Myself, Captain Dobson, and one incoming freshman. That's it."

With an electric buzz and an impressively deep-seated creak, the black gates opened and Stedge quickly returned to the station wagon. Dobson drove the station wagon through the gates, which closed like a sprung trap behind them, and guided it along a paved, russet-colored roadway edged in brick that led into thickly wooded terrain.

The last stage of their journey had been a forty-hour drive with few rest stops and only an abbreviated night's sleep in a motor court. Normally, neither Dobson nor Stedge would be saddled with the tedium of escort duty, but Cliff was different from other students, most of whom had enrolled voluntarily, understood what they were getting into, and paid for the privilege themselves, either in full or on the school's installment plan, which included permanently altering one's will to leave a tidy bequest to the blandly named Alumni Fund.

After driving a mile along the wooded roadway, Dobson abruptly stopped the station wagon and muttered, "Okay, let's do it here." Cliff anxiously wondered what "it" was and grew even more concerned when, after being assisted out of the car, he heard what sounded like a switchblade flicking open. As his arms stiffened, Dobson soothed, "Relax, Cliff, the sergeant's just cutting off the bandages, now that we're inside the gate." The gauze was expertly slit and removed in one piece . . .

———————————————— ♠ ————————————————

From the Journal of Cliff Iverson

I had no notion how long I'd been in transit, dear X, slipping in and out of my drugged state. Three days, six? My, how time flies when you're having Finn (Mickey). I remembered being on the water at one point, but whether it was a lake, a smooth transatlantic crossing, or down the mighty Mississip' on the paddle wheeler Natchez Queen I couldn't say.

My bandages were cut and fell from my face. I had to squint from the sudden light after prolonged darkness but I could see I was standing near a grove of birches. Freed of the bandages' filtering, a rush of sweet woodland odors invaded my nostrils. Pine, pear, fermenting fallen apples—

"You want a last cigarette?" asked Stedge.

"Not if it's followed by the words 'ready, aim, fire,'" was my reflex and apprehensive response. "My eyes are just getting used to the light and I was hoping to see another sunrise."

Dobson gave Stedge a look of reproach for his thoughtlessness. "The sergeant means you won't be able to have another smoke after this. No smoking for students anywhere on campus. Cigarettes and their butts can betray you with investigators. Lipstick prints or brand names on a cigarette butt, tobacco stains or identifiable ashes, a misplaced matchbook, all certain trip-ups. Besides . . . smoking can kill you."

I hoped someone other than these two strange cops would soon explain what was going on. Thus far, I had only their say-so that I wasn't being kidnapped . . . and incidentally, I was. But they'd been surprisingly decent traveling companions this last day and a half while the induced stupor was allowed to ebb slowly from my brain. I'd rambled a bit about Fiedler and his reign of terror at Woltan Industries, but they seemed to know almost as much about this as I did, even that he was considered to be the most likely catalyst in the unexpected suicide of Cora Deakins, a young woman at Woltan whom I had very much cared for. Likewise the death of my colleague and friend Jacek "Jack" Horvath.

The trees were spaced so tightly together in this part of the woods that the forest seemed to be closing in on me. The leaves were tinged yellow as if with a touch of jaundice—

Suddenly something swept across me as if my chest had broken the tape at a finish line. In the same instant, there was a loud punching sound on my right. I turned to see an arrow now embedded in a white birch tree, its fletching feathers quivering as if from fright . . . but of course I was the frightened one, adrenaline surging into my chest where it might have been skewered.

I was even more alarmed to see a uniformed squad approaching me, men in navy gym shorts and tee shirts, women sporting scarlet-belted PE suits with notched collars. They were clearly being led by a robust, chestnut-bearded man in his early thirties, from whose right hand dangled a formidable longbow. He announced to the gym-clad group in a tuneful accent, "There now, you see? The Hunting Accident! So straightforward, regrettable, and forgivable! Where else can you take a jaunt on a sunny day carrying weaponry whose sole purpose is to kill whilst bearing a government license permitting you to do so? Now, if you spotted a stranger in the underbrush behind your house carrying a double-barreled rifle, you'd call the police. Yet put a red peaked cap and hunting vest on him . . . and he's an outdoorsman!" He sobbed in mock hysteria,

"I—I heard a rustle in the bushes and fired, not knowing it was dear old Trevor bagging a quail he'd just shot!"

The group's amused reaction annoyed me and as I felt my heart still pounding like a toy tom-tom, I glared at the bearded man and snapped, "Hey!"

"Yes?" he responded, taking me in for the first time.

"You could have killed me!"

The bearded man gave me a bewildered smile. "Well . . . of course."

The others snickered, the lone exception being one young woman who remained silent. She stood out from the crowd because she seemed considerate, because her short, ruddy-copper hair strikingly framed her honey-brown face, and because she'd stand out in a crowd. I knew that for the rest of my life, I'd recall her as the woman who hadn't laughed at me.

She half raised her hand and responded to the bearded man, "But I think some of us aren't good enough to hit a target from that distance, Coach Tarcott." Her accent was English, sort of, but not that of the upper class, with a charming inflection as if she'd just bitten into a plum.

"You don't have to be good enough, Gemma. Anyone?"

The bearded man offered the question to the group as I studiously filed away that the young woman's name was Gemma. Apparently, I'd wandered into a bizarre gym class, or rather, it had wandered into me.

With no volunteers, the coach reluctantly sighed, "Very well, Mr. Sampson then, as bloody usual."

He yielded the forest floor to a lean man around my age who sported more blond hair than was considered appropriate outside of grand opera, and his British accent evoked a storybook villain with a name like Prince Pernicious. He enlightened his classmates in a world-weary tone, "You only need the skill to fire an arrow enough distance that you <u>might</u> have done it. Invite your human target to your home and have a chaise longue ready for sunning themselves after a few extremely stiff G and Ts. You ensure there's only the two of you around. You walk two hundred yards away and fire a few arrows at a target located not too far from where your victim is pleasantly dozing, these arrows intended to be found by the police later on. You then drop your bow as if you were startled by an outcry, race to your sleeping quarry, automatically creating the footprints of someone running to see what dreadful accident has just ensued . . . and at your victim's side, you stab your dozing target through the heart with an arrow."

Sampson looked pretty pleased with himself and peered at the group as if expecting applause. Discovering none, he continued a bit sullenly, "Just be sure to wear rubber gloves, not only to avoid leaving your prints in the center of the arrow, where one would rarely hold it, but also to assist your grip for the stabbing. Once the deed is done, leave the gloves by a flower bed alongside a hedge clipper, and ring for the police in a state of well-practiced hysteria: 'I shot an arrow into the air, Sergeant, and it fell to earth, oh Christ, not <u>there</u>!'"

"But how do you get your target to doze off?" Gemma asked. I could now detect a tinge of the Caribbean in both her burry British accent and her appearance. "That's a lot to assume, don't you think?"

The sergeant, who'd been listening with interest, opted to fill in the blanks. "When you study toxins with Monsieur Tissier, you'll learn nothing beats a couple of really stiff banana daiquiris enriched with yogurt. The bananas have tryptophan and magnesium to make your target dozy and potassium to keep them that way. The yogurt delivers melatonin, tryptophan, and calcium, and to seal the deal, they make a 168-proof rum in Barbados that might as well be knockout drops. By the way, you'll never taste anything better in your life."

"Or after, I'll warrant," voiced Tarcott. "Well said, Sergeant, and greetings, Captain! Back from the big city, I see." He waved his longbow in my direction and inquired, "One of ours?"

"One way or another, Coach," replied Dobson. "We'll know more after the dean's given him the once-over."

Tarcott's reply was a single spiked clap of his hands. "All right, class, back to your lodgings to change into civvies," he directed, and set a brisk pace along a path that retreated out of the woods, his class obediently falling in place behind him.

I watched, as I suppose men have watched for centuries, to see if Gemma would give me a backward glance, and in that same rich male tradition, I admit I was vastly disappointed when she didn't.

The captain, sergeant, and I returned to the car and we drove for another half mile until we reached a huge oval of tan gravel, spread out like a floor mat before the vaulting doors of a manor house. My eyes were now accustomed to the light, but I was dazzled all the same and gave a low whistle.

"I don't suppose you've ever seen anything like Slippery Elms," said Dobson, apparently referring to the mansion. "Few people are supposed to."

So, dear patron for whom I'm writing all this, what were my impressions upon viewing for the first time the manor where you'd had me brought? My initial thought was "Toad Hall." This was, of course, an inadequate comparison but the best I could muster considering the limited number of books I'd read that centered on soaring Gothic structures. (As a boy, I went nine pages into The Hunchback of Notre Dame before realizing it wasn't a football story.)

The exhaust engineer in me reflexively began counting how many slim chimneys rose from the mansion's various roofs, but Dobson and Stedge hurried me through a functional business entrance to the far left of the manor's towering doors and into a reception hall teeming with activity. We navigated past a dozen smartly attired individuals all heading to appointments within or outside the mansion, then skirted a broad staircase more appropriate to an opera house. We then passed through a trio of connecting rooms where folding chairs and lecterns were being removed by custodians in dark gray uniforms, none of whom gave a glance to anyone but each other. At last, we arrived at double doors bearing the gilt-lettered words "Office of the Dean." Dobson opened these doors and gestured me into an anteroom and toward its Chesterfield couch.

A lone woman in a tweed suit, the tight bun of her hair skew-

ered by a pencil, looked up from a file drawer and offered a warm, "Good afternoon, Captain Dobson." Apparently, I was invisible.

The hard-faced man almost threatened to smile. "Afternoon, Dilys. This is Mr. Iverson, he has a three o'clock with Dean Harrow, if that's still convenient."

"There's still two minutes," she said, nodding toward a cuckoo clock in the shape of a chalet, which housed more doors than a bedroom farce I'd seen in New York. Dobson departed without farewell as Stedge sat guard, thumbing the pages of an Italian fashion magazine.

Frankly, I was grateful to have a moment to collect both myself and my thoughts regarding this bewildering setting and my situation. The windows of the anteroom looked out upon a broad terrace with a grand, multitiered fountain, beyond which stretched a long, formal lawn with reflecting pools. By the fountain, I was alarmed to see a woman holding another person's head underwater while several men and women in blazers watched with studious interest. Maybe it's a baptism, I thought, ever the optimist.

After more than a minute, the submerged individual (a man, as it turned out) was allowed by his submerger to surface and was handed a towel by an older woman clearly in charge of the session. She pointed to the nose and mouth of the man drying himself, with both the drowner and still-gasping drownee nodding calm affirmation.

The clock launched an appearance by the much-awaited cuckoo, who piped the hour of three, and the woman named Dilys said pleasantly, "Mr. Iverson, the dean will see you now."

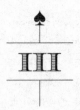

From the Journal of Cliff Iverson

"Well now, let's have a look at you!" said a distinguished-looking man with unwarranted chumminess. From behind a massive desk at the far end of the room, he set down the brass fountain pen in his hand—although it didn't look as if he'd been writing anything—and rose to greet me. He wore black-striped charcoal pants, a dove-gray double-breasted vest with rounded lapels, and an open black jacket, the image of a Harley Street physician, not that I'd been to Harley Street, or London for that matter (unless I was somewhere near London right now, which, for all I knew, I was).

The walk to shake his outstretched hand was not a short one. The dean's office (I assumed this was the dean, for an oak nameplate on the desk bore the name "Dean Harbinger Harrow") was an immense space with tall, mullioned windows spanning the entire wall on his right and, opposite, twelve-foot bookshelves requiring a wheeled ladder. Behind his desk were diplomas, degrees, and accreditations, surrounded by framed letters and photographs of Harrow with notables, many of whom I recognized by sight: singing-cowboy film star Gene Autry, the UN's Dag Hammarskjöld, former vice president John Nance Garner, director Frank Capra, comedian Danny Kaye, radio evangelist Rex Humbard, and actress Loretta Young.

Harrow waved me toward one of two captain's chairs facing his desk. "Make yourself comfortable, please. How was your trip?"

I hesitated as I seated myself. "Well, that's kind of hard to say."

The dean smiled at his foolishness. "Of course. Idiotic of me to ask. I imagine it was most disorienting. At least I hope it was. Well now, do you understand why you're here?"

"Sort of. On the last part of my trip, when I was awake, we talked a bit, to pass the time. It was clear that Captain Dobson and the sergeant knew I'd tried to commit—" I found myself unable to say the next word.

"Murder," Harrow supplied, "although that is not a term we use here. And you failed, which we most <u>definitely</u> don't condone."

"They made it sound as if I could either come here or, uh, face the music back in Manhattan." I omitted a third option foremost in my mind, that of getting out of this madhouse and back to Baltimore where Fiedler was still ruining or endangering the lives of others.

"And did Captain Dobson explain to you precisely what our institution is?"

"He just said . . . well, at first I thought he was making a little joke. We'd been driving quite a while, and he said this is a finishing school for finishing people off."

The dean paid lip service to a smile. "And he told you why he was bringing you here?"

"Yes," I said. "To stop me from committing another stupid murder."

"Precisely."

"So . . . I'm unclear." I squirmed in my seat. "Is this a reform school for failed murderers? A sanitarium for homicidal maniacs? Because I want to make it clear I'm not a serial killer. There's only one person in the world I've ever wanted to, you know, <u>harm</u>."

"A fortunate few come to the applied arts with innate gifts, but most must learn. McMasters was established to serve that need," he explained with a note of pride. "One's target should not have to risk losing his life at the hands of an amateur."

There was a courtesy knock on the door and the woman named Dilys entered, bearing a tray that she placed on one side of Harrow's large desk. On it was a cut-crystal decanter and matching glasses, and a folder that she lay before the dean. "Mr. Iverson's file," she identified and withdrew.

Harrow immediately opened it and perused its top page. "Mm, yes, orphaned at the age of nine"—he looked up at me with surprising empathy—"tragic accident, I'm most genuinely sorry." His eyes returned to my curriculum vitae. ". . . raised by aunt and uncle, both now deceased—further condolences—no siblings, fine grades, MIT under the Weiss Endowment . . . Caltech magna cum laude . . . and now Woltan Industries, which is of course where your current problem began." Something in the notes drew his interest. "Spelunking?"

"Cave exploration," I explained. "I think the British term is potholing. I also enjoy mountain rappelling because the emphasis is not on getting to the top but how you come back down to earth."

"You have a more diverse range of interests than I'd expect from a science whiz . . . water polo at Caltech—excellent, we're in need of a goalie—varsity baseball, and you play piano?"

"Stride piano. A subset of ragtime. I'm self-taught, which means I had an idiot for an instructor, but I'm decent, I suppose." Why was I answering all these questions, dear sponsor? Because I wanted my captors to think I was resigned to going along with this madness.

"No major romantic involvements, I take it?" came the next question. Really?

"I'm no monk. But in college, I was carrying a full study load while working nights to pay for room and board, and it didn't leave me the time or budget for dining and dancing. At Woltan, I'd only recently gotten set enough in my work to start giving my social life some thought, when suddenly I was . . . dismissed."

"Any one person you had in mind? Socially?" I didn't answer right away and he scanned my folder, finally offering: "Cora Deakins?"

So they knew about her as well.

When it became clear I had no intention of discussing Cora with a stranger, no matter how genteel the cut of his clothes, the dean resumed what I hoped was the end of this unsettling interview. He did seem intrigued by my pastime of restoring war monuments in Baltimore's Louden Park near Fort McHenry, nurturing grave-stones made indecipherable by moss, algae, and pollution back to a state of legibility. It was peaceful, reflective work in a verdant setting, my aim being to let the headstones again tell their stories and memorialize the soldiers' sacrifice by name once more . . . a welcome respite from the demands of Woltan.

Dean Harrow ghoulishly observed that we shared a common in-terest in maintaining tombstones. I replied with an edge, "I restore them, I don't create them."

He gestured toward the cut-crystal decanter and glasses that the woman named Dilys had left on his desk. "Sherry?" he inquired. "A solera Del Duque I'm told, although I have my doubts."

This guy is batty, I thought, no matter how plush the surround-ings. I wasn't much of a sherry drinker but the escape plan I'd been slowly cultivating for the last few minutes could use a decent slug of corked courage to fortify my nerve. As the dean measured out two schooners of trembling amber, he said with a tinge of sad-ness, "Well . . . I'm dreadfully sorry you've come such a long way just to hear me say this, Cliff, but for a plentitude of decades I've been aiding and abetting many of the best and keenest homicidal talents of our time. Where it comes to killers, I know the very instant when I <u>don't</u> see one." He gave me a a pained but compas-sionate look. "Nothing personal, but you simply don't have the makings of a deletist. You barely got away with your utter deba-cle this time—thanks only to the intervention of Captain Dobson and his sergeant, I gather—but try again and you'll make a rum go of it, only heightening the fanatic anti-homicidal fervor sweeping the globe." He handed me my glass as if it were a consolation prize. "You mustn't feel bad. Many worthy human beings are unable to commit murder, yet still go on to live productive lives, even if they can't end each other's. As for your intolerable employer, I'm afraid you'll have to adopt 'live and let live' as your motto." He raised his glass. "So, before we toast: I put it to you that this was a fool-hardy enterprise on your part for which you are ill-suited. Pledge you won't make another attempt and I'll have the good Captain Dobson return you to your home tout de suite, having arisen from your descent into madness and living the rest of your days with a clear conscience." He touched the rim of his glass to mine, sounding the warm 'ting' of fine crystal. "What say you, Cliff?"

I drew myself up straight. "Your words make sense, sir, and I'm sure I'm inept at this. But I made up my mind months ago. Merrill Fiedler must die or I'll die trying."

As I brought the drink to my lips, the dean's hand flew at me with remarkable quickness and my glass went flying, shattering against a gaming table by the window. I stared at him, bewildered.

"Sorry," he offered. "Had no choice. The sherry is poisoned."

With outrage and genuine fear I rasped at him, "You would have <u>killed</u> me?"

"Oh yes, quite reprehensible, I'm so ashamed of myself!" said Harrow with mock regret. "You're here because you attempted to murder another human being and yet you're aghast because I might do the same to you?" His voice grew steelier. "Let me explain, young sir: There is no drive back home with Captain Dobson, nor are you changing your mind. Your course was set the moment you learned of our existence. If you do well, you will graduate and commit your deletion, whereupon you will have every reason to keep your crime and our existence to yourself, even as you fondly recall your days here. But if you're a washout at McMasters, then you yourself will be the victim." The dean permitted himself a withering smile. "Not that we'd take any pleasure in killing you. You'd simply present a threat to every graduate of McMasters and its faculty. So I'm afraid it's sink or swim for you, and here's hoping you stay afloat."

My mouth had gone dry as alum. "You mean if I fail . . . ?"

"Yes, we'll have to scrub you, I fear. Your 'die' has already been cast, pun intended. Once a student sets foot on campus, there are only two ways to depart: either as a fully accredited graduate or in an attractive urn. But there are two bright sides to this: First, our graduation rate is nearly eighty-three percent."

"Oh my God," I croaked, hoping that "I croaked" would not be my epitaph. "And the other bright side?"

Harrow set down his untasted sherry. "If we're forced to kill you, you meet a really first-class end! Without warning, painless, all over in a second. I only hope when my time comes—"

A rap at the study door made him pause as Dilys entered, along with a custodian bearing a dustpan and broom. She bore a short stack of books and smiled merrily. "I heard the sound of breaking glass. I take it congratulations are in order?"

"I believe so. And, efficient as ever, you had janitorial assistance at the ready!"

She smiled knowingly. "Well something would have to be removed from this room, one way or another." Her quick glance at me made me feel like a corpse in progress as she indicated the books in her arms. "I also brought in some of Mr. Iverson's required reading. Save him a trip to the campus bookshop, since he's arrived late for term."

"Oh, you're a wonder! Mr. Iverson, please meet my trusted associate Dilys Enwright." As she gave me a pleasant nod, Harrow took the thickest volume from her and offered it to me with reverence. "Here you have it, Iverson: Our bible, albeit with far fewer killings than the Holy Scriptures. Principles of Successful Termination by Guy McMaster himself. To be fair, Duer did a major revision decades ago and it was long overdue, Lord knows. The chapter 'Horses and Carriage Houses' was scrapped completely and another regarding personal servants was unacceptable even in Guy's time. Ninth edition, printed just last year. You might"—he opened the book toward the back—"take note of the appendix by a certain H. H. It has received some generous comments, I blush to say."

I mumbled something about reading it with real interest, although my real interest was in one particular cane in the umbrella holder near the dean's fireplace, which I was now thinking might facilitate a way out of this madhouse.

The dean thumbed nostalgically through the remainder of the books. "I'm afraid you won't relish many of these other volumes, though. All required reading for first term. Chitham's Fundamentals of Murder . . . everyone hates it, I did, so will you. You'll think it irrelevant but most successful deletions draw upon it one way or another. <u>Advancing the Cause of Death</u> by Langenus, <u>Tredici Passi Da Evitare</u> by Cardinal Rafael Dorando, in a new translation that finally captures the vitality of his ex-eminence. And <u>The Police Problem: Keystones to Its Solution</u> . . . your traveling companion Captain Dobson has thankfully brought this old creaker up to the present day." He turned to Miss Enwright. "Please have these sent to Mr. Iverson's quarters. I'll be showing him around the campus and don't wish us to be burdened."

Dilys Enwright said that could easily be done and Harrow stepped to the door. "Come along, then. Term started weeks ago and you have tons of catching up. I fear your botched attempt in New York demonstrates how far you have to go and I dread to think what your sponsor would say, were I to inform them of your abject failure."

"My sponsor?" I asked, foolishly thinking for the briefest moment that I was beginning to understand things.

"Oh yes. You couldn't afford a McMasters education were you not on scholarship. We know heaps about you, lad; we've been quietly monitoring you for some time, at the request of your patron. It was only your impetuous blunder on the subway platform that forced our intervention ahead of schedule."

I shook my head, utterly baffled. "Someone is <u>paying</u> for me to be here? Who—?"

"We can talk about it on our walk." He stepped around the custodian, who was sweeping fragments of glass from the floorboards. "Unless of course you'd prefer another sherry."

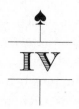

IV

FROM THE JOURNAL OF CLIFF IVERSON

The dean was soon leading me across the paved esplanade of the fountain gardens just beyond the manor's grand patio. Although I tried to display keen interest, I felt as if I were being given a personalized tour of Gay Paree that might culminate in a surprise visit to the guillotine.

"Now that fine building with the tall portico there, that's our science center. The chemistry lab is below ground, just in case. And the poison gardens are directly behind." He smiled wryly. "We have to make sure they're nowhere near the kitchen gardens, as you can well understand. One gust bearing the wrong seed to the green bean beds . . . think of it! And these fatal flowering plants and toxic berry hedges continue all the way up those terraces to the hillside's crest, home to the world's largest formal fungus garden."

"Imagine that!" I enthused, although why anyone would want to imagine that was a mystery to me. He rhapsodized about death caps and destroying angels, then pointed to a nearby timbered building whose tall windows mirrored the sun in near-blinding fashion.

"Our mess hall, converted from the great stable at Oxbane." He scowled. "You're too late for lunch, I fear. You could take high tea at Chadleigh House, purchase a Ploughman's in the Market Hall or a spot of something at the Student Union to tide you over until din— Ah!" He pointed to a spotless white truck approaching on a paved service lane as the childlike sound of jingling bells could be heard. "You like ice cream, I assume?"

The exuberant sky and bucolic setting of this murderous campus, the smartly dressed male students in their blazers, the women in pleated skirts and saddle shoes, all seemed as surreal to me as any of the extraordinary events of my recent life, including the round-bumpered ice cream van stopping before us. A driver in bleached white uniform leaped from his perch, moved quickly to the rear of his truck, and opened the silver handle of the icebox door as the smoke of dry ice billowed out into the warm afternoon.

"Afternoon, gents," said the driver, a cherubic-faced young man, who looked as if he sampled much of his own stock. He offered a small salute against the brim of his cap. "Cold treat on a warm day? Last call for the afternoon."

The dean fumbled in his vest pocket. "My treat, I insist, and I'll confess I'm a complete mark for toasted almond. You, Iverson? I'm told Americans adore shredded coconut." The man had nearly poisoned me and now we were sharing ice cream notes in merry fashion, bringing new darkness to the words "Good Humor." But since Dobson and Stedge had seen to it that I had no money on me, I thanked him for his generosity and requested a chocolate-covered vanilla bar.

The ice cream fellow reacted apologetically. "Sorry, you're the tail end of my route today, and all I have is"—he peered into the frozen vault—"yup, just Popsicles, except we have to call them Frosties."

Harrow pouted. "Well, for lack of anything else . . . what flavor do you recommend?"

"Orange is our number one seller because that's all we have. Orange for you, too, my friend?" Soon I was struggling to rip away the wrapper from the bar, some of the paper refusing to separate from its white-blanched frosted surface. "Careful your tongue doesn't freeze to it," warned the vendor with a good-humored laugh. "I had a student stuck to a fudge bar for five minutes before it thawed."

I smiled and opened my mouth to bite into the ice pop when the dean was obliged to bark at me yet again. "Don't eat that!" he cried, and seized my frozen pop, rotating it to study its crystallized coating as it caught the sunlight. "Something on the surface . . . ?" he asked the vendor with clinical curiosity.

"No, ground glass, sir, throughout," the baby-faced driver proudly declared. "Impossible to differentiate from ice crystals within the popsicle. And any abrasion he might have felt on his tongue he'd have attributed to freezer burn. He'd have been hemorrhaging his guts out in a matter of minutes."

I wanted to deck the driver but realized my justifiable rage could be better utilized as misdirection. I bided my time as Harrow grunted to the student, "First-rate conception."

He beamed. "Thank you, sir! I know my work thus far may not have met with as much approval as—"

"First-rate conception and despicable execution!!!" snarled Harrow with contempt. "You're a disgrace to McMasters, picking on a student who hasn't even registered yet! I only played along to see how far you'd take it. You know our policy is to stop short of the finishing stroke, as with fencing or karate. Get your rapier squarely upon your opponent's heart, but don't make the final thrust. This is a very dark blotch on your already disreputable record, Terhune. You've been skating on the thin ice of a hell that froze over for you last term!"

"Oh, but sir," protested the driver, hopping on one foot, "the cleverness! I admit I was surprised when he took the bait so quickly and I was just about to warn him when you intervened. Besides, I didn't know he was a freshman, sir."

Six years at the finest engineering schools in the world, I thought, and this little cherub is calling me a freshman. Next thing you know I'll be going to the Sadie Hawkins dance with the sweetheart of Sigma Chi.

Dean Harrow was not buying his excuses. "He's barely been here an hour, Terhune. Do you even know his name? Any fool can kill a stranger. If that's your goal, you have no need for us, nor we for you. The two most unacceptable words in the McMasters lexicon are 'innocent bystander.' We do not kill those with whom we have no quarrel."

"But we kill other students, sir, or rather, we try to," Terhune began.

"Soldiers play war games with live ammunition, but the goal is not to decimate one's own army before engaging the enemy. Where'd you get the truck?"

"The motor pool. It's the old Chevy pickup, with many hours of body work on my part."

"A shame you didn't go into forgery. There, at least, you seem to have some talent."

The young man extended his hand toward me. "Cubby Terhune, I'm very sorry about trying to murder you. Hope you won't hold a grudge."

The dean stage-whispered to me for Cubby's benefit, "Don't trouble yourself to memorize his name, Mr. Iverson. He bought his way in here and at the rate he's going, he'll soon simply have 'bought it.'"

"That doesn't change the fact that this twerp did his best to murder me," was my melodramatic response. "I ought to knock his block off!" I swung at Terhune in what I hoped looked like a credible roundhouse, and he feinted back reflexively. My left leg went useless beneath me and my body twisted to the ground.

Harrow looked concerned. "Have you hurt yourself?"

"It's all right," I said, miming pain. "Bum knee, injured it in high school. One hard twist and I'm like rubber on my feet for the rest of the day. Probably didn't help that I was sitting in the back of a sedan for God knows how long."

Cubby assisted me to my feet and helped me walk a few unsteady steps. Harrow suggested, "We can fetch a stretcher and take you over to St. James." He saw my puzzled look. "Our infirmary. Vesta Thripper is a certified nurse practitioner in addition to being Dean of Eroticide. She could bandage that up for you in a trice."

I shook off the suggestion. "It's not that bad. I suppose if you could loan me a cane—I think I saw one back in your office that looked practical enough. Not the shillelagh or the sword stick, just that simple wooden one with the curved handle."

The dean directed Cubby to fetch the cane from his office on the double, then offered me a steadying arm as we crossed the expansive quadrangle, along which buildings of Tudor and Georgian design were neatly lined like a Monopoly board late in a game. Of course, I didn't really need the dean's help, beyond obtaining the cane that Terhune was retrieving. Ever since I'd spotted it in the dean's office, I'd been plotting how to acquire it, which accounted for my unceremonious spill to the ground. I had to escape these halls of poison ivy and nail Fiedler before the bastard gave any further thought to his brush with death in the New York subway.

The dean and I sat facing a colonnaded building on the far side of the Quad upon whose mantel were chiseled the words "Roebuck Memorial Auditorium." (I found myself wondering if Mc-Masters had helped Mr. Sears dispense with his former partner and this edifice was the result of his guilty conscience.) A parade of pedestrians appropriate to any cosmopolitan boulevard ambled past us, all cordially greeting the dean, who bestowed a paternal smile and cheery wave of his hand to all. In terms of countries of origin, the student body appeared to be a veritable United Nations, and while most students were in their twenties and thirties, there were others ranging all the way to retirement age, universally vigorous and clear-eyed. Apparently, you're only as old as you kill.

Since some students might hope to accomplish their goal in the guise of a femme fatale or Casanova, I was not surprised to see more than a few mannequin-types sporting haute couture and strutting the Quad's diagonal as if it were a fashion runway. But there were just as many wholesome Becky Thatcher and Joe College types.

"All walks of life walk here," commented the dean, clearly capable of reading my mind, which was not good news for me.

"And all nicely dressed," I observed. "I take it the impoverished need not apply?" Having been obliged to work my way through college, I'll admit I've never shaken a mild grudge toward those who'd had it easier.

"Far from it," countered the dean. "Tuition is determined on a case-by-case basis. Our fees are nothing to sneeze at for those who can afford to pay through the nose." He glanced to see if I appreciated his tortured wording, but my poker face (I was supposed to be in pain after all) seemed to disappoint him. "Billing on a scale allows us to offer scholarships to the deserving but deprived. In such cases, we also supply a first-class wardrobe, since dressing to kill is a vital factor in many a successful deletion. It's a sad truism that those who appear affluent often evade the scrutiny of law enforcement."

I looked around what I could see of the impressive campus, and it was a lot to take in. "But surely this place can't be supported by tuition fees alone?"

The dean conceded, "Well, our curriculum has led many alumni to a state of financial security, and they rarely forget their gratitude, just as we never forget their addresses."

"You blackmail them for the crimes you helped them commit? How nice of you." I was instantly concerned I'd been too snide, but the dean didn't seem to mind.

"Like all colleges, we keep in touch with our alumni in the hope that they'll be a soft touch for whatever they can painlessly afford. When graduates successfully delete an obstacle to their happiness or security, and go on to lead productive and prosperous lives, we encourage them to express their school spirit with an affordable tithing. We also accept endowments, bequests, and, as in your case, personal sponsors."

"But how can I have a sponsor?" I objected, and the question bewilders me even as I write this for you, dear benefactor. "I have no wealthy friends or relatives."

"Suffice it to say you're on the road to someone else's ruin via the faith and financial backing of one who wishes to remain anonymous . . . and that's all I can tell you about that. Ah, Miss Mown, a word?"

A vivacious woman, perhaps in her thirties but looking younger by virtue of her gamine-style haircut, approached at the dean's summons. She was wearing a sleeveless blue taffeta evening dress and white satin opera gloves completely inappropriate to the time of day and her surroundings. Harrow offered with some ceremony, "Miss Mown, may I present our newest student, Cliff

Iverson? And this, sir, is Dulcie Mown. She's been here barely six weeks and has taken to McMasters like potassium cyanide takes to sulfuric acid."

"Oh, I'm a quick study," she said with a charming if clearly well-practiced laugh. She instantly reminded me of someone but for the life of me, I couldn't place who.

The dean gestured toward her formal outfit. "A lovely gown, but I don't remember any special ball or reception this afternoon."

"It's for Basic Stratagems," she said. "Just homework, not really suited for my own thesis, though there are some small applications. I'm fresh from the firing range where opera gloves are a girl's best friend, preventing fingerprints while protecting the hands and arms from gunpowder residue." From her clutch bag she withdrew a .22 revolver. "I was seeing how satin gloves affected my aim. Too thick and slippery. I'm going back to goat skin."

Harrow approved. "Yes, I almost said it's the one instance in which you should treat your victim with kid gloves, but I caught myself just in time. But why the evening gown on a sunny afternoon?"

She adjusted the shoulders of her dress. "Well, one can't walk around in opera gloves without arousing suspicion, thus the gown, which camouflages the purpose of the gloves. I could stop in to see my target, purportedly on the way to some nonexistent gala, leaving him unconcerned until the moment I produce the gun."

Dulcie struck me as exactly the type who went to galas, real or invented.

The dean turned to me and stressed, "Context is everything, Mr. Iverson. Never approach your target with a knife unless you're polishing the cutlery. Never hold an axe unless you're chopping firewood. And never don gloves in front of your victim unless he thinks you're about to wash the dishes, shovel the driveway, or perform a tracheotomy." He turned to Dulcie. "And what would you do with the gloves afterward, my dear? Your hands and arms may not bear gunpowder residue but the gloves certainly will."

Dulcie seemed bored. "Please. I'd wash them in a bowl of vinegar. It destroys nitrates."

"Spot on, or rather, spot off," the dean remarked with approval. "But what do you do with the vinegar?"

"Add three parts oil, two shredded heads of lettuce, walnuts, tangerine segments and serve it at my victim's wake."

"Sheer poetry," lavished the dean, "although sending the vinegar down the drain and washing the bowl with Borax will probably do just as well. Take heed, Mr. Iverson, take heed! Miss Mown's thinking is precisely the sort we embrace."

Dulcie Mown was clearly a model student. She might also have been a model. But as she departed for her next class, I despaired at her savvy answers, for they only demonstrated how out of Mc-Masters' league I was. If the conservatory executed washouts, I'd have been safer committing an inept murder, pleading guilty, and hoping for a life sentence.

But why does she seem so familiar?

We briefly interrupt young Mr. Iverson's journal. —HH

To answer the question beggared by Cliff Iverson, I should explain that no one was more devastated than "Dulcie Mown" herself to learn that simply by cropping and dying her hair, shunning makeup, modifying her accent, and changing her name, she could go unrecognized on campus as renowned Hollywood cinematic star Doria Maye.

Naturally, "Doria Maye" is not her real stage name (a name you would likely know the instant it was mentioned). And of course, her *real* stage name was not her *real* birth name either, so it is layers upon layers. But even this many years after the events here chronicled, we respect the privacy (and anonymity where law enforcement is concerned) of all McMasters students, as we would yours should you attend dear old McM.

I'd suggested to Miss Maye that if others learned her identity, it might interfere with her studies and the secrecy of her mission, adding that the faculty were only human as well and might show her preferential treatment. She assured me this would not present a problem, as she'd been receiving preferential treatment for years. In the end, however, she agreed to relinquish the spotlight, dye and trim her hair, adopt a Savannah lilt and become, God forbid, a civilian.

When she'd first arrived at McMasters, I'd personally escorted her to Foxglove Cottage, a rare single dwelling just a half mile past Mead Mere. Seeing its thatched roof for the first time, she cooed, "Oh, this is wonderful! From the outside it looks just like a humble peasant's cottage, and on the inside"—she entered, her eyes widening in horror—"it looks like a humble peasant's cottage! You don't expect me to *live* here, do you?"

I regarded with admiration the hearth set within rough-hewn stone walls, the snug but deep box bed with its patchwork quilt, the room's rude table and chair in a tiny corner kitchen. "But this is one of our most charming dwellings, my dear. It's original to the estate."

Dulcie was agitated. "When I opted for a private cottage, I thought it would be a bungalow with two bedrooms, dressing area, wet bar, two-and-a-half baths. And where's the pool?"

"You take the Number Three shuttle to the Bathing Pavilion."

Dulcie stated she'd have to have her decorator, Mr. Arnold, do a complete makeover of the cottage. I'd explained that if he did, Mr. Arnold's life would have to be terminated when his work was finished. "Could he be whipped instead?" she asked. "He may actually charge me less if that could be arranged."

♠

From the Journal of Cliff Iverson

At this point, much to my relief, a breathless Cubby finally returned with the cane I'd requested, offering it with a terrier's eagerness as if nothing would make him happier than for Harrow to toss it, crying "Fetch!" I noted with relief that the cane did indeed bear a rubber tip, crucial to my plan.

Cubby looked up at Harrow, as if hoping the dean would slap a gold star on his forehead. "Anything else I can do, sir?"

"Do <u>better</u>, Mr. Terhune! If you'd paid attention in Poisons and Panaceas with Professor Redhill, or stayed awake during Monsieur

Tissier's Great Last Meals, you'd have known ground glass is generally harmless to anyone who doesn't have angina. Now take your ice cream truck back to Automotive Arts and help the garage restore it to its former lack of splendor!"

As Cubby ran off and Dulcie bid us good day, Harrow walked me toward my quarters, grousing, "I'm at the end of my rope with Terhune, who may wind up on the end of his."

"I don't think I'll be any more competent," I said with utter sincerity.

"You're a sponsored recruit, not a volunteer. We know that. You'll have a grace period, and your RA at Hedge House will give you practical advice. Meanwhile, one of our students will be monitoring your progress, for your benefit and our own."

"Who will that be?" I asked.

"Sorry, if you knew, they'd never get an honest glimpse of you. Better you don't have to second-guess everything you do and say around him or her."

Great, I thought, now I'll have to second-guess everything I do and say around everyone.

We left the quadrangle and a graveled path led us past a few thatched abodes, one of which bore the hanging wooden sign "Bookshop & Sundries." The path widened and verged onto a ring of cottages encircling a spacious village green and a vast, irregularly-shaped pond, along whose banks several willows wept about their age. The structures there leaned toward the rustic or, in one case, simply leaned. "The students call this area the Market Hall," explained the dean, "although the actual hall is that pavilion there." He gestured toward a ragged iron shelter at the far end of the pond. Its arched legs supported a windowed roof and clock beneath which vendors were busy hawking their wares. "Among our busiest social centers," he added. "The Skulking Wolf serves cask ale and tavern fare. That's the Tuck Shop with blue shutters, they do picnic hampers as well. The Asian structure is Jade Flower Spring. And many students can't go a week without a savory cheese tart they call a 'pizza' sold at the back of Scarpia, our romantic Italian restaurant in that miniature villa on the other side of the Mere."

"The Mere?" I inquired.

"The pond's full name is Mead Mere. Not very deep, but useful for submersion experiments and the like."

I cast a glance at the pond and, as if granted a wish, spotted the young woman from the forest who'd chosen not to laugh at me. She'd exchanged her gym outfit for a short-sleeved blouse and jumper, and was snapping back a fishing line with a graceful arc of her russet arms.

The dean followed my glance. "That's Gemma; she loves fly-fishing, used to do it with her father, I'm told. We stock the Mere with brown trout, but one must throw them back. No need ending a life if you've no appetite or quarrel." Gemma had gathered up her gear and was waving goodbye to a woman wearing a straw sun bonnet above a ruddy complexion who was tossing breadcrumbs to the swans that ornamented the pond.

"And that's Miriam Webster, who decided to call herself 'Mim' after she married a fellow with an unfortunate last name . . . although she now has a much better reason for trying to delete him. And there's our Toma Sasaki, dean of math. His monograph 'All Time Is Relative When Killing One,' is a landmark." Sasaki had white hair but a youthful face and he was capturing the tranquil scene in watercolors. "You'll likely have him for Odds and Getting Even. And that chap with the Byronesque mane who's sprawled on the grass is Matías Graves, English and Spanish literature." Graves, in his late thirties or youthful forties, dressed in cable sweater and corduroys, was engrossed in evaluating and marking papers. It surprised me that a still-youthful fellow, maybe only ten years older than myself, would sequester himself here in . . . wherever we were. I wondered if the faculty got to leave the premises whenever they wished.

We were by now in the midst of a small village neighboring the market hall: a gathering of tiny shops and stalls clustered together as if to better gossip with each other. Short, cramped streets, cobbled courts, and intriguing passageways made a miniature maze of the snug little town. A Dickensian pawnbroker's shop displayed many curious items in its curved, compartmented windows, and

from its doorway stepped the blond-maned young man from the archery class who'd all too cleverly answered Coach Tarcott's question. He held in his hand a mahogany case about the size of a portable chessboard.

The dean inquired, "Pawned something, Mr. Sampson?"

"Traded my old musical instruments for new surgical instruments." He opened the case, revealing a gleaming array of scalpels and probes nestled in crushed velvet. "Jack the Ripper, eat your heart out."

"I believe he did," said the dean. "Or was it a kidney?"

"I thought they'd inspire me more than my clarinet and sax, though I've murdered 'Rhapsody in Blue' with both." He stared in none-too-friendly fashion at me. "You're that newly landed fellow the coach almost skewered, yes? The name's Simeon Sampson. I might say let's be the swellest of chums, but students are marked on a curve here so, to be candid, I'll be doing whatever I can to see you fail, and at first glance, I doubt it'll be much of a challenge."

I was delighted to see him leave and my spirits were further lifted as I saw Gemma approaching from the Mere. As if I had willed it, the dean beckoned to her and I thought, 'Come on, tell me her last name!' Once again he read my mind.

"Gemma Lindley, this is Cliff Iverson, who's just arrived today."

"I know," said Gemma in a more neutral tone than I would have liked.

"I crave a boon," he continued. "I'd have asked Mr. Sampson but he's a bit, you know . . ."

"Full of himself?" supplied Gemma.

The dean smiled. "Yes, he's almost as smart as he believes he is. I was just escorting our Mr. Iverson here to Hedge House but we got sidetracked by Cubby Terhune and now I'm woefully behind schedule. Would you mind showing him the way for me? You reside there, yes?"

"I wish I could afford Hedge House," she said with a laugh. "I'm in the women's dorm, but it's not far from Hedge. I still have Wump at five but that's by the Dovecote." This last sentence was complete double-talk to me but I'd have enjoyed hearing her read a logarithm table.

"Well, I'm sure Mr. Iverson won't protest your taking over, eh Cliff? How's the ankle?"

"Knee," I corrected. "I'll be fine as long as I have this." I raised the cane a bit, hoping he wouldn't ask for it back.

"Consider it yours until you no longer require it. And as I've said, if you need any further help or advice, your RA at Hedge House is the personable Mr. Champo Nanda."

"Unusual name," I noted.

"He hails from Rangoon. Have you ever been to Burma?"

I said I hadn't but Gemma slyly asked, "Are you sure you're not there now?" which elicited a chuckle from the dean. She added, "The only thing I know about our current location is that we're not in Tobago. I was born in England but I've visited my mother's family there and the air reeks of spices and wild poinsettia." She inhaled the summery breeze. "Not Tobago."

I was about to ask Harrow if there were any students who were privileged to know the school's location but he was already walking away with a cheery "See you at dinner!"

Not if I can help it, I thought. I was aiming to be long gone by then.

"Hedge House then," said Gemma, starting off. I hobble-skipped to catch up with her and apologized for the slow pace of my feigned trick knee. She said not to worry, and nothing more.

"What's 'Wump'?" I tried after an awkward silence reminiscent of my adolescence.

"Campus nickname for Wardrobe, Makeup, and Prosthetics," was her minimal response.

I counted to five before trying again. "Been at McMasters long?"

This time I thought she wasn't even going to answer. Finally, not turning to look at me, she offered, "A bit more than two weeks."

"What brought you here?"

"A car driven by Captain Dobson," she said.

"From?"

She stopped walking. "Look, if you want to know who I was and who I want to delete and why . . . I don't talk about that unless a faculty member demands it of me. Some people here, that's all they want to talk about, but not me. It's taken my life savings to pay for a single term. I'm here for an education, not the best time of my life. I don't mind showing you where you'll be living but we'll never see each other again once we leave here." She paused. "If we leave here."

I thought that Miss Lindley (for we now seemed to be on a last-name basis) was equally willing to kill an enemy or a conversation, and I wondered who had treated her so cruelly that she'd enroll in this seminary for slaying. Her hard stance belied her soft features . . . or maybe she was every bit as cold-blooded and driven as I was but had simply inherited memorable ginger hair as I'd inherited my grandfather's height.

I did know how it felt to reach a point in one's life where murder seemed the only way to go on, just as for some bedeviled souls like Cora, suicide seemed the only way out. But did my attempt to kill Fiedler prove that not all murderers are monsters, or simply that I'd been a monster all my life and not known it?

I heard the wrought iron clock above the Market Hall chime. "Sorry, I have to get to Wump," said Gemma. "Hedge House is around this turn." She moved away briskly, and for the second time today she left my company without a backward glance.

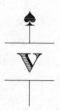

From the Journal of Cliff Iverson

I had decided to escape from McMasters only minutes into my interview with Dean Harrow. The poisoned sherry, Cubby Terhune's lethally intended popsicle, and the fatal sentence for flunking merely confirmed this to be my only sane option. But appearing compliant before making my break for freedom seemed a wise move, and checking into my intended future residence was a part of that subterfuge.

Hedge House might easily have passed for a large colonial bed-and-breakfast in a quaint New England town. I half expected to find a revolving postcard display near the reception desk, but instead found a matronly woman who resembled a less-imposing Mahalia Jackson. She wore a tweed skirt, stiff-collared blouse, and pale blue cardigan that bore a few crumbs of muffin.

"You'll be Cliff," she said with a smile, looking up from paperwork that littered the counter. "I'm Mrs. Forage, rhymes with 'porridge'—oh dear," she vexed, noticing my cane. "No one told me . . . I've put you on the third floor and of course there's no elevator."

I reassured Mrs. Forage that my affliction was only temporary and that I could manage the stairs with no difficulty, which of course happened to be the God's honest truth. Much relieved, she took down a key from a peg board and led me through a chintzy front parlor that served as the Hedge lobby. On a cork bulletin board, I eyed a title card labeled "Thought for the Day," below which bore the calligraphy:

> *When a man dies from a bullet entering his chest,*
> *it's a homicide.*
>
> *When a man dies from a meteorite landing on his head,*
> *it's a tragedy.*
>
> *Don't use bullets. Use meteorites.*
>
> *Don't commit a homicide. Commit a tragedy.*
>
> —Guy McMaster

I followed Mrs. Forage up a narrow set of stairs once intended for servants and pretended to need a moment after the second flight, owing to my troubled knee, while Mrs. Forage commented on the extended summer we were having. Eventually, we emerged in the third-floor hallway and I was shown to room 3E.

"You have a southern exposure; most people like that, especially with this extended summer we're having. You share a bathroom with your neighbor, Miss Jäeger." She looked a bit embarrassed and explained, "Normally we try to keep the sexes matched but you being a late arrival, 3E was the only vacancy. The bathroom doors bolt on both sides, but always knock two or three times before you go in just to be safe, okay? And you'll make sure the bathroom is left as you found it, and to unbolt the door on her side whenever you leave."

I gave Mrs. Forage my solemn word I'd leave the bathroom precisely as I found it, because with any luck I'd be leaving it forever in only a few moments.

"There's daily cleaning service but students are expected to keep their rooms tidy. If there's anything I've forgotten, just have a word with me between eight and five, yes?"

My intended quarters were efficiently snug. The bed wasn't big, but the mattress was impeccable, the sheets nubby cotton, the bedspread nicely weighted. There was a Mission writing desk and chair and a compact leather reading chair. A brown Bakelite radio sat on a mirrored bureau. I turned it on, wondering with great interest what stations I would hear. As I waited for its tubes to warm up, I opened a small closet and was surprised to find a half dozen shirts, a similar number of pants, and several sports jackets waiting there, all my size, as were several shoes and sneakers on a shelf above.

I went back to the bureau and opened its top drawer. Undershirts and boxer shorts were neatly folded, the drawer below holding socks and blue gym shorts.

Through the miracle of thermionic emission (I'd been obliged to study air band spectrums at Caltech), the table radio was now producing music, something Baroque it seemed. I waited for the piece to end, hoping I might hear an announcer identifying the station, perhaps even its city of origin.

There was a leather portfolio by the radio, embossed with the McMasters emblem, and a handwritten note was paper-clipped to its cover:

Mr. Iverson, welcome! Please enjoy your first day on campus. If you have any questions or problems, I'm in rooms 2A & B at the top of the larger stairs. Always knock first on 2A and wait, as I might be meeting with another student.

The note was signed:

Champo Nanda, Men's Resident Advisor, Hedge House

I opened the portfolio. There were a number of printed pages and pamphlets tucked into its left and right pockets, including a map of the campus for which I had no need since it did not show any environs and I already knew the escape route I planned to take. A dining schedule reminded me how very hungry I was.

MEAL	DAYS	HOURS	LOCATION	NOTE
Breakfast (English)	M–Sat	7-9:30 AM	Mess Hall	Classroom dress
Breakfast (Continental)	M–Sat	6-10 AM	Lounging Room	Classroom dress
Lunch	M–Sat	Noon-2 PM	Mess Hall, Sun Porch or (weather permitting) West Patio	Classroom dress. Boxed lunches are available if ordered before 10 AM.
High Tea	W & Sun	4-5:30 PM	Chadleigh House Library	
Dinner	M–F	7:30-9:30 PM	The Great Hall	Tie and jacket required for men. Ladies, appropriate dress please.
	Sat	8-10 PM	The Ballroom at the Manor	Saturdays after-dinner dancing to recorded music in the Ballroom.
	Sun	see below	———	
Sunday Brunch	Sun	9 AM-1:30 PM	Conservatory	Dinner dress required.
Sunday Dinner	Sun	see note —→	Mead Mere	Sunday dinner can be purchased at locations around Mead Mere.*

On its reverse were further advisories:

ALCOHOL—McMASTERS RULES

Excessive indulgence in alcohol is discouraged, as your studies are sober work. However, there is a specialty cocktail (limit one per student) served at seven each night in the Drawing Room, and an appropriate wine from our extensive cellar is selected by Monsieur Tissier and served with your entrée each night, one-glass limit per student. Hand-pulled ale is available at the Skulking Wolf on Mead Mere, one pint per customer.

PECUNIARY NOTE

Students with low or depleted McMasters financial accounts may sign up for Sunday afternoon work assignments (kitchen, grounds, clerical, etc.) posted

on the bulletin board in the Student Union each week.
As recompense, a free serve-yourself meal of hearty soup,
bread, and salad is served that evening in the common
room adjacent to the Kitchen Gardens. However, also
note that Dr. Pinckney, dean of medical arts, states
that skipping an evening meal once or twice a week is
healthful to the system and stimulating for the brain.

Beneath this dining schedule was a slim manual of some dozen pages, its blue-gray cover of textured paper bearing the words "McMasters Rules and Regulations." It was dated the previous year. I started to open the manual, then realized there was no reason to learn the rules at McMasters since in a few minutes I would be attempting to break its first implicit commandment: Thou Shalt Not Leave.

The radio offered up another Baroque composition, identical in tempo and mood, minus any announcer's introduction. It might even have been the same piece. I tried tuning into a different station, but the radio's lone knob was simply a combination volume control and on-off switch. There was a notice glued to the back of its Bakelite chassis:

OPERATING YOUR TABLE RADIO
To hear Bach's 5th <u>Brandenburg Concerto</u>, turn radio ON.
To not hear Bach's 5th <u>Brandenburg Concerto</u>, turn radio OFF.

I chose the Off option and searched the room for any detail that might help me discern where on earth (and for once I actually meant that phrase) I was. I could safely rule out the Arctic, Antarctic, and desert locations, but beyond that, I hadn't a clue. Some nondescript notepaper, pencils, even the light bulbs in the bedside table lamp bore no indication of their manufacturer. My top bureau drawer had a wood-handled toothbrush, a safety razor, and a comb-and-brush set, all anonymously made. I longed for a brand name. If I managed to get beyond the school's electrified gates, it would have been nice to know if I were behind the Iron Curtain, on the road to Morocco, or down in the valley where the green grass grows.

By the bed was a carafe of water covered by a glass tumbler. I downed a glass and poured a second, knowing that if I successfully escaped, food and drink and lack thereof might figure in my survival. I had no idea how far I would have to travel before reaching any kind of refuge or shelter, and obviously I had no money, the sergeant having impounded my wallet at the start of our journey. Again miming a limp, I descended the narrow stairs, waved vaguely at Mrs. Forage, who barely looked up from her paperwork, and retraced the route I had taken with Gemma Lindley and the dean back to the manor house Captain Dobson had called Slippery Elms.

A miniature Swiss chalet I passed en route dubbed "Mussel's Tuck Shop on the Mere" might have provided some sort of snack for my journey, even if I'd had to pinch it, but unfortunately it had closed for the day. I would have to make my break on an empty stomach and pray there were apple or pear trees among the foliage surrounding the manor. I wasn't going to put off my escape until I was better prepared. I had my hands on the rubber-tipped walking cane and who knows how long they'd let me keep it. Besides, at the gate, Captain Dobson had mentioned not remembering today's password, which I'd luckily heard Stedge using. Tomorrow it might be changed.

There were few students about now. They were probably in their rooms doing homework or dressing for dinner, as per the dining schedule in my room. Once past the manor house, I dropped the pretense of a limp and moved down the long drive that would lead me back to the school's electrified main gate.

In the time that my head had been bandaged, I'd found my other senses had become more acute. Once Sergeant Stedge had exchanged passwords with the gatekeeper's amplified voice, the car had continued on a smooth roadway for some two minutes until we stopped at the thicket of birch trees where my bandages had been removed. I had detected no sharp turns or diversions along this stretch and was confident this road would lead me back to the electrified gate and fence, which Dobson had reminded Stedge "packed a punch."

Beyond a woodpecker's sporadic hollow drumming, the woods

were silent, no sound of others in the brush or a motorcar's purr in the distance.

I'd been able to memorize the exchange between Sergeant Stedge and Gatekeeper Pashley. The irony of Stedge's code name, "Thomas de Quincey," had not evaded me. I'd read his "On Murder Considered as One of the Fine Arts" when seeking moral justification to kill Fiedler.

Now I saw the gate for the first time and it did not fail to impress. When I'd heard it swing open, I'd pictured something more functional and less ornate than this imposing entryway. The tightly spaced, razor-sharp prongs topping the fence's tines looked more lethal than broken glass or barbed wire. I'd wondered if any overhanging limbs extended past the fence, allowing me the chance to climb above and beyond it and drop to the ground outside the gate, but no such luck, which was probably just as well since I wasn't much good at tree climbing and a fall directly above the fence would surely impale me.

A sign confirmed that the fence was electrified. Whether it would be as deadly for me as for the deceased squirrel now resting in peace alongside it was an experiment I had no interest in conducting.

My desperate hope was that the intercom Stedge had spoken into was either attached to the other side of the fence or standing just in front of it. I was relieved to see that the green metal box was indeed mounted to a waist-high pole just two feet beyond the other side of the fence, which would have been beyond the reach of anyone trying to squeeze their arm between the bars of the fence without coming in contact with them. The wooden cane with its rounded handle and rubber tip was now my most prized possession. Not only would it extend my reach, but wood was a poor conductor of electricity, and the providential rubber cap at the cane's tip would be the pièce de résistance, quite literally. If I held the cane only by its rubber-capped tip, I should be invulnerable to the fence's charge.

I gently slid the handle end of the cane between the fence's iron pickets, moving it just past the pole on which the box was mounted, so that the tip of the curved handle pointed toward the face of the intercom. I pulled the cane back slowly. There was a squawk of feedback, identical to the sound I'd heard when I'd been bandaged in the car, and it gave me hope as I released the button.

"Hello, how can I help you?" came the tin-can rasping of the man Stedge had called Mr. Pashley.

I again pulled the cane toward myself and attempted an impression of Sergeant Stedge: "The Knocking at the Gate!"

"Here's a knocking indeed!" replied the voice. "State your name."

"Thomas de Quincey."

"Sergeant Stedge . . . ?" came Pashley's voice from the intercom, sounding bewildered.

I suppressed a curse as the cane chose to slip off the button, and I fumbled to depress it again. It was an odd angle and the cane popped out of my hand like a squeezed bar of soap in the shower, dropping in the grass on the wrong side of the fence. I heard Pashley say, "Sergeant Stedge? When'd you go out again?"

There was no time for me to consider my options. I thrust my arm out between the electrified pickets, grabbed the cane's rubber tip in the grass, and yanked the end of the cane back to my side of the fence. Only after I had the rubber tip back in my hand did I realize how close I might have come to electrocution, as I again managed to depress the Talk button.

"Captain Dobson assigned me to find any security holes in our perimeter but I got myself locked out. Let me back in, Mr. Pashley, if you please."

With an electric buzz, the black gates swung open. I dashed between them, out from McMasters and back into sanity, feeling like my good, free self for the first time since Dobson and Stedge had knocked on my hotel room door. I looked at the face of that blessed intercom box from the "come and go as you please" side of the fence, and pressed the Talk button, this time with my thumb. "Thanks, Mr. Pashley, I'm coming in now. You can close up behind me."

After a few seconds, the gates swung shut, locking me out . . . thank God. I noticed a sign on the gate reading "McMasters Home for the Criminally Insane." Truth in advertising, I thought.

Keeping the cane as a potential weapon, I ran with both the elation and terror of a death row inmate who'd been mistakenly released and was anticipating the error's discovery. I sprinted along the edge of the paved road as it curved slightly to the left, in case I had to quickly duck into the dense woods. What would be the first non-McMasters structure I would see? At some point, no matter where the conservatory's grounds were located, they would have to yield to someone else's property, public or private.

I'd done some NCAA cross-country running at Caltech, and I quickly realized there was no way I could sustain my feverish pace as long as I'd like. Yet it would soon be dinner and my empty chair in the Great Hall would certainly be noted. Which raised the question: To what future was I escaping? Were Dobson, Stedge, and Harrow the only ones who knew of my attempt to murder Fiedler, or were the real police aware of it as well? Was I behaving like an ingrate, dear benefactor? Trading in a luxurious, landscaped asylum (complete with chic restaurants, a rustic pub, and extremely interesting women) for twenty years in a cellblock with brutal men and no adjoining bathr—

Car coming.

I strained to decipher the sound, yearning for it to be an airplane or approaching thunder. But damn, no such luck. It was definitely a motorized vehicle approaching from behind me, undoubtedly from McMasters. At least the curve of the road had been continuing leftward, which gave me a few seconds before the vehicle came into view when I would be seen. I made a frenzied dash into the woods and hid behind a broad oak.

As I tried to regain my breath, I took stock of how grisly the consequences of bolting the conservatory might be. If McMasters imposed the ultimate fail mark on students who simply couldn't make the grade, what sentence would they levy against me for fleeing the school with full knowledge of its existence and purpose?

Of course, I'd weighed all this before making a run for it, but now that I had no way to turn back, the grim weight of the risk I faced was more fully registering on me. Scaring me, too.

My anxiety was raised to the fourth power when my ears detected the car slowing as it neared me. Its engine faltered and choked a death rattle. I heard the grind of the car's ignition, a failed sputter from the motor, silence again, and another ignition grind. Lord have mercy, did the car have to break down right at this very stretch of road?

Or was this a heaven-sent opportunity?

I heard a door slam, footsteps scuffing, another door opening, and the sound of metal scraping. Someone uttered an expletive. Whoever was pursuing me didn't sound very calm or methodical. Maybe I wasn't being hunted, I dared to speculate. After all, McMasters couldn't be totally self-sufficient, some deliveries would have to be made on a regular basis. Please, please let the breakdown be a civilian returning from just such a drop-off! Could I pass myself off as a hiker in need of a lift? It was surely worth risking a look. I carefully peered around the side of the tree.

Oh, for the love of God, it was Cubby Terhune's goddamn ice cream truck! And yes, there was Cubby, sweaty and florid, pouring a can of gasoline into the truck's gas tank.

I <u>had</u> to hijack that truck. I looked about and saw a broken oak limb that would make a more threatening weapon than my cane. I had no intention of using it on Cubby (although it would be poetic justice, since he'd tried his best to murder me and I was certain I could take him in a fight if it came to that). But having a weapon in hand might make my demands more persuasive, and every minute counted before the McMasters crowd got wise to my absence.

Luckily, Cubby was absorbed with filling the gas tank, permitting me to approach him very closely, unnoticed. Standing almost directly behind him, I growled as gutturally as I knew how. "Ter-HUNE!"

The young fellow whirled, terrified, as his eyes went to the club in my hand. "Please don't kill me," he quietly implored.

"Finish filling the tank," I ordered, keeping my distance since, after all, he did have a can of gasoline in his hands. He might also have a match.

"The can's empty," said Cubby, following my own train of thought and turning the can upside down to demonstrate his harmlessness.

"How many more of those do you have?"

"Four. I hid them in the ice cream locker, gasoline won't freeze unless it's like a hundred below. I figure God knows how far the nearest gas station is from wherever the hell we are."

"You don't know either?"

"None of the students do. Please don't kill me, there's no need."

"Toss me the keys to the truck. Now!" Under certain circumstances, being a bully can be a refreshing change of pace.

Cubby looked embarrassed. "They're in the ignition, I didn't think to take them out. Please take me along, won't you? I've been on academic probation for two terms. I'm a total washout, they plan to expel me, and I know what that means. That's why I'm breaking out."

"How'd you manage it?" I demanded, less interested in how he'd managed it and more concerned with whether he'd likely drawn a posse after him.

"I was driving the ice cream truck back to the garage, near the loading dock where they get deliveries from the outside world. The gate there is a standard-issue fence but electrified. Then it dawned on me that the truck has rubber wheels, and as long as I didn't touch metal, I was safe. So I rammed it through." He looked at me beseechingly. "You might need an extra pair of hands. I speak a little Italian, German, who knows what country we're in?"

"How come they're not right behind you?" I said, moving to the driver's side of the truck.

Pride flashed across Cubby's face. "I put the confectioners' sugar I used to make the ground-glass popsicles into the gas tanks of the trucks at Automotive Arts before I made my break. Regular sugar's unreliable but powdered sugar works great. They'll have to call Headquarters." He looked back down the road anxiously.

"I bet Stedge'll be along any second on his motorbike, he loves to open up that thing."

I deeply regretted hearing myself say, "Put the can back in the icebox and hop in."

Cubby's eyes grew wide and worshipful. "Oh, thank you, you'll never regret—"

"Just hurry, dammit!" I slid into the driver's seat and started the engine. Cubby jumped into the passenger seat and we were off.

"Will this thing go over seventy?" I asked. "It may need to."

"I have no idea," said Cubby. "What do you think the speed limit is?"

"Speed limit?" I yelled. "Hell, I don't even know which side of the road to drive on!"

As I floored the lumbering truck, I reasoned there was only so far we could travel without seeing some sort of road sign, one which might offer a clue as to what part of the world we were in. A posted speed limit of ninety would suggest either a metric country or certain parts of Texas. My other thought was, if we were pulled over by a cop for speeding, would that be a good or bad thing for me? If I were to rat on McMasters, surely Dobson and Stedge would not hesitate to reveal my attempt on Fiedler's life, something they'd both witnessed firsthand.

The road continued curving left and I was thrilled to see a sign approaching. I didn't care what the hell it said: Slippery When Wet, Ende der Autobahn, even a Deviazione sign would speak volumes.

It read:

Slow 放慢
Hospital Zone 醫院區

"Well, it's in English," said Cubby helpfully.

"And Chinese? You think we're in some British possession? Hong Kong, maybe?"

"Maybe the— Oh no."

"What?"

When someone says "oh no," and you say "what?" it's safe to bet what follows is never going to be great news. Cubby was looking into the passenger's wing mirror. "Stedge is behind us," he cautioned. "Quite a way back, but I know his motorbike. You have to go faster."

"If it's a hospital zone, then there has to be a hospital. It's our best hope." We both saw it at the same moment, a low, V-shaped concrete building up a slope to the left. I swerved toward the hospital's gates which, unlike McMasters', were wide open.

"Get out!" urged Cubby. "Go in and get help for us, and I'll lead Stedge away from here to buy you time! He may not even know you've escaped yet. Odds are he's only after me and the ice cream truck." What he said actually made sense, and I braked the truck by the entrance. Cubby slid over to the steering wheel. "You were willing to help me even after I tried to poison you. Just promise if they catch me, you'll try to come back and save me."

I swore I'd do so and Cubby revved the truck back onto the roadway. I ducked behind a sign and watched Stedge race by, hunched over the handlebars of a Triumph motorbike. Once he had passed, I looked at the front of the sign with intense interest. It read simply:

VETERANS' HOSPITAL
医院的老战士的

An offshoot in the hospital's crescent driveway led to a side entrance, possibly for an emergency room, I reasoned. I certainly had no intention of remaining outside one second more than necessary, just in case Dobson and others were closely trailing Stedge.

This side door was propped open by a crate labeled "Surgical Gauze." I stepped in and confronted a short corridor with linoleum flooring, fluorescent lighting, and pallid green walls. A very tall man in surgical gown, cap, and mask was vigorously washing his hands while a nurse shook talcum powder into rubber medical gloves. His hands dry, he thrust them deep into the gloves held by the nurse and both entered double doors marked "Operating Room 2."

I debated what to do but realized time was of the essence where Cubby's fate was concerned, so I opted for reckless: Moving quickly to the same sink station, I pulled a surgical mask from a steel dispenser, employed wooden tongs to pull scalding-hot gloves from a steamy bin marked "Sterile" in both English and (I assumed) Chinese, donned mask and gloves, then pushed through the double doors myself.

An operation was in progress. The bright overhead lights made it hard to see, but the very tall surgeon and nurse were now alongside an attentive anesthesiologist, who was monitoring a ventilator with its signature pumping and releasing sound like an unreliable metronome. As I squinted beneath the bleaching light, I heard whispers between a stout surgeon and an assisting nurse regarding sutures, cotton, and gauze while the nurse I'd followed hung a bottle of hemoglobin on a stand. A third surgeon stood ready to aid with suction.

I cleared my throat. "Excuse me," I said.

All in the operating room looked at me. The nurse at the portly surgeon's side said sharply in a thick accent, "We are performing an operation, sir."

There was no time for diplomacy. I responded forthrightly, "I realize this is hardly the appropriate moment or setting, but an institution just up the road from you, one that calls itself a home for the criminally insane, is actually a boarding school for would-be murderers, and a student there is risking his life so that I can tell you this. There's no saying what they may do to him." Of course I realized how absurd this sounded; they would reasonably assume that I was an escapee from the aforementioned institution, and in point of fact, they'd be correct. I added, "I'm perfectly willing to be questioned by a psychiatric expert to detect if I'm paranoid or delusional. Believe me, I find this as inconceivable as it sounds. But someone needs to call the authorities."

The lead surgeon continued his work but asided in a deep-fried southern twang, "Nurse Brumley, would you be so kind as to show this poor gentleman out?"

"Doctor, I need your help <u>now</u>," I demanded.

The assisting surgeon, who'd been holding the suction tube, lowered his face mask with a sigh and said in a steely British accent, "Mr. Iverson, you've all the timing of a prophylactic salesman in a maternity ward. Now silence please while we continue our exam."

It was Dean Harrow.

My eyes were finally adjusting to the light and I could discern students above the operating theater seated in stadium-style chairs. The stout surgeon pulled down his own mask, revealing a rosy nose and shaggy white mustache. He said, with a generous helping of Alabama patois, "All right, I suppose as long as we've stopped— you can sit up now, Bob, by the way."

Bob was apparently the patient, who sat up quickly on the operating table and listened attentively as the well-rounded surgeon continued, "Don't let this unpropitious interruption distract from the point I'm trying my level best to make here: In this whole sweet world, there is no setting better suited to a deletion than a first-class, fully equipped hospital, where every single, sunshiny day people kick the bucket for all kinds of strange reasons and nobody thinks they should call in the police."

Oh dear God, I thought, they're all from McMasters! I whirled to race back out the double doors but discovered a smiling Sergeant Stedge blocking my way. Next to him, Cubby Terhune shrugged apologetically.

Dean Harrow lowered his mask again. "Mr. Iverson, pray take a seat with the other students. Up there by Simeon and Miss Webster."

I looked back at Stedge, who cracked gum while casually resting his hand on a holstered Colt revolver. All sense of purpose, energy, and self-esteem that I'd felt in making my escape drained from me.

In that moment, dear sponsor, I believed there was no challenge so big that I couldn't find a way to fail at it.

VI

FROM THE JOURNAL OF CLIFF IVERSON

I stumbled up to where the students were viewing what was clearly a staged operation and slunk into an aisle chair near Simeon Sampson in the third row. The woman named Miriam Webster, whom I'd seen feeding swans at the Mere, was a row above me and she leaned down to offer comfort. "You're not the first to attempt a premature exit, sweetie. Don't let it bother you."

Simeon offered his own note of support. "Pathetic failure."

The surgeon from the South continued, "And for those of you still paying attention, tell me where else could you get your target unconscious in such a professional way without a struggle?"

The dean turned to the class. "But I'm sure Dr. Pinckney doesn't wish to give the impression that hospital deletions should be confined to the ER or operating theaters. Semi-private rooms, oh, rich opportunities there! But let's see how Mr. Helkampf and Miss Lindley have made out." He looked around. "Are they with us? With all the surgical masks, I can't tell."

Doc Pinckney couldn't help but interject, "Well doesn't that just <u>prove</u> exactly what I'm saying? The dean himself don't know who's in this room! In a hospital, you get to wear a mask to cover your face, a skull cap to hide whether you're blond or balding"—he pulled off his own cap, revealing a matted crown of silver hair—"a loose-fitting gown to hide your eye-catching figure, surgical gloves to prevent fingerprints, and not a single soul would give it the least thought. You could have a surgical saw in your hand and no one would raise an eyebrow!" He raised his own tufted eyebrows to emphasize the point. "Now Mr. Helkampf, Miss Lindley, identify yourselves please?"

The surgeon and nurse whom I had followed into the operating room both removed their masks, caps, and surgical gowns. The faux surgeon was a very tall man in his thirties, prematurely bald on top but with a generous amount of dark hair above both ears, like a scary circus clown, although in my book, "scary circus clown" is the exact opposite of an oxymoron.

The nurse called Miss Lindley was, of course, Gemma. "Both present and accounted for, Dean Harrow," she said cheerily, giving a wink to the man named Helkampf. This friendly signal to her companion stung me as if a poison-pen letter had been hand-delivered to my heart, minus the letter.

The dean said, "Please share what each of you were up to, had your mission not been interrupted by the histrionics of Mr. Iverson."

The students' amused sniggers made my cheekbones burn as Helkampf gestured toward me. "Well, this jackass ended up assisting me, unintentionally. I'd been planning to create a diversion on the other side of the operating theater by tossing a cherry bomb that way. But his dramatic entrance caused a different distraction and while you all gave him your attention, I switched the tubes between the oxygen and ether tanks. As the patient started to fail from too much ether, the anesthesiologist would have tried to save him by increasing oxygen and decreasing ether—or so he'd think he'd be doing—until he cut off the oxygen completely. In the ensuing panic, I would have raced out of here as if to find one of those new defibrillating devices, slipped out of this medical gown in the surgeon's disposal closet where I'd first put it on, and departed the building as a civilian who had no connection to this unfortunate mishap."

The dean turned to Pinckney. "Doc? Your verdict?"

Pinckney frowned. "You'd toss a cherry bomb in an operating room, near ether and oxygen tanks?"

Helkampf smiled with assurance. "A fire would doubly assure my target's deletion."

"I'll pretend I didn't hear that, sir!" snapped the dean. "You'd have us all dead as well, were this not a simulation. We don't condone cold-bloodedly murdering a team of dedicated physicians just to achieve your self-serving deletion. As Guy McMaster often said, 'By all means commit murder but not by all means!'"

Bob, the designated patient on the operating table, asked Helkampf, "But, Jud, what if I—meaning, your stepfather—didn't die but spent the rest of his life in a coma? That wouldn't do you much good if you're looking to inherit his fortune."

"Oh, my stepfather doesn't have a fortune," said Jud. "I need a good malpractice suit against the hospital. Then he'll have a fortune for me to inherit. The biggest awards often go to victims who survive but are dependent on life support for the rest of their lives. A coma would be just fine." He smirked. "I just love my veggies!"

My back bristled at this loathsome joke, and those around me gasped or gaped in revulsion.

"Wrong in every way!" hammered the dean. "Despicable language, Helkampf, and contrary to McMasters philosophy, we strive for quick, clean deletions."

"It's also inept understanding of the law," I spoke from my seat of exile, where I might as well have been wearing a dunce cap.

You may or may not know, mystery patron of mine, that I have more knowledge than I wish about comas, owing to my father being in one for several weeks after his and my mother's accident. For the last few weeks of his life when I was fourteen, I learned about inheritances and comas, until his death and bankruptcy rendered the subject meaningless.

"What do you mean?" Helkampf came back icy-creepy, and for the first time since I'd sat down, Stedge took his eyes off me. It was probably stupid of me to challenge him but I'd been stewing away from being made a fool of by the likes of Cubby Terhune, resenting Gemma's apparent coziness with Jud Helkampf, and grimly realizing that the conclusion of this seminar might also mean the finale of me. I thought I might as well try to reclaim my dignity, particularly if it might be the last thing I do.

"Pray, what has Jud misconstrued?" asked the dean, but I aimed my answer straight at Helkampf's tightly paired eyes.

"In the case of a coma," I said evenly, "any award stemming from a lawsuit would go to a trust fund dedicated to maintaining the victim for the rest of his days."

Harrow allowed himself a thin smile. "He's right, you know, Mr. Helkampf. All your work and risk would have been for nothing."

"Not after I've deleted him the second time around," countered Jud, yielding no ground. "My stepfather can't alter his will when he's in a coma, can he, sir? So, after I win the judgment on his behalf, the trust becomes an asset of his estate, which he made the mistake of leaving to me. I've been such a devoted stepson in recent years." He caught himself grinning and reined it in a few seconds too late.

The dean eyed him warily. "You're deeper and darker than I thought, sir. This is not the situation you outlined for us when you enrolled."

Jud blinked twice, his shining scalp and the thick dark hair on the sides of his head giving him the appearance of an ostrich egg in an eagle's nest. "Oh, this isn't what I'm really going to do, Dean Harrow. I was only answering in the context of this particular scenario." He smiled blandly. "Scout's honor."

The dean looked unconvinced and turned to Gemma. "And your plan, Miss Lindley?"

Gemma looked troubled by the previous exchange, but then, she'd looked troubled every time I'd seen her today. "For the purpose of this assignment, I intended to inject our victim with air."

Dr. Pinckney groaned. "You'll find that procedure is way overrated."

"A sixty-milliliter syringe, Doctor, via the vertebral artery into the brain."

Pinckney thumbed his suspenders. "Well yeah, sure, that would do it."

She removed a large syringe from her medical gown pocket. "I'd stand by the patient's head and ask if anyone thought the patient's feet were turning blue. When everyone looked at his feet, I'd inject air into his neck, under cover of adjusting his gas mask and tubing."

Bob the "patient" countered, "But then you'd be standing there with that large syringe in your hand. What if someone sees it?"

"Oh, I'd make <u>sure</u> it was seen," she said with a quiet confidence I couldn't help but admire, even as she curdled my blood. "The moment I'd injected the air into you, Bob, I'd plunge my still-empty syringe into this vial of atropine," and she produced the same from the pouch of her gown, "as if I were readying the syringe to inject into your heart, if the head surgeon deemed it necessary. I'd be viewed as both level-headed and well-prepared. Cause of death would be cerebral aneurysm, there'd be nothing unaccountable in your system, and the murder weapon"—she flourished the hypodermic—"would be filled to the brim with unused atropine."

"How would you justify asking about his blue feet?" I asked her.

"His toes <u>will</u> be blue. A fountain pen on my clipboard will have intentionally leaked ink onto my gloves, which I unwittingly transferred to the patient when I adjusted his feet on the operating table. Just enough blue on his toes to justify my concern and the attention of all." It was the longest conversation we'd had to date. I joined the burble of approval from the students in attendance, but Gemma shook it off. "No, you don't understand. It's just an intellectual exercise, I would never be able to do this."

The room went silent.

"*Pourquoi pas?*" inquired Harrow, despite there being lots of ways to ask "why not?" in his primary language. Pretentiousness aside, his face registered concern.

"Too many careers would be ruined just to serve my self-interest," said Gemma. "And it would be bad for the hospital itself. I work at one. A death like this could do harm to the community's trust, and keep people from having vital surgery."

She'd let too much compassion into the room for Doc Pinckney's liking, and he said to the class as a whole, "Well now, I realize medicine is not a calling for most of you, but do remember that your target is under anesthesia, there's no pain or suffering, just a transition from induced sleep to big sleep. And that, to me, embraces the very soul of the most important commandment you'll find anywhere in your <u>Principles of Successful Termination</u>: 'Do in others as you would have others do you in.'"

A bell rang and the students, pleased to reach the end of a long day, filed out. I wasn't sure if I was supposed to join them or not. Was I still a student, or had I revealed myself as a duplicitous traitor to both McMasters and you, my charitable sponsor?

Just what did they do with turncoats at the McMasters Conservatory for the Applied Arts?

"Come along, Mr. Iverson, you must be starved to death," said the dean. He saw my startled look and added dryly, "That's an observation, by the way. Not a decree."

VII

From the Journal of Cliff Iverson

The snub-nosed yellow school bus marked "Route 6: Labs–Residence Halls–Student Union" was lying in wait for us in the dark, for the sun had made an early night of it while we were fretting over matters medical. I took a vacant window seat toward the back, wanting to nurse my wounded ego in private, but my own personal traitor Cubby sat down next to me, apologizing yet again for his attempts to undermine me twice in the same day. He explained, as I had already guessed, that we had never left the McMasters "Ring Road" during our seeming escape. Had we continued much farther, we would have eventually come to the loading dock where deliveries are made, then a security gate for an area currently under construction, and then around to the main gate again. In retrospect, I realized the road had been curving gently to the left the entire time. Apparently, the outer perimeter of the Ring Road had an electrified fence of its own, concentric to the inner one and the main gate.

"But if the Ring Road only circles the campus and is fenced in as well," I asked, "how does anyone get onto the road from the outside world?"

"There's talk of a tunnelway. I'm sure you took it yourself when you came here."

"And the signs in English and Chinese . . . ?"

Cubby explained to me that the Labs were akin to a movie soundstage, re-creating real-life environments such as diners, art galleries, a dentist's waiting room, the stock market trading floor, the balcony of a Manhattan penthouse, basically any setting where students might commit their thesis, this being the term for one's graduation deletion. At today's PreMed-(itated) class, it had been an operating room, and the dean had playfully arranged the signage as a Veterans' Hospital in Free China. Tomorrow, the Labs were going to be a dining car on the Super Chief about three hours out of Chicago.

"And when you pretended to run out of gas, how'd you do it so near to where I was hiding?" I asked sullenly.

"You found me, remember? I would have pretended to be out of gas as many times and as noisily as I had to until you hijacked my truck. Cliff, you gave the wrong password at the gate. The few faculty members approved to come and go freely have multiple passwords and rotate them after each use. When I saw Sergeant Stedge on his motorbike getting ready to go after you, I volunteered to round you up instead. He followed me as a backup in case I failed, but thanks to you, I've gained points for initiative and invention, and I'm back in Harrow's good graces. I won't forget that, or that you were willing to take me along on your escape route."

Simeon Sampson came down the aisle and said in a voice intended for all, "Thanks for warning us about the evil students at McMasters. I'm sure everyone on board will show their appreciation, each in their own way."

Cubby groused, "When was the last time you helped anyone here, Sim?"

"As the first homicidalist in creation once said, 'Am I my brother's keeper?'" His refined features shifted smoothly into an expression of contempt. "Any escapee represents a threat to our safety. If I had my way, I'd flunk you here and now."

I turned my attention to the window. The moon was in retreat behind dense clouds as the bus's headlights helped it burrow through the gloom to find its way back to the main campus. A rebellious gust of wind robbed the overhead trees of a few odd leaves that had been clinging for dear life to indifferent branches. Soon I could perceive radiant gas lamps outlining the Quad and its many diagonals; clearly this straight dirt road we were taking was a considerably shorter route between the Labs and the campus than the lazily rounded Ring Road. Now I could see the fountains of Slippery Elms frothing brightly, water lit from beneath, and the bus pulled onto the paved road that hugged the Mere past residential bungalows and cottages.

The bus stopped just before Hedge House, and as the students rose from their seats, I saw for the first time that Gemma had been sitting with Jud Helkampf and was now following him off the bus, perhaps because this was the closest stop to her dorm, or perhaps because she was keeping company with him despite his earmuff hair, his disturbing grins, and his deformed plans for murder.

I asked Cubby in a low voice, "So what's <u>his</u> story?"

Cubby responded, "Helkampf? I don't know why he's here."

"For the same reason as everybody else." Even Gemma, I thought to myself.

"No, you got me wrong, Cliff, I know he's capable of murder. I just don't know why he would need any guidance from McMasters. I think he's a born sadist."

We both exited the bus. The evening was cool but windless for the moment. The gaslight lampposts evoked England, Ireland, or Beacon Hill, and in their golden glow, I was surprised to see a young couple walking hand in hand. So, romance on the campus was not out of the question. Which of course brought Gemma Lindley to mind. When I'd decided to flee McMasters, I'd regretted I would never see her again. And now there she was, just twenty feet ahead.

I called out and she turned expectantly. "Well hello again," she said brightly, then registered dismay as I drew closer. "Oh, I thought you were Jud." She began again, "I guess you've had quite a day, haven't you?"

I winced. "It's as if I'm a plebe cadet on his first day at West Point and a laughingstock since the moment I got here. Except you were kind enough not to laugh."

"My mum and dad taught me not to laugh at people who aren't laughing," she explained. "Besides, I think in life, the joke usually turns out to be on us." A colder gust of wind rudely brushed between us and she shivered, her teeth clicking reflexively and, well, charmingly, but she was all business. "The reason I'm here and what led me to enroll is no cause for levity."

"I can't picture you killing someone." Was I really saying that to her? "The few students I've met so far, I can kind of imagine it. As for me, I know now that I'm at least capable of trying. But you . . . the plan you outlined in the Labs was really smart, but I wonder if you're like the brilliant medical student who discovers she can't stand the sight of blood."

Oddly enough, now she _did_ laugh at me. "Stand at attention, Cadet. You don't pull any rank with me. This may be my first term at McMasters, too, but you're talking to a veteran."

"I don't understand."

"I've already committed murder." She stepped away at a clip that informed me my company was sought no further. I should have known I still had at least one gaffe left in me for the day.

Returning to Hedge House, I found Mrs. Forage putting messages in the residents' cubbyholes. "Is that trick knee of yours better now?" she inquired. "One time it seemed to go to your other knee, which caused me concern." I told her the pain was gone and not likely to return.

My room was as I'd left it, except that the bed had been turned down, there were a pair of folded navy blue pajamas and an identically colored robe with white piping across the foot of the bed, and Dean Harrow was seated at my writing desk. I would have found this ominous had the dean not been smiling.

"I was thinking that after the grueling day you've had, it might be humane of me to let you skip a formal dinner in the Great Hall and allow you to dine in your room." He removed a large Jacquard napkin from my desk, revealing a silver tray laden with a variety of finger sandwiches, a silver tureen of still-steaming green soup, and a crystal carafe of straw-yellow wine nested in a small silver bucket of crushed ice. "Simple fare but Girard's _potage de cresson_ is the standard by which all others are measured. I envy you your first taste."

First taste of my last meal? I wondered. "Would you like something yourself?" I asked in my most careless manner.

The dean laughed warmly and stood. "Yes, of course, pick me a sandwich . . . any one you like." I chose for him, and the dean ate it without hesitation. I waited, feeling guilty for either distrusting Harrow or for killing him, but if the words that followed were his epitaph, he'd decided to say it with smoked salmon and crème fraîche in his mouth. "We're not upset with you in the least, Mr. Iverson. Your escape attempt was fully anticipated, especially after your request for the cane. But we would never delete you so soon after your arrival—if only because it would be bad business to accept tuition fees for special students and then murder them on Registration Day. But now it's time you were asked the Four Enquiries. First: Is this murder of yours necessary?"

"For me, it is," I said resolutely, and stuffed an egg salad and pancetta sandwich in my mouth, for I realized that whether it was poisoned or not, I had been dying of starvation the entire day. So the hell with it. "If I had escaped, my first aim was to try once again to end Fiedler's life. The only lesson I've learned is that I'm hopelessly inept at this. Perhaps terminally so."

"But have you tried all other remedies? Will no one mourn your victim? And will this tawdry world be better off without him?"

I responded affirmatively in each instance. The dean nodded and poured some wine for himself, drinking it to demonstrate it was safe, then poured a healthy measure for me. "Excellent. You've learned there are only three ways to leave McMasters: by escaping, which is near-impossible and we'd be obliged to hunt you down; by shuffling off this mortal coil as a failed student; or by graduating fully trained and ready to perform your thesis in the outside world. I suggest that choice three is easily the most appealing. What say you, Cliff?"

I've been alone since being fired from Woltan, dear sponsor. I grew up with a kind aunt and a begrudging uncle as my only family. In college, partly out of financial necessity, I made my studies my life, then proceeded directly to Woltan where I traded in studying for designing. My propulsion engineer, Jack Horvath, was a dear friend but more like a supportive uncle . . . and now, of course, he's gone. Fiedler's claims about my radical leanings (the sum total of my politics being that Jimmy Stewart would make a good president) caused those from work to keep their distance after I was fired.

But now, thanks to your mysterious generosity, I have mentors willing to teach me a craft, and classmates with a shared intent. I might even make a friend or two.

And so I've decided not to think of McMasters as a luxurious prison, but as a blessed and unexpected opportunity, a second chance I haven't earned but for which I am deeply grateful. Whoever you are, you've provided me this miracle, wanting me to not only better myself but to worsen Fiedler. I owe you a much better effort than I've made thus far.

Just now, I took a last sip of wine and turned to the textbooks that had been left on my desk. One volume interests me most, and is clearly offered with my specific mission in mind. It's bound in black leather with gilt trim. A strong, intricate pattern evokes the spiked fence of the school, edged with flowers bearing ominous thorns. It bears the emblem "McM" in two diagonal corners and, opposite them, the same strange symbol I'd seen on the conservatory's main gate.

I opened the book, feeling (I would imagine) something like an archaeologist who unseals a tomb immediately after reading an inscription placing a curse on all who enter.

But I opened the book all the same.

The frontispiece quietly restated its title: Murder Your Employer, naming Guy McMaster as its author, but crediting other contributors to what was clearly a newly revised edition. The names included Dean Harbinger Harrow, Captain (ret.) James Dobson NYPD, and an R. M. Tarrant. I plunged into its preface, which began with a few sentences surely penned by the dean himself, as they sound exactly like him. I copy them here so that you know I clearly have my work cut out for me.

"Let us inform you of the bad news as early in your studies as possible. Those who wish to delete their employer embark upon a treacherous path. What might seem, on the face of it, one of the easier pursuits undertaken by a McMasters graduate is actually among the most perilous.

"Oh, to do in one's dentist (never a completely bad idea) or, better yet, any clerk at the department for motor vehicle registration! Simplicity itself.

"But to delete one's employer, whether—"

The lights have just gone off in my room and the luminous clock by my bed says it's precisely ten. I'm writing by the light of that dial at the moment so I apologize if my words are hard to read. Sleep seems like the second-best thing in the world right now, the first being a second chance to spare the world from Merrill Fiedler. Thank you for granting me this remarkable and unforeseen opportunity. I will try to do right by you and wrong by him. Good night.

VIII

Although Cliff Iverson would have considered Gemma Lindley and Doria Maye (a.k.a. undergraduate Dulcie Mown) to be comfortably niched within our student body, he might have been surprised to learn that but a few months prior to his own arrival, both women had known as little about the conservatory as had he. And since we will be following both women's progress throughout this text, I take you (very briefly) back to their own first introduction to the McMasters Way. —HH

Standing at the back of the faux-Jacobean banquet hall in Little Bavington, in the English county of Northumberland, Gemma Lindley reached into the right pocket of her suede jacket and, for moral support, touched the folded application form within, while Adele Underton, administrative executive of St. Ann's Hospital, was honored for her innovative House Call program, this being a mobile clinic for the elderly and infirm.

"Thank you, really, all," began Underton in a surprisingly common accent. She twisted the mahogany-and-brass plaque to catch the beam of a spotlight as the spiffy crowd turned their chairs away from their blancmange to view the stage. "Thanks for this honour. But our House Call program was truly a group effort."

Gemma clenched her teeth. *There was no group. I did it alone.*

"And while this may have been my dream . . ."

Liar. I dreamt it up.

". . . it requires a team to make something this big happen."

There was no team.

"And so I accept this not only for myself . . ."

Don't accept it for yourself.

". . . but for all those who unfortunately I haven't time to name here . . ."

Take the time to name me here. 'My assistant Gemma Lindley, for the idea, and for the execution of said idea, and all that she does', for which you take all the credit.

". . . and so I thank all the team, and particularly all of *you* gathered here tonight for this single-most honour . . ."

Gemma could not help but think how hard she'd worked. The good she'd done had been its only reward, and she'd been fine with that until what rewards there were had gone to Adele, whose grip she was in, tight as a hemostat.

". . . and so, let's have a grand night!" Adele declared to a last round of applause.

You'd need a big vat to boil a person in oil, wouldn't you? Would I put her in the vat and slowly bring the oil to a rolling boil? Or would it already be boiling as I drop her from high above, after dredging her in egg yolks and flour? What a gorgeous sound she would make!

She tightened her grip on the application form. Three months earlier she'd accepted an invitation from her late father's cousin Julia to visit her newly acquired home in Italy atop a truncated mount near Livorno. Julia had purchased the rustic but now well-appointed villa after the unexpected death of Lymon, her husband of many years. Gemma had admired how courageously Julia had moved forward with her life, donating Lymon's collection of antique wind instruments to the British Museum and exchanging her predictable perch as the widow of a chartered accountant for the food, wine, and sunlight of the Tuscan coast, despite so many of her new male neighbors being considerably younger than *la splendida Giuliana*.

When Gemma, after a few too many glasses of Vermentino, had shared with her friend the soul-crushing despair of life under the unrelenting thumb of Adele Underton (although keeping to herself the dark hold Adele had over her), Julia revealed that when she had felt similarly oppressed, she had gone back to college for some courses that helped her cope.

"This was after Lymon passed on?" asked Gemma.

"No, before. But it was very helpful in terms of my new life. In fact, it made my new life possible." And then she spoke straightforwardly about how a sabbatical from the hospital might provide the Rx to remedy her current ills.

After the awards ceremony, Gemma returned home, knowing her mum would already be well asleep. Her mother was senior cook at the nearby Imperial Chemical Industries (ICI) factory, and on weekdays she had to be up at dawn to oversee the baking of bread for the employee canteen. Gemma sat at the kitchen table, unfolded the application form, uncapped her fountain pen, and filled in the spaces for name, address, telephone, occupation, annual income, and estimated financial worth. The next question read:

What is the motivation and justification for your thesis?

Julia had also explained to her what the word "thesis" meant in this context. Gemma thought for a moment and then wrote, from the heart:

Blackmailers shouldn't be allowed to live.

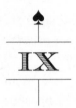

IX

Doria Maye had never been required to wait in Leon's waiting room before. For her, Leonid Kosta's reception area had simply been the next-to-last portal in the procession from her bungalow on the studio's back lot to Kosta's palatial office, whose twenty-two-foot mahogany doors would be gaping upon her arrival, framing the five-foot-five studio head, his arms beckoning. "There she is!" he'd cry. "There's the Regent Diamond of my crown jewels, there's my goddess, Doria darling, come, my doors are always open for you!"

His doors were now closed for her. And in the reception area just outside them, Doria's four-inch heels were growing cooler by the minute.

She complained to Kosta's receptionist, "He asked me to be here at three, I arrived at three twenty, and now it's three-thirty. That's half an hour I've been waiting."

The receptionist looked up from a magazine. "I'm sorry, did you say something Miss Maye?" she asked. "I'm afraid I was buried in thought."

"Yes, and I'm sure it was a shallow grave," Doria remarked. "How much longer am I expected to sit here? I've had marriages that ended sooner than this."

"I guess we're both paid to sit here," remarked the receptionist in unacceptably egalitarian fashion. She returned to her magazine and did not look up until 3:40, when she glanced at her watch and said, "Mr. Kosta will see you now."

There'd been no sound of an intercom or buzzer and Doria was compelled to ask, "Did he *instruct* you to make me marinate here until this moment?"

"I wouldn't keep him waiting," recommended the receptionist.

Doria rose to her feet and approached the doors, not sure if she should wait for Kosta to open them from within or for the receptionist to rise and do so for her. Neither event transpired, so she managed the job alone, if with some difficulty.

Leon Kosta was reading a script, and as his feet were resting on his immense desk, the soles of his shoes were the first greeting she received. "Did you read this Paramount script I sent you?" he asked, not looking up.

"I'll just sit here then, shall I?" she said, moving to a chair across from him.

Kosta lowered the script. His face could have been that of a Mediterranean fisherman, a thriving black marketeer in Izmir, or a Hollywood titan. He had, in his time, been all three.

"Did you like it?" he asked.

She hesitated. "It's . . . Leon, it's wonderful. I read the novel two years ago and, if possible, I think Hal's adaptation is even superior to the book. What few changes he made only help us understand Ember better."

He reached for the novel on his desk, *Ember Morgan Comes Home*, its now-trademark cover depicting the title character standing on the roadside, caught in the headlights of an approaching truck, unashamed in her green top with black stripes and black satin skirt, her traveling bag resting next to the ankle straps of her glossy shoes. The image had been seen in every bookstore window and paperback display around the country.

His eyes glistened with eagerness. "The role would suit you?"

"More than—" She stopped herself. "I was born to play the part. I may not physically resemble her, but Edith can pad me in all the right places and you'll remember I went redhead for *Make a Grown Man Cry*, so it won't startle anyone to see me that way. Soft-hearted strumpets used to be my trademark, and I think the public would love to see me play a self-sacrificing floozy one last time."

"I agree." He opened a mahogany humidor and she could smell its Spanish cedar lining. "Cigar?" he asked.

She didn't know what to say. "Uh, no. Thank you."

Kosta selected a chestnut-colored Habanos. "Paramount wants me to loan you out to them for *When Mason Met Miss Dixon*. But then you couldn't do this, and you for this makes sense."

"Yes, it does make sense, Leon," she said, using the grateful voice she'd come up with for *The Loves of Florence Nightingale*. "After all, for the last eight months the only lens I've been in front of was held by my dermatologist. You should be putting me through my paces. Why loan me out to stud for another farm?"

It was absolutely the worst way she could have phrased it, as if her voice had been hijacked by what Edgar Allan Poe called the Imp of the Perverse.

Kosta guillotined the head of his cigar employing a replica of the one he'd built for the opening scene of *Waterloo*. "I hear Marc Danner is some stud, too."

Suddenly the torment of her exile for the past year burst from her. "Leon, we were filming in Moab-bloody-Utah. It was *you* who stuck us out there. Marc was doing rewrites every night trying to reinvent a role written for Laraine Day. We'd run new lines at dawn in a camper smaller than your desk, we were so cramped it was physically impossible *not* to have sex."

Leon reached for a massive lighter on his desk and she wondered if he were going to throw it at her. "Three years," he pronounced. "For three years I tell every actor and director on this lot to respect you and not even think of making a move on you, confiding in them that not even I, King Kosta, can nail you . . . and then you screw the new head of production for Republic!"

"But that was months before he got the position at Republic, he was just a writer at the time! Sex with a screenwriter doesn't count, it's barely masturbation! How was I to know he'd get a job with another studio? We had a one-night stand, and I mean that literally, the trailer was so tiny we were forced to stand. And you'll notice he hasn't offered me any films since he's been at Republic. Can't you forgive me? I had no idea anyone would hear about it. He and I were the only ones who knew—"

"*He* was the one who told me!" bellowed Kosta. "He's told everyone. You've made me look like a fucking *eunuch*!"

"I believe 'fucking eunuch' is an oxymoron," Doria responded, wondering if there was anything she wouldn't do to land this part. She searched deep into her soul and thankfully came up empty. "Well, let's get our little revenge on *him* then, shall we?" she chummed up to him in a mischievous voice. "Let's start seeing each other. Let the rumor mill spin into high gear, and I'll let it be known that in my little black book Leonid Kosta is a man among moguls." She giggled. "The mogul I ogle. I like that. Do you like that?"

"You're saying you'll screw me now?"

"My pleasure," she purred, knowing those two words would never enter into the equation.

He singed the tip of his cigar with the desk lighter's flame, took a quick puff and blew the smoke across the desk and directly into her memorable eyes. "Why would I sleep with you now? I sleep with skillful harlots, eager ingenues, and stars. You're a has-been in the making."

"Only because you've put me in cold storage during the winter of your discontent with me. But here I am, thawed out and rendering unto Caesar what is Caesar's: You came, I thaw, you conquer. But once I play Ember, I'll at last be a star worthy of your"—she pasted a smile over her internal cringe—"big entrance."

He ignored her dangling proposition and poured a glass of water from a silver carafe, opened a pewter pillbox on his desk, and swigged down several blue pills with a pained grimace. Then he held up the Paramount script and, with the lighter, ignited its lower right-hand corner. "You're never playing this part, 'Doria Maye,' a.k.a. Doris May Taplow. The only reason I had you read the script was because I wanted you to understand what you've lost."

She watched the burning pages curl back on themselves in their death agony. Kosta tossed the flaming script into the wastebasket, poured water from his carafe to snuff it, opened a drawer, and removed another script. "You're under exclusive contract to this studio for the next six years. All I'm obliged to offer you is two pictures a year, but you have the right to refuse. Here's the first." He slid the script across the desk toward her.

"What is it?" she said, with all the wariness of a new mother being handed the swaddled spawn of Satan.

"Based on a nice children's book that's coming out. Its publisher gave me an advance look. Story of a smart spider and a condemned pig, made me bawl my eyes out and it's about time we gave Disney a run for his money. You'll do the voice. You won't be on camera, but still, a picture's a picture."

"I'd be the spider?"

"Oh, you don't want to be the spider. She dies at the end and I'm doing a whole series. You're going to be the pig. I'm making you as big as Francis the Talking Mule."

An actual grin came over his hard face, and she understood. "I see. So that in the future, everyone who sees one of my old movies will laugh and say, 'Hey, I know that voice! She's the talking pig!' Like being unable to see Bert Lahr without thinking of the Cowardly Lion. I'd never be cast in a serious role again!" She stood, attempting to summon her dignity, or at least some indignity. "I exercise my right to refuse your offer."

"I'm sure you can use the exercise. Listen, cherub, there's tons of stinking scripts in this town and I intend to offer you all of them. But the next time you appear in a quality role will either be when your contract has expired, along with the public's memory of who you were . . . or over my dead body."

Slowly panning across the mental image of his dead body, she turned on her heels and exited his office, attempting to slam the doors behind her, a difficult task considering the size of the doorknobs alone. She yanked at one, then pulled the other, and stormed through the waiting room.

"You need to change agencies, Miss Maye."

Doria stopped and turned. The receptionist was still the only one in the room, adjusting an arrangement of royal-blue delphiniums on a pedestal near where Doria was standing. "Were you speaking to me?" asked the actress.

The receptionist never looked up from the flowers but continued in a low, precise voice, "It sounds as though you could use my fiancé's help. He's the fastest-rising agent in this town."

Doria had had enough of her cheek for one day. "And he's such a success that his future wife has to work reception?"

"I don't do this for the salary. I do it for the information I acquire on his behalf. These walls can talk, Miss Maye, and I listen."

"What firm does your fiancé work for?" she asked.

"Roger Holland Associates."

Doria laughed. "Roger Holland is a despicable human being."

"I agree. Vile and loathsome. But he isn't anymore."

"A change of heart?"

"Yes, it's been donated to science. He died last month under pretty seamy circumstances while vacationing in Patong. The agency is trying to keep it under wraps while my fiancé reorganizes the firm. Here's his card. And you should take this with you to the meeting." She handed Doria what appeared to be a miniature satin playing card. On one side was the silhouette of an ace of spades, while engraved on the back were the letters McM. "He can explain when you meet."

"I don't understand," Doria asked. "Is this some sort of casino or resort?"

"No," said the receptionist, giving the delphiniums a final primp. "It's a school where they'll teach you how to act."

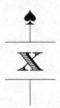

From the Journal of Cliff Iverson

Dear sponsor (and from hereon I'm going to address you as "dear X" because you're beginning to sound like a brand of toothpaste or shampoo): Today was my first full day at McMasters. It began with my usual disorientation when I wake in unfamiliar surroundings, assume I'm still in my bedroom at home, and wonder why someone has, during the night, relocated my window to a different wall and moved my dresser to where my front door had been. Then my brain slowly re-deals the hand I was dealt the day before, one card after another gradually reminding me (in this case) of the extraordinary circumstances leading to my now occupying a smart if simply furnished dormitory room on an idyllic campus nestled in the verdant woodlands of God knows where. Outside, a confident morning sun seemed to be taking full credit for gifting me with a new start in life, and a shaft of its light helpfully pointed out that a slim notebook had been slipped under my door while I'd slept.

I rose quickly from my bed, donned the robe I'd draped over the Mission chair at my desk, and plucked the notebook from the carpeted floor with curiosity. It resembled the kind of small composition book with a pale blue cover that's distributed by school monitors for essay questions. A note clipped to the cover from my resident advisor explained that all students are required to state the reason and rationale for their projected thesis, this statement usually submitted as part of their evaluation for admission. In my unusual case, however, this statement was still due. The booklet was blank except for the question at the top of page one:

What is the motivation and justification for your thesis?

*From Cliff Iverson's file, we are able to here
share the answer he gave.—HH*

If my mother could speak to me from beyond the grave and she knew what I'd been up to of late, I'm sure she'd say, "God in heaven, Cliff, what happened to you? Why would you dedicate your life to removing another person from the planet? Did our death when you were so young leave you bitter toward all those who continued to live?"

To which I'd say, "Forget about <u>me</u>, Mom, what is heaven like and where the hell is <u>Dad</u>?!" I know I shouldn't joke about such things, but my life's gotten so simultaneously sinister and absurd in recent days that my best option may be to laugh until I cry, especially since I got much of the crying part out of the way months ago.

Trust me, I do understand the frailty of existence and that a human life comes only one to a customer. But then you get older and discover there are people in this world who rob others of their lives or make life too hard for others to live. And too often these people thrive and profit.

Maybe this is convenient to say, but I believe lots of people have at least one individual in their lives about whom they think, "I could never murder anyone. Except maybe . . ."

That's who Fiedler is to me.

Usually, the threat of capital punishment or life imprisonment is enough to deter us from committing that one murder we might otherwise rationalize. But then again, when people commit self-murder (meaning suicide), aren't they sentencing themselves to in-stantaneous execution? Yet, tragically, even that punishment isn't always enough to deter them.

So if sensible people can kill themselves because life no longer seems worth living, then I suppose a sensible person might kill someone who makes other people's lives unlivable, or who endan-gers the existence of others. It's the "Could you assassinate Hitler?" clause. Are there not little Hitlers who try to rule our lives? What army protects us from them?

It took three strikes for me to place Fiedler in this context, and the second one alone was enough to justify Fiedler's end: He posed a daily threat to innocent lives. I told him, "Fiedler, there's now a potentially deadly series of flaws in the W-10."

Fiedler looked up from his couch where he was reading a magazine. "Close my door," he said, and after I did, he continued, "A little late in the day to be telling me, don't you think?"

"It was safe as designed," I answered, enraged he'd try to shift blame onto me. "The production modifications you've made change all that."

"Don't be stupid," he said. "We'll make our sales. There'll be some initial flights. Maybe a problem will be reported. We'll offer on-site modification for an additional surcharge."

I lowered my voice. "Or a plane we constructed will drop out of the sky, killing all souls on board after as terrifying a free fall as any human will ever experience. This includes the flight crew, who will have the technical knowledge to understand that their lives are over and there's nothing they can do except pray they picked the religion that delivers an afterlife."

Fiedler's next strike occurred when Jack Horvath, my propulsion engineer, was discovered in Ellwood Park with a .29 blood alcohol level, dead from a direct gunshot wound to the heart. No one would accuse Fiedler of having murdered him. I knew better, and that's when I started thinking in dead earnest how I would ensure Fiedler met a fate no worse (but no better) than death.

But before any of this, there was Cora. You at McMasters seem to already have something in my file about her, but for the record, Cora Deakins was Woltan's inventory supervisor. All my requisitions needed her approval, whether I asked for a fresh crate of yellow legal pads or a gross of Hamilton camshafts for testing purposes. In her quiet and patient way, she was probably one of Woltan's most powerful employees, but those at the top had made sure not to tell her this.

I liked her from the outset. A lot. I'm sure there's such a thing as love at first sight, although I suspect many people recall it more in retrospect than experience it in their initial encounter. But I do believe in seeing someone in a different light for a first time, suddenly realizing that this person you've been passing in the hall for months is someone you might be prepared to share your life with, even though the previous day you'd barely given them a thought, or at least a conscious one.

Cora, whose features and facial expressions had always received a warm welcome from my eyes, loved to rib me about some of the strange purchases the design team would submit for her authorization. There were the ten braces of dead turkeys that Jack Horvath and I (both of us strapped to one end of the Woltan wind tunnel) hurled into our latest engine's cowling to see how the W-10 might survive a flock of migrating geese being sucked into the spinner. Cora not only witnessed our messy enterprise, for which she said we should be tarred since we were already feathered, but also approved the solvents we ordered by the barrel to remove the literally fowl odor from the tunnel. After a hogshead of pine, lemon, and clove oils failed, she suggested cranberry jelly, chestnut stuffing, and mashed potatoes. In that moment, now that my evenings no longer consisted of studying for an exam or working a night job to pay for those studies, my mind focused on the relative vacuum of my social life. In Cora, I believed I might have had the dumb luck to have discovered the remedy to that state of affairs, and perhaps so much more.

The next day, while she was reviewing my latest requisition requests, I concluded, ". . . some Melton epoxy for the wing models, ten Zeitner display stands, and maybe you'd like to take in a movie this weekend, and, oh yeah, a new K-5 compressor."

"A movie?" she asked. "Which one do you have in mind?"

Did she think I was requisitioning one? "Anything that interests you. Don't limit yourself to black-and-white. Money is no object. And this would include your own bag of popcorn, you wouldn't have to share."

She looked intently at her clipboard. "You don't even know me."

"Well, that was the idea. Get to know you."

"By sitting side by side for two hours, making no eye contact and not talking?"

"Well, I'm terrified of awkward silences," I said, as much honest as flippant, "and you notice them less during a western."

As far as I could tell, she was more amused than alarmed by me, and her reply was fair enough. "Tell you what: You pick a movie you'd genuinely like to see. That should tell me something about you right there."

"I suppose I should rule out any Popeye cartoon festivals?" I ventured.

She smiled just a bit. "It's all up to you. I'll pick the restaurant for after the movie, and that may tell you something about me, because it will be inexpensive and we'll split the check."

"Oh, this date's going to cost me?" I said with alarm. "Geez, now I'm not so sure."

We made it for the coming Saturday, which on Monday felt several light-years away from the cold feet I sometimes develop as an eventful day approaches. She had no cause to drop by my offices in Woltan Tower for the remainder of the week, and by midday Saturday, I thought I'd best ring her, just out of thoughtfulness, in case she'd had a particularly strenuous week and wished to postpone. Perhaps, even like myself, she was wondering what we would talk about outside of work. I would certainly understand her reticence, just as she would probably understand mine if I'd had any. I mean, there had been talk that Merrill Fiedler had taken her out once or twice. She might be afraid I couldn't match the expensive nightspots or restaurants his expense account afforded. Sure. Fine. Let her go out with Fiedler if that's the kind of man that interests her. Would I want to be with the same kind of woman that Merrill Fiedler would squire, impressed by his expensive watch, his private office, his stenographic pool? She probably thinks she's too good for me, and I probably pressured her into making the date. I should call and see if she wants to cancel. I looked up her number in the company directory. Her phone was listed under "Mr. and Mrs. J. Deakins," which made me assume she lived with her parents . . . unless Cora was the "Mrs." in "Mr. and Mrs. J. Deakins," in which case how shameful of her to go out with me on a Saturday night!

A raspy male voice answered, "Yes?" He sounded as if he had a case of strep.

"Sorry," I apologized without knowing why, "my name's Cliff Iverson. I work at Woltan. I was wondering if Cora could come to the phone?"

"No, she can't," he said. Then he must have dropped the phone, for I heard it clatter loudly against a wood surface as he cursed and recovered the receiver. "I'm her father—" He started to cough repeatedly.

"Well, may I leave a message for her?"

"No, you can't. She's _dead_." I heard a moan the likes of which I hope I'll never encounter again. ". . . She's dead," he repeated, and hung up before I could say anything further.

By Monday, most of Cora's friends at Woltan seemed to know it had been suicide. The word "Nembutal" was being whispered. She'd been having trouble sleeping of late.

I took her death hard. I realize this must sound ridiculously overdramatic, and I hate it when people try to graft themselves onto someone else's tragedy. But I felt as if some part of my future self might have died with her. Foolish. However, the design and production deadlines for the W-10 made no allowance for the grief of a man whose only claim on Cora was "the date that might have been." My associate Jack Horvath, Dutch uncle that he was to me, saw to it that I had lots of thorny issues to keep me busy. (This was all before I discovered the cost-conscious design changes Fiedler had made to impress the Woltan boardroom.)

About two weeks later, I went for what I thought would be a quick drink after work with Keefe Maguire, the head of Woltan's structural assembly division. He was being relocated to the company's small branch in Dortmund, which he said was an industrial part of Germany most admired by those who love smokestacks. Keefe had always treated my designs with care and I asked if I could buy him a farewell round at the nearby Shandon Star. His first rye with Rheingold chaser soon turned into three, which unfortunately had also turned me, in Keefe's reddening and watery gaze, into a confidant. The subject of Cora's suicide had come up—probably because I was still so haunted by her death that it only took the lone beer I'd been nursing to mention her name.

Keefe's head waggled in a knowing way. "Something you should know about Cora," he shared with me slurringly. "Last month, me and some guys from work bumped into Fiedler at a strip club on The Block. He was at the bar, buying ginger ale at champagne prices for a trio of pros while he kept knocking back gimlets. Got himself drunker than I am now." This reminded Keefe to order another round for himself but this time he dumped his fresh shot of rye straight into his brew and chugged the mix down. "Guess he was embarrassed I caught him paying for bar girls, so . . ." He leaned into my face, beer froth clinging to his lips as if he were rabid, and confided, ". . . he showed me two pictures he had of Cora, buck naked in his office."

I wanted to smack the world-wise expression from his face, and you should keep in mind I had always liked Keefe until now. If Fiedler himself had walked in at that moment, God knows what I'd have done to him. "You shouldn't be telling me this," I growled through clenched teeth. "If Fiedler found out, it could cost you your job."

He slammed his glass stein on the bar as if it were a gavel. "Why the hell do you think I'm being transferred?" he yelled, causing the stranger on his left to move farther down the bar. "As soon as Fiedler woke the next morning and remembered what he'd shown me, he started arranging my exit. That's what he does. If you know too much or he distrusts you, he ships you off to where you won't be heard from again. In Cora's case, she spared him the trouble."

Keefe further related (at this point I needed to order a shot of rye for myself) that Fiedler had boasted of an ingredient he could add to a drink that heightened his "hypnotic power" . . . and that he photographed the end result more to keep his guests in line than to paste in his scrapbook of golden memories.

For me, this was easily a fourth strike for Fiedler, but as you at McMasters somehow already know, he was able to discredit me before I could design a plan to end him. The funny thing is, he wasn't even aware that I cared for Cora. I was simply the person who knew too much about the W-10's vulnerabilities, owing to Fiedler's production modifications, something that only myself and Jack could likely detect or even prove without a catastrophic failure.

When you create an airplane, a submarine, a bridge, you knowingly make necessary but informed compromises within the tolerances of your design, factoring in where stress is likely to occur, circumventing your most vulnerable pressure points in the empennage or crown. However, Fiedler's modifications were, like himself, both stupid and arrogant. They assumed nothing else could possibly go wrong, but things _can_ go wrong, and several things going wrong simultaneously must never happen at ten thousand feet.

Once I told him about this, Fiedler dealt with it in decisive fashion, by immediately planting Woltan's confidential research in my car and in Horvath's locker, falsely staining us a reviled shade of pink, effectively destroying our careers and credibility.

The damage Fiedler has caused can't be undone. But if I can get it right this time, I could at least stop him from doing any further harm for the rest of his life. How? By making sure the rest of his life ends a whole lot sooner than he has reason to expect . . . and the sooner the better, because it's not as if Fiedler has no further projects or people he could endanger.

And I've come to realize in writing this that whatever plan I might develop to—what's the word they use here at McMasters?— "delete" him, it also needs to alert others to the flaws in the W-10 in a way that the higher-ups at Woltan will notice and believe, hopefully before the W-10 ever takes its first commercial flight.

"But killing Fiedler won't bring back Cora or Horvath," I can imagine my parents saying. "That's just an eye for an eye."

To which I'd say I'm truly sorry Fiedler only has two eyes.

That's as much of an answer as I can give to this question this morning. I know I have a lot ahead of me today, so I hope this serves its purpose.

Clifford Iverson
Hedge House

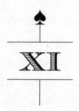

XI

FROM THE JOURNAL OF CLIFF IVERSON

Dear X: My first term is proving to be every bit as pastoral, frantic, and surreal as my first day.

As happens in one's early weeks at any new college, I made a few initial acquaintances due more to schedule, classroom seating, and housing than affinity. I have come to like (or perhaps "be impressed with" would be more accurate) Dulcie Mown, although I haven't yet figured out why I feel I've already met her before in the world beyond the conservatory's electrified fence.

Most of the students here have a "live and let live" attitude toward others, which is slightly hilarious considering the intent of our studies. Jud Helkampf (the sick-minded "surgeon" from Labs) and fair-haired Simeon Sampson both seem to have decided independent of each other that I represent a challenge to their goals, which would amuse me if I weren't worried they'll try to permanently eliminate the competition. The one personality I can't crack is Gemma Lindley, who seems determined to avoid me since revealing she'd already murdered someone.

One day, after class in the Gonzago Bower, I'd asked her if she'd like to join me for dinner at Scarpia that Sunday evening, when the dining hall is closed and students must fend for themselves. She'd said no without the thanks. I settled for one of the trattoria's pizzas, sharing it with the often-inescapable Cubby Terhune from down the hall and my RA, Champo Nanda, after which I turned my attention to chapter three of <u>Murder Your Employer</u>, which enumerated all that mission's pitfalls, i.e.: "Never commit a deletion using your victim's trade: 1.) Do not electrocute an electrician (as past exposure may have made him resistant to shock) 2.) Do not poison a pharmacologist as he or she may have knowledge of and easy access to a remedy . . ." and so on, in discouraging fashion.

Owing to my disgracefully inept attempt on Fiedler's life, the date of my arrival at McMasters had been moved up a term, and most of my electives had to be chosen for me in absentia by Registrar June Felsblock, whose imposing but strangely enthralling frame had greeted me on my first full morning in her second-floor office at the manor house.

"Yes, I'm afraid I had to sort out your study load myself," she confirmed, "but as it happens, most of your classes are mandatory for first-term students anyway." Reviewing my file, she said cheerily, "So. Murdering Our Employer, are we? Well, don't think it hasn't crossed _my_ mind more than once!" She laughed, looked around the room as if concerned about hidden microphones, and considered my schedule card.

IVERSON, CLIFF J.	TERM 1	Recruit (Sponsored)		MAJOR: Delete Employer		SUPERVISOR: Dean Harrow	
	MONDAY	TUESDAY	WEDNESDAY	THURSDAY	FRIDAY	SATURDAY	SUNDAY
7	P.E.	⟶	⟶	⟶	⟶	⟶	Sleep in!
8	Breakfast	⟶	⟶	⟶	⟶	⟶	
9	Penmanship	Language I		Practical Electronics	Language I		Sunday Brunch 9–1:30
10		Herbicide (Gonzago Bower)		All Creatures Venemous & Small (The Serpentine)		Shabbat Morning Kiddush (opt.)	Chapel (opt.)
11	Headquarters	Principles of Deletion	P. of D.	P. of D.	Headquarters	Seasonal Gameplay (currently Underhanded Tennis)	Sunday Brunch (ends 1:30)
12	Lunch	⟶	⟶	⟶	⟶		
2	Arts & Letters	Odds & Ends	Arts & Letters		Arts & Letters		**ASSEMBLY**
3	(Mc)Master Class (Employer) Dean Harrow		Remains to be Seen	Sporting Chance (gym clothes)	(Mc)Master Class (Employer) Dean Harrow	WMP	Lecture, Slide-show, Concert, Play, Film (attendance required)
4			High Tea (opt.)	Shower		High Tea (opt.)	
5		Ways & Means at The Labs		Ways & Means at The Labs	Eroticide (Vesta Thripper, RN) (one-time consultation)	Free	Free
7:30	Dinner	⟶	⟶	⟶			
9					Track when announced (compulsory)	Dinner & Dancing in the Ballroom*	No evening meal*

"I wondered about Greek as my foreign-language elective," I began.

"Oh, it's our most popular language course," she counseled. "It sounds foreign to everyone and no one can identify it. Sometimes I think the Greeks make it up as they go along. And their alphabet is utterly unreadable to most other nationalities."

I also questioned Penmanship, pointing out that I was already an expert draftsman.

"Forgery and related crafts," she patiently explained. "Did you know that if you trace your own signature, police experts will testify with absolute certainty that someone else was attempting to counterfeit your name? Helpful when you wish to appear you've been framed."

"But why would I need to master forgery if I'm going to, say, run somebody over with my car?" I asked, not unreasonably.

A shimmer of disapproval flitted across the registrar's bold features. "Molding the well-rounded deletist is the McMasters way. How can you understand a symphony if you only know the oboe part? Even the best-laid plans can go amiss, requiring improvisation in the field of battle while you're far from the protective confines of McMasters."

There was one remaining entry for which I keenly wished an explanation. "What is, um . . . Eroticide, may I ask?"

June Felsblock offered me a vixen-like smile. "I think it's best for Vesta Thripper to lay out the syllabus for you herself. It's purely an introductory course at this stage where your thesis is concerned, and I'm certain you'll enjoy it. Professor Graves teaches the women's version, and associate professors Laurel and Thorpe accommodate those who need to ply their skills on alternate sides of the street, so to speak. I realize such studies might be considered progressive to some, but romance, desire, seduction, and heartbreak are among the most potent arrows in the McMasters quiver. Never forget that Cupid is armed and dangerous, Mr. Iverson!" She raised her eyebrows playfully.

I swallowed and probably blushed, feeling as nervous as a foot soldier who's just been told that paratrooping is part of basic training. But I decided I'd jump off that bridge when I came to it, and was glad to change the subject. "Are there any courses that will get me outdoors?" I inquired. "I've been cooped up in windowless labs for quite a while."

"Oh, Coach Tarcott runs a very aggressive PE department, you'll be in wonderful shape by the time of your thesis. And I've got you down for Herbicide in the Gonzago Bower with tutorials at the Menagerie, that's our animal version of the poison gardens. There are some jellyfish and blue frogs currently on exhibit at Watery Villa that you shouldn't miss. Many students take great pleasure in little living killing things."

I also saw that I'd been put down for Track and confided to June Felsblock that running was not my best sport.

She smiled at my naiveté. "You don't understand. Track is not a noun. It's a verb."

I readily accept, X, that I'm not a natural where murder is concerned. But I soon discovered many of my classes didn't feel much different from my studies at MIT and Caltech: Lectures intoned to the hypnotic tattoo of chalk on slate, centered around a textbook written or updated by one's instructor. But naturally, most courses and extracurricular activities resembled nothing found at a traditional university. "Weaponry Around You" (a weeklong seminar within Principles of Deletion) focused on ordinary objects that could serve as deadly weapons; an hour was devoted to the spatula alone. Students also learned that a person is more likely to have a lethal accident in their bathroom than on a commercial flight, causing Cubby Terhune to believe that the bathroom on an airplane must be the most dangerous place in the universe.

As for the universe itself, McMasters possessed a modest but fully mechanized observatory, with its potentially catastrophic confluence of revolving domes, rotating piers, and gear teeth. The respected astronomer Signe Childs, all of five feet with owl-eyed glasses, demonstrated that an unattended telescope, with its filters and lens covers removed, could be left pointing to where the sun would arrive later in the day. "At a precise and calculable moment," she explained in a thick Swedish accent, "powerfully magnified sunlight will beam through the unshielded right-angled eyepiece, aimed wherever you wish a conflagration, while you, the perpetrator, are miles away, leaving no telltale inflammatory device at the 'scene of the flame' beyond the benevolent light of our sun. To the police—and in contradiction to Shakespeare—the fault will lie not in ourselves but in our stars."

Campus life has proved to be both delightful and harrowing. There is always the likelihood that a picnic, nature walk, touch football game, or square dance may suddenly reveal itself to be an unadvertised educational lesson. A seemingly dreamy "necking session" at the Labs, where volunteer students parked in engine-less cars on a fake cliff overlooking projected city lights below, had been deceptively billed as an Eroticide-sponsored "Meet Your Classmates Mixer." But it was quickly subverted into an Automotive Arts tutorial on how to clandestinely render a parking brake nonfunctional and ease one's unfaithful mate and one's disloyal best friend into a canyon below. Another parked car, this one with fogged-up windows, was used by Dr. Ward Pinkerman to demonstrate how an exhaust pipe can be refitted to have two ducts, switchable from outside the vehicle, one of which feeds back into the car should one's unfaithful mate be parked with one's disloyal best friend in frigid weather while the engine's running. All aspects of our daily activities were laced with the underlying purpose of McMasters' existence, no less than a Bible college would be with religion, or West Point with warfare.

I quickly learned that McMasters students proceed along two parallel paths, one of which leads to that well-rounded background articulated by June Felsblock. That's why I found myself in Winning Combinations, an ancillary elective in combination locks and safe-cracking, wondering how this acquired skill would help me destroy Fiedler. (On the bright side, the class placed me at the same workbench as Gemma, who seemed intensely keen to master the craft, for reasons she kept to herself.)

But on the alternate path, it is tacitly understood that all undergraduates are here with a specific target in mind. (My RA told me the school would never knowingly accept a serial killer or someone who was antagonistic toward, say, all DMV employees in general.) And it turns out that at least half a student's studies are dedicated to the specific strategy for one's thesis, which as I've already mentioned is McMasters parlance for one's culminating off-campus deletion. Toward that end, a designated faculty member works directly with each student, and I am fortunate to have no less than Dean Harrow as my advisor. Because he teaches so few classes himself and is only accountable to the board of directors and Assistant Dean Erma Daimler (who is also the school's chief financial officer), the dean has been free to lavish extra attention on my tutelage, and has kindly shown awareness that, because I had not enrolled voluntarily, some allowances might be made as I evolve as a full-time student.

My own attitude, dear X, has become "in for a penny, in for a pound," bolstered by my indebtedness to you. You've provided an ample trust fund for me, but I'm determined to spend as little of that as possible, for as my plans to delete Fiedler have been shaping, I suspect they may require a modest bankroll. So I've taken part-time scullery work in the Great Hall's kitchen to try to work down my debt to you.

The job has also provided me with some excellent tutorials-on-the-fly from Chef de Cuisine M. Girard Tissier, whose knowledge of poisons is far-ranging. In the aftermath of dinner, while scrubbing burnt syrup from one of the great copper sugar pots, I learned that uncooked red kidney beans can be deadly in sufficient quantity. While scraping lamb drippings from the two roasting ovens, I also overheard Girard reprimanding sous-chef Arnaud, "Non, mon brave, the acid hydrofluorique may not hurt or burn on contact but it soaks through tissue, corroding away the bone. I cannot approve of filleting a living human being, not with methods more humane at hand." I've also found food for thought regarding lead acetate as a sweetener, Condy's crystals as a neutralizer, and toxic but tasty green potatoes for a St. Patrick's Day shepherd's pie.

Pocket money from my kitchen chores has allowed me the indulgence of a fresh-pulled pint at the Skulking Wolf most evenings before bed, generously dispensed by Wilfred Mussel, proprietor of both the pub and the Tuck Shop. Since only one drink is permitted per customer and tipping is unheard of, it's been a relatively frugal indulgence . . . and when I've been encouraged by Mussel and classmates to play a few "rag" numbers on the upright piano secreted in the corner, the pint has always been on the house.

I've found convivial company at the Wolf with a number of students. Some find it therapeutic to discuss what had brought them to McMasters and what they intended to do about it when they left, each trusting that his or her secrets were safe with the others, owing to the bond of our common cause. Dieter Seidel and Enzo Gentilini often share thoughts with me over the Wolf's smooth but tangy ale. Dieter is second double reed of the Leipzig Philharmonic and covets the first chair, occupied by the imperfectly pitched nephew of its musical director, whereas Enzo is a Sicilian postal inspector who wishes to delete—without instigating a vendetta against his family—the local *caporegime*, whose drug trade led his son to addiction and death. Both are gregarious, warm-hearted men who make for excellent drinking companions, as does the ruddy-faced "Mim" Webster, whose cheery good nature has been a tonic whenever I've felt low or lonely. The friendship of Cubby Terhune has been cloying at times, but his unremitting hopefulness is almost endearing when it isn't a nuisance.

I might mention that the Skulking Wolf was once a true half-timbered inn from the 1700s, with low beams and skewed walls, and a few small, impeccably clean rooms are available on a nightly basis for private pursuits. One evening early in term I spotted Gemma at a fireside table with Jud Helkampf, he of the clownlike hair. Gemma was talking earnestly, Jud only half listening as his dead eyes kept wandering toward a narrow staircase leading upstairs. He made a terse comment to her that I couldn't hear. She looked as if she didn't know what to reply, Helkampf shrugged with a humorless smile and Gemma left.

I downed the remainder of my ale, made a hasty goodbye to my friends and followed her. She was walking quickly toward her dorm. To stop her would require calling after her, and if I did, I wasn't sure what I wanted to say. As my benefactor, I'm sure you'd agree that the last thing I need at this time is a college romance. The very phrase sounds silly, considering I'd finished my postgraduate studies several years ago. So I consciously if regretfully let go of the impulse and headed home to claim my most treasured possession these days, which is a solid night's sleep.

A typical weekday begins at 6:30. I knock on the bathroom door to make sure my next-door neighbor isn't already occupying the space. Early on I'd forgotten to lock the door to the adjoining room and Audrey Jäeger had entered just as I was about to doff my robe for a shower. I'd seen her face around Hedge House and on campus, but this was the first time I'd realized said face belonged to my (semi-detached) roommate.

"Sorry, my fault," I apologized to the curly-haired Audrey, who was wearing an identical robe to mine. She began putting eyedrops in her eyes, which looked red as if from crying. "My name's Cliff Iverson. I believe we're sharing this bathroom."

"Not for long," said Audrey in a flat voice.

I objected, "Well, it wasn't <u>my</u> idea—"

"I meant I'm not long for this place, or this world," she said, retrieving a hairbrush by the sink. "Never done anything smart my whole life. Parents bought my way through private school, I was a poor student but didn't give that any thought when I enrolled here, and now I've clevered my way into a death sentence, which is funny because I meant to be sentencing someone else. Serves me right, getting a taste of my own poison," and she closed the door behind her.

"And great to meet you, too. I'm sure we'll get along swell," I said to the door.

Each morning by seven, I take the stairs to the homey front parlor, where gym-suited Hedge House residents plucked cups of steaming beverages from the sideboard. Coach Tarcott invariably pops his head into the parlor and cries out something along the lines of, "Right, who's for double rounds of PE this morning?" to an antiphonal chorus of groans. "We're off to the bocce ball court and back!" We all dash after the coach along one of the school's many clay paths, and soon my throat is burning from exertion but cooled by the morning mist.

The student body arrived at McMasters with a variety of physiques, but with Tarcott issuing encouragements and rebukes in a range of argots, his charges are already arriving at the best shape of their lives, toned and trim. If looks alone could kill, McMasters is making deletists of us all. I do note, though, that the apparently doomed Audrey Jäeger is a frequent straggler, often in a photo finish for last place with the huffing Cubby Terhune.

After PE, I change, shower, and savor a brioche with a bowl of smoky café au lait in the manor house's morning lounge, declining the staggering English breakfast available in the Great Hall. Soon I'm off to my first morning class in the Hall of Science. This is McMasters' most modern edifice, a low-slung building that also serves as the de facto "lid" for the chemistry laboratories two substories down.

I'd thought, given my extensive background in circuitry, that I'd catch up quickly with my classmates in Practical Electronics. But the key word is "Practical." McMasters' objective was not to create electrical engineers or electricians but electrocutioners.

My instructor for this short course was adjunct professor Silvana Sparchese (who prefers to be called "Sparks" and hurls spools of insulated wire at anyone who calls her "Silvie"). On this particular morning, she was sporting her trademark green mechanic's jumpsuit (worn for no reason other than comfort) and making the point that the Hollywood cliché of a gangster turning up the radio to cover the sound of a beating or killing was problematic. Cranking a radio too loud, she said, is just as likely to draw a visit from an angry neighbor or landlord, probably not a good idea if you're trying to drown out the sounds of, say, a drowning. She spat out ideas faster than our pens could write them down. "Of course, the good side of using a radio to cover a bathtub immersion is that if all else fails, you just flip the radio into the water. However, an alumnus at Bell Labs tells me they're about to launch transistor radios which operate on a nine-volt battery. Nine volts wouldn't kill a goldfish, 'kay? Good news is, record players still need wall power and are superior in every way. With a radio, you risk your cover-up music being interrupted by a news bulletin or an unexpected four-bar rest. On a portable electric phonograph you pick the music that best serves your dark purposes and still have good old AC or DC ready if needed, 'kay?"

I looked around the room and saw the class scribbling away: heiress Prisha Sunder, who intended to delete her penniless fiancé and her female spiritual counselor, once she'd learned the two were lovers; two-thirds of the Callaghan triplets, Faith and Charity (whose intentions toward their absent sister gave new meaning to the phrase "abandon all Hope"); my doom-laden dorm mate Audrey; poet José Régio, whose inept play on my water polo team has resulted in haunting sonnets about the emptiness of victory; six-foot-eight ballet dancer Illarian Volkov, whose target was the current director of the Ballets Russe de Monte-Carlo; and slim Milton Swill, whose flaming-red hair made fire engines green with envy, but about whom I know very little.

Of the many fountain pens in the room, the only inactive one was uncapped and pressed against the lips of Simeon Sampson, who seemed to enjoy displaying disinterest.

Sparks also asserted that Wagnerian opera was an ideal source for cover-up sounds, as few can differentiate between a victim's shrieks and a contralto singing Brünnhilde's battle cry from *Die Walküre*. She also stressed that rhythm and blues was ripe with possibilities. "Amateurs plugging ungrounded microphones and electrified guitars into the same amplifier at an outdoor concert where a summer shower could start up out of the blue?" she demanded. "To ignore a setup like that would be nothing short of criminal, 'kay?"

Here's an incident that may give you a sense of the competitive spirit on campus, dear X: Two weeks back, as homework for Practical Electronics, Simeon requisitioned a Columbia record player for these long-playing discs that record companies are selling. Using techniques advanced from Dean Harrow's Entering Without Breaking, Simeon planted the record player in my room in place of my table radio, as if an upgrade had occurred. He then hid beneath the bed, knowing I would be returning from dinner any moment. On the turntable, Simeon had left a recording of Ravel's *Boléro*. He had also removed the notched volume knob from its metal axle, turned the axle to the two o'clock position, and replaced the notched knob so it appeared to be in the eight o'clock position; thus, when the needle dropped, the volume level would appear low but already be high.

I arrived in my room and was pleased to see any device that could play something other than the fifth Brandenburg Concerto. I dropped the needle, turned up the volume to what I thought was a modest level, and Ravel's usually near-inaudible but pulsating vamp began. While I'd often had trouble hearing the opening minutes of *Boléro* on the radio without reaching for the volume control, the record player amplified the disc commendably, and it was the first time I'd heard its opening flute solo clearly. I stretched out on my bed and let the mesmerizing theme give my overworked mind a breather.

Some ten minutes later, I realized that *Boléro*'s gradual but unrelenting crescendo was much too loud for even Ravel's most devoted disciples. Any moment my dorm mates would be banging on my door, complaining about the noise. I jumped from the bed and rushed to the player, the flurry of which covered the sound of Simeon sliding out from under my bed and spearing me between my shoulder blades with the end of a wooden coat hanger, as if it were a knife. The blow was so unexpected and forceful that I fell to my knees.

As I regained my breath and composure, I watched Simeon turn off the record player as a grinning Champo Nanda came through the open bathroom door, having secretly witnessed the experiment. "Great job, Sampson," said Champo Nanda. "Executed exactly as proposed. Simple but effective. *Boléro* is instantly appealing."

"Who doesn't love *Boléro*?" preened Simeon.

"And Ravel and Toscanini did most of your work for you. You've earned bonus points, but I'm afraid it's a demerit for you, Cliff."

"I don't understand, Simeon," I complained, having endured

weeks of snide comments and contemptuous looks from him. "I get along with most people here. Why are you so damn hostile to me?"

Simeon unplugged the gramophone and closed its lid, taking possession of the requisitioned player. "I'm here because I made a determined choice. You're here because you were pressed into service. In the thick of battle, I'd rather have an eager enlistee at my side than a half-hearted recruit. You could cost me my life."

Ten days later, Simeon returned to his rooms on Hedge House's uppermost floor, where the apparently privileged character had a suite with a study and private bath. One of the side benefits of the trick he'd played on me was retaining possession of the record player for a month. This evening, he found a 78 disc waiting by the turntable, with a note on Champo Nanda's stationery reading: "Understand you're a Doris Day fan. Just got this advance acetate from a Hollywood alumnus. Thought you might enjoy it."

Simeon examined the record's label: "Doris Day – It's Been a Long, Long Time." Finding nothing unusual, he set his phonograph's speed to 78 rpm and played the record as he dressed for dinner. Two minutes into the song Doris intoned, ". . . Kiss me once, then kiss me twice, then tick-kiss me twice, then-tick-kiss me twice, then-tick-kiss me twice, then-tick—"

Simeon realized it would go on like that until he did something about it and lifted the tonearm of the record player with his fingers. The instant he did, a black wall struck him, hurling him across the room, victim of an electric shock that left him stunned on the floor.

I entered from his study. "Pretty simple," I said to Simeon, who was rubbing sensation back into his right hand while looking at the singed blond hair above his knuckles. "I located a recording of Doris Day singing this song among the big band transcription discs McMasters plays at its weekly soirées, transferred it to magnetic tape, then spent two hours at the Labs editing it to sound as if it had gotten stuck at two minutes and twelve seconds in. I then transferred my edited version to an acetate disc on the sound department's mastering lathe. Next, I rewired the tonearm so that when it reached an angle of twenty-nine degrees from its détente position, a paper clip I soldered to the tonearm's pivot screw would come in contact with an intentionally loose live wire, making the tonearm a live electrical source."

The smug prig made a choking noise that pleased me fine. "Where'd you learn this?" asked Simeon.

"A three-day tutorial at the Labs called 'Sounds Like a Hit to Me,'" I patiently explained, "which focused on the practical applications of tape recording. Of course, the electric wiring I knew from my work. Just be thankful I was humane enough to add a ground interrupter, limiting how much of a shock you received. Without it"—I turned to Champo Nanda, who'd entered behind me—"Well, I defy any human not to reach for the tonearm of a skipping record. In this case, the tonearm was, uh, armed."

Champo Nanda helped Simeon to his feet. "Just as you outlined in your proposal, Cliff. Excellent work hoisting Mr. Sampson by his own petard."

"Well, I couldn't imagine him not listening," I said modestly. "I mean, who doesn't love Doris Day?"

From the Journal of Cliff Iverson

Dear X, my successful retaliation against Simeon seems to have marked an upswing for me. Word that I'd taken Sampson down a peg quickly circulated across the chatty campus and I found myself greeted more often with a "Hi, Cliff!" than the curious stares of the past. Soon after, I was invited to take dinner at the dean's table. Cubby made it clear this was quite a special honor, purportedly a reward for the results I had achieved the day before in Wigs, Makeup, and Prosthetics, which I took to naturally, due to the aesthetic skills I'd developed in aircraft design. I'd modeled in putty and clay to create more aerodynamic noses on jet planes, so it was not surprising I could create a convincing false nose for myself. But I also suspected the invite was a good-hearted attempt on Harbinger Harrow's part to officially acknowledge my acceptance into the student body, as well as his faith in my worthiness.

At seven-thirty each weeknight, the Great Hall is filled with the pleasantly reverberating garble of students and faculty beneath the octagonal chandeliers hanging just above a sweeping mosaic of octagonal tables. Above the double doors to the serving kitchen is a minstrel's gallery, where hidden speakers feed music into the great room.

The waitstaff are formally uniformed in McMasters crimson and black. Orchids at each table, weighty silverware, Limoges place settings and linen napkins, crystal decanters of wine, and the clean scent of butter pats on ice all evoked a great ocean liner's dining room.

Table One was on a velvet-carpeted dais dead center against the south wall, where one chair larger than any other commanded a sweeping view of all those seated in the hall. I correctly assumed this would be the dean's chair, and a place card indicated I was only two seats to his right. Around the table, I noted Coach Tarcott; Champo Nanda; Professor Matías Graves, looking like a young Spanish nobleman; and the charismatically ample registrar June Felsblock.

On my right was a woman with a matriarchal air about her, definitely a blue blood because one could see her veins like a diagram of the human vascular system. "I assume you're Cliff Iverson," she said, submitting and withdrawing a hand that had no interest in touching mine. "Erma Daimler, assistant dean and chief financial officer of McMasters, how are you?"

"Starving," I confessed.

"Yes, it is a great responsibility to hold both positions but somehow I manage," she said. She signaled to a waiter who sported three small aces of spades on his jacket, indicating decades of service. "Anton, this student is in need of food," said the gaunt Erma. "Bring us the bread basket and celery tray now."

"It's my pleasure, Dean Daimler," said Anton.

"No, it's your job," she corrected, and Anton hastily stepped away.

My resident advisor, Champo Nanda (who'd enlightened me that in Burma there are no first and last names . . . or perhaps he just dreaded being called Champo, which made him sound like a pugilist Marx Brother), tried to ease me into the table conversation. "Coach was just maintaining his long-held contention that the sword is mightier than the pen."

"And usually sharper," added the coach.

"But the fountain pen's a lot easier to pack in an overnight bag and ideal for dispensing poison," countered the English and Spanish literature chair. "And never underestimate the power of a skillfully worded faux love letter or blackmail note."

"What's your major, Mr. Iverson?" asked Erma Daimler without much caring.

"Employer," answered June Felsblock on my behalf as Anton carried a basket of rolls baked so fresh their aroma enticed me from the far end of the table. "Certainly an increasingly popular major."

"A postwar phenomenon, I suspect," commented Erma, "now that unquestioning obedience to the military and industry is no longer crucial to the war effort. The world is changing, as I must continually remind the dean."

Felsblock tore open one of the steamy rolls and lathered it with butter. "Mmm, murdering one's employer now easily surpasses deleting one's rival on the job or financial advisor. Of course, all three still lag well behind spousal deletions." She turned to me. "That was my major, and my husband Dale's as well." Her gaze turned to an eye-watering stained-glass window depicting King David flanked by two of his most famous victims: Goliath and Uriah, husband of Bathsheba. "He and I came here as strangers, wanting only to be done with our cruel and unloving spouses. And then, lo and behold, a campus romance . . . oh, it can happen, Mr. Iverson! Moonlight walks down Boot Hill, picking the castor beans come spring, our first kiss under the Jacobean eaves of the Lonomia Caterpillar Pavilion . . ." She caught herself. "Sometimes I share my bliss too readily."

Dean Harrow arrived breathless and slid into his seat. "Sorry to be tardy. Iverson, delighted to have you. Now where's Girard?"

As if that were his cue, a diminutive gentleman in a tuxedo approached. His slender shoulders and hips were of equal width, and his gleaming hair and mustache had clearly been dyed to match his suit. "*Bienvenue, mon capitaine!*" he cried with the verve of just-uncorked champagne. "*Mille fois pardonne.*"

"He's French," Daimler advised me, in case I thought Tissier had terrible diction. Of course, I'd already gleaned much from him simply by eavesdropping during my stints of kitchen scullery work, but we'd never formally met.

Dean Harrow pivoted toward me. "Mr. Iverson, may I introduce you to the man in whose hands you have been placing your palate as well as your life this past month: Monsieur Girard Tissier, our chef de cuisine, who also lectures on toxins. Winner of the Silver Toque, a Chevalier de l'Ordre Mérite agricole"—Tissier stiffened with pride—"and co-owner of the renowned Le Carcajou in Paris, until the fateful day his partner disagreed with Girard . . . after which Girard cooked something that forever disagreed with his partner. Are we ready to serve, *mon brave?*"

"Excuse me one moment before Chef Arnaud tries to behead *le poulet* for the Coq St. Veran himself. With sauces, he is a genius, but at animal slaughter, the man is a butcher."

Tissier stepped away hurriedly as the dean rose and tapped his spoon against his water glass. The Great Hall quieted instantly. "Good evening," he said in a well-modulated voice that seemed to carry impressively around the room until I noticed a microphone dangling above Harrow's head in Damoclean fashion.

"Good evening, Dean Harrow," came the uniform response widely across the room.

"Let us bow our heads in a moment of reflection." I thought it bizarre that a school with McMasters' intent would say grace, but all lowered their heads, many folding their hands, as Harrow intoned: "Heavenly father, who gave life to all creatures on this earth and then thought it would be just as good an idea to give us death . . . thank you for the bounty we are about to receive, and also for the bounty which is not on our heads. Give us this day our daily bread—and may I just say how delicious the brioche was today, my compliments to our baker as <u>well</u> as to our maker—and forgive us our trespasses, as we forgive those who've trespassed against us once we've deleted them. And may all of us soon be saying 'Amen' at the funeral of our targets. Amen."

"Amen" resounded across the room.

Individual supplications in other languages and religions having already come to an end, the sociable sound of creaking chairs and resumed conversations filled the dining hall, but the dean continued, "This will be a working dinner." Immediate groans from all corners. "<u>And</u> we'll have none of your grousing, thank you. In the course of your meal, an attempt will be made to poison you."

Coach Tarcott muttered under his breath, "*Ach-y-fi!* Every bloody week, God forbid a man could have his dinner in peace."

"I believe we're excluded at this table," Graves counseled us. "Except perhaps for Cliff."

The dean continued, "Some ingredient in this evening's meal—when administered in enough quantity and lacking any remedy—has the ability to end your life. Bear in mind it is not enough to merely know the name of a poison and how to obtain it. The psychology of its presentation is vital. Be sure you take that into account with this evening's 'oral exam.'" Erma Daimler gave a single snort at Harrow's turn of phrase. "If you feel you have identified the toxic ingredient, stand and call my name. First student to identify the poison will have his lowest exam grade this term raised to one hundred. Quite the prize. Guess incorrectly, though, and your highest exam grade will be lowered to a sixty. Should you fall ill and not recover despite our best efforts, you will be remembered at a touching ceremony this Sunday and entered into the McMasters annals with a citation for valor, despite showing such poor taste." He waited for a laugh but the room was stony silent, it being an axiom of show business that the condemned are an extremely tough crowd.

"He's kidding, right?" I asked Champo Nanda in a low voice.

"It's so hard to know," my RA answered with a tinge of anguish.

"However," Dean Harrow reassured the room, "the outcome of a fatality is unlikely. The dose should not kill you." He turned to Tissier, who had just returned to the dean's side, and inquired softly, "It won't kill them?"

Tissier seesawed the flat of his hand.

"It will not kill you," repeated the dean. "And we have the antidote at the ready." Again he murmured toward Tissier, "We have the antidote at the ready?"

The Frenchman shrugged.

"And the antidote is at the ready," confirmed the dean. "Now let's hope that justice, as well as dinner, is served."

With that, a line of uniformed waiters proceeded in serpentine fashion from the serving kitchen into the Great Hall, each carrying a bone-white porcelain tureen and matching ladle. The diminutive

Girard signaled for the dean's overhanging microphone to be low-ered further, and the Frenchman spoke into it as if hosting a fash-ion show. "Tonight's dinner begins with *le consommé*, employing my patented beef stock which won the 1947 Lyons Festival and combines fresh tarragon from France with Poet's Marigold from England, strained to offer a simple but introspective broth to bet-ter prepare you for the courses ahead. Bon appétit!"

At our table, Anton the head waiter respectfully ladled out a steaming pale brown bowl of consommé for me alone. Champo Nanda encouraged me to eat up and I cautiously did so. Despite the fruits of Tissier's genius that had been delighting me week after week, I was surprisingly unimpressed by what was little more than brown boiled water.

"Well?" Dean Harrow asked. "What do you think?"

"It's certainly very warm," I said diplomatically.

Erma Daimler turned to Tissier. "Apparently, the kitchen is to be commended for their successful use of fire."

The Chef de Cuisine scanned the tables about the hall with great intensity, but the soup was being consumed with no immediate ill effect, other than some rumblings of disappointment over the me-diocrity of the broth. The deadly dish was clearly yet to come, I thought, for it was hard to imagine any poison tasting this bland.

The dean shared a soft word with me alone. "You could build upon your good start by winning this exercise, young Iverson. The neutrality of the soup should give you a clue. Consider—"

There was a sharp clatter as a chair fell over with a student in it: a slender young man with flaming-red hair was clutching at his stom-ach. I recognized him from Practical Electronics as Milton Swill.

A striking woman in a fluted metallic cocktail dress rose from her own table and moved to the student's side, pouring something into a napkin and holding it under his nose.

On the other side of the room, another student was stricken. It was Cubby Terhune. He, too, fell to the floor.

This commotion was punctuated by Simeon Sampson and Jud Helkampf, who both stood up from the same table, one hard upon the other. "Dean Harrow!" each called out.

The dean rose and pronounced, "A photo finish, I think?"

Gemma rose quickly from the same table and, as she took a glass of water to Cubby, protested to the dean, "Jud figured it out first! He told Simeon and Simeon immediately stood up."

Simeon looked perplexed. "That's not true!"

"No, she's right!" barked Helkampf.

"Well now, let's see," said the dean. "Mr. Helkampf, what have you?"

The young bald man with bookends of hair said, "The poison is in the saltshaker."

"And what leads you to think that?"

"This kitchen would never create a soup this tasteless. At first, I thought maybe it was my tastebuds not being sensitive enough, but I found myself reflexively reaching for the salt, something I've never done here before. Then I realized tonight's the first time I've seen salt and pepper shakers on the table. I might have noticed sooner but a saltshaker looks so normal on a table. So I waited to see if anyone else used the salt, and Swill did."

"Very sporting of you to let him do so," said Harrow dryly, and he made the aside to me, "Never poison your target, Iverson. Your target should poison himself. Got that?"

"Yes sir, got that," I said, as easily and falsely as "It's all taken care of" and "There's nothing to worry about."

Harrow called out to the still-standing Simeon. "Care to venture what the poison is?"

Simeon shook the "salt" into his palm. "Well, there are some colorless crystals among the salt grains. My guess would be dear old potassium cyanide. But Monsieur Tissier, why didn't I smell cyanide's trademark odor of bitter almonds?" This seemed a good example of a bright student asking a question simply to show off his knowledge.

Tissier responded in despair, "How many of us have ever smelled bitter almonds, what would that be? Some say arsenic is more the scent of old sneakers. And one out of every ten people cannot smell cyanide at all! It is a flaw génétique."

"And how are our victims, Vesta?" Dean Harrow inquired of

the arresting woman in the metallic dress. I would learn that Vesta Thripper was the world's only advanced registered nurse practitioner to also be represented by the Eileen Ford Agency. Her eyebrows and lips were fine lines set below a high brow, and it was obvious Milton Swill felt it was almost worth his stomach cramps to have her taking his pulse in such close proximity. I wondered if he were ailing or simply swooning.

"They'll both be fine," Vesta pronounced in a handsome voice. "The dose was small and diluted by the soup. I gave them a whiff of amyl nitrate and a charcoal tablet. A tall glass of milk and a good night's rest should find them better in the morning."

The dean offered the school's collective thanks to Monsieur Tissier for abandoning his art for the sake of the exercise, and with that, the unwarranted saltshakers and bowls of insipid soup were removed. The real soup was now brought in by the same solemn conga line of waiters, even as Swill and Terhune were assisted from the hall, while Tissier proudly announced his legendary Chaga fungus balls in hot squid ink with thyme-roasted shallots, tansy, and ground ivy.

I watched Gemma give Jud a quick hug to acknowledge his victory as she returned to their table. I couldn't fathom why she liked the unprincipled fellow, but then, in my limited experience, every couple makes total sense if only you knew more about them. If you could be privy to their most intimate conversations, riffle through their dressers, closet, or that shoebox at the back of a high shelf, then the equation usually balances out perfectly, once you factor in their needs and fears.

The real soup having now been sampled, Tissier took in stride the enthused compliments around the dean's table. Emboldened by a second sip of the heady Haut-Brion being served, I chimed in, "I have to say this soup sounded awful when you described it, but it's . . ." Searching for a description, I came up short. "I've never tasted anything like it in my life."

"Not like <u>anything</u>?" asked the Frenchman eagerly.

"No, not ever."

Tissier rapped his knuckles against the table. "And this is *exact-*

ement what I always tell the Coach Tarcott, who declares *les sports* to be the perfect medium for deletions, while I maintain the most efficacious *méthode* for the concealment of toxins is the cuisine *exotique*. The more one's guests expect you to surprise their senses, bombarding their tongues with undreamt-of tastes, the easier to conceal some deadly ingredient. Having the reputation for innovative dishes sets the table for murder!"

"I concur," chimed Dean Harrow. "We all have an idea of how chicken pot pie, New England clam chowder, or franks and beans should taste. But what flavor is loup in Bishop's Lace and henbane reduction, I ask you? Tell your status-hungry guests they are the first to be offered Girard's beef trifle with jellied blowfish confit in sauce *pourri* and they'll fight for a portion even if it kills them . . . which, of course, it would."

"That's fine for those with a knack for cooking," I said. "But I can screw up cornflakes."

"Can you not grind twenty cherry pits to create cyanide or fresh nutmeg to make myristicin?" asked Tissier encouragingly. "Or place apricots in an industrial blender with their lethal pits intact, giving you a poisonous puree that can be added to any number of desserts?"

"And with what accompaniment would you serve such a poisonous puree to your guests?" I asked.

The Frenchman considered and shrugged. "I would let them eat cake."

This may have amused the table . . . yet in the course of this one dinner alone, Dean Harrow had adroitly imparted certain wisdoms to me that I soon would incorporate into my quest to rid the world of Merrill Fiedler.

XIII

If the narration of our next chapter seems less conspiratorial and exuberant than the tone struck in this volume's foreword, you may attribute this to the distasteful nature of the person upon whom it focuses. Additionally, more than any other chapter, it relies heavily on outside sources, including interviews with others at Woltan Aviation. —HH

While Cliff Iverson was studying to become the homicidalist he had never intended to be, Merrill Fiedler continued to kill dreams and crush hopes as if by second nature.

Fiedler was known to take pride in his physique, whereas pride and Joan Beeson were no longer on speaking terms. He had a 9 a.m. appointment with her but he wasn't at his desk when she'd timidly knocked on the doors to his office. "Come on in," he shouted from his full bathroom, the only private one in Woltan Tower. "It's not locked."

He stepped out of the bathroom in one of his long terry-cloth robes, patting dry his bronze and silver crew cut with a gold velvet towel. "Right on time," he commented. "Scoot yourself in."

Joan looked behind her, worried that his greeting her in a state of near undress might be witnessed from the reception area. "I'll come back later, Mr. Fiedler," she offered. Fiedler had decided she should address him as "Mr. Fiedler" during office hours.

"Don't be silly," he scoffed. "If Woltan doesn't want its staff seeing me in my robe on occasion, I guess Woltan shouldn't expect me to work so late that I have to sleep here." That had been his rationale to the company for the convertible bed in his office. Fiedler often stayed overnight at Woltan, which might seem symptomatic of a hardworking executive, if you didn't know better. "After all, it's not the first time you've seen me in a robe, or out of one for that matter."

Although his words might have sounded like an overture to seduction, Fiedler's sex life was no more about his desire for women than the Lincoln Tunnel was a monument to America's noble president. Fiedler simply measured his power by how fully others yielded to him or tolerated the intolerable. One day this might take the form of breaking off an affair with company switchboard operator Janice and starting up with stenographer Shari, which meant that switchboard operator Janice would have to put through his calls to her romantic replacement. On another day, it would be discrediting Caltech's Clifford Iverson even while taking credit for his work in an industry publication. On a good day, it would be both, and more.

He might have shed the robe and dressed in front of her, but he still bore a yellowish bruise on his back where he'd struck a subway platform column while being attacked by a crazed New Yorker two weeks earlier. Two plainclothes cops had saved him from falling into the path of a train and the resultant contusion had been slow to fade. He didn't want Joan Beeson to know he was capable of bruising.

Fiedler had learned what little he knew about aeronautics as an air force technician and, opting not to re-enlist, had taken a position at Woltan, whose government contracts made him exempt from recall after Pearl Harbor. With most of the male competition otherwise engaged, it had been easy for Fiedler to shoulder his way past the 4F rejects and working women as the country's war machine drove Woltan's assembly lines to nonstop production. But now, with a new generation of bright young tech graduates freshly hatched from college and chirping at Woltan's doorstep, Fiedler stayed on top by relying on his real skills: fragmenting the self-esteem and confidence of his charges, spotlighting their stumbles, and hijacking their successes.

Where women were concerned, Fiedler had additional tactics. He openly denigrated those who, by his narrow standards, were plain or drab. For the more attractive, he had a different policy. Joan Beeson was the latest of his flames whom he'd transformed into a burn victim.

He gestured her to his convertible bed, currently in sofa mode. It was upholstered with a dark, textured wool. Leather would have been more Fiedler's style, but he often sat naked on it and didn't like his skin sticking to its surface. It felt unprofessional.

He slid past a waist-high antique globe nested in a Mediterranean wrought iron frame alongside the couch and settled down next to her. "Well Joanie, I understand big things are in store for you in Michigan," he said, trying to sound envious. "I guess you got word last night."

"Are you mad?" Her eyes were wild and uncomprehending. "How can I move to Michigan? I can't leave Baltimore."

He draped an arm around her. "Now you don't have to worry. I go to Michigan at least four times a year. We'll still see each other."

She brushed away his arm as if it were a spiderweb in a crawl space. "You think the reason I'm upset is because I won't get to see you? I have a sick husband, a child in school, relatives, friends, I don't know anyone in Michigan."

"It's not just Michigan, Joan," he said with significance. "It's Lansing. The state capital. And my understanding is that this new position pays much more than women make here."

She stared at him. "*You* did this, didn't you?"

"No, this is all New York's decision." He looked chagrined. "Guess I shouldn't have told them what a great job you do for me." It was a half-hearted effort, and he had it in him to do better, but he didn't feel like taking that much trouble with it. He just wanted this woman out of his office, the state, and his life. He'd been done with her months ago. "It won't be the same here without you."

"You can't let this happen, I know too much about you," she said, which of course was precisely the reason he'd let this happen.

"Joanie," he said, knowing she hated the name. "You ever hear of a Land Camera? It's not much known yet. Self-developing film. Baxley in security planted one for me in this globe. The lens is up here at the Arctic Circle, see?" He rotated the antique globe, which stood slightly higher than the couch, so that the North Pole was pointing at her. "When I turn it on, it takes a picture every minute for fifteen minutes. I told Baxley I needed it to catch any snoops looking at blueprints."

He picked up a manila envelope from his coffee table and handed it to her. She opened the envelope, uncertain what to expect, and withdrew four snapshot-sized images of herself, engaged in an act that was technically illegal in several states, including both Maryland and Michigan. Fiedler had modestly managed to remain out of frame.

"Feel free to rip them up," he offered cordially. "I have shots with much better focus."

She felt sick, as she often did after leaving his company. "It was the drinks, or something in the drinks," she protested, as if owing him some explanation. "And after that, it was just not knowing how to say no to you. I'm begging you, for my family's sake, don't make us move."

He tied the belt of his robe into a double knot, which she knew from past experience meant he was ready for her to leave. "Look, Joan, we both had our fun . . ."

"I don't remember any."

Fiedler was relieved. If she was going to insult him . . . "Then I guess you won't miss me as much as I thought." He opened the door for her and made sure that, as it closed, it smoothly nudged her rear out of the room for good.

This had gone so much better than how things had finished with Cora. She'd ranked as acceptably attractive to his appraising eyes, and he suspected she was starting to fall for Iverson, which was completely unacceptable. The last two times he'd needed to overtly blackmail her to sleep with him, and she'd taken the photographs too seriously.

How can you tell which people will kill themselves and which won't?

He intercommed Meg, who'd held her job because he wasn't interested in her. "Is Eric Gottschalk out there?"

"Yes, sir."

"Send him in. No incoming calls."

There was a rapping at the door and Fiedler bid Gottschalk enter. It irked him that the bespectacled young man had not changed out of his lab coat, as if he were only stepping away momentarily from more important work.

"Eric," he said. "Sit."

Fiedler moved to his desk, still in his robe, and Gottschalk proposed, "If you want a moment to change . . ."

Fiedler shook him off and pointed at the low chair across from him.

Gottschalk asked, "Does this concern my memos about the design flaw in the W-10?"

"There is no design flaw in the W-10," he corrected him regarding the plane currently backordered by Pan American, BOAC, and Turkish Airlines, even though no aircraft had yet been completed.

"I've recently discovered margin notes in the schematics made by my predecessor, Clifford Iverson," said Gottschalk. "In the current design, all the electronics for the elevators and rudder go through the cargo hatch, rather than in a separate canal below it, as he intended. If for any reason the hatch doorway blew out, the pilot would be manning a one-hundred-and-thirty-ton glider with no way of controlling its descent."

He waited for Fiedler's response, which was to open a folder on his desk. The two panoramic window walls in Fiedler's corner office commanded vistas of the flatland outside Baltimore, and his desk and chair were situated at their point of intersection. When one sat across from him in chairs which were also, by design, as low as a coffee table, Fiedler seemed to float in the sky, while the manufacturing plant and low-lying hangars below him simply vanished from sight. The sun at this hour was positioned directly above Fiedler's head and there was no way for Gottschalk to discern the expression on his face.

"Eric," he inquired as if he didn't know the answer, "did you ever belong to the Pan-Pacific Student Union?"

Gottschalk looked bewildered. "In college. What's that to do with the design flaw?"

Fiedler smiled. "We're talking now about the flaws in you. Are you aware that the Pan-Pacific Student Union is on the attorney general's list of subversive organizations?"

The young man removed his glasses and began to polish the lenses with the lapel of his lab coat. "I didn't participate in any activities. I just attended a few meetings with a friend."

"George Bridwell," read Fiedler from a page in his hand. "That correct?"

Gottschalk shifted slightly in his seat. "Yes."

"You and he are currently roommates in the city?"

"Yes, we share the rent."

"A one-bedroom apartment, I believe?" asked Fiedler blandly.

Gottschalk blinked twice. "There's a convertible sofa in the living room. We toss a coin each month and I seem to land tails more often than not."

"I thought you might. Mr. Bridwell is not the same color as you?"

"What of it?"

"Nothing, just of interest. Confirmed bachelors, both of you?" Fiedler let the words hang in the air for a moment. "So you cohabitate with a non-Caucasian in a one-bedroom apartment. This makes you a security risk at a company engaged in defense projects. Once entered into your file, the information will follow you everywhere."

"So I'm fired," Eric finally voiced. "Ruined, too."

"No," Fiedler informed him, "I've known this for quite some time and intend to keep it private as long as I can. But I hope you appreciate the risk I'm taking. I'll expect you to inform me of any disloyalty to Woltan or myself among your coworkers, and always share with me any bright new ideas you come up with before you discuss them with anyone else."

It was so quiet in the room that Fiedler could hear Gottschalk swallow. He poured his employee a glass of water, and Gottschalk's dry mouth needed it in order to say, "I . . . won't forget your giving me this second chance, sir."

"What I expect you to forget is this nonexistent design flaw in the W-10. And I wouldn't take seriously any other notations you find by Iverson. He and his associate Jack Horvath were caught at the main gate with government documents in the trunks of their cars."

"I hadn't heard about that."

"Oh yes. They were stopped before any harm was done and I allowed them to resign rather than create bad publicity for Woltan. Competitors like AirCorp would have made hay with it. As it happens, the shame may have led to Horvath's death, and Iverson has vanished from the face of the earth. All that matters now is getting as many orders for the W-10 as possible. Once delivered, if we decide there's a concern, we can always issue an advisory."

Fiedler rose and motioned toward the door. Gottschalk stopped at it to tender a meek "Thank you again for hiring me, despite what you knew about me."

"No need," Fiedler advised him. "I hired you *because* of what I knew about you."

Alone now, he put his bare legs on the coffee table. He envisioned a day when everyone in the company would be in bed with him, one way or another.

He picked up his phone. "Janice?" he said to the switchboard operator who had a butterfly-shaped birthmark on her inner right thigh. "Get me Shari Dougan. She's a secretary in Accounting."

"She's a lot of things," responded Janice. "I'll get her for you now."

He noted that Janice always refused to call him Mr. Fiedler. He'd been pretty awful to her, even by his standards.

"Hi, this is Shari," came a promisingly breezy voice.

"Shari, it's Merrill Fiedler. Come up to my office, pronto. And fix your makeup before you do."

"You're such a joker," she said and waited for a response, but Fiedler had already nestled the phone back in its cradle. Getting up from the couch, he banged the bruise he'd acquired in New York. It still hurt and might remain sore for a week or two.

Otherwise, life was good.

XIV

We now review the progress of Gemma Lindley and Doria Maye (a.k.a. Dulcie Mown) before resuming the journal of Cliff Iverson. —HH

Having no sponsor or personal wealth, Gemma could not afford the privacy of Cliff's efficient room at Hedge House or Dulcie's rustic peasant cottage. The women's dormitory was tourist class for those just barely able to scrape together tuition, and Gemma shared quarters on the third floor with three other women. The good news was that McMasters treats everyone as equals in its classrooms and dining hall, so one only felt underprivileged a few waking hours a day.

The always affable Miriam Webster had the bed on Gemma's right, with a small night table between them. When they'd drawn lots for sleeping accommodations, Gemma had been lucky enough to win the berth with an overlook of Mead Mere and the beguiling shops and narrow cobbled streets of its curious little village. It was dark now and, lying on her bed, she studied the blue electrified lights dangling from the willows that encircled the great pond. They were an alternative firmament reflected and rippling in the black mirror of the Mere's surface. Warm gold lanterns were strung about the cafés and pavilions, and the uncountable profusion of gossamer fairy lights precisely outlined the entire hamlet like latticework.

It had been weeks now since she'd said too much—far too much— to Cliff Iverson about being a murderess. Despite liking him and sensing something kind about him, she'd avoided him as much as possible since then and kept all conversation and eye contact to a minimum.

She wondered if her subconscious was attempting to stymie any attraction she might feel toward him, knowing that her precious time at McMasters could ill afford the kind of affair that might culminate (as was rumored around campus) in one of Vesta Thripper's "assignation rooms" under the intentionally blind eye of the annex's liason officer. Why had she told Cliff her secret?

"Your secret is safe with me," Adele Underton said at St. Ann's Hospital the year before, while they worked side by side in admin, both the same rank but Gemma with seniority.

Gemma looked up very slowly from her calculations. Her heart had recommenced beating, although unsteadily. "What secret?" she asked with feigned calm.

"That's precisely right, just as you say. What secret?" Adele beamed. "You see? There's no need for anyone else to know about it or to judge you."

Gemma waited for more, but that was apparently it. Adele returned to reviewing documents and each calm flipping of a page made Gemma want to scream. She knew the longer she didn't challenge Adele about her strange words, the more it affirmed she did have something to hide, which she of course did. She *had* to say something . . . but what? She tried, "Do you want a coffee?"

"Oo, yes please," said Adele.

Gemma rose and went to a machine just outside the door that dispensed scalding-hot coffee in painfully thin cups. "White or black?"

"White, extra sugar please," said Adele.

Gemma held down the appropriate buttons. "Did you see they've posted a notice that Glenda is retiring?"

"I did indeed. They're taking applications from within before they advertise for a new admin head. That's very thoughtful of them. Were you thinking of submitting your name? The moment I saw the announcement I imagined you would."

"Yes, I was planning that," she said, scalding her fingertips as she withdrew the cup.

"But you haven't done so yet?"

"No."

"Oo, that's good. So then, don't."

Gemma had been handing Adele her coffee but froze. "What? Why wouldn't I?"

"I don't think you could manage the hours. From prison." She trilled on a giggle. "Joking, of course."

She set Adele's coffee down, avoiding her eyes. Adele added, "But you know, they wouldn't hire you, once they knew. Only they won't, because I know how to keep a secret."

Gemma went back to her seat, having forgotten to get coffee for herself.

Adele chirped, "Only I'm going to put in my own name, and I'd be very grateful if you'd write a letter of recommendation."

"For you?"

"I thought a note from one of my peers—"

"Peers?" Gemma had been at St. Ann's for five years, Adele barely that many months.

"It wouldn't be a lot of work. I've typed it up for you already." She handed Gemma a folded letter. "On hospital stationery. I don't think I've exaggerated my merits, and I did come from a better business school than you. And Dr. Ellisden says I lift his spirits. Or lift his something." She giggled again.

Gemma began reading the typed letter and suddenly felt as if she'd forgotten how to breathe. "This isn't a letter of rec— It's an accusation that I . . . stole pentobarbitone and a syringe from the dispensary to use on my—"

Adele snatched the letter back with a playful laugh. "Oh, I *am* sorry, wrong letter! The stationery's the same, you see. *Here's* the recommendation. And we can just tear up this silly letter." She did so and let the pieces fall into the paper bin, with a cheery, "Don't worry, it's just a copy, I have others if you ever want to review it for accuracy. So you see? Your secret couldn't be safer." Adele took a sip of her coffee. "Oo lovely, just how I like it."

XV

Dulcie Mown was late for Alibis and had no excuse. She tried to make her entrance without being noticed, which went completely against her nature, of course. Captain Dobson, his hat on his head, tie knotted at half-mast, looked at the wall clock and then at Dulcie. "I'm sorry," she said for the first time in a decade. Another new skill mastered.

For celebrities, a surefire gauge of their current stardom is how readily their tardiness is accommodated. In the Movie Star Time Zone, dinner begins when you are seated, scheduled commercial flights do not depart until you arrive at the airport, and a morning film shoot cannot commence until your director has apologized. It was hard to suddenly be accountable to clocks, appointments, and professors. She was, after all, the same woman who'd caused a New Year's Eve celebration to delay singing "Auld Lang Syne" until well after 2 a.m.

She'd hopped off the Number 3 shuttle bus at the foot of the Flora & Fauna hillock and rather than wait for the connecting tram, opted to leg it from there to "Headquarters," the campus name for the Tolson School of Police Procedures. It was a quick climb up the fragrant Poison Gardens' terraces, staying well clear of Gonzago Bower. (Doria Maye was exempted from all studies at the bower owing to a life-threatening allergy to bees, attested to by a Chopard medical bracelet in rose gold with an engraved warning flanked by pink opals and diamonds.) Then down a slope called Boot Hill, home to the Menagerie. Toward the bottom, she skirted the Victorian glass pavilion housing the Snake Pit (a name which was not metaphorical) and trotted past thatched cottages designated for faculty only, entering the illuminated pedestrian tunnel through a smaller knoll adjacent to Boot Hill. With students' voices reverberating off the tunnel's cream-colored tiles, Dulcie soon emerged at Bowling Green and the neoclassical façade of Headquarters, its broad steps having the grandeur of a Hall of Justice, although much of its façade was plaster passing for stone. Entering its faux marble lobby, she headed down the left hallway, lined with numbered doors.

Dobson's lecture room at the end of the hall was dreary, the first truly unattractive location Dulcie had seen at McMasters since arriving two months earlier. The captain's constant concern was that the cozy surroundings and polite nomenclature of McMasters might distract some students from the solemn fact that the enemy (meaning the police and district attorney) were to be taken dead seriously.

Today being the first in a series of required lectures, Dulcie looked around for friendly faces. There was an attractive woman in her thirties or forties named Blossom Shing who'd confided she was here to delete two men who had destroyed both her family's business and her father's will to live. She greeted Dulcie with a small smile, as did a sweet, white-haired widow in her late seventies named Constance Beddoes. She was worth millions and would soon be marrying an extremely attractive Italian fortune hunter. Constance had said that after they were wed, she suspected her husband might attempt to murder her for her money. Thus, she had enlisted at McMasters to be one step ahead of him, if it came to that.

"But if you think he might kill you for your money," Dulcie had asked, "why on earth are you marrying him?"

"Well, I'm really looking forward to the honeymoon," said Constance. She assumed that, for at least that phase of their romance, her Lothario would be on his best behavior. If after that she feared for her safety or grew tired of him, she doubted anyone would suspect her of killing him for his lack of money.

Dobson's classes were no-nonsense. He refused to indulge in the euphemisms of McMasters, saying words like "murder" and "kill" without pulling any punches. Many students found his bluntness refreshing at the end of a long day.

"Here's the bad news, boys and girls: The police are real and we are not stupid." Dobson still referred to the police as *we*. "Nine times out of ten we know within a few hours who the killer is. We don't start an investigation with an open mind and we don't worry much about the least likely suspects because usually the most likely suspects did it."

Blossom Shing called out, "So if you can spot us coming a mile away, what do we do about you?"

"Always have an alibi," said Dobson flatly. "That's why Alibis is a required course. You can have means, motive, opportunity, but with an unshakable alibi, we can't get you. The sergeant here has a saying, how does it go?"

Stedge was pleased to supply it. "If it looks like a duck, swims like a duck, quacks like a duck but has an alibi, it's not a duck."

"So, if your victim was shot to death at dawn in front of St. Patrick's Cathedral in New York, make sure you were photographed at noon the same day in the Vatican with the pope." The captain paused. "Keep in mind that's not always as easy as it sounds."

"But how can we be somewhere we're not?" asked Constance. It was a valid question that bordered on the metaphysical.

The captain came toward Dulcie as if about to make an arrest. "Miss Mown, the last person to arrive for any class of mine gets called upon first."

Dulcie accepted her medicine. "A body double?" She realized by the blank expressions around her that she'd used a term from her trade. "Meaning, someone who resembles you?"

Dobson frowned. "No accomplices. Ever. Show me two individuals who commit a murder and I'll show you one individual who'll make a deal with the district attorney to implicate the other. In fact, I'll show you *two* individuals willing to do that."

Dulcie fidgeted in her chair. "So, if I need another person to give me an alibi, but I'm not allowed to have an accomplice, I suppose they'd have to be unwitting accomplices. But I still don't see how I can be in two places at the same time."

Dobson's face softened. "Well, we'll be explaining ways to achieve that. But keep in mind there's no reason why your alibi has to mean it's *you* who were 'somewhere else' at the time of the murder. It could be that the scene of the crime seems to be somewhere other than where it was. Or that the time or day of the murder was different." He flicked a pencil against his desk with impatience. "I recommend you review the mimeo sheets, Dulcie."

At dinner in the Great Hall that evening, still worrying over the conflict of "alibi is vital but accomplice is forbidden," she found comfort in Girard Tissier's lamb Wellington and, even better, a solution in its accompanying cruciferous side dish. It was the first time a vegetable had offered her a way out of a dilemma since she portrayed the title role in *Jaqueline and the Beanstalk*. The dish was one of Girard's proudest creations. Rapini (which Dulcie knew better as broccoli rabe), whose flowers, leaves, and stems were separated, each cloaked in its own treatment: the stems done in gorgonzola with brazen chunks of garlic, forthright and almost beefy; the crowns bathed in a seething chili glaze that clung to the florets, giving them the ruby finish of a candy apple; and the leaves creamed like spinach in a nutmeg and cinnamon sauce, turning them into something akin to a Christmas pudding. The trio had arrived at each table in a segmented rectangular white serving platter, looking like nothing less than the Italian *Tricolore*. Dulcie was fascinated by the one vegetable passing itself off as three. Even its name on the bill of fare card was charming: *Rapini Masqué en Trois Sauces*, conjuring concealment and the guises of a masked ball. It proved only a short leap from this colorful conceit to the possible solution to the paradox that had until that moment been vexing her.

Gemma, on the other hand, found no comfort in the evening meal. Walking home from dinner that night, she could barely keep pace with Jud Helkampf, who seemed disinterested in the pleasure of her company. They'd reached the fork in the walkway where the path to the women's dorm began and she tried to say something engaging to evoke a minimal good night from the self-absorbed Helkampf, but he'd left her with hardly a send-off. She wondered why she even bothered, and then remembered: she had to.

Continuing on alone, she saw a sign outside Oxbane Chapel announcing that confessions would be heard that evening. On impulse, she entered the Gothic church via an arched side portal set between lancet windows. Alone, she entered the chapel's solitary confessional booth.

"Father, forgive me for I have sinned," said Gemma through the dividing screen.

The priest responded, "How long has it been since your last confession, my child?"

Gemma hesitated, then responded, "Forever. I'm not Catholic."

"Oh, sod that then," said the priest, "neither am I."

He exited his side of the confessional, suggesting Gemma do the same. Sporting a cleric's collar, a chummy grin, and a mane of black-and-tan hair like that of a Yorkie, he energetically explained, "I'm Episcopalian but very inclusive, I serve all faiths here. I even whisper sweet nothings to the atheists. I hear confessions for the Catholics, but I call them 'concessions,' and I have a prayer for them that's a bit of a 'Hail Mary' pass, as it were. Rest easy that I strictly adhere to the sanctity of the confessional. Whatever you wish to share with me will go no further. By the way, I'm Father Pugh," he said almost apologetically, for of course he pronounced "Pugh" as "pew."

The thought of a priest named Pew forced Gemma to suppress a smile and the cleric read her mind, a skill acquired from many a bad joke having been made at his expense. "I know, I know," he lamented in chagrin. "Most everyone here just calls me Padre."

"Gemma Lindley. Let me understand, though: You *are* a real priest?" She didn't wish to bare her guilty conscience to just anyone.

"Super priest," he clarified with an awkward flourish. "I can also pronounce food kosher and officiate at a Daoist wedding."

"But how . . . ?"

"Dispensation from the chief rabbi at Beersheba and the same from the Zhengyi Monastery at the Celestial Master's Mansion in China. McMasters alumni can be found among the hierarchy of most religious orders."

She looked at the lovely interior of the Judith of Bethulia Interdenominational Assembly Room—formerly St. Stephen's Church of Oxbane, until its deconsecration prior to disassembly by Guy McMasters. She wondered if its rose window, graceful beams, nave, and transept were all a sham that belonged more properly in the Labs.

"But your faith, Padre! The fifth commandment. How do you rationalize serving here?"

"I know," he conceded. "Yet doesn't a priest walk to the execution chamber with the condemned murderer? Doesn't the army chaplain pray with the soldiers before they go into battle, knowing their goal is to kill as many of the enemy as they can manage? And hear ye the word of the Lord: 'Now go, attack the Amalekites and totally destroy everything that belongs to them. Put to death men and women, children and infants. Now kill all the boys and every woman who has slept with a man.'" He smiled blandly. "Numbers 31. We can do this all night."

"But for you, a priest, to condone murder—"

"Every staff member at McMasters has committed murder. Didn't you know that?"

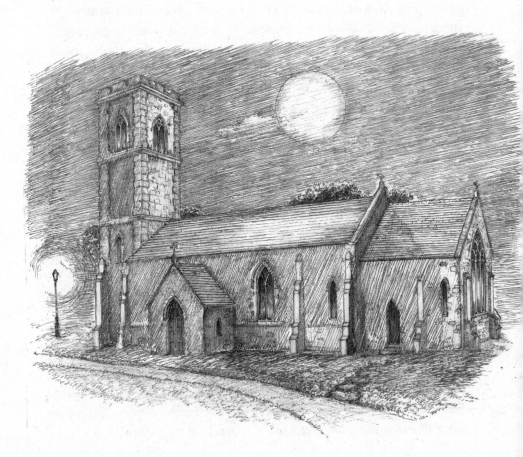

The hair on the nape of her neck riffled as if an electric storm were approaching. "I don't think I ever thought that through. I assumed *some* of the faculty had, but everyone? You too?"

"We all had our reasons, just as you do, no doubt. I murdered a bishop and would do so again without a moment's hesitation—meaning *that* particular bishop, of course, not just any." He confided, "More often than not, it's God's work we're doing here at McMasters . . . that is, if you believe in a just God. So if you wish to unburden yourself, you may share what troubles you have in utter confidence. I'm not judgmental in the slightest and, unlike an overpriced psychiatrist, I can grant you absolution at the end of the session."

"I wish to confess to murder," she said.

The padre sighed. "Better to me than the D.A."

— ♠ —

After dinner, Dulcie walked back to Foxglove Cottage and was glad to see a low fire had already been observantly lit by McMasters' turndown staff.

Those in Hollywood who knew actress Doria Maye socially might have characterized her as flighty, but that was only because they had never worked with her on a film project. She researched her scripts with the diligence of a scholar, and as Dulcie Mown, she approached her studies with similar focus and dedication. The Four Enquiries were framed on the wall, as they were in every dorm room, cottage, and classroom on campus. The first, **Is this murder necessary?** was followed by a near corollary: **Have you given your target every last chance to redeem themselves?** Was she certain of her own answer to each?

That last day at the studio, before an announced vacation would serve as cover for her time at McMasters, she was fully convinced of the unswervable affirmative to both. She'd been walking to her bungalow when she saw Claude Revenson, chief financial officer for the studio, departing the commissary with a studious man in his early twenties.

The sun had had its merry way with Claude Revenson after a weekend of navigating his yawl in lazy eights around the Anacapas off the Santa Barbara coast: His brown hair was now a sandy blond, his usually pink complexion the shade of creamed coffee. He looked more like a film studio's swashbuckling star than its economic navigator, and his teeth caught the light as he made an introduction.

"Doria, I wanted you to meet our new boy wonder, Laddie Graham. A protégé of our beloved Leon. But excuse me, I'm late for a budget review."

He trotted off, leaving Doria with Laddie, whom she would more likely have imagined as head of his class in college, and he might have skipped a grade of high school at that. His curly hair was tousled in numerous directions, and he sported a belted tweed jacket that he wore open. "I've been looking forward to meeting you, Miss Maye. Just wanted to say how very much I've admired your work since"—he was at least diplomatic—"since I, and the world, first took note of you. I find your acting to be focused, detailed, and mesmeric."

Doria made a few purring sounds, wondering why he'd omitted "unparalleled," but one can't have everything.

"I have a few scripts on my desk I'd love to share with you, written by a passel of playwrights I've brought in from the East. Strong, psychologically driven stories. With an established star like yourself in a pivotal role, tautly directed, they could rise above their B-movie budgets, like *The Maltese Falcon* and *Cat People* did a decade ago."

"B?" asked Doria in shock.

"We're also giving some of our staff writers the chance to direct, because we think they'll see to it that storytelling and character remains at the forefront."

"B?" inquired Doria further.

"It's just a shame that Mr. Kosta is so determined to see you in this animated film series he's planning. But he says he wants to remake your image, turn you into America's very own honey-cured ham, won't even consider you for any other project." He lowered his voice. "I thought maybe if you came to him with a script you discovered and loved . . ."

She was really not savoring the direction this conversation was taking. But still, if she deigned to lend her A-name to a street-savvy B-picture, one that would garnish awards for its gritty realism, it might actually help her career.

She gained access to Kosta in his office and touted Laddie's merits. Kosta needed no convincing. "Yes, that boy is a genius. I'd call him my wunderkind but he's barely a *kind* yet. Imagine what he'll do in the years ahead. He loves you, and oh, the scripts he has up his sleeve. He's got these writers . . . you taste the dialogue in your mouth like the wines of Peloponnese."

"Give me a real film, Leon, and I'll work for scale!"

Kosta exhaled with a snort. "Okay. You have a deal."

"I can work with Laddie?"

"No, you can work for scale. On the cartoon." He beamed at her. "My pig."

She sat now at the crude wooden table in Foxglove Cottage. Dobson had advised her to review his commandments and she intended to do so before retiring. She opened a black three-ring binder and studied the mimeographed sheets referred to as Dobson's Rules. The first stated simply:

RULE 1. <u>NO ACCOMPLICES</u>

but it had two corollaries listed directly below.

COROLLARY 1A. <u>NO LOVERS</u>. Never commit a murder with your lover unless you both plan to be faithful for as long as you live and, by the way, that doesn't happen. The kind of love that leads to murder is hot-blooded by nature and grows cold at almost the same rate as your victim. Together, the death you cause could do you part.

COROLLARY 1B. <u>NO HIT MEN</u>. If a man you don't know is willing to kill a man he doesn't know for a modest amount of money, is this who you want to trust with the biggest secret of your life? If your hired killer is arrested for committing your murder, or for committing anyone's murder, or for driving over the speed limit in a hospital zone, he will gladly offer the authorities a list of all his past employers to get an easier sentence. Why wouldn't he? Professional courtesy?

RULE 2. <u>LET GEORGE DO IT</u>. (The <u>big</u> exception to NO ACCOMPLICES.) If you hate someone enough to kill them, chances are someone else hates them just as much. So let's say you want to kill Fred and a guy named George finds his wife in a motel bed with Fred and there's a loaded gun conveniently sitting on the night table. Let George do it. Create and manipulate the situation so that George has means, motive, and opportunity. Then let human nature take its course. God helps those who help others to help yourself.

RULE 3. <u>CREATE IGNOMINY</u>. A two-dollar word for "disgrace and dishonor." If possible, have your victim die under sordid circumstances. It tends to make even the police think, "Well, he sort of deserved it, didn't he?" or "Boy, he really got himself into this mess." Taking the edge off a detective's outrage may be the difference between him tenaciously pursuing leads and giving up the case for dead.

She paused in her reading.

Doria was a self-made diva who'd wanted as much control as possible over how she appeared on-screen. To effect this, she'd learned more than most film stars about all aspects of filmmaking, from wardrobe and makeup to lighting and lenses. Now grasping the importance of being in two places at the same time, and being reminded of the helpfulness of ignominy, a scenario was materializing in her mind, with a starring role for studio head Leonid Kosta.

The box bed whispered her name from across the room and begged her to keep it company. She was so tired. And as with any script or character that presented a puzzle to her before she slept, she knew she'd awake in the morning and have the answer.

In the morning, she did.

♠

It pleases us with this volume to make available for the very first time something you would never see were you to be an on-campus student: three candid faculty appraisals. —HH

Mid-Michaelmas Progress Report

Student: Cliff Iverson
Faculty Advisor: Dean Harbinger Harrow

To the Board and Whom It May Concern:

As Mr. Cliff Iverson is attending McMasters on full scholarship, this will be a more extensive report than usual, as it is intended not only for review by the board but for the eyes of his sponsor as well.

To Mr. Iverson's sponsor: Your copy of this report arrived in an airtight cylinder. Upon exposure to oxygen, the ink on this page will vanish within minutes, so please read this in full now, as it will be your only chance. As with all our prior communications and discussions, sharing the existence of the conservatory or the contents of this report with anyone other than Mr. Iverson is strictly forbidden and, I must stress, irrevocably enforced.

Striking a more pleasant note: I'm delighted to state that Mr. Iverson is advancing commendably, which is not always the case with "draftees." In his initial month, he kept very much to himself, but he is by nature congenial, lacking in airs and attitudes, and, unlike a number of our students, does not blame the world or class-mates for the woes that brought him here. He does a good job of confining his hatred to one specific executive (i.e., target), and that hatred is commendably fueled by his compassion for other victims of said executive's cruelty.

While Mr. Iverson's studies occupy most of his very busy day, he has taken a scullery job in our kitchens following dinner and uses this modest income to purchase whatever treats he allows himself, rather than dipping into the generous account which you his sponsor have established in his name. In doing so, he has also been gleaning a more profound understanding of toxicology from Chef Tissier, and I would not be surprised if this unexpected tutoring will come into play in his graduating thesis. I am also personally pleased that he does not get needlessly embroiled in the philosophical aspects of the McMasters Method, as too many students do. During an outdoor session of our Sporting Chance course, on a day where Coach Tarcott was focusing on croquet and the many effective uses of mallets, balls, and even well-sharpened hoops, Cliff's democratic nature made him visibly restless with the effete nature of the sport, with its finger sandwiches, lime cordials, and the impracticality of getting men such as his own target to consider playing such a genteel game. He respectfully suggested it would be easier for him to hurl a thing called a beanball (apparently the most dangerous "brushback" pitch) during a pickup game of baseball at a company picnic. It seems Cliff was a varsity pitcher in high school, possessing both the velocity and accuracy to make such a pitch deadly. When Coach Tarcott suggested Cliff might employ that method, he replied that, sadly, it's hard to pitch at a company picnic when you've been fired from the company.

You might be interested to know he has joined the water polo program in our newly refitted sun-roofed swimming lido, as he apparently played for Caltech and has become our most dependable goalkeeper and a fan favourite.

Further relating to sport, young Iverson has taken full avail of our vigorous athletic opportunities where his physical condition is concerned. His recent years shackled to a drafting table have been more than erased by his "all-in" approach to exercise and sports under Coach Alwyn Tarcott. Cliff's superior physical condition should serve him well at our year-end track meet, which can provide a springboard to early matriculation and the pursuit of his thesis, which might lessen the cost of your gracious sponsorship.

All told, you could likely not be supporting a more decent fellow, and I imagine this is a primary factor in your desire to underwrite him. He has readily taken to McMasters methodology, shaping it to fit his own sensibilities and experiences, and is admirably results-oriented, perhaps because of his background in aircraft design, where deadlines are crucial and miscalculations can terminate in tragedy.

His resident advisor, Champo Nanda, informs me that he has befriended a number of residents at Hedge House, the coed residence where he stays, and I have personally observed him being a big brother to several of our more hapless cases.

There are few negatives to report at this time. However, in his first months here, Mr. Iverson has acquired a competitor, a male student whom we frankly now regret having accepted into our fold. We are trying to contain this situation, which is more our fault than Mr. Iverson's.

To the board, I would say this is a manifestation of recent efforts to slacken our screening process in order to increase profit, as advocated by our chief financial officer. We *must* learn a lesson from our experience with Mr. Helkampf.

However, this situation is not entirely problematic, as it has stimulated Mr. Iverson's otherwise dormant competitive streak. My primary concern as his faculty advisor has been that his thoughtful nature might cause him to falter in a critical moment during his thesis.

And once again to his most generous sponsor: While I am not allowed (and you would not want me) to reveal details of his proposed deletion, thus making you an accessory, I will say that it involves a financial stance atypical of these "go-getter" days. Toward that end, I have asked our Padre Pugh to leaven him with de facto sermons regarding God's love for the cheerful giver and remind him, as Luke advises: "Give, and it shall be given to you." Please know that your faith in the future of Mr. Iverson could not be better invested.

Mid-Michaelmas Progress Report

Student: Gemma Lindley
Faculty Advisor: Coach Alwyn Tarcott

To the Board:

The Padre here, all blessings! Coach Tarcott has asked me to speak on his behalf, owing to the demands of his recreational schedule, which seems to get more intense as the lowering temperature has brought it indoors.

We're both concerned about Miss Lindley's progress. Mind you, they don't come much brighter or more diligent than our Gem. She applies herself to her studies and if it were only a matter of grades, she'd be in like Flynn.

Our apprehension is toward the underlying hypothesis of her proposed deletion, one which we think may be fatally (in the wrong way) flawed. Her method is sound but relies upon what may turn out to be a false assumption: that she can manage to befriend a woman who is blackmailing her and entice her into a weekend lark in the countryside. She aims to convince Miss Underton to join her on a brief hiking tour around Bolton Abbey and Barden Tower in the Yorkshire Dales. Hours of research in the tombs of the McMasters library have led Gemma to a location less than thirty minutes northwest of Harrogate, a seemingly pastoral brook at some points only a few feet wide called the Strid.

As an inveterate nature lover and ex-Queen's Scout, I hope you'll forgive me if I abandon professional detachment for a moment and share my enthusiasm for this toxic torrent that Gemma has unearthed. The meandering creek called the Strid seems at some points narrow enough to cross in a single stride (hence its ancient name), or by picking one's way across a few black rocks standing amid its energetic waters.

But slip into those waters and the Strid will devour you alive, because it is not a brook or creek. Even at seven feet in width, the Strid is the River Wharfe, a broad, powerful river forced to turn ninety degrees on its side by a yawning but incredibly narrow gorge in the landscape. The ribbon of water atop the gorge gives it the harmless appearance of a stream, and its slick, moss-covered banks hide twisting shafts that drain to the abyss below, where lies a network of underground tunnels and caverns carved over eons by the river. One slip and the doomed are either battered against its craggy sides or, more often, sucked down its rocky arteries into watery caves from which there is no return. The ratio of slippers-to-survivors over the last forty years is 17:0, and no one would be surprised to learn that an inexperienced hiker had been the first death of the season. The Strid rarely yields a corpse.

All well and good on the face of it. Coach Tarcott has been tutoring Gemma in the Shukendo school of jiujitsu, to master the subtle technique of pushing away an outstretched hand to topple her victim's balance while seeming (to both her target and bystanders) to be assisting them.

When I expressed concern that this method entails more peril to Gemma than we at McMasters condone, she said she preferred it this way. Apparently, as the above method entails considerable risk to herself, Gemma actually feels less hesitant employing it! More than most students, Gemma has had great difficulty setting aside feelings of guilt about her proposed thesis. I've assured her that drowning is considered a relatively placid death, but she parries by asking upon whose testimony this belief is founded. In her own mind, if she slipped and water-chuted to her downfall with or without her target, it would simply serve her right, and she'd have no cause for complaint.

Coach Tarcott and I find this to be an *extremely* unhelpful attitude and we are troubled that Gemma may fail because, in her decency, she may subconsciously feel she deserves to.

Toward remedying this dangerous attitude, the coach and I have specifically given her a thankless assignment that hopefully will prove to her that trying to befriend one's blackmailer is an enterprise weighted toward failure. Better to learn this lesson here than on the field of battle.

The urgency of our intervention is made even greater because, due to a lack of finances, Gemma can only afford tuition for one academic year. Unless we can get her to consider a different stratagem, she will be embarking on a thesis that may be ill-fated, and for which she will have precious little time to improvise an alternative.

We have additionally added a series of sessions with Vesta Thripper of Eroticide in the hope that another woman's counsel may be more effective than that of a priest who once removed a depraved bishop from Life's chessboard without contrition, or a former Olympic coach who once pinned a heartless champion's bronze medal to their chest with a nail gun. I close this report noting that we both personally like Miss Lindley a great deal, thus our heightened concern.

Mid-Michaelmas Progress Report

Student: Dulcie Mown
Faculty Advisor: Professor Matías Graves

To the Board:

Dulcie Mown is an exemplary student, the kind we hope for each time we approve an applicant. I've been starving like a polyphagian Pollyanna for a student with the range of skills and readiness of Miss Mown, and Dulcie is a seven-course meal from soup to nuts (she's also a little nuts, by the way, but engagingly so): extremely intelligent, a fast study, asks sensible questions and expects sensible answers back, turns in homework assignments on time and spot on, and participates with admirable spirit in all extracurricular activities. She is clearly sophisticated but does not force her worldly awareness on her schoolmates or, as far as I can tell, any of her professors. There are times when I wish she would take a little more time to enjoy the social whirl here, but she seems dedicated to assisting someone back in California (possibly a sister, close relative, or best friend) whom she clearly worships and for whose cause she possesses a level of devotion and dedication almost Harpy-like in its singlemindedness. May we all have such avenging angels beating their wings, feathers ruffled, against our enemies.

Afterthought: After giving Captain Dobson an advance look at my progress report, as I frequently do, he enlightened me as to the identity of this person "back in California" to whom our Dulcie is so fervently dedicated. He said that he spotted the true identity of "Dulcie Mown" within minutes of her arrival here, whereas I have been completely taken in this whole term. The captain theorizes that getting to the top in Hollywood and—in particular—staying there requires a certain animal cunning and that he'd "bet the farm on her to win, place, and show no mercy . . . a real natural."

XVI

FROM THE JOURNAL OF CLIFF IVERSON

Dear X: My differences with Jud Helkampf have escalated this term. A typical example surfacing in a semifinal round of intramural water polo, this being a sport I'd enjoyed while at Caltech, as you may or may not know. Matches are held at the Swimming Lido, whose indoor pool, tiled patio, and zinc bar beneath a glass roof make it a welcome place for study, gossip, plotting, and even swimming the whole year long.

Jud and I have proved ourselves more than adequate goalkeepers for our respective teams, although Helkampf's contempt for the rules would not have held water in an Olympic competition. According to regulations, goalkeepers alone may touch the bottom of the pool with their feet. Taking advantage of this, Helkampf smuggled a narrow-gauge dock line under the high waist of his trunks, swam beneath Cubby Terhune's feet, yanked him underwater, and quickly tied bowline knots around both his ankle and the bottom rung of the pool's metal stepladder. When I saw that my closest-positioned teammate had suddenly vanished, I dove and spotted Cubby drowning mere inches below the surface, and while I struggled to untie the knot, Helkampf attacked my untended net and scored the winning goal for his team. When I protested to Coach Tarcott, who was refereeing the match, his only response was a smile that read: "This is how life works. Don't expect help from me now and don't expect help from the police against your Mr. Fiedler." And while the coach personally despised Helkampf, there was no ignoring the efficacy of his method.

I had my chance to exact some seemingly harmless revenge at the very same lido, not in the pool, but while speaking at the school's biannual meeting of the Return to the Scene of the Crime Club, a student organization formed to support those who had failed at a deletion prior to McMasters. My participation was not only requested but (as with this journal) required; however, I was relieved to learn I am not the only failed murderer among the student body.

The assembly drew a robust and thankfully receptive crowd, with seating on both the patio and the risers behind the pool. Apparently, getting to hear firsthand accounts of fellow students' past ineptitudes made most attendees less embarrassed by their own fallibilities and insecurities.

At the podium, the rally's host, Matías Graves, brushed back a thick swatch of hair and began, "*¡Saludos y bienvenidos!* It's gratifying to see such a fine turnout! Let's first give our thanks to these brave souls coming forward today to share their experiences with us." He addressed the designated speakers near the podium, which included me, Mim Webster, and (much to my surprise) Gemma Lindley. Graves continued, "No one is here to judge you for any past failure. You did your best, lacking the education and fellowship this institution provides." He turned back to the crowd. "And as Demosthenes said, 'He who fights and runs away may live to fight another day' . . . although Guy McMaster preferred the more succinct 'I'll get you next time!'"

The first speaker, Miriam Webster, was an appealingly blowsy woman, much given to head tossing, who always looked as if she'd just been interrupted while planting amaryllis. She admitted attempting to poison a controlling and miserly husband, cleverly spending a year breaking the bulbs of large wall thermometers (so much less suspicious than purchasing rat poison, and no signature required) in order to stockpile a huge dose of red mercury, only to learn after pouring it in his morning coffee that if the mercury in a thermometer is red, it isn't mercury. Apparently, her effort wasn't a complete failure: The upshot was that after her tight-fisted husband tasted the doctored coffee, he demanded they switch from Grand Union coffee to Chock full o'Nuts, a premium brand.

Gemma was up next. She began cautiously, as if each syllable might choose to attack her, and her voice trembled, which I suspected was more from repressed emotion than simple stage fright. "Unlike others speaking here today, my . . . attempt went exactly as planned. So the operation was a success and the patient died." I was sitting to one side of her and noted that sunlight had caused the gloss of a tear's trail on her face. "And yet it was a miserable failure, because I did not think beyond my single murder, and that's why I now have to commit another." It was the first time I'd heard the word "murder" spoken aloud in weeks, and as I wrote it just now, I half anticipated armed guards bursting into my dorm room to confiscate my pen.

She glanced toward Matías Graves, faculty chair of literature. "I should have studied my Shakespeare, Professor. 'Blood will have blood.'" She quoted this as if issuing a warning to the muted crowd. "Murder can beget murder. My successful deletion was not the end of things. Now I'm obliged to murder a second time, for a motive far more tainted and self-serving, one that goes against my nature. But I have to do this, or the already wounded heart of an innocent bystander—my mother—will be destroyed. So let my own experience warn you: Think beyond your mission. When you murder, you may believe you're done with your victim, but murder may not be done with you."

This was taken in by the crowd like a temperance lecture at a bacchanal and only a spattering of hands beyond my own accompanied Gemma back to her seat. It was likely a good thing for her that Dean Harrow was only now entering the lido to join Dobson and Stedge at a patio table, for he might not have approved of her distinctly downbeat sentiments.

I would have offered some supportive words to Gemma but it was my turn to speak. I hadn't relished recounting my ineptitude to my assembled classmates, but the dean and Champo Nanda had separately explained to me the obligations of a sponsored student, pointing out (perhaps more candidly than I'd have liked) that others might benefit from my past incompetence. I tried to be a good sport, admittedly in the hope that acknowledging my past idiocy from the outset might diminish any open derision.

Had I been striving for laughs, I could not have done better. Even the stone-faced Dobson nearly cracked a smile as I described my oversized "disguise." The one stark exception to this was Helkampf, who topped the crowd's generally sympathetic laughter with a few snide jeers of disdain.

When my narrative came to an end, Matías Graves joined me at the podium and asked if I'd share with the assembly any positive lesson I might have taken away from my misadventure. And while my murder attempt had certainly been a spectacular botch-up, I did feel I'd cleverly executed something, if not my victim.

I began, "Well, the one thing I may have done right—"

"You couldn't do the right thing if they cut off your left arm," heckled Helkampf.

I gave him the tolerant smile of a parent about to gift his ingrate son the keys to a new sports car. "You know, Jud, you're going to feel very guilty in a minute," I advised him good-naturedly, then directed my words to Harbinger Harrow, now seated on the patio. "Dean, might I present the award now rather than at the end of the assembly as we scheduled?"

The dean, beaming with magnanimity, approached the lectern. "Absolutely, Mr. Iverson. A fine time for the award, to be sure!"

"Thank you, sir." I cleared my throat and announced, "Classmates and faculty: I've been given the privilege of presenting the midterm Student of the Semester award to the undergraduate whose work has most embodied the guiding principles of McMasters. So would you be kind enough to step forward and receive the award now, please . . . Jud Helkampf!"

I led the surprised crowd in obligatory applause and an equally shocked but very pleased Helkampf stood and joined me and the dean at the podium. Harrow shook Jud's hand and enthused warmly, "Well . . . congratulations, Jud, we haven't always seen eye to eye, but this is a tribute you've richly earned."

The applause had ended quickly, lacking any real enthusiasm from the crowd, and in the silence, Jud stepped to the microphone and began, "Well, first, I'd like to say—"

"Oh, shut up and sit down," snarled the dean and a communal

gasp swept across the crowd. For a moment, I thought Helkampf might actually strike the dean, but Sergeant Stedge was already standing at the ready, so Jud had to make do with casting a venomous glance in various directions. I had learned in Zooicide that most poisonous snakes have slit pupils, and damned if his eyes didn't seem to possess them as well. As he slithered back to his table, the dean addressed the assembly. "Just to be clear: There is no 'Student of the Semester' award, and I suspect Mr. Iverson invented it just now to demonstrate one of the most powerful weapons any of you can use against your target, especially those of the male persuasion. 'Vanity of vanities, saith the preacher, all is vanity!' Most of us are readily prepared to believe the best about ourselves no matter how far-fetched."

As it happened, my cloudy misadventure in New York had seen at least one glimpse of sunlight, which I proceeded to recount to the now attentive crowd: how I'd used Fiedler's vanity to get him to stand precisely where I wanted him . . . on the incoming end of an uptown IRT subway platform.

I'd called Fiedler from a drugstore opposite the Hotel Buchanan.

"How'd you know where I was staying?" was Fiedler's greeting. The true explanation was that Fiedler's chatty secretary, Meg Keegan, had once told me that whenever the great man went to New York, he invariably took a suite at the Buchanan consisting of a large bedroom flanked by two adjoining drawing rooms, one strictly for business, one strictly for not.

I answered as if I was still accountable to him. "Oh, I'm in the city myself. Word gets around about you." Fiedler was big-headed enough to believe that Manhattan was abuzz about his arrival.

"And what are you doing here?"

"Looking for a job. I'm out of work, remember?"

I could hear Fiedler flipping through papers on the other end of the line. "You call for any reason?"

"Just wondering if you'd heard of any openings anywhere."

The paper rustling continued. "I have work to do. Don't call me anymore."

"I read that piece about you in the trade magazine," I said. "Nice picture."

The rustling ceased. "What trade paper?"

"New York Business Weekly, as if you didn't know," I voiced jealously.

"Business Weekly?" asked Fiedler.

"Really? You haven't seen it? Well, you probably won't find it now, it was last week's edition. I was glancing through it at a sub-way newsstand, looking for job listings, and what's the first thing I see? A full-page article about you." I struck a bitter tone to perfection, probably because I didn't have to fake it. "What a great start to my big trip to the big town!"

"Read 'em and weep, as they say," said Fiedler, who was one of the "theys" who said that.

"Cora's standing right behind you in the picture," I added, which silenced Fiedler for a moment. As it happened, Cora was not in the picture, because there was no such picture or article, although New York Business Weekly was a real publication available at city newsstands.

"She was attractive but confused," he finally pronounced as if it were a coroner's verdict. "Shame what she did. Where'd you say this newsstand was?"

So much for Cora's eulogy, I thought. "As it happens, I read it on a subway platform right across from where you're staying, at the start of the IRT uptown platform. If you're going to the trade show, you could take the subway from there to Columbus Circle."

I could hear the smirk in his voice. "I wouldn't be caught dead on the subway."

You will be soon enough if I can just get you on that platform, I thought. "Yeah, that's probably why you didn't see it. The edition might still be in the subways because they hang on to their stock a little longer. Captive customers, you know?"

"The IRT, you say?"

"Uptown train, two flights below the street," I offered smoothly as a floorwalker.

"New York Business Weekly . . . what's on the cover?"

"I don't remember, I didn't buy it. I can't afford to buy myself magazines right now."

"That's why they have libraries. S'long."

I heard a click and hoped I'd enticed Fiedler to go exactly where I needed him to be on the subway platform.

"Yes, you did well back there," affirmed the dean at our private consultation the day after the lido assembly, "and ridiculing Jud Helkampf was a droll way to demonstrate—paraphrasing Mr. Wilde—that flattery is a most sinuous form of incapacitation. Luckily, your target is likely unaware that you enlisted his own vanity to reel him in, so he'll probably not recognize that strata-gem if you employ it again in your thesis, as I've recommended you do. His readiness for adulation is a bottomless vessel into which you can pour praise without him protesting, 'Please, sir, may I have less?'" Harrow reached for some sherry of the nonpoisoned variety. "However, a note of warning, young Iverson: I fear you may have further aroused Jud Helkampf's ire and I would be most watchful where he's concerned."

I thanked him for both the sherry and the warning, and asked if he had any further comments on the formal proposal for my the-sis. Harrow scribbled something on a slip of notepaper. "Well, I've already given you Ecclesiastes One-Two on the subject of vanity, so I'll now prescribe you Acts Twenty-Thirty-Five, coupled with a very brief tutorial from Professor Sasaki."

I wondered what mathematics could possibly have to do with my thesis. Glancing down at the words Harrow had written, I was surprised to read: "It is more blessed to give than to receive." I raised my eyebrows, and the great man responded, "If you give generously to your Mr. Fiedler as if there's no tomorrow, the day may soon come for him when there won't be."

XVII

From the Journal of Cliff Iverson

It has become necessary, dear X, for me to keep a wall calendar in my room to demarcate the passing days as they've accelerated into weeks, then months, because autumn seemed to be playing hard to get for the longest time. But at last the colors of Slippery Elms' abundant woods turned and the grounds became a pageant of pastels. Mim Webster, who seems to know her stuff where arboriculture is concerned, identified the oaks, maples, sweetgums, and dogwoods whose leaves were now as cranberry red as the mane of Milton Swill (the bantamweight who was poisoned the night I dined at the dean's table). The trees from which Slippery Elms took its name were yellow as a hazard sign, while the estate's hickories and poplars shed gold leaf as if nature had divested itself of costume jewelry. It made a dazzling setting for outdoor classes in Rake and Hoe Wielding, particularly coupled with the always useful cultivator.

As the school year progressed, we had a few light dustings of snow, the first of which arrived so precisely on Christmas Eve that rumor was Dean Harrow had seeded the clouds in order to deliver a picture-perfect holiday. No great fuss was made about Christmas except on the day itself, but then the school celebrated as heartily as the born-anew Scrooge. By the dean's decree, all campus skullduggery was forbidden until midday on the twenty-sixth, even as he asserted that nothing was more conducive to a successful deletion than the false comfort and joy of the Yuletide season. Despite the armistice, Jud Helkampf tried his best to lace the eggnog with an overdose of nutmeg (which in enough quantity can cause amnesia, acute anxiety, palpitations, and, in some instances, death). Luckily, its rich odor alerted others, and Helkampf was sent to his room without his pudding.

But while Christmas spent at least one of its twelve days at McMasters, winter was very much to our content and passed quickly, which only caused the student body to further speculate regarding where in the world they were. For a while, Milton Swill insisted on Nepal, but the monsoon season never arrived and he later claimed he had said Naples. The night sky might have offered clues, but unless your thesis depended on the constellations, students taking an undue interest in the heavens were advised to look down and mind their step, lest they have a nasty accident. The one exception was the moon, which McMasters felt belonged to everyone.

I had gotten in the habit of wandering as close to the perimeters of the estate as a casual walk would permit, not for purposes of escape but merely to see if any local features might offer a clue as to where I was. Toward the west (the sun's rising and setting at least gave us the four compass points) I had found an old stone well with some kind of runic symbols etched into its ledge, but the characters seemed recently carved and I suspected misdirection.

I'd been excited once when, ambling by the Automotive Arts depot on the very far side of the campus, seemingly miles from the main gate, I'd spotted an ambulance bearing the name "Our Lady of Mercy Hospital, Santiago." But the truck bore no license plates and had appeared at the Labs a few days later as part of an experiment on how to escape a crime scene at ninety miles per hour with the unwitting assistance of a police escort. It wouldn't have surprised me to learn that the vehicle had once been Cubby's ice cream truck.

One Sunday, though, in what I decided was surely early spring, I made my way through the Tangle and the bamboo forest beyond it, hiking upward to see if there were any elevated parts of the estate from which I might get a more commanding view of the outlying area. As the terrain rose and became rockier, I arrived at an unexpected crevice, as if I were atop a slot canyon. On the other side of this chasm, a stone castle was set into the hillside, with a single Rapunzel-like turret spiring toward the clouds. On closer inspection, the fortress proved to be an ornamental folly built with forced perspective on the considerably higher side of the ravine, giving the impression of being farther away and more imposing than it really was. It might only have housed a single room. Still, the peak across

the crevice was discernibly higher than where I stood, and ascending it might gain me a better view of the surrounding terrain.

I'd expected a trestle or rope bridge of some twenty feet to span the narrow chasm, but instead discovered a small aerial tram parked at a platform on the far side, suspended from a rope pulley that stretched back to a similar platform only a few feet from me. The tram was hardly bigger than a Ferris wheel's enclosed cab . . . but how to summon it from my side?

I peered down into the ravine but couldn't discern how far it dropped, for the crevice narrowed to barely the width of my body. Fuming up from the aperture, the entrails of brimstone-scented vapor obscured what lay below. A grim fate, I thought, to fall and find oneself wedged between two walls of rock, knowing that the best result of wriggling free would be yet another fall to an unknown depth.

I made a mental note to sign up for whatever activity would allow me access to the other side of the ravine and possibly gain me some better sense of where—

"Iverson."

I flinched in surprise and spun to find Simeon Sampson directly behind me, although I'd heard nothing prior except the stirring of the wind and some random cackles from the rooks nesting within the castle. His thin lips pursed into an icy smile as he picked up a small rock and, as if trying to skip a stone on a lake, flung it past me into the ravine. It dropped out of sight and I failed to hear it land. "Taking another of your ambitious strolls?" he asked. "You'll cease being the dean's pet pupil if he thinks your feet are getting itchy again. And an isolated perch like Raven Ravine and Castle Guy is a particularly unwise terminus. I could gain a few extra credits merely by giving you a quick push. Hanging from this ledge, my mercy would be your only ally." He smiled. "That's incorrect grammar but it makes you a dangling participle."

Sampson had been among those assembled when I'd recounted my failed attempt to push Fiedler off the subway platform. I did my best impression of a snarl. "You're forgetting I'm the one who tried to shove another smug prig to his death."

This amused Sampson to no end. "Your intended homicide victim is living proof of your ineptitude. I'd start focusing your attention on the track meet at the end of term. It's where the gloves come off, paranoia becomes a sensible frame of mind, and things that go bump in the night may be a lead pipe coming in contact with your cranium. Let's make it a date, shall we?"

With that, he stepped behind a heap of boulders.

"Look, I've had it with you!" I yelled and dashed around the rocks to pursue him, but he'd vanished. Fearing an ambush, I looked in every direction including up, but my adversary had disappeared as effectively as a master magician who had no interest in taking a bow.

XVIII

From the Journal of Cliff Iverson

Because crowded social gatherings can be an excellent smoke-screen for deletions, McMasters holds a lot of dances, the way an army holds war games every few months. This evening, the Grand Ballroom at Slippery Elms hosted its third Valentine's Day mixer of the term, even though we'd said goodbye to February weeks earlier. June Felsblock had drawn head chaperone duty and was displeased at the meager number of students warily mingling on the ballroom floor. "I will not watch you wallflowers poisoning the punch bowl all night!" she barked, which caused her corsage to catapult from her left dress strap. "This next number is a Ladies' Choice, and you have ten seconds to acquire a dancing partner or suffer two demerits."

If her edict sounded combative for a soirée, dear X, you should understand that amorous activities are serious business here at Mc-Masters, even if the word "love" never appears in the curriculum catalog. By now we'd been instructed that the arrows of flirtation, infatuation, desire, lust, covetousness, jealousy, and heartbreak all have their place in the McMasters quiver, if purely as a means to someone's end and not as road signs along the steeplechase of an affair. Just last week, the dean challenged the assertion that each man kills the thing he loves, countering, "To the contrary, our purpose is to help you kill the thing you loathe, and if wearing the mantle of affection helps you achieve your goal, so be it. At Mc-Masters, romance is a verb, not a noun."

Dance Craft is a required course, since ballrooms and night-clubs present many unique opportunities for guile while one's target is distracted or intoxicated. So although I always dreaded sock hops and such in college, I've done my best to honor your sponsorship and willingly tripped the light scholastic with whoever might have me.

Now, with June Felsblock decreeing a Ladies' Choice, I found Audrey Jäeger, my neighbor at Hedge House, tapping my shoulder and drawing me into a two-step to the recorded strains of a society band. "I need your help," she whispered, brushing away oat-colored ringlets from her face as her lower lip began to tremble. The reflex sympathy she elicited made me as annoyed with myself as with her. "I'm done for," she groaned, blotting tears from the right side of her face against the display handkerchief in my school-issued blazer.

I squirmed uncomfortably within our clinch. "Look, Audrey, I'm not unsympathetic, but just because I've been situated next door to you doesn't mean we're family. I really don't know much about you. You might even be some kind of test or informer where I'm concerned. I have so much on my plate already. Can't you turn to someone else?"

"There is no one else. Please."

What might she be getting me into? "Well, it would depend on what kind of help you want. I mean, obviously, I wouldn't kill somebody."

She gave me the strangest look. "But isn't that why you're here?"

"Change partners, still a Ladies' Choice!" announced June Felsblock, and Dulcie Mown efficiently slithered into Audrey's place, while Audrey sought refuge with Dulcie's vacated partner, Milton Swill, who dutifully whisked her away.

Dulcie was an accomplished dancer, smooth if a bit on the showy side, and I wisely opted to be led by her. "A favor," she began, and I detected no question mark at the end of the phrase. "You mentioned during one of our croquet matches that you were a baseball pitcher in high school. Matías reviewed your records and tells me you were an MVP." I'd already noticed Dulcie's tendency to refer to most faculty by their first name, in this case, Pro-

fessor Graves, her faculty advisor. She continued, "I need someone
to throw batting practice for me, now that the weather's warmer.
Challenging pitches. For my thesis. I may throw like a girl but I
need to bat like a Ruth."

It took me a second to decipher this. "Babe."

"Sweetie," she responded. "Of course, I could use a ball suspended on a string but that's not the same thing as a pitch coming
at me with only half a second to calculate and clobber." Nestling
closer, she said, "I'm sure there's some way I could repay you down
the line with a little something from my own bag of tricks."

Clearly Dulcie was dangling a reward like a ball suspended on
a string, but it was impossible to tell if her offer was laced with
suggestive innuendo because everything she said was laced with
suggestive innuendo, or seemed to be . . . even ordering oatmeal
at breakfast. "I've done a bit of acting in my time," she went on,
turning her face toward mine as if to reveal more of herself to me.
"Should your own plans require a thespianic turn or two, I could
certainly give you some pointers."

There was something very credible about her when she said she
was no stranger to acting. She struck me as both tantalizingly familiar and instantly appealing. And my thesis, now well-evolved
at this stage, did in fact require some role-playing. I was about to
agree to the deal when June Felsblock commanded everyone on
the floor to change partners and, much to my even greater interest,
I found Gemma in my arms.

Is ballroom dancing the greatest achievement of the human species, X? Imagine swooping down upon a stranger on the street,
encircling their waist with your right arm, clutching them to your
chest, and spinning about the sidewalk with your cheek pressed to
theirs . . . they'd call the cops! However, add a musical combo to
the equation along with the words "May I have this dance?" and
you're above reproach.

As I held the graceful Gemma, I heard myself say—despite my
bliss—"Sorry to keep you away from Helkampf for even a second." I couldn't believe the bitterness in my voice.

Gemma's reflex response was a mirthless laugh, followed by a terse "I loathe him."

"You'd never know from the way you behave with him," I groused.

She looked over my shoulder, perhaps monitoring to see if Helkampf was near us on the dance floor. "It's not really any of your business, but it's part of my studies. An assignment."

I instantly reveled in her nonexplanation. It had been hard for me to reconcile her slavish devotion to Helkampf with her otherwise endearing nature. I began to hold her less stiffly, and she seemed to relax in my arms. "They've given you a hard subject to warm up to," I offered.

"Well . . . I chose to come here, accepted their methodology, and shouldn't complain. But it would be nice one evening to do something that isn't dedicated to murder. To have a spring break, if only for one afternoon."

I found myself telling her about the castle I'd discovered on the far side of Raven Ravine and the quaint aerial gondola by which it could be reached, trying to make it sound like a visit to the Swiss Alps. I offered to show her the place sometime.

She shook her head. "Sounds like a lovely date," she said. "But we aren't going to have a lovely date and I could be leaving any day."

As we drifted about the ballroom floor as idly as an unmoored canoe, I remembered that once we left McMasters, I would never see her again. I didn't even know if Gemma was her real name. Chastened by this thought, I tried my best to enjoy the dance, knowing it was likely our last.

XIX

From the Journal of Cliff Iverson

It was Coach Tarcott's firm belief that the solution to all problems in life lay in some aspect of sport, whereas it was Professor Grave's firm belief that Coach Tarcott was an idiot. The truth probably lay somewhere between the two extremes, but as the coach tried to find a sports application for my upcoming thesis, I countered, "The only sport my target likes to play is the ponies."

"Polo? Great!" exclaimed Tarcott. "One of the most neglected of the deadly sports. Croquet mallet in a stampede? Lovely!"

"No, I meant ponies as in horse racing, betting. My target loves long shots but can't endure losing. If you want to get in good with him, you pass along a tip, but God save you if the horse doesn't win."

"That's worth serious thought," advised a suddenly sober Tarcott. "Find a person's passion and you'll usually find their blind spot as well."

"Cliff!" The voice bore a tantalizing familiar intonation and I saw Dulcie Mown heading my way across the momentarily vacant playing field. "Now would be a great time for that batting practice I mentioned to you. Just let me change and we can put in a half hour before dinner." She didn't ask if this would be as great a time for me as for her but, to be fair, she had already lived up to her end of the bargain by giving me some extremely useful acting and makeup tips at Wump over the last few weeks.

At her private cottage, I turned my back (although she didn't ask me to) as she shed her stylish outfit and shimmied into standard-issue dungarees and a school sweatshirt. From behind her box bed, she produced a Louisville Slugger. The quartermaster's office had only let her requisition the baseball bat for personal use after Coach Tarcott confirmed it was to be used as weaponry and not simply for sports.

The school's American baseball diamond and British oval cricket pitch coexisted at opposite ends of a huge pasture, both turfs having a slight downward slope as a reminder that McMasters does not believe in a level playing field . . . and that the advantage should always go to the striker.

Dulcie asked me to mix the location of my pitches but to feed her nothing but fastballs. Concerned I might accidentally bean her, I asked the coach to provide her with a batting helmet. While strapping on a catcher's mask, he was compelled to mention that few disguises are more natural than that of a home plate umpire, whose own mask, loose black uniform, and chest protector obscures both shape and face. I commented this was useful information if one wanted to delete a contralto for murdering the national anthem when Dulcie yelled in her best Brooklynese, "Come on, Cliffy, put one out over the plate!"

I pitched from the stretch and Dulcie swung under the pitch by a foot or so, but that was irrelevant as the ball had already reached Tarcott's glove before she'd begun her swing. "Just need a little warm-up to get my timing right," she explained, but after fifteen minutes, Dulcie had still not connected with a single pitch. She threw the Louisville Slugger to the ground and suggested gutturally an unusual use for it that may not have occurred to its manufacturer.

I tried to console her. "Don't feel bad. After all, at least six times out of ten, the best players in the game get an out."

Dulcie choked up for a moment, not on the bat but in her throat. "You don't understand, Cliff," she lamented at last. "I can't afford to miss on my first swing. If I do, it'll be my third strike."

XX

A few years before Cliff Iverson's arrival at McMasters, Eroticide was changed from a voluntary elective to "mandatory when proposed by a faculty advisor." This was done because while most female students displayed a willingness to improve their knowledge of stratagems *sexualis*, the majority of male students were erroneously confident that they had nothing further to learn.

Eroticide is a customized, one-on-one tutorial (two-on-one being a rare exception) under the auspices of, and on some occasions *with*, Vesta Thripper, Advanced Practice Registered Nurse (as well as Miss Indiana 1951 and Miss Rheingold 1952). The curriculum is tailored to each student's specific mission with the referral coming from one or more faculty advisors stipulating that the amatorial arts are relevant to the student's thesis. After all, not all deletions are crimes of passion. The initial consultation is invariably a private student-teacher conference, for which Vesta employs the seating arrangement of psychiatric therapy, couch in a darkened room. To this layout, Vesta often places a lit candle on an end table near the student's feet for its hypnotic and focusing quality. The seating arrangement is also designed to alleviate any embarrassment regarding the matters and methods under discussion.

"My thesis involves becoming my target's friend," Gemma explained once the initial consultation was underway. A cold current of revulsion passed through her. "She has an absolutely malicious hold over me, yet somehow I have to convince her I'm no threat."

"I've read your proposal and Father Pugh's private notes," Vesta advised. "So I'm aware your thesis depends on getting your supervisor"—she consulted her notes—"Adele Underton, to go hiking with you in the Yorkshire Dales, this although she's blackmailing you and would have every reason on earth to distrust you." Despite her training, Vesta betrayed vexation as her faint eyebrows rose. (She wore no makeup during consultations, as students were frequently intimidated by her features.) "Really, Gemma? You need to make your blackmailer *like* you? A tall order, don't you think?" She added gently, "Unless, of course, you wish her to *desire* you. That's a different thing altogether."

Gemma flinched. "No, that wouldn't work. I don't think I'd be convincing. Besides, Adele is only interested in men."

"As marital prospects, possibly. But you'd be surprised how often a woman can find herself attracted to another. A form of adolescent crush that continues into adulthood."

Gemma shook her head. "No, I think trying to arouse her sexually would only arouse her suspicion. We have to become 'best mates' somehow. That's why Coach Tarcott gave me the assignment of getting a particular student to befriend and trust me the way I'll have to manage with Adele. I was hoping you might be able to guide me with that as well."

"And the student is . . . ?"

Gemma paused. "Jud Helkampf."

Vesta shuddered. "Jeekers," she responded, betraying her midwestern farmland origins. Although as au courant in her peg-top silhouette dress of hammered satin as the mid-Atlantic accent she'd acquired via the Eileen Ford Agency, when surprised or startled, Vesta often reverted to her Hoosier self: a registered nurse at Mercy Hospital in Cicero, where she'd been discovered by a New York fashion designer who'd had an emergency appendectomy while visiting family. "I've interviewed Mr. Helkampf and if he ever did any soul-searching, he'd find there was nobody home . . . and you're supposed to get him to *like* you?" She shook her head. "Of course, I believe I could advise you how to *seduce* him. Monsters are often quite easy."

Gemma sat up on the couch. "No, Coach Tarcott has prohibited me from doing anything overtly enticing or seductive, not for any moral reason, but since I won't be using seduction on Adele, trying it on Jud would be pointless. Plus, honestly, he does give me the creeps."

Vesta knew that Alwyn Tarcott was an intelligent man and she couldn't help but wonder why he'd given his student the impossible assignment of gaining Helkampf's trust. Perhaps it was to demonstrate to Gemma, while still in the protective cocoon of McMasters, how hopeless her current deletion plan might prove.

Vesta asked if she'd offered to do Helkampf's homework to better gain his confidence, but Gemma explained that she and her advisor had ruled out that tactic as well because, back in civilian life, Gemma already did all of Adele's work for her . . . so this would bring nothing new to their relationship.

"Have you considered sports with Jud?" tried Vesta. "You know, the camaraderie of teamwork?"

Gemma slid around to sit up on the edge of the couch. "I've helped him cheat at water polo, volleyball, even badminton if you can believe it, but he acts as if being his accomplice is both my obligation and my privilege."

Vesta closed her spiral notepad with a flip of the wrist. "I'm sure you know there are emotionally warped people who feel that every other person on this planet exists solely to advance or gratify their malformed ego. In psychology, it's called narcissistic personality disorder, which has always felt off the mark to me, since these people aren't actually in love with themselves. Quite the contrary. Someone like Helkampf operates from a lack of self which, early in his life, mutated into an unquenchable thirst for adulation. For those like him, the glass is neither half-full nor half-empty because life is not a glass but merely a funnel. And when adulation falls short—as it always will for such people—it triggers a fearsome and wounded rage." She instantly regretted saying this, for it might cause someone as sensitive as Gemma to view Helkampf (and, worse, her true target, Adele Underton) with compassion . . . a terrible emotion to instill in a would-be deletist! Tarcott and Father Pugh had referred Gemma to her in the hope that a woman who was expert in the McMasterian arts might better counsel the novitiate. But there was precious little she could recommend.

"Gem, I'm not sure there's anything in my particular field of study that I can offer. It would be easier to hijack your Miss Underton than to get her to voluntarily join you on a short hiking vacation." She leaned toward Gemma. "From what you've told me, your target is not as warped as Jud and probably twice as cunning. Are you absolutely sure your method of deletion is the best choice you could make?"

The River Strid had seemed to solve so many problems for Gemma, if she could only get Adele to cross it with her. She resisted the suggestion, saying, "I'm squeamish by nature, but this method would let nature do all the dirty work for me. The body would be gone in an instant, it would be viewed as a dreadful accident . . . all I have to do is help her to slip."

"It would hardly be like murder at all," acknowledged Vesta, who'd heard this kind of rationale many times before. There were good people, murderously intended, who could handle every aspect of their studies except the fact that they had to kill someone. Vesta rose to snuff the lit candle on the end table and turned on a lamp. "The best I can suggest is that you acquire a well-groomed, well-dressed English boyfriend for whom you care little and about whom Adele knows nothing. It's okay if he's a bit of a dunce, a . . ." she tried to recall the British term, "a *twit*, you know? Let's call him Alistair. Confide a few times to Adele that Alistair is secretly coming into a fortune when he turns thirty-five, mumble something about Cadbury or Cunard, but say that for now he lives on a stipend and doesn't like anyone knowing about his financial prospects. Let Adele see you wearing expensive accessories—you can buy them yourself and return them the day after you wear them, saying, 'Oh, this? Just another trinket Alistair got me, the dear.' This should interest her no end. Your Alistair will certainly already have a friend named, say, Nigel, who has difficulty getting dates. Male twits tend to travel in twos and threes, like ducks in the park. Let Adele overhear you trying to find a woman to join you, Alistair, and Nigel for a weekend in the Yorkshire Dales. Adele will push herself on you, because she'll see it as an opportunity to steal wealthy Alistair away from you. I'm sure she thinks she's more alluring than you, as most predators have a high opinion of their own charms. You'll reluctantly acquiesce, owing to the hold she has over you, and Adele will think this was all her own idea. Once at your Yorkshire vacation site, while her full focus is on how quickly she can conquer Alistair's heart, you and Adele leave the boys to watch a cricket match in the hotel's bar while the two of you take a walk along the nearby Strid. Her mind is plotting how to peel Alistair away from you, not on you and the brook. She carelessly suggests, 'Maybe the four of us could go dancing after din—' and oh dear God, she's in the drink!"

It was as plausible a solution as Vesta could concoct and Gemma looked half-convinced. She asked, "Are there any . . . negatives to the plan?"

Vesta hesitated. "Well, pragmatically speaking, you may need to memorably seduce your 'Alistair' in advance of the trip, to guarantee he'll go to Yorkshire with you whether he likes hiking or not. The mere promise of consummation might not be enough. It could require making him eager for an encore performance."

"But then I'd be a common prostitute."

"No, you'd be first-rate, I'd see to that, promise."

Gemma's internal debate ended quickly. "Sorry. It's just not me."

Vesta pleaded, "Are you *sure* this is the only plan that suits you, Gem? You realize there's every chance you'll fall into the Strid with her . . . or that you die rather than her."

"If I did, it would serve me right, don't you think?" said Gemma, much to Vesta's dismay.

FROM THE JOURNAL OF CLIFF IVERSON

I'd finished my briefing on the end-of-term track meet and was making a fast jog of my own back to Hedge House when—okay, I'll admit it—my heart sank at the sight of Gemma leaving Eroticide by the lodge's side door, one of which bore the words "Comparative Religious Studies – Exit Only!" This signage was clearly a face-saving device for those departing from a consultation (or a "conviviality session" in one of Eroticide's private rooms, rumored to resemble an ocean liner's cabin, minus the porthole). It was widely known among the student body that anyone making their exit via that door was either considering something indecent as part of their thesis or honing their skills at same.

A dull despondent ache filled my chest and I confess to you, X, that in that moment I was humiliated to discover I apparently have an embarrassing puritanical streak. "So she's <u>that</u> kind of person!" I thought with indignation. (Of course, had she been that kind of person with <u>me</u>, I would have found it a forgivably touching reflection of her openheartedness and sensuality.) But I was genuinely surprised to see Gemma departing from Eroticide's side exit. After Cora had ended her life, and there was talk of a sordid relationship with someone (I've already told you who), the prudes at Woltan had tut-tutted, ". . . and she seemed like such a nice girl!" I still think that about Cora, no matter what happened between her and Fiedler. After all, if he could make a murderer of me, how easy must it have been for him to send her off the rails, especially with pharmacological assistance.

Gemma did seem more resigned to life's harsh realities than Cora had been, based on what little I knew about either of their situations. Where Cora had seemed in free fall and unable to cope with the future, Gemma struck me as determined, if darkly bitter, about her mission.

This had made me both admire her and sympathize with her. But now I'd discovered she was undoubtedly planning some sexual angle under the expert tutelage of Vesta Thripper. "Or maybe she doesn't need much guidance at all," I sullenly confided to a squirrel who was gorging himself on winged seeds as they helicoptered down from the maples of early spring.

And yet, was I any more virtuous . . . when my own thesis called for me to seduce the insatiable vanity of Merrill Fiedler?

Dulcie Mown (a.k.a. Doria Maye, occasional headliner in scandal columns) had responded dubiously to the dean's recommendation of a consultation with Vesta Thripper. She was far from a naive novitiate, after all. "I admit certain isolated components of seduction, or at least the illusion of same, are central to my thesis, Harby." (Dulcie had taken to calling Dean Harbinger Harrow by a sobriquet lacking precedent or permission, and he swore to Captain Dobson that if she persisted, he might have to give her a taste of her own curriculum.) She went on to reassure him, "But it's unlikely I'll do anything I haven't already done on screen or in an audition." It should be noted that, where Doria Maye's earliest roles and auditions were concerned, this was not quite as wholesome a reassurance as it might sound.

The dean scribbled a quick note as if writing a prescription, put it in an envelope, and sealed it with wax. "Give this to Vesta when you see her. It will be the finishing stroke to your endeavor, designed to ensure your victim's final infamy." He almost chuckled, smothered it with a cough, and handed her the envelope. "I believe you're glory bound, m'dear."

Despite the arrival of spring, Eroticide's lounge was still staged for the winter term in the guise of a plush ski lodge with a central open fireplace and high-backed sofas tucked away to create "quiet little tables in the corner" all around the room. In warmer months, this same facility would resemble a Polynesian bar at a swank hotel in the tropics, the sound of breakers piped onto the terrace outside. The underlying theory was that nothing lowers resistance to romantic entanglements more than a resort environment in an isolated location, fostering the attitude of "Oh, you're on vacation, live a little, no one back home will know!"

Vesta gently explained to Dulcie, in highly clinical terms, the unusual procedure the dean felt she might include in her thesis and the unique challenges it presented. "There's a range of possibly unfamiliar accessories and logistics for you to master. And right now you may wish to visit the restrooms," suggested Vesta.

"For what purpose?" asked Dulcie. "Are we going on a long trip?"

"No," said Vesta, "our trip will end there." She led Dulcie to the men's and ladies' rooms. Since the current illusion was that this was a swank skiing chateau in Switzerland, the doors were labeled as they would be in Gstaad. Dulcie started to walk toward the one bearing the word "Damen."

"Sorry, wrong door," advised Vesta, pointing across the hall. "The door marked 'Herren' is the one we'll be wanting."

XXI

From the Journal of Cliff Iverson

Dear X: In terms of luxury, gastronomy, personal attention, and sheer beauty of surroundings, I imagine McMasters is rivaled by few schools . . . for which I offer many thanks, generous sponsor! Its one notable deficiency seems to be a lack of a graduation day, an occasion when I might have hoped to finally meet you. But my resident advisor, the always straightforward Champo Nanda, tells me students depart McMasters the moment their advisor and review board deem them ready. There is usually no advance notice, as this lessens the opportunity for students who have grown close at McMasters to make rendezvous plans for that time after they have rejoined the outside world. In the safe setting of the conservatory, reunions like this may sound viable and exciting at the time, but Champo says they are as unlikely as a tobacco heiress reuniting with her steward from a Mediterranean cruise once she's returned to her old Kentucky home.

But tonight's track meet very much resembled a graduation ceremony, which feels appropriate where I'm concerned, since my own thesis seems as primed as I could hope it to be.

The designation "Track Meet" is a bit deceptive, if you picture relay races and hundred-yard dashes. Cubby, who attended last year's edition, says a more accurate description occurs when you add words that are omitted but tacitly understood by all: <u>track</u> your quarry, <u>meet</u> your quarry, and delete your quarry, at least to the point where your success or failure can be determined by the school's judges. Restraint is advised where any "coup de grâce" is concerned, but restraint can be a hard thing to come by when winning is genuinely a matter of life and death.

Cubby informed me that Track Meet is always held in the evening and outdoors, weather permitting, commencing with a ceremony on the playing field for the entire school. Tonight, a raised platform hosted a dais for the faculty, a podium for those speaking, and two long tables bearing hundreds of diploma-like tubes ready for distribution. As students assembled in the bleachers, the pep band played the campus fight song, school pennants whipping about in the brusque evening air. Coach Tarcott lit a towering bonfire by firing a flaming arrow into the night sky. It fell dead center into a hummock of bone-dry branches and firewood that had been well-salted with chemicals by Professor Nan Redhill (Practical Science's department head) in order to sustain a livid-colored blaze throughout the ceremony.

After singing the school's alma mater (set to a classical theme whose title I can't reveal because it also serves as a code between alumni in the outside world), we sat at the ready. The spring night air bore the stimulating scent of nature returning to life, seasoned with the knowledge that we soon would be flirting with death. The track meet was intended to prepare us for the real thing, just as pilots must face simulations of engine failure and police must race through obstacle courses beneath bursts of live ammo.

"I will dispense with levity," said Harrow, apparently assuming he would normally be a laugh riot, "in order to make clear that each year's track meet is to be taken in dead seriousness by all. This evening represents your first foray into the realm of freeform deletions and the grade you receive will carry great weight in calculating your average for the term and readiness for your chosen thesis. For those of you who have been doing poorly, this is a superb chance to overcome that. For those of you doing just satisfactorily, a poor showing tonight could drag you under. Obviously, tonight is an improvisational effort for which you've had no way to prepare, and we factor that into our grading process. But to those hunting, it is vital you demonstrate to the judges that your target could well have expired owing to your efforts. Conversely, if you are the quarry, you must demonstrate that you might have terminated your hunter. As with fencing and Asian fighting arts, you are expected to pull short of a final thrust or blow. There is no need to cause actual termination . . . but then again, to quote Casca, Cassius, Cinna, Trebonius, Cimber, Ligarius, and Brutus after the fatal stabbing of Julius Caesar, 'Accidents will happen.' So keep in mind this evening is much more than a chummy game of hide-and-seek. We shall now commence the selection process."

The campus and village were already in a state of readiness, with the Labs and Wump standing by for emergency use by those improvising deadly scenarios. The shops and restaurants of Mead Mere were brightly lit and spouting music, their staffs braced for a rush of late-evening customers who had murder on their menu.

Now the dean began trumpeting last names of the assembled students in alphabetical order. Once I heard "Ibanez" and "Imlauer," I joined the briskly moving line directly behind Sergei Ivanovich, whose broad back I'd come to know well during fire drills. Soon I was stepping onto the platform where a young man from Dilys Enwright's staff consulted a ledger and directed me to the first of the two tables. "Take tube three, seven, or thirty-five, the choice is yours but only one," he advised, giving the proceedings at least the air of randomness. "Once you've opened your tube, be sure to keep your blue assignment slip, as it's the only proof of who your quarry or hunter was."

We were required to remain in our seats until the last tube had been distributed, to ensure that all students began the hunt (as I choose to call it) at the same moment. The sound of a gunshot creased the air, and I thought the first deletion of the night had occurred when I realized it was Coach Tarcott's starter pistol signaling that we could open our respective tubes. But I refrained from doing so until I was alone. In my card-playing days at MIT, I was told that where poker faces were concerned, mine was about as inscrutable as an "Eat At Joe's" sign outside a diner called Joe's. I feared that if I knew the identity of my target and encountered them prematurely, I might tip them off with a mismanaged glance or a shifting of my eyes. So I trotted head down to Hedge House to discover if I were a predator or prey, when I heard footsteps running toward me and my name being called in a stage whisper. This soon? I thought.

To my relief, it was Cubby Terhune. "Don't worry, you're not my target, see?" From the pocket of his brown corduroy zip-up jacket he withdrew a blue slip which read:

YOU ARE A <u>HUNTER</u>.
YOUR QUARRY IS GEMMA LINDLEY.
YOU ARE ALSO SOMEONE'S QUARRY.
GOOD LUCK.

I was actually relieved to read those words. If Gemma had to be someone's quarry, the least likely person to put her at risk (other than myself, of course) was the inept Terhune. I soberly counseled, "Well, keep in mind you lose more points for a failed attempt than for no attempt at all. You can't afford any negative numbers at this point." Of course, I had no idea if this were true, but I hoped it might prevent him from doing something impulsive that could harm Gemma.

"Who do you have?" asked Cubby, eyeing the tube in my hand.

"I don't know yet, and if I did, I'd probably keep it to myself. Now be careful. Gemma usually hangs out with Helkampf and you don't want to get in <u>his</u> way, right?"

With that, I departed, but not without looking back to see Cubby heading in the direction of the women's dorm where Gemma lived. Likely he thought she might visit her room to retrieve something useful for her own hunt. From the shadows between the gaslights along the walk emerged the figure of large man whose bare scalp glowed dim in the weak moonlight. He stopped Cubby and moved in closer to him. I couldn't be sure but the man might have been Jud Helkampf. If Cubby was Jud's target, it would certainly be an early evening for them both.

Two minutes later, I was sitting on my bed, praying I wouldn't hear the beseeching knock of Audrey Jäeger at my bathroom door. The Fates, reliable as ever, heard my fervent prayer and acted upon it.

"Cliff?" A muffled Audrey spoke to me through the door on my side of the bathroom and I wished she could muffle herself even more.

"No, Audrey."

"Please. The track meet would be a perfect cover for them to expel me. You know what I mean by 'expel,' don't you? You have to let me in."

I emitted what I'd come to call the Audrey groan and set my still-unopened blue tube on the bed . . . but doing so caused me to consider the possibility that Audrey might have drawn my name. Opening the door could be the worst next move I could make.

"I'm sorry, Audrey. We're not supposed to trust anyone, especially not during Track Meet." No sooner had I said this than I realized that if I had any brains—and apparently I didn't—I should first see if "Audrey" was the name in my blue tube, in which case I'd be more than delighted to let her in the room. "Hang on a second," I said. "Maybe . . ."

I opened the tube and removed the enclosed blue slip. Typed on it were the last words I had expected to read. I was now utterly bewildered, for the words were:

YOU ARE A HUNTER.
YOUR QUARRY IS CLIFF IVERSON.
GOOD LUCK.

As I tried to make sense of this, Audrey continued from the other side of the bathroom door. "You don't understand, Cliff. The name I drew. I don't know what to make of it but it can't be good. I'll slip it under the door and you can see for yourself."

She did so and I noted that the paper and typeface were identical to my own. She could hardly have had time to find matching paper and a printing press to create a counterfeit for herself. Bizarrely, it read:

YOU ARE A <u>HUNTER</u>.
YOUR QUARRY IS AUDREY JÄEGER.
GOOD LUCK.

I unlocked my side of the door and showed her my slip of paper indicating that my quarry was me. "Unless the curriculum has suddenly swerved toward the metaphysical," I said, "I think this is a mix-up."

Audrey pointed out that she had been standing directly behind me when the tubes were being distributed, Iverson being most immediately followed by Jäeger. Was the unimaginable possible: McMasters had made an error?

Audrey plonked herself down on my bed as if we were bunkmates at summer camp. "What do we do?"

"In a way, this could work to our advantage," I reasoned. "If I was supposed to hunt you and you were supposed to hunt me, we're both aware of that now through no fault of our own, right? And we don't really want to do each other any harm, right?"

"Oh no, Cliff, you've been very patient with me."

"So . . . if we stay together and out of harm's way, in the morning we can declare that we both managed to delete each other at the same time."

She appeared game enough but still puzzled. "How would we manage that?"

I started to dope out an approach without knowing where it might lead. "Look, we share the same bathroom, so I know you use tooth powder instead of toothpaste, and you know I drink a couple of glasses of water when I wake—you always complain about the water carafe being nearly empty by the time you're up." I walked into our shared bathroom and reached for some talcum powder in a medicine cabinet. She joined me as I started to sprinkle some into a tin of tooth powder by her toothbrush.

"What are you doing?" she asked with keen interest.

"Putting strychnine in your tooth powder. This talc will stand in for the real thing. The judges don't expect me to kill you, just demonstrate that I could have."

She looked dubious. "Where would you have gotten strychnine at this hour?"

"The apothecary shop at the Mere is open all night for Track Meet. And in the outside world, rat poison's easy enough to come by. Hardware stores and nurseries all carry it." I replaced the lid. "Your turn now. Put some tetrahydrozoline in the water carafe. It's tasteless and enough of it can bring on coma and death."

"Where would I come by this tetra-something without a prescription?"

"You already have it." I reached for her bottle of eye drops. "It's the active ingredient in these drops you use after your crying jags. Over-the-counter, easy to keep in a pocket or purse. When I was doing scullery duty, Chef Tissier said the powder rooms of a lot of swank restaurants have eye drops alongside the mouthwashes and hair tonics on their marble sinks, which is good to know in case you ever want to rejoin a dinner companion, wanting to lethally spike their soup or champagne. It's safe in your eyes, but not in your stomach. Of course, instead of adding your eye drops, I'll add a symbolic dash of Listerine to the water carafe instead." I did so and replaced its stopper. "All set. So we'll explain the timing to the judges this way: Early tomorrow morning I drank my two glasses of water, took a hot shower—which happens to accelerate the sedative effect—became dizzy, and lay down. Meanwhile, you followed routine, so I wouldn't think you were up to anything unusual, and brushed your teeth while waiting for me to die . . . and the strychnine I put in your tooth powder acted so fast I might actually have heard you hit the floor moments before I went into convulsions."

Audrey caught on fast. "So we can both claim we successfully pretend-deleted the other, and with no way to prove which of us died first, they'll have to give us both a passing grade." She seemed pleased, as was I, and we agreed to spend the rest of our night sequestered in our rooms until the morning, when we could report our mutual mock murders to the judges.

I sat down at my desk and began writing this account for you, when I heard a single knock or bump of something on my door, which was locked, of course. I rose quietly, picking up the wooden chair at my desk in case I had to defend myself, and pressed my ear against the door, straining to hear any sound from the hallway . . . breathing, a cough, a footstep.

Nothing.

I am now seated at my desk again and, as I write this, I'm feeling newly concerned. First, I think I got too full of myself by telling Audrey about eye drops being poisonous. I will not under any circumstances drink the water in the carafe or any other liquid that she might have access to. After all, there is no way I can completely rule her out as my hunter.

Second, in writing to you about Cubby's note, where he had been designated both a hunter and a prey, and with the sound at my door just now, it dawns on me that someone in addition to Audrey might be assigned to hunt me. To be candid, dear X, I wouldn't put it past McMasters to have intentionally switched Audrey's slip and mine so that we both might lower our guard, and I'm beginning to wonder if the very last place either of us should be right now is sitting here in our rooms where anyone can find us. I have a thought about where we might sequester ourselves for the night, although I'll have to acquire the skill that dolphins have, of letting one side of my brain sleep while the other keeps a single eye open to watch for potential predators . . . including Audrey Jäeger.

Unlike the circumspect Cliff Iverson, Dulcie Mown had immediately opened her own cylinder at the crack of Coach Tarcott's starter pistol. She was, after all, an experienced actress and felt she would have no problem maintaining her poise even if her designated target were standing directly beside her. She read the blue slip of paper and found its words to her liking.

A huge poster board at the playing field's refreshment kiosk displayed the photographs and names of undergraduates, so that if a student wasn't acquainted with their prey, their image and place of residence on campus would be readily available. Dulcie noted that the ruddy-faced Miriam Webster was looking in the "S" section, her eyes locked on one particular picture. Dulcie commented, "Milton Swill? I wouldn't try poisoning him if I were you, Mim."

"Why shouldn't I?" asked Miriam reflexively, and instantly realized she'd tipped her hand, although she could see no harm in doing so.

Dulcie explained, "Ever since he unwittingly consumed that poisoned salt in his soup, he's wary of everything. Shouldn't be hard to locate him on campus, though, his mane is the color of a stoplight." She looked at her own slip of paper. "Lucky me," she commented sarcastically, switching to her best Dietrich accent to intone, "I've drawn *Herrrr* Helkampf!" She bid Miriam good luck and ambled toward the well-lit building that housed Wump, where wardrobe changes, makeup, and even prosthetics were still available for the evening's escapades.

Gemma had never seen the campus more alive, for the entire student body was now either trying to avoid their unknown tracker or locate their assigned quarry. Going to bed (or at least going to one's *own* bed) was out of the question. Some students in their early twenties foolishly behaved as if the event was some sort of society scavenger hunt, their misguided bursts of laughter occasionally punctuating the night. But most took this nocturnal fox hunt in dead earnest, their visages determined, guarded, wary, or simply frightened. The profusion of students anxiously seeking a safe haven (or stalking those who sought one) was augmented by the faculty who were stationed to serve, when summoned, as proctors and adjudicators of all encounters.

The slip of paper in the tube she'd selected had not been what she'd hoped for.

YOU ARE SOMEONE'S <u>QUARRY</u>.
GOOD LUCK.

Story of her life! As she understood the rules, her task was to remain undeleted until dawn. She considered returning to her room but remembered that since she shared the space with others, she could not lock herself in. And if one of her roommates proved to be her hunter . . .

As she considered what to do next, Jud Helkampf came walking toward her from the direction of her dorm. He was whistling cheerily to himself, which was uncharacteristic and thus all the more creepy. And now he'd spotted her and there could be no pretending she hadn't see him, so she fell in step, as she'd been constrained to do all term. "Well, Jud, this is the happiest I've ever seen you," she tried gamely.

"Because of who I drew in the lottery. It's going to be a pleasure to get him."

Gemma tried to imagine which male student would give him such joy to kill and one name instantly came to mind. "Cliff Iverson?"

Jud didn't answer but his suppressed smile seemed confirmation enough. Gemma was surprised to find herself worried for Cliff and wondered if it would be against the rules to warn him, for Jud really *might* kill him. But how to find Cliff while he was on the hunt or in hiding? And why did he matter more to her than any other imperiled student? "Well, best of luck and all that," she said. "I have my own assignment to tend to, so I guess we should part ways for now."

"Are you hunter or quarry?" Jud asked.

She forced a knowing smile without one iota of confidence behind it. "I guess that depends on who you find in the net after the trap is sprung." Gemma hoped this sounded knowing, even cunning, in the total absence of a plan.

She truly did wish she could warn Cliff, but Jud certainly wouldn't appreciate her disloyalty. She reminded herself once again that the only reason she'd enrolled at McMasters was to address her own plight and not that of others. Tonight, as one of the hunted, her first obligation was to find somewhere to hunker or, preferably, bunker down until dawn.

She remembered a site Cliff had described to her during their last Valentine's Day dance that sounded like a perfect sanctuary: some kind of castle beyond the bamboo forest, reachable only by a small, hand-powered tram car that traversed a ravine. The good thing about the gondola, Cliff had explained, was that the only way to bring it back from the castle was for it to be cranked by a passenger within it, so once you were across the ravine, no one could reach you without advanced mountain climbing gear or a block and tackle, neither easy to come by at this hour. Of course, she'd be alone there, frighteningly so. But whereas anyone in a crowd might be her hunter, at the castle they would have to reveal themselves while being unable to get at her. She decided to wait in safety, if total isolation, until daylight.

At first it wasn't a very lonely walk to the Tangle, because so many hunters and hunted were on the same paths, albeit most moving in the opposite direction. But as she reached the bamboo forest, the student body thinned to the point of emaciation, for only a fool (or someone like herself with a plan) would traipse through such an isolated area.

She feared she might stumble into the ravine Cliff had mentioned, but as she approached the rocky terrain beyond the bamboo forest, the moonlight was less diluted from the competing light of campus buildings and streetlamps.

Now she was walking on harder ground and, in the deep quiet, the uneven scuff of her steps was slapped back at her with faultless precision by the stone walls around her. She rounded a slight turn and was rewarded with the stunning sight of Castle Guy across the ravine, dramatically lit from beneath, the upward shadows making it lofty and imposing. Its glow helpfully illuminated the quaint gondola resting on its wood perch on her side of the gorge. Hidden lighting shone down into the misty ravine, the beams absorbed by a murky, sulfur-laced fog, leaving its depth scarily indeterminate. She thought, It's like the Strid, but without the water.

Approaching the toylike gondola poised upon its departure platform, she was surprised to feel a foolish wave of dejection as she realized that the waiting tram meant that Cliff had not come there as well. It was a reaction she'd not felt since her teenage years in Northumberland: going to a party with the hope of seeing, say, "Andrew," taking hours with her appearance, changing outfits more than once, asking her mum if this went with that, and, upon arrival, carelessly asking "By the way, is Andrew here yet?" only to be told that Andrew's family was in London for the holidays. She had vaguely hoped that Cliff might also have sought haven here, imagined him calling out to her from across the ravine, riding the gondola back to pick her up, the two of them spending the night at the castle, safe from all others. Who knows where that might have led? But no, she would be taking the small tram alone to the castle side and spending the night listening fearfully for any sound of an approaching stalker. Not her favorite way to spend the hours after midnight. But things could be worse, she thought.

Then the electric lighting on the castle chose to extinguish itself. "Welcome to worse," she murmured.

The thick gloom that instantly tautened around her might have been deadly, considering how close she already was to the edge of the ravine. Luckily, two guttering torches, nested in iron mountings, flanked the castle's portcullis, and the flickering pulse of their flames managed to intermittently push away the inky night like a receding tide. She looked at her watch dial. It was 10 p.m. She assumed the electric lights shut off automatically at that hour, as did most other lights on campus. In one way she was grateful that, when it came time to cross the ravine in the tram, it would be impossible to see the ominous drop below her. She groped her way forward and managed to reach and open the gondola's door. Clambering in, she was blindly fumbling for the crank that would move the car along its guide rope when she touched a hand that was not her own.

Audrey was hiking to the Tangle at a far more hurried pace than she had ever displayed in PE, for she wanted to stay as close as possible to Cliff, who was leading the way. The two drew stares simply for traveling as a duo, the track meet being an "every student for themselves" event where tag teams were discouraged if not forbidden. Cliff was not a fool, so he still entertained the possibility that Audrey had somehow swapped the tubes herself and might at any moment clutch his throat with an exultant cry of "Consider yourself deceased!" If so, he hoped the journal he'd left on his desk might gain him some points for ingenuity before she'd "deleted" him.

But Cliff was also capable of seeing both sides of an issue, and he reasoned with empathy that Audrey—terrified of terminal expulsion from McMasters—might fear he was acting on behalf of the school to permanently "dismiss" her and intended to use the track meet as his cover.

Of course, Cliff knew he was *not* up to something but he certainly wouldn't blame Audrey for thinking he was. So, each vigilantly watching the other, they made their wary way beyond the bamboo forest path and reached where the ground became rocky, requiring them to employ the flashlights they'd brought with them. As they did, the shape of another person appeared a hundred yards in front of them, outlined against the glow of Castle Guy's twin torches on the far side of the ridge. "Who's that?" asked the figure, and Cliff recognized the voice as Cubby's. Cliff held his flashlight up to his face and Cubby came trotting toward them, his open corduroy jacket flapping in the stiff wind like pelican wings.

"What are you doing out here . . . *and* you?" Cubby asked Cliff and Audrey in turn. "You're not allowed to track me together, that's against the rules!"

"We're not tracking anyone," Cliff told him. "What are *you* doing here?"

"I was following Simeon and doing a good job of it, had him in sight all the way from Laundry Cottage past the Thistle Maze and the Primrose Path up through the Tangle. Then he went up this ridge and vanished."

Cliff swept the area with his pocket torch. "The ridge is so open here, you'd think the only way someone could vanish would be to hurl themselves into the rav—" He whirled on Cubby. "Wait, you say you were tracking Simeon? I thought you said were supposed to track Gemma?"

Cubby straightened with pride. "I traded quarry with Jud."

"*Traded?*" asked Audrey with unexpected concern.

"Simeon has always been insulting to Cliff, and I thought I'd try to put him in his place! Thinks he's so smart." He added, "Of course, he was able to vanish on me, so I guess he is smart."

Cliff wanted to shake Cubby senseless. "You let Helkampf loose on Gemma, knowing how warped he is?"

"I thought they were pals; they're always hanging out togeth—"

A penetrating scream rang out, doubly frightening because it was abruptly silenced at its peak. Cliff whipped his head left and right, as if there'd be a remnant of the shriek lingering in the air to indicate its location. "Where'd that come from?" he asked Audrey, who was peering down the path they'd taken, when a much shorter cry sounded from the direction of the castle.

Cliff sprinted up the rocky incline to the gondola platform and Audrey followed, easily besting Cubby (much to his surprise), as the three raced to the tram's launch pad just above the slot canyon. Reaching the platform, Cliff cursed, for the gondola was on the Castle Guy side, with no way to bring it back until whoever was on that side cranked it over.

Cliff could now hear Gemma pleading with someone from the other bank of the gorge. He discerned two figures struggling below the castle's torches, and while he couldn't see any facial features, the taller of the two had a head whose outline resembled a truncated three of clubs. It could only be Helkampf, his hair like oversized earmuffs over a domed head.

On the castle side of the ravine, Gemma had been using every skill she'd acquired in Asian Arts to delay Helkampf's attempts to close her throat. His voice was like that of a demented aunt coaxing a child to take medicine that didn't taste so bad at all. "Don't fight, you're making it worse than it needs to be," he sickly soothed Gemma as she tried to counter with a guillotine headlock, knowing she could not maintain it for long. "I just need a photo of you unconscious to prove I deleted you."

"I thought—we were friends!" she managed to get out.

His falsetto giggle terrified her. "The opposite. I know when I'm being buttered up, you little con artist."

For Helkampf, the thrill of "legally" stalking Gemma instead of the assigned Simeon was so enticing that he'd gleefully accepted Cubby's offer to trade quarry slips, even if this might constitute a bending of Track Meet rules. The possibility of a sanctioned murder excited him more than was healthy for Gemma or anyone who stood in his way. He'd shadowed her until it was clear she could only be heading for the tram car to Castle Guy, whereupon he'd circled ahead at a fast sprint in order to lie in wait for her just before the castle lights had snuffed out. He savored the fact that he would be deleting her in a location no one else on campus could reach. How many bonus points would he be awarded for that?

"I can pose dead the way you want, I won't move, promise!" Gemma vowed.

"No, it'll look fake," he said as he broke out of her weakening hold. "I need your eyes open with only the whites showing and your tongue sticking out." Dear God, thought Gemma, this is his punch list! Could he possibly complete it without killing her? He added, as if this were sufficient explanation, "They're not happy with me lately and I need a high score."

McMasters had clearly made a disastrous error in their review process, thought Gemma, and apparently she was going to pay for their mistake. Helkampf's hold on normalcy was slipping even as his grip on her neck was tightening. "Don't fight me, Gemma, or I could hurt you," he advised. It was a laughable statement but she had no breath left in her with which to laugh. Her vision grew dim and she kicked at him, fearing if she went under, she'd never return.

From the opposite side of the ravine, Cliff bellowed Helkampf's name but it had no effect. Gemma swiveled her head at the sound of Cliff's voice and managed a kind of bleating sound.

Audrey bellowed, "Let her go, Jud! You're not supposed to really kill anyone!"

"Unless it can't be helped," he grunted, struggling with the work at hand.

"It's an exercise, Jud!" yelled Cliff. "A game!"

"Games have winners! I'm here with my quarry and you're over there, losers!" He sounded terrifyingly like a schoolboy who "won't share toys with others."

There was so little side light from the castle's flailing torches that Gemma and Helkampf were merely shifting inkblots in the night, and in Rorschach fashion the shapes became Cora and Fiedler in Cliff's mind. He could not bear for her to die again. From the tram's launch platform, Cliff peered down into the shadowy mist of the ravine and tried to convince himself that although the drop was daunting, the crevice itself was not all that wide. He wondered if he could sustain a grip on the tram's pulley rope and inch forward, hand over hand, across the gorge to the castle side. If only he had protective gloves . . .

"Give me your jacket, Cubby," he snapped, and Terhune quickly shed his corduroy zip-up. Standing at the edge of the platform, Cliff draped the jacket over the tram cord, silk lining against the rope, corduroy facing out for him to grip.

"What are you doing?" cried Audrey, but all Cliff could hear was a last sputtering gasp from Gemma across the gorge. Holding the jacket with both hands, he let his feet slide off the platform, the way a person committing suicide will allow the chair beneath a noose to slip out from beneath them. The slight downward angle of the pulley rope caused him to slide away toward the long, welcoming mouth of the slot canyon.

The rope leveled off and he came to a stop dead center above the ravine. Frightened as he was of falling, he was even more terrified he might drop and become wedged between the rock walls that nearly intersected below and find himself pinioned for minutes or hours—unreachable by any immediate rescue effort—knowing the best option the future held for him would be to writhe free of the stone vise only to complete his delayed fall toward death. He'd heard of people who'd been wedged between a subway train and its platform, able to listen and speak, and to whom rescue crews and a hastily summoned priest could only explain that the moment they were freed, their demise—delayed—would now be arriving on Track 2, and did they have any message for their loved ones before they were released from both their pinion and existence?

He knew the act of looking down would destroy what little nerve he possessed, so he shimmied the jacket along the rope, grateful that the ribbed corduroy was saving his hands from friction burns. "Hang on!" he called repeatedly to Gemma, though he knew he was talking to himself.

Helkampf was startled to hear Cliff's cries growing closer, and he ceased choking Gemma for a moment. As she dropped to the ground, he ran to the castle's gate, grabbed one of the two burning torches, and walked it back to the platform on his side of the ravine. "I'm sick of you trying to show me up!" he snarled and held its flame to the pulley rope.

"If you burn the rope, you'll be stuck there," Cliff responded hoarsely, trying to reason with the lunatic.

"We're witnesses!" shouted Cubby from the safety of the other side. "He's not your quarry, you'll be expelled!"

"He's lousing up my hunt and bringing down my average!" countered Helkampf, as if this explained everything. The rope was burning now without assistance from the torch, so he turned his full attention back to Gemma.

Audrey hissed to Cubby, "I've got to get help!" and ran toward the Tangle faster than he would have predicted based on the labored slog of their morning runs together. He wondered what possible help she could reach in time to save either Gemma or Cliff, and continued to loudly protest Helkampf's actions, albeit from across the ravine.

Cliff had gently edged forward to where the rope was aflame, hoping he might extinguish it with Cubby's jacket. He realized that, in snuffing it out, he'd be applying his full weight to the charred stretch of the rope, but anything was better than waiting for it to burn all the way through. He dared not look into the geyser-like exhalation rising from within the gorge. Its brimstone odor now seemed ominously prophetic where Cliff's immediate future was concerned, as he helplessly watched Helkampf bending over Gemma's half-conscious body.

There was a deafening sound of iron grating against stone—so loud it might have been electronically amplified—as the portcullis of Castle Guy rose, revealing Simeon Sampson lit by a blinding spotlight shining down on him through the castle's murder hole directly above his head. Dressed in a slim white suit, shirt, and tie, he seemed an emissary from the angels, his blond hair halo-like in the beam. He decreed, "All right, Mr. Helkampf, I think that's quite enough."

"How'd you get to this side without the tram?" grunted a startled Helkampf, momentarily distracted from Gemma and utterly dazed by Simeon's seemingly divine intervention.

"Oh, the staff of McMasters get around the campus in ways of which you have no notion," he informed him.

Helkampf slowly straightened. "Since when are you staff?"

"Since completing my deletion four years and seven months ago," said Simeon with a tinge of pride. "Luckily, I'm the recipient of my parents' youthful genes, which allows me to mingle with students as their peer while monitoring their progress." He turned to address Cliff, who was still hanging, his arm muscles burning almost as fiercely as his lifeline. "My primary mission this term has been to watch after you."

"At the moment I'd say you've done a really lousy job!" despaired Cliff as he watched the flames eat through the last filaments of rope.

"Yes, I'm sorry about that," said Simeon with genuine regret as the rope split.

The last sound he heard was Gemma calling his name in horror as he dropped into the void below.

As Dulcie Mown had predicted, the bright and blowsy Miriam "Mim" Webster found her quarry Milton Swill easily enough, for his tabasco-pepper-red hair was such an incendiary crown that to disguise it he would have had to shave his head or wrap it in a babushka (neither of which Milton was likely to do, track meet be damned). Swill's trim

frame and modest height had made it easy for Mim to rule out most of the students hastening across the quadrangle in search of safer or more shadowy sectors of the campus. It made for a bizarre footrace in all directions, particularly for those whose blue slips had notified them they were someone's target.

Like Cubby, Miriam had been instructed to hunt a quarry (Milton) but also advised that she was some unknown student's prey. She adopted the philosophy that being a moving target was more tolerable than waiting for one's hunter to find you. But Track Meet was a marathon lasting until sunrise, and she was learning that one can only keep moving so long.

She found Milton Swill at the Obelisk, an authentic Egyptian spire on the Slippery Elms estate. Students enjoyed nestling on benches to watch the sun set behind it, though of course they had no clue where the sun was setting. Rumor maintained there was a secret entrance into the Obelisk, and a spiral staircase leading up to a summit from which a vertical aperture would allow a vista said to clearly reveal McMasters' location. But no student had ever credibly claimed to have found a way into the tapered monolith.

The usually withdrawn Swill had clearly decided to let romance overrule self-preservation, for Miriam spotted him just before dawn beneath a gas lamp, blithely necking with a blonde on a park bench near the Obelisk, the two swaddled in a large cashmere throw to stay warm (not that their amorous nuzzling wasn't generating its own heat). Milton had his back to her but his fire-engine hair betrayed him, while the vaguely familiar-faced blonde, whom Mim couldn't quite place, had her eyes closed in rapture. Thus, neither noticed Miriam's stealthy approach as their kisses deepened and sweet nothings passed between the twosome. Who knew the diminutive Swill had it in him? she thought. Still waters run short, it seemed.

As she closed in, armed with a fallen tree branch she'd found in a nearby grove of sycamores, she saw the blonde's eyes were not so much closed as squinting as she huskily moaned encouragement to Swill. "*Now,*" the blonde urged.

Miriam, a gentle soul, announced, "And with just one more step I'd have struck and you'd be dead, Milton."

Swill whirled and plunged a concealed rapier into Miriam's side. "*Au contraire*, 'tis I who've been waiting for you, dear Miriam!" said the purported Milton who, removing a red-headed wig on loan from Wump for the evening, revealed Dulcie Mown's close-cropped head of jet-black hair. "I'm afraid I lied to you back at the photo board," she explained to the stunned Miriam. "*You* were my quarry, not Jud Helkampf. Luckily for you I'm expert at fencing, so no harm done." It was vexing for the Hollywood star not to mention her title role in *The Countess of Monte Cristo* with its famous Duel on the Parapet scene. "See how perfectly I thrust my dull rapier between your left arm and rib? A sharpened tip and a foot more to your right, you'd have been dead on your feet."

"And I'm witness to that, of course," said the blonde who'd been necking with Dulcie. She removed her golden tresses, revealing the sensitive features of Milton Swill, sporting lipstick that matched his genuine scarlet mane. Milton had been delighted to linger in Dulcie's experienced embrace while watching over her shoulder to alert her to any approaching hunters. It was quite the symbiotic arrangement: Dulcie serving as decoy for Milton's hunter, Milton being the camouflaged lookout in "Milton's" arms. And while Swill may not have realized he'd been necking with an established Hollywood romantic lead, he'd delightedly found her feigned passion more memorable than any prior necking session during his relatively sheltered life.

Cautiously, Mim withdrew the perfectly placed rapier from where it had been adroitly tucked between her arm and side, with no harm done beyond a small tear to her sleeve.

Dulcie turned with new energy to Milton. "Now, let me help you catch your quarry, whoever they are," she insisted. "A promise is a promise."

"Oh, that's all right, Dulcie," said Milton, using a handkerchief from his prop purse to slowly wipe away the lipstick he'd applied to his mouth. "As it happens, *you* were my designated quarry, and when you told me to disguise myself as a woman—at least from the neck up—I *might* easily have used a lipstick that Professor Redhill helped me develop for my upcoming thesis. It's permeated with melittin, phospholipase, apamin, hyaluronidase, and histamine . . . the equivalent of bee venom. Odorless, tasteless, and deadly to those like you and my future target, who both have a life-threatening allergy to bees." He pointed to the Chopard medical bracelet she always wore in public and called out to a yellow-vested McMasters proctor, who approached, clipboard in hand. Milton concluded, "I could have killed you any time we were necking, Dulcie. All I had to do was transfer it subcutaneously by giving you a hickey or nipping at your earlobe. Consider yourself dead as well."

Dulcie reflected and dryly replied, "Bite your tongue."

Cliff was deeply delighted to discover that there was indeed an afterlife, but greatly surprised that one could feel physical pain there. Even more unexpected was that the first spirit to greet him was not that of poor Cora or even his late coworker Jack Horvath, but Audrey Jäeger, who looked down at him with almost maternal concern as he floated buoyantly on a thick cloud.

"Y'okay?" asked the wingless angel. "Sorry for the scare. But the determination and nerve you demonstrated tells us you're more than ready for your thesis."

"Tells *us*?" Cliff asked.

His eyes were adjusting to the space, which had all the personality of a boiler room. A steel box on the far wall was churning out steam and the reek of sulfur was no longer subtle.

"Yeah, I'm afraid I'm McMasters staff," answered Audrey apologetically. She descended metal steps from a catwalk a few feet above him. "Sorry for all the hangdog expressions and crying on your shoulder. Dean Harrow needed us to keep tabs on you, since you didn't voluntarily choose to attend McMasters. I was supposed to make sure you weren't planning another escape or getting overly despondent, so I went into my 'misery loves company' routine." She made an Audrey face and laughed. "What a pill I was! Truth is, I love it here, who wouldn't? I'm hoping to lecture next year."

The sponge cake cloud on which Cliff lay served as a perfectly fitted carpet for the oval room, above which a railed catwalk outlined the chamber's circumference. Dull steel doors were located at all four compass points around the walkway. Audrey stepped onto his confined cloud, gently bouncing toward him on sneakered feet and offering him her hand. The cloud felt like a yielding trampoline as Cliff stood and unsteadily wobbled about on it. "A crash pad," Audrey explained. "Used all the time in the movies. The crevice through which you fell is slab-stock foam rubber molded to look like rock." Cliff peered up to see the last of the promontory rocks through which he had fallen some twelve feet above. "Raven Ravine was quarried out of a rocky hill before my time but its vapors, stench, and seeming depth is no more real than the Labs or Mastertown, our mock city block behind Headquarters. It was paid for by a bequest from a Swiss financier's widow after her husband successfully met with a mountain-climbing accident in the Austrian Alps. Some colleges spend their alumni's donations on football teams. We spend it on workshops and simulations." She indicated the dull steel door on his left. "That leads to the inside of Castle Guy."

Castle Guy . . . He suddenly remembered, "Gemma! Is she—?"

"She's fine. Well, I mean, physically. But of course she's stricken that you've died."

Cliff made a quick move toward the steps leading up to the catwalk but the pad beneath him yielded as if he were wading through chocolate syrup. "I have to let her know I'm okay. How do I get out of here?"

Audrey shook her head soberly. "No, Cliff, we have to wait here for faculty. But since you ask, the door facing you leads to a camouflaged manhole near the tram, useful for disappearing acts such as the one Simeon pulled on both you and Cubby. The door on your right is to an underground tunnel with a four-seat railcar to the Tangle, Headquarters, and Slippery Elms. The last door, well, I can't tell you about that, seeing as you're leaving us."

Leaving us? Cliff thought with dread. Had he miraculously escaped death only to face expulsion, with all that word ominously implied. "Why, because I failed to stop Helkampf?"

Audrey noticed his eyes darting from door to door as he considered making another attempt to escape. "Don't be alarmed. All's well. Jud Helkampf broke every rule of the track meet, so he disqualified himself. You died, kind of, trying to save Gemma from a completely prohibited assault, so your grade point average is in fine shape. And Gemma gets top marks for attempting to defend herself as skillfully as she did. All of us assigned to you were concerned Helkampf might try to harm you while using the Meet as cover, which is the reason for the apparent mix-up in our tracker cards. That way I could stay close to you while Simeon simultaneously monitored you from a distance—we call that a 'loose tail.' But then Cubby messed things up when he traded cards with Helkampf, who then went after Gemma. That's when I had to leave and get help."

"But if Gemma thinks I'm dead, I have to let her know—"

"It's for the best, really," she said soothingly, as if she had returned a boy's pet frog to the pond where he'd first found it. "Simeon and I will verify Cubby's undoubtedly breathless account of your heroism and demise which he, too, believes was real. You really did make a spectacular exit, you know. But although Gemma seems to have been more taken with you than any of us realized, Vesta Thripper feels your loss will make her focus even harder on her own challenging thesis, heartless as that might sound."

Cliff suddenly felt very alone and—silly word to use—estranged from the conservatory. McMasters had been so civilized, inviting, and pretty damn delicious as well. He'd made some extremely interesting acquaintances with more intelligence across the board than he'd known since his days at MIT and Caltech. And although he was aware from the start that he had a mission, he hadn't realized it might come to such an abrupt ending. Gemma, Dean Harrow, even Cubby . . . was this the last he'd ever know of them?

The steel door that, according to Audrey, led up to the castle slid open and the white-suited Simeon emerged from behind it. "Well now, Cliff," said the refined fellow. "Deepest apologies for being so damn unpleasant to you throughout. Tricky assignment for me. A thousand pardons."

To Cliff, Simeon's past brusqueness seemed the least of the issues he had to tackle. "That's okay, but can you tell me what's going to happen to Gemma . . ."

"She'll be departing shortly as well, although I wish she could afford at least one more semester. I'm not at all certain she's as ready as you."

Cliff heard the *whoosh* of the portal door to the castle again sliding open and a somber Captain Dobson and Sergeant Stedge stepped into the chamber. This was becoming quite the secret clubhouse meeting and he eyed the two plainclothes detectives warily. "And why are *you* here?"

Stedge removed a gunmetal flask from the breast pocket of his snug jacket. "A farewell drink. Time for another road trip."

"I won't be coming on this one," Dobson advised. "We don't think you'll try to escape, seeing as you're headed home."

Stedge smiled. "Graduation Day, Cliff. It's how we do things here."

"The same way death ought to come," added Dobson, almost wistfully. "No time for last words, apologies, retractions, rewrites. The good you did, the mess you made, that's what lives on."

Cliff thought: *So . . . I'm done?* He pictured his journal sitting on his desk back at Hedge House. Would the school pass it along to his unknown sponsor, and let him or her know he was about to take his final exam?

As if to counterbalance the captain's austere words, Simeon tossed in, "I've been made privy to your thesis, and I truly do believe it can work."

"Yeah, but I'd be real careful about the last part," cautioned Dobson. "It could backfire on you like a shotgun with two blocked barrels." He tipped two fingers toward his hat as a modest salute. "Nice knowing you, Cliff."

"But what about Dean Harrow . . . and don't I learn who my benefactor is?" Cliff sputtered, feeling rushed as Stedge measured out four fingers of the flask's contents into a silver flagon, one likely borrowed from the castle above.

"You might hear from Dean Harrow after you complete your McMasters thesis. *If* you complete it, that is." Stedge handed Cliff the flagon with an encouraging nod.

The captain and Stedge had saved him from death row once, and he'd just survived death a few minutes earlier. Time for Fiedler to do the dying now.

He figured he could drink to that.

XXII

The conference room at Slippery Elms had once served as Guy McMaster's library, reached via the formal staircase in the Grand Reception Hall. At the top of the stairs to the left, one enters an extremely wide anteroom whose glass-enclosed shelves are host to a staggering display of rare bindings and first editions. It was a priceless collection, literally speaking, for none of the books had ever been purchased; rather, they'd all been hand-selected by Guy McMaster himself from the libraries of stately homes where he'd been a delightful houseguest.

The anteroom also serves as an aural buffer zone for the boardroom beyond it, preventing those walking in the hallway from overhearing the oft-heated conversations when Dean Harbinger Harrow crosses daggers with Assistant Dean Erma Daimler, who believed that removing the word "assistant" from her title would be one of McMasters' most worthy deletions.

"Gemma needs another term, at the very least," Dean Harrow quietly protested.

"Then you pay for it," instructed Erma Daimler who, like the other members of the review board, was enthroned in one of a dozen deep-buttoned leather chairs around the Norman banqueting table of the original dining hall at Oxbane. The operation of McMasters was an ongoing debate between the two, Dean Harrow's viewpoint being philosophical and artistic, Daimler's economical and pragmatic. "I dislike hypocrisy, Harbinger. It's all very well to shroud our purpose in cozy euphemisms and plush surroundings, but McMasters is a business."

"I prefer to think of it as a way of life. And death, of course," said the dean.

Coach Alwyn Tarcott murmured to Captain Dobson. "And we're off."

Daimler responded, "It could yield more profit if it were run in a sensible and less sentimental way. Our housing is strained at the seams, or haven't you noticed? Imagine tripling the school's revenue while modestly lowering tuition. The average student stay is two or three semesters. I'd reduce that to six weeks, in and out, in an accelerated program."

The dean laughed. "I can't make anyone a well-rounded deletist in that brief a time."

"They don't *have* to be well-rounded!" Erma retorted. "We're wasting their time teaching them how to poison potato salad or boobytrap a power mower when all they really want to know is how best to press a pillow against their aunt Pilar or wreak vengeance on the swine who stood them up at their senior prom. They should tell us whom they wish to delete, we should tell them how to do it, cue 'Pomp and Circumstance,' and next please!"

"You overlook one minor snare," advised Harrow.

Professor Graves pushed a thatch of hair away from his eyes, knowing the dean used that expression when an opponent had the dean precisely where the dean wanted them. With keen interest, Graves dryly inquired, "Pray, what would that snare be, sir?"

The dean answered with an eye on Erma Daimler. "If a history teacher tutors you on the Spanish Inquisition and its torture devices, and you then go out and perforate your best buddy in a homemade iron maiden, that is not the teacher's fault. Similarly, Dr. Crippen received training at the Cleveland Homeopathic Medical College, which helped him wield poisons more effectively, but no one suggested bringing their staff to the dock. Even the hypothetical examples we cite here on campus are abstract exercises, imparting historic general principles from the distant or not-so-distant past. But if we tailor a plan for each of our students, with customized timetables, weaponry, alibis, as you suggest . . ."

"Yes?" asked Erma, not knowing where this was going.

". . . we would legally qualify as accessory to every crime committed by anyone who attends McMasters."

This silenced Erma Daimler for the moment, and Padre Pugh clutched at the opportunity. "Might we return to the students up for review? The dean's concern that Gemma Lindley may not be prepared for her thesis echoes my own apprehensions."

"Well, she isn't a deletist by nature, is she?" posed Graves. "Students who come here to rid themselves of a blackmailer are invariably victims who under any other circumstances would never have considered the conservatory."

The coach clearly agreed. "It's the bloody English lawbooks have it wrong, boyo. Murdering your blackmailer should be an act of self-defense."

It was rare for the school's dean of literature to side with Tarcott. "Yes, you'll recall Sherlock Holmes wouldn't raise his magnifying glass to identify the killer of the extortionist Milverton. I quote: 'There are certain crimes which justify private revenge. My sympathies are with the deletist, not his target, and I will not handle this case.'" He smiled at Dean Harrow. "I paraphrase, of course."

The padre pointed out reluctantly, "Yet I'm afraid Gemma really *must* go home, no matter what our feelings. She received a maternity leave from the hospital . . ." He noted several pairs of upraised eyebrows around the conference table. ". . . a request which was pure deception on her part, to be sure, but she'll be dismissed if she doesn't return on schedule, and her thesis requires proximity to her target."

The dean shook his head. "Very well. I suppose there's nothing to be done. Captain, you'll let me know if McMasters needs to intervene? Which brings us to . . ."

"Dulcie Mown," said Dobson, and a chuckle went around the table.

Tarcott rolled his eyes. "She could teach *us* a few lessons, I'd say."

"Once she got a handle on our modus operandi she had a thesis proposal on my desk in a few days," said Dobson in an unusual display of approval. "Her approach wouldn't work for all our students, but she arrived here with extra wire cutters in her toolbox, if you get what I mean."

"So she'll be well on her way, yes, all agreed?" Erma polled. "I have quite the waiting list for Foxglove Cottage." There was general assent around the table.

Dean Harrow continued, "And now our Mr. Iverson. He's already been dispatched with the sergeant, I gather, after beginning to show an unhealthy amount of emotion risking his life for Miss Lindley. Any longer stay here and I'm afraid his resolve might soften, the way the Greeks believed the Mixolydian mode of music might weaken an army. Has his sponsor been told of his departure?"

"I dictated a letter just this morning," the assistant dean confirmed.

"Which leaves only . . ." he scanned the list before him and his expression soured.

"Helkampf?" asked Coach Tarcott, eager at the prospect.

Dean Harrow looked searchingly around the table. "How did this happen?" he posed in a quiet but exacting voice. "How did our screening process so completely fail? Our mission is to create focused deletists, with a specific, approved mission . . . not to assist Jack the Ripper to up his score from five harlots to a dozen! Erma: the board of admissions is your bailiwick, what went wrong here? Who accepted Jud Helkampf, who reviewed him?"

Assistant Dean Daimler consulted a few lonely pages in a dossier. "He, uh, seemed to have met the financial qualifications. And his application form was in order."

The dean cast her a withering glance. "And who interviewed him?"

"Uh . . . I believe we allowed him to submit written answers, owing to"—she had found a short typed letter—"the difficulty of arranging a personal interview where he lived."

"And that would be?"

"He said the city of"—she consulted further—"Metropolis." She looked around the table. "I would imagine that's in Greece?"

"Erma," intoned Harrow in a sub-whisper, "would you ask a member of the faculty—I'd suggest Vesta Thripper or Nan Redhill, but I leave the choice to you—to review past applications of our current student body who haven't had an in-person interview?"

Coach Tarcott leaned forward eagerly. "You want me to deal with Helkampf for you, Dean? He's not worth you soiling your hands, and I owe him a full deck of yellow cards."

The dean shook his head. "No, Alwyn. You mustn't deny me the pleasure."

— ♠ —

"Dulcie Mown" had wondered for some time what purpose was served by a vent in the stone wall just to the left of the hearth in Foxglove Cottage, and had she not retired as the odorless vapor quietly hissed into the room, she would have learned very quickly. But she was already in that woozy transition where idle musings start to fragment and drift into nonsensical thoughts and then into sleep. She was envisioning the glorious day soon to come when she would let it be known to her classmates just "who" had been walking in their midst all this year. Yes, I'm *that* Doria Maye! she'd affirm with a gurgling laugh, and they'd marvel and say they'd *known* that voice from somewhere but had never dreamt . . . and then the gurgle surrounded and overwhelmed her as the gas suppressed all thoughts conscious or otherwise, and she was as "under" as any anesthesiologist could wish. And now, slipping in the front door, here indeed was an anesthesiologist—among other medical titles—in the opulent form of "Doc" Clement Pinckney, dean of medical arts. He listened to her heart with the stethoscope he always wore like a bolo tie and counseled two attendants bearing a stretcher, "Yeah, she all done, put her in the van."

Thus it was that Dulcie Mown was now ready to make her Hollywood comeback.

Gemma was yet again on the couch in Vesta Thripper's office, believing she was about to receive further guidance from her counselor, who was finding it difficult to conceal her uneasiness regarding her student's looming departure. She'd grown fond of this young woman and apprehensive that McMasters might have failed to fully prepare Gemma for her thesis. It was a bit like seeing off a kid sister in Plum Tree, Indiana, as she boarded a bus to the big city where all the wicked people live.

She'd lit the meditative candle at the couch's end, then pretended she'd forgotten her notes and excused herself to get them, asking Gemma to stare at the candle as a focusing exercise, counting backward slowly from a hundred while concentrating only on her mission. She paused at the doorway before departing and said warmly, "You're a good human being in an unacceptable situation, Gem. Your target brought this entirely upon herself. Keep that in mind when the time comes, because when you're dealing with an opportunist, you must seize any opportunity before they do." Then she was gone, more completely than her student realized.

Gemma doubted that most McMasters undergraduates got this kind of pep talk. There was something wrong with her, she knew it. If only Cliff, brave Cliff, were still— She heard a faint, steady sibilant sound in the room. Was this how McMasters expelled their failures?

She tried to rise from the couch, but found herself sinking deeper into it than was physically possible. Her last thought before blacking out was to wonder, were she ever to open her eyes again, if she'd see her mother—who was alive when she'd departed for McMasters—or if she would be greeted by her father, whom she had killed.

"Well now, let's have a look at you," said Dean Harrow congenially to Jud Helkampf, who was standing at the open doorway of his office. He'd been escorted there by Coach Alcott and Captain Dobson, but the dean had waved the faculty members away with a pleasant air. "You can wait outside, gentlemen. I wish to have a private word with our rambunctious charge here." He beckoned the uneasy student forward. "Come, don't be shy, I'm not going to bite your head off. Sherry?"

"Uh, sure, I'd guess I'd like some," responded Helkampf, his demeanor unusually docile, although a death adder can seem blissfully asleep before it strikes and recoils in one-thirteenth of a second.

Following Helkampf's assault on Gemma, and Cliff's plunge into Raven Ravine, Simeon and four husky school monitors had escorted the reprobate from Castle Guy to his living quarters, where he was restricted until his case came before the student council, which in turn forwarded its recommendation to the faculty review board. He didn't expect to get off without some form of censure but the offer of sherry seemed a better start than he'd expected.

"Please help yourself," said Harrow, but as Helkampf moved toward a cut-crystal decanter and glasses on a table near the window, the dean warned, "Oh, no, Jud, that sherry is poisoned! I rely on it whenever I find myself in this room with someone I can't tolerate. Here, best let me pour." He measured out two schooners of a marigold-colored liquid from a smaller decanter on his desk. "And here's to your damn good luck that no real harm came to Miss Lindley. That would have made your punishment far graver, I fear." He proffered a glass to Helkampf, who only had it in his hand for a second before it slipped through his fingers and fell on the carpeted floor.

"Sorry," said Jud apologetically, who was not fooling the dean for a second. "Lucky for me it didn't break. But I'll be glad to pay if I stained the rug."

"Oh, that's the least of the bills you'll need to worry about where we're concerned," the dean countered. "Once you've completed your thesis and come into your inheritance, we will be extracting a stiff penalty fee to compensate for your deletion of Mr. Iverson, which was uncalled for." He clicked his tongue. "Really, Jud! He was a sponsored student, quite profitable for us . . . but we can hardly continue to charge his benefactor now. You'll be expected to make up the difference down the line. Nothing you won't be able to afford when that time comes, I'm sure."

Helkampf was in fact relieved by the dean's offhanded dismissal of Cliff Iverson's lost life and gratified that the school's response was based on avarice and recompense, not reproach and condemnation. But why would he have expected anything less cold-blooded from a school where Cain is viewed as a patron saint?

Harrow quaffed the last of his sherry and set the glass down. "Now then. Let's discuss your other problem, that being your absolutely unacceptable attack on Gemma Lindley. *That* will require a personal apology, my friend."

Helkampf did his best to look contrite but could only manage an expression that read as bilious. "I wanted to show the school that I'm the best student you have and that I don't pull any punches."

The dean dearly regretted he had to pull his own punches where Helkampf was concerned, but he continued his seeming negotiation. "Well, we've asked Miss Lindley what she'd wish by way of restitution. She reflexively asked for your hide, properly tanned and cured, but then more seriously requested that you personally create Cliff Iverson's last earthly resting place."

"I have to dig his grave?" Helkampf asked with a tinge of belligerence.

"No such thing. You see, the question has arisen whether an urn for Mr. Iverson's cremated ashes would be appropriate, or whether the standard coffin with a burial here on the grounds would be more meaningful. Miss Lindley feels that if you were involved in the decision process, you might better appraise your foolhardiness. So she has asked—demanded, really—that you choose for him, as if it were for yourself: either an urn for his ashes or a coffin for his remains, fashioned by your own hands . . . as was his death."

The dean's captivating delivery lent this utter fabrication, of which Gemma Lindley knew nothing, the Solomon-like air of reasoned justice.

Helkampf considered. "Well, I don't know much about that kind of thing."

The dean lit up. "Oh, Handicraft is an admirable course, what they call 'shop' in your country, I believe. I'm going to turn you over to Mr. Koniec of Ceramics and Woodworks, a true artisan: powerful hands, strong forearms, wonderful with lumber. He could build you a home that would last you a lifetime with hardly a nail, all joints tight as a drum." He rose and walked toward the office door. "But it's completely your call, mind you: an urn will be just as acceptable to Miss Lindley, and to us. I'm afraid that's the price you must pay for Mr. Iverson's sad end and your despicable assault on a fellow student. Best get to work quickly and be done with it. Sublevel Two."

"In the basement?"

Harrow blinked. "Oh yes, *sub*-basement actually. Ceramics makes use of a powerful kiln adjacent to the furnace room. Two flights below the main level. Sorry to send you below"—his eyes danced at the quip to come—"but you had no problem sending Mr. Iverson six *feet* below, did you? Off with you now, Mr. Koniec awaits. Just be grateful you got off so easy."

Jud uttered a quick grunt of discontent and left without so much as a "thank you, sir." And with the very brief exception of Mr. Koniec, no living creature ever saw or heard from Jud Helkampf again.

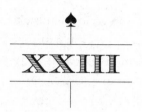

XXIII

FROM THE SECOND JOURNAL OF CLIFF IVERSON

Dear X, my departure (Sergeant Stedge reminded me repeatedly that it was not yet a graduation) from McMasters was unexpected, but I assume the journal I left behind at Hedge House has been conscientiously conveyed to you. I found a new journal waiting for me here at home, its blank pages eagerly implying I should continue my account until the completion of my thesis (or of me).

During my trip home from McM, every few hours (or maybe days, since my senses were unhitched from time) I would half wake from my hibernation and Stedge would speak to me in short, supportive sentences. I could hear the sound and feel the vibration of churning engines as I lay in the comfortable nest of some kind of cabin or cargo bay . . . all possibly a deception, of course, but whether real or staged, I would stir for a moment or two, then slip back into mindlessness.

I awoke for good over the course of some gradually less woozy hours before realizing I was in my home, the one I thought I might never see again when I'd followed Fiedler to New York. Yet here I was, restored to the suburbs of Baltimore, less than five miles from Woltan Industries and Fiedler, free to go anywhere and do what I wanted for the first time since Dobson and Stedge had knocked on my hotel room door in Manhattan.

I was obliged to remind myself that I was no longer in the "civilized" environment of McMasters, where the deletion of certain kinds of people was deemed appropriate—a topic which could be discussed as freely as the Joint Chiefs of Staff at a conference table planning the assassination of an acknowledged despot. I was now in an enemy camp, where I had to assume that everyone I encountered was, either knowingly or unwittingly, working against me.

How I was already missing McMasters.

Please know, dear X, that I never for a moment thought, "Was it all just a dream?" McMasters had been real and I have serious business to attend to.

I got up from bed and instantly fell backward, having been off my feet for God knows how many days. Gradually getting my sea legs, I found everything as I'd left it. (Who am I kidding? It was tidier.) I shuffled toward my narrow kitchen to get some water, using the walls and furniture for balance, and arrived at the refrigerator. A note was taped to its door:

Welcome home. Your cover story for the time you've been gone is that you found work in Montreal at Canadair, which is now a subsidiary of General Dynamics here in the States. An alumnus has ensured that there is a record of your employment on file there. While gone, you sublet your home to a John Michael from Greenville

I smiled at the name and location because I'd been taught in Principles of Deletion that the most easily forgotten pseudonyms consist of two first names, such as James Andrew or Mary James, and that there is a Greenville in most every state of the Union.

Michael from Greenville, who was researching the Baltimore military during the Spanish-American War, a subject that no one will be interested in hearing about. He paid you cash in advance, which you will find at the bottom of the contents of an unopened box of Rice Krispies in your kitchen, along with a generous endowment from your benefactor and the not-inconsiderable money you earned and saved while with us. Your automobile remains in its allocated parking space with a full tank.

Memorize and burn this note and make no attempt to contact us, which is subject to the penalty of expulsion. We will contact you only if appropriate or necessary. Please note the ledger book on your kitchen table. You are still required to keep an account of your progress for your generous sponsor. Skipping this continuing assignment will result in a Fail no matter what the outcome of your thesis. —HH

I was happy to see my drafting table still in its corner of my living room, along with all the tools I'd need to ply my craft. It would be time-consuming but not a great challenge to replicate my designs for the W-10, no harder than asking a mother for a detailed description of her child. I'd not only been co-designer and drafts-man of the W-10 but had overseen Woltan's presentations to man-ufacturing partners and airlines, handling questions and technical issues, with the exception of Fiedler's opening and closing self-homages, in which he'd given others the impression that he'd not only created the W-10 but the miracle of flight as well.

I was pleased to find some of the earliest sketches for my brain-child still safely locked away in a trunk at the foot of my bed. These would help me retrace (literally, in some cases) my design process. My plan was to re-create my blueprints so that anyone with a smattering of expertise would notice the potential for di-saster in Fiedler's cost-cutting changes to the routing of the plane's flight control wires and hydraulics. When I'd privately pointed this out to him, Fiedler's instant and clearheaded response as a trust-worthy executive to his catastrophic mistake had been to terminate me and my associate Jack Horvath and decimate our reputations.

That sure fixed that potentially lethal design problem, all right.

I intended to back-create a schematic diagram nonchalantly comparing the altered routings with the reassuring legend No risk to empennage control systems unless decompression occurs and blandly note on page two that there is no cockpit indicator for disengaged door pins and so on. It would be hard for any profes-sional not to follow this breadcrumb trail and grasp that the recipe for an appalling tragedy lay dormant in Fiedler's nickel-and-dime modifications.

My mouth was arid from my protracted, drug-induced sleep. I returned to the kitchen, ignited the welcoming letter at the burner on my stove, and washed its ashes down the drain. Someone associated with McMasters had considerately left a pitcher of iced coffee and bottles of fresh milk and cream in the fridge. I poured a tall tumbler for myself and set about my work.

XXIV

Gemma Lindley had been returned to Northumberland—presuming she'd ever left, for there was nothing to say McMasters wasn't within hiking distance of Hadrian's Wall.

It gave her quiet delight to again be boiling brussels sprouts with her mother in the kitchen of the two-up two-down home in which she'd been raised so cheerily by her parents. Their half-house was but one slim volume in a snug row of smoke-stained brick dwellings, all invariably spotless and tidy within. Her street, Hemming Terrace, was bookended by a view of factory chimneys at one end and the banks of the almost-river from which the town of Throckington Burn took its name.

She was putting a tray of potatoes under a small roast to catch the drippings once the gas was lit beneath, and she tried to sound conversational as she asked, "Mum, would you have wanted Dad to be alive longer than he lasted in hospital? Have you ever wished you'd had more time to say goodbye?"

Gemma's mother, Isabel, who'd been called "Isa" her entire life, turned her attention away from the turnips she'd been peeling, a task which she, as head cook at the ICI factory's canteen, performed with expert efficiency. Despite her Tobagonian origin, her accent was of the North. "Eee-up, love," she said. "Him passing so sudden were a blessing. I'm sure he willed himself to let go, knowing the burden he'd be, and . . . the pain, you know?" She assaulted a last turnip as if it were partially responsible. "Your father was tough, went to the construction site every day until he couldn'a rise from his bed. But when he said quietlike, 'Isa, I can't take it na longer,' I knew we'd run out of happy endings. So I thank merciful Jesus for taking him quick as he did. I told you that then and I'm telling you that now. And what more could I have said to him after all the years? He knew I loved him first, right enough, first and only."

"And if anyone ever made you think I hadn't loved him, you'd pay it no mind, yes?"

Isabel lay down the peeler and gave a familiar sigh that tapered into the last moments of a laugh, a sound that had comforted Gemma since her earliest years. "Who'd ever say that, I wonder? A more devoted child than you neither of us could've had, our Gem."

It had been a blissfully simple and happy home for the three of them, and there was surprisingly little tension in her life over her parents' marriage, beyond the expected childhood name-calling where color was concerned. Most in the town indulged her white father taking a former Tobagonian as a wife. However, Gemma was not so naive as to believe—had her parents' hues been reversed—that their family would have been as tolerated by neighbors or classmates.

While at McMasters, she'd written her mother each week, her letters forwarded to Isabel (as is most McMasters mail) from an accommodation address in Tórshavn, capital of the Faroe Islands, so chosen because few know of the archipelago or its location.

Gemma had convinced her mother she'd been living there for nearly a year as part of a training program for hospital administrators. But she'd presented a much different excuse to her employers at the hospital. It had been a most uncomfortable scene to enact, bypassing Adele Underton and requesting directly from the board a sympathetic leave of absence for approximately nine months to take care of a "family matter." She added hesitantly that a boyfriend of her own had recently "let her down in a big way" and she was in urgent need of a change of venue.

Among the predominantly male board there was some clearing of throats and shifting in seats. The board head asked if she would like a glass of water, and another fellow left to get one for himself. Gemma was asked if she were certain she would be prepared to return to a full-time work schedule after her nine-month issue was . . . resolved. Gemma said yes, she had a married sister up north who couldn't have children and she thought she might be able to make a contribution to the couple's lonely life.

The head of the board clicked his teeth on the stem of his briar to indicate the gravity of the moment and pronounced Gemma was doing the right thing. He said she could have her old job back upon her return, providing her immediate superior, Adele Underton, approved. Gemma knew that her cover story, proposed by the McMasters recruiter with whom her Livorno cousin Julia had put her in touch, would stymie Adele during her studies; she'd never dare countermand a ruling by the hospital's trustees.

But her studies had ended, all too soon perhaps, and Gemma now had to come to terms with her thesis.

She had awakened a week earlier to find herself in a bed-and-breakfast only a short bus trip from her family's row house. The very next day, after a lovely catching up with her mum, she took down her bicycle from where it had been hanging in the coal shed and went for the jaunt she'd promised herself during her studies: to Little Swinburne, down toward Cragback Farm, east to Great Bavington, and at last to where the How Burn (a creek, not a question) meets the River Blyth. She reached the outcrop of rocks near the harbor where she and her father used to search for the tiny molting crabs that hid in the rock pool when the tide went out, shedding their old shell to make way for their next. These peeler crabs, as her dad called them, were irresistible bait for almost any fish coming in from the sea, especially in the winter. To purchase such expensive bait was beyond the means of her family, but they were free enough for those willing to rummage through the rock pools, especially a child whose hands could fit between the small boulders draped in seaweed. After she'd proudly filled her sand bucket with the tempting lures, she and The Dad would head for the estuary's breakwater, where they invariably landed sparkling cod and coalfish, fit to be expertly cleaned, filleted, dredged, and panfried at home by Isa for a supper the gentry themselves couldn't top.

She'd hoped revisiting these soothing, fondly remembered sites might provide enough of an emotional lift to inspire some improvement to the plan she'd presented for McMasters' uneasy endorsement, now that she was free from the pressures of her academic surroundings. She'd sensed her professors were not overly convinced of her proposal, perhaps because it tended to hinge on nature, always a capricious accomplice at best. At least her first step was clear enough, and certainly the most crucial, because nothing else would succeed if she failed at that.

She and Adele had the horrific (where Gemma was concerned) arrangement of sharing a private office, Gemma positioned in the corner with a small desk overwhelmed by a mountain range of paperwork, Adele's desk twice the size and barren save for twin telephones and a bonded leather desk pad with matching dual pen stand. The impression given any visitor was that Adele clearly got more work done than Gemma, who seemed by comparison a hopeless drudge, this being an appraisal Adele would often privately confirm.

The door of their shared office was kept shut unless Adele wished to lure a promising resident surgeon into her lair, in which case Gemma would be dispatched for beverage and biscuits. Thus, when the two were alone, Adele could freely say to Gemma whatever she wished without fear of being overheard.

"It's been a very trying time for me in your absence," Adele informed her on her first day back. "Nothing got done." A portending avalanche of paper was clear evidence that "all work and no play for Gemma" was high on Adele's agenda.

"I apologize for being away so long," offered Gemma. "You realize it was a family matter I was attending to." She let the context set in. "I had to let matters run their full course."

There was not much to say to this, other than the sympathetic inquiry about the mythical offspring's fate, which Adele might have made but, naturally, didn't. "Least said, soonest mended. Your replacement wasn't half-bad where her own work was concerned, but she barely helped with mine."

That's probably because you didn't find anything to blackmail her with, thought Gemma. But she bit her tongue lest any sign of suppressed hostility might make Adele more wary. She could hear the dean as if he were seated at her side: *Always give your victim the same sense of well-being as the condemned man whose doctor pronounces him perfectly fit for tomorrow's execution.*

"Well . . . I'm back and dedicated to making things work as smoothly as before," Gemma vowed. "Better, if anything."

"If I ever thought you might 'flew the coop' so to speak," wafted Adele, "I'd be forced to share what I know with the board, not to mention our constabulary. I hope you haven't forgotten the envelope I've entrusted to Old Riggins."

Gemma had certainly not forgotten the envelope. She'd encountered it just prior to her departure for McMasters. It had been of the buff manila variety, into which Adele had inserted three letter-sized envelopes with an air of ceremony. "One for the hospital board, one for the police, and one for the *Northumberland Gazette*," she'd said cheerily, then lit a stick of red sealing wax and dripped it copiously along the manila envelope's flap while advising, "Just to be on the safe side. Not implying you'd ever try to do something to silence me, but, well, you *have* already killed one person, haven't you?"

Gemma made her usual quiet protest that she'd done so to spare her father any further suffering, to which Adele had responded, "Call it what you will, love, you and your mum accepted the death benefits, didn't you? Now, what I know about your father's end is in these three letters, and I'm sending them on to nice old Mr. Riggins at Riggins and Sons." This was the local soliciting firm that handled most of the hospital's legal affairs, excluding such tawdry matters as malpractice suits, which were delegated to a tougher outfit in Newcastle. The manila envelope containing the letters had sat on Adele's desk for hours, its maroon seal of clotted wax lending it all the charm of a gaping wound, until the mailroom boy picked it up. Adele had then blithely phoned old Mr. Riggins, with whom she'd flirted at several receptions, and explained that she'd just mailed him an envelope she hoped he'd keep safe for her. "It looks awfully melodramatic, you know, '*To be opened only in the event of my unexpected demise*,' but it's just a few letters to relatives, as I'm taking some flying lessons this summer and one never knows, does one?" She had winked at Gemma as if this were all a grand lark, but of course, Adele was serious to a fault.

Gemma had recounted this repellent incident on one of her very earliest days at McMasters, and Dean Harrow, Padre Pugh, and Vesta Thripper each sternly advised her that something would have to be done about the manila envelope before her thesis dared commence. Gemma hoped the challenge of removing a sealed envelope from a locked safe in a solicitor's private office, without the safe's combination or even a few helpful sticks of dynamite, might better steel her gentle nature for the deletion of Adele Underton.

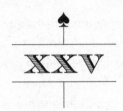

XXV

Master's Thesis

Deletist Aspirant: Dulcie Mown (*alias* Doria Maye *alias* Doris May Taplow)
Proposed Executive: Leonidas "Leonid" Kosta
Location: Los Angeles and environs

Doria Maye had no need to be briefed on her cover story as to where she'd supposedly been during her time at McMasters, for she had written (with ample assistance from Professor Graves) a detailed if utterly fictitious account of her travels across Europe, Africa, and Asia in monthly dispatches appearing in *Collier's* magazine. She'd also sublet what she gaily referred to as her "minor manor" in Beverly Crest to a young sheik whose oil interests were of the suntan variety, to be massaged by him into the backs of starlets whose figures were well-matched to Doria's hourglass-shaped pool.

Now she and a rented chauffeur were pulling up to the studio's main gate in Doria's slightly dated Lincoln Cosmopolitan. Once off the lot, the driver was to deposit the Lincoln with a dealership in Ventura that had purchased the car for cash, along with the promise never to advertise its filmland pedigree. The sale would help bankroll Doria's thesis, while some unlawful lessons she'd learned at McMasters would provide her with a suitable vehicle when she would be needing one.

Since the end of the Second World War, the security gate on Jacaranda Drive had been occupied from 4 p.m. until midnight by Finton "Finny" Flood. Early in his tenure, he'd realized it was advantageous to tend to the predilections of studio royalty while also being the trusted repository of their secrets, all with the fawning manner of a maître d' seeking a healthy tip. He registered the requisite amount of gush upon seeing the Return of Doria.

"Oh, and it's you, Miss Maye, tell me you're back to stay!" he exclaimed, laying on the brogue as if landing the punch line of a joke about an Orthodox rabbi, a Buddhist monk, and an Irish priest.

Despite the still-cropped hair of Dulcie Mown, Doria was once again sporting her trademark tresses, courtesy of an excellent wig. "I'm back if they'll have me, Finny! I have an audience with the man who put the 'potent' in potentate," she blithely quipped from the back seat. "I called the tune and now the piper must be paid!"

Flood consulted the day's schedule and saw that Doria was indeed penciled in for a five o'clock appointment with studio head Leonid Kosta. Reaching for the parking pass forms, he asked, "And will it be back to your old quarters after that?" Her bungalow had been vacant since her departure, except when Kosta held screen tests there for starlets, minus a crew or camera.

"I'll find out if I still have lodgings after I've danced for Herod. He may hand me my own head!" she answered. Finny laughed merrily with her, even though he had no idea what she meant. He scribbled the date on a gold pass, tucked it under the Lincoln's windshield wiper, and wondered, as the car drove on, if Doria Maye had talked that way when she was twelve.

"No bungalow. You have no need for it," said Kosta from his office couch, where many an actress had promoted herself from extra to bit part by opting for the best-laid plans of Kosta. The prize was usually—as Doria liked to put it—a cameo role in the hay. He had not bothered to rise from his reclining position to greet her, but had remained rudely supine, with throw pillows propping his back as he marked up scripts. "It's all nice of you to come back here agreeing to do the pig flick after wasting our attorneys' time and money. But when I originally put you up at the bungalow, it was for two reasons only, the first being you should have somewhere to entertain in private—"

"Somewhere you'd hoped to entertain *your* privates, you mean," she said reflexively, quickly defusing this with a playful smile.

"—and the second, to give you as much beauty sleep as possible before you reported to Makeup on morning shoots. But doing a cartoon voice, you no longer have to look your best. In fact, you can look like *skatá.*" Doria needed no translation. "So bye-bye, bungalow. You didn't care who you slept with, so now I don't care where you sleep."

She desperately wanted to say, *But Leon, it's central to my thesis that I stay at the bungalow. I'll only need the place for as long as you live, and that shouldn't be very long at all!* Luckily, she'd had the benefit of a McMasters education and her response was well prepared.

"Fine, but if you're going to put me out to pasture this way, you may not want to seem like such a cad in the Hollywood press. Think of it from a public relations angle: I can either announce that my formerly famous face has been axed by a heartless studio head . . . *or* I can announce I'm retiring from the spotlight over the protests of my beloved mentor, Leonid Kosta, who has kindly put me up in my old bungalow while I pack up the accumulated souvenirs of my years at this cherished studio. As it happens, I've already scheduled a farewell interview next week with *Collier's* in the same bungalow to explain how my global travels have altered what I seek from life." Needless to say, she had no such interview scheduled but if she were successful, Kosta would not live long enough to learn this. Dean Harrow had taught her that one may promise any future event in a target's future in order to lure or coerce them, as long as the expiration date for said target's future precedes it. Timing is everything.

She knelt at his feet *(as many a starlet, see earlier)* and beseeched, "Just a few more weeks at the bungalow to save face, Leon, that's all I ask! Give me that and I'll be the voice of your precious pig and squeal for you without a squawk."

The inhuman Kosta proved only human in that moment, for he savored the applause of opening nights and awards ceremonies, sopping it up with a paternal countenance. He liked to call himself "Papa Kosta" and viewed the studio's female contract players as his own dear family with whom he could commit incest on a regular basis. Thus, he was sensitive (only in this one way) to how he might look to the rest of the industry, and Kosta grudgingly granted her use of her old bungalow, with the proviso that the end of the month was his absolute deadline.

"Leon, that's a promise," Doria vowed with utter sincerity.

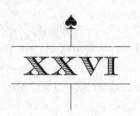

XXVI

"I wish to be placing the bet on all horses in race three, four, and fives," said the gold-bearded man in red-framed sunglasses wearing a canary-yellow tropical shirt adorned with purple parrots. He had clearly learned English as a second language from someone who didn't speak it that well in the first place. "Can this be done?"

It was a particularly lovely day at Santa Clarita Racetrack, and since it was not even noon and no other bettors were waiting, the teller opted to be patient, even helpful.

"Well now, sir," said the teller, "there's certainly no law against it, and I'll be glad to do that for you, but since my Maker cursed me with a conscience, I feel obliged to mention there's very little chance you'll come out ahead that way. The management has already thought through most of these angles, you see? That's why we have parimutuel betting with a fixed commission for the track and taxes for the state. Sure, picking every horse, you're guaranteed to win but you're also guaranteed to lose a dozen times or more, and while you might bet more heavily on a long shot to compensate, there's a reason why long shots are long shots. They have this tendency to lose. Still want to do it?"

"I do," said the man, who lowered his voice to confide, "I have a system."

"Oh, a *system*!" remarked the teller, with mock deference. "I didn't know you had a *system*. That changes everything!" A minute later he was handing the man a wad of tickets neatly secured by a rubber band. "There you go, every horse in the third, fourth, and fifth. I'd wish you good luck but you've kind of removed that element from the transaction. So I'll just say you win some, you lose more."

Cliff took the wad of tickets and stepped away without further comment, offering the teller a parting glimpse of his pulsating shirt. In a public library, his appearance might have raised eyebrows and seemed cartoonish. At a racetrack on a Tuesday afternoon, when people with real lives were busy at work, he was the epitome of the confident loser.

It was one of several characters that Dulcie Mown's tutelage had helped him create at McMasters, with a backstory detailed enough to make him feel real in the moment.

Cliff flipped through the bets, knowing that mathematically, he had three certain winners in his hand, albeit amid a plethora of also-rans, deadbeats, and nags.

He was feeling lucky.

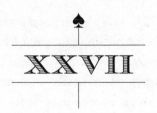

XXVII

Gemma wondered how on earth she could get into Old Riggins' antique safe without having to drill it open or blow it up. Then she'd recalled Dean Harbinger Harrow's lecture series on Break-ins, Break-outs, and Passive Egression. "When a portal is locked, ignore the door and focus on the oaf who's been entrusted with the key!" he'd asserted. "For every inescapable and impenetrable prison, there is an underpaid milk van driver who comes and goes free as a bird. For pity's sake, get to know the milkman!"

Chumming up with solicitor Riggins's secretary, Kaye Cookson, had been child's play, almost literally, for Kaye had been a few forms behind Gemma in school and was a sweet naïf whose main attribute had been a flair for touch typing. Gemma commenced her mission by dropping off innocuous mail at the law firm, such as a hospital fete announcement or a blood drive appeal, purportedly to save the hospital postage costs "as it's right along my way," although it wasn't. She and Kaye struck it off the instant they discovered a shared passion for Delft embroidery, a craft which Gemma—who didn't know the first thing about it—was now condemned to master in private, cursing that Kaye (who herself somewhat resembled a Dutch girl on Delft teacups and tiles) had not instead developed a passion for F. Scott Fitzgerald or, even better, Ella Fitzgerald. But as Gemma dropped off irrelevant mail in the early morning hours before Old Riggins arrived, and shared updates with Kaye regarding their respective blue windmills on lace-trimmed handkerchiefs, Gemma would casually look around the premises, with Riggins' safe or strongbox being the object of her inspection.

The offices had been in the same location in the High Street since the Edwardian era, in what had previously been a fishmonger's shop, and Gemma could swear its foyer still bore the pleasant whiff of fresh-caught plaice and haddock nesting on beds of freshly shaved ice. "Old Riggins" was in fact the grandson of the founding Riggins, whose solicitor son eventually became "Riggins," who then persuaded his only offspring to abandon a passion for chemistry and become the "Son" in the firm's name. The office's cast-iron safe clearly dated from the senior Riggins' time, a venerable Milner model easily approaching five hundredweight.

This was not what Gemma had hoped for. Knowing she could not attempt her thesis until she'd already nullifed the threat of the manila envelope containing Adele's accusatory letters, she'd invested hours in Winning Combinations at McMasters studying padlocks (surprisingly simple to crack owing to their shackle-and-ruts design of sticking and resistance points) and modern safes, which she had managed to open using a rare-earth magnet wrapped in a headscarf. But there was no artful way around these vintage safes, short of a deafening drill or dynamite. This was where a well-rounded McMasters education served students best, for its curriculum focuses relentlessly on the weakest link in the chain, that link so often human.

"Oo, what a beautiful old safe!" said Gemma, brushing her fingertips along the flowery lettering and gilt trim on its door. Above it hung a framed antique chart of the periodic table dated 1908. "I had an uncle who turned a safe like this into a wine and liquor cabinet. Then he forgot the combination and never touched a drop again!"

Kaye giggled, pleased to hear a joke that she both understood and was not about her. "You'd think after all these years Mr. Riggins would have the combination committed to memory," she said chattily as she prepared to type a letter. "But he complains he has to look it up more and more these days. Age, you know."

"So, of course, *you* have to tell him the combination each time," submitted Gemma as gently as Ben Hogan finessing a seven-inch putt.

"Not on your nelly!" she said with a snort. "He'd never trust me or anyone else with it. He'll just groan and say, 'What's that darn combination again?' except he doesn't say 'darn.' But by the time he's walked across the room to the dial, he's remembered it again, silly thing. He said he'd forget it completely if it weren't for an element of luck."

Gemma tried to disguise her ravenous interest. "I wonder what that means."

Kaye shrugged. "He acted as if he'd said something funny, but if it was a joke, I didn't get it. Of course, I don't get lots of jokes."

"Probably has it written down in one of his drawers," Gemma said as idly as she could manage.

"More likely written down in his *pair* of drawers," joked Kaye, thrilled to hear Gemma's friendly laugh and to have been so sophisticated. "He stands, says 'Now what's that blinking combination?', but magically comes up with it by the time he's gotten to the safe, as if it were written in the air."

"I don't think they make invisible ink for skywriting," said Gemma, circling around the topic in case she could turn up anything further.

"He could probably make some invisible ink. Mr. Riggins told me he always wanted to work in chemistry—he did rocket fuels or something during the First World War—but his father persuaded him to go into law, to keep alive the good name of Riggins and Son. I think he always regretted it." The framed chemistry chart above the safe now made more sense to Gemma, as a wistful nod to The Road Not Taken. "I didn't like chemistry in school," Kaye went on. "It smelled awful. And everyone called me Potassium."

Gemma turned, puzzled. "Why that?"

She lowered her voice. "The symbol for potassium is K. You know . . . *Kaye*?" she winced. "And this boy I had a crush on—Ronald Lockwood, do you remember him? No?—he was the first to call me that."

Gemma patted her arm. "Children can be so cruel."

"Yes, and adults as well," said Kaye, as if life had not been particularly kind to her.

"Take in the cinema tonight? They've a drama with Kieron Moore. We could have a bite beforehand at Alberto's."

"Alberto's?" asked Kaye, as if Gemma had suggested going to Nicaragua.

"In Bexley Street. They do a nice spaghetti marinara for only two and six and the waiter always gives me a glass of wine on the house. I bet if we flirt with him, we might even get refills."

Coming back from the pictures, their chumminess enhanced by a blood-warming Chianti and a shared admiration for Kieron Moore's profile, they passed Riggins and Son and, as it happens, Gemma had an unexpected "visit from a friend" and needed use of a powder room. There were no nearby pubs, and all the shops were closed, but Kaye said not to worry and led Gemma through the passageway between Riggins's and the adjacent tobacconist, to the cobbled mews behind the building where she worked. Three wooden steps led up to the rear entrance. "I'm afraid I have to ask you to turn your back," apologized Kaye. "I've orders not to let anyone know where the key's hidden, awfully sorry!" Gemma obliged, assuring Kaye that she understood completely. Simply knowing a key was hidden outside the premises was more than enough for Gemma's future plans. She heard a rasp of stone, the sound of the door being unlocked, another scraping sound, and Kaye whispering, "It's open now. Come in quick and mind your step. I mustn't switch on the lights."

As she entered the dark office, Gemma asked why no burglar alarm had gone off, and Kaye explained, "Mr. Riggins bought a sticker for the door that says we have one, but that's as much as he wants to spend. He says that's for jewelers, banks, and shops that sell things. We don't keep any valuables on the premises. The most you could steal would be a pair of his briefs!" She laughed with pleasure, two naughty jokes in one day clearly being a milestone for Kaye. "Come on, I'll lead you to the loo."

Gemma estimated that, on a return visit, it might take her all of a minute to locate which brick, stone, or tile the key was hidden under or behind. Now also learning the happy news that there would be no burglar alarm to deal with, Gemma planned to return the very next evening. She didn't want to stitch one more blue windmill than was absolutely necessary.

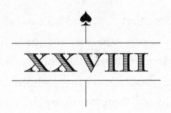

XXVIII

FROM THE SECOND JOURNAL OF CLIFF IVERSON

Well I'm pleased to report, X old buddy, that we've had some luck where money's concerned. Of the winners in the three races where I bet on every single horse, okay, yes, one was the favorite and we profited minimally. But the second turned out to be a bit of a long shot, paying 10 to 1, and the third was a total surprise: Ganymede, who'd just been raised a grade (if it sounds like I know what I'm talking about, trust me, this is just what Coach Tarcott was able to cram into my brain about "the gee-gees" before I departed dear old McM). Not much was expected of Ganymede but he came in <u>first</u> at 32 to 1! So as beginner's luck would have it (although there was actually no luck about it), two of my three guaranteed winners had impressive payoffs.

Buoyed by this good fortune, I dialed the number for Woltan Industries from my home, asked for Fiedler, and waited for the switchboard operator to put me through.

"Merrill Fiedler's office?" Meg Keegan's greeting always sounded like a question.

In my heartiest chamber of commerce baritone I enthused, "Yes, Miss, I'd like to speak to your boss about serving as head judge of our annual debutante swimsuit competition here at Rockvale Country Club." I was asked to wait a minute and in considerably less time than that, Fiedler was on the line. I know my man, all right.

"Hello there, how can I help you?" asked Fiedler, eager to do his civic duty.

"Murray, it's Bob."

"It's Merrill, not Murray."

"Oh, sorry, my mistake." I hung up. Having ascertained that Fiedler was at the office, I then headed to the luxury apartments barely ten minutes from Woltan where Fiedler made his home. Once or twice in the past, I had dropped off designs and renderings for him there and I knew a twenty-four-hour doorman presided over the entrance from a podium near the elevators, with a public telephone booth just across the lobby.

The doorman (whose name tag identified him as Ricky) was new to me, although the previous one I'd encountered would not have recognized me in my clear glass horn-rimmed spectacles, my navy blue work shirt and pants, and the heavy stubble I'd purposely grown while replicating the W-10's blueprints. "Dropping off a package for Mr. Tim Tunney," I said.

"I don't know any Tim Tunney. What's the apartment number?" said Ricky, taking the package from me and immediately handing it back while rolling his eyes at my incompetence. "Look at the address. You want 6 Meredith Street; this is 6 Meridian."

I apologized and went to the lobby pay phone. I called my home phone, memorizing the number on the pay phone's dial as I informed a nonexistent dispatcher that I was running late. I then walked around the block to my car and drove home.

I'd purchased a battered Underwood portable typewriter from a pawnshop on Old Maiden Choice Lane in Arbutus, where I'd also acquired an unrelated photo scrapbook inscribed "Property of Theodore Stevens, Ottawa."

Wearing latex gloves, I placed the three winning tickets from that day's race in an envelope and typed a letter on Hammermill paper, stocked by every stationery store in the country. X, I'm including a carbon copy of that letter in this journal for your reference.

As follows. —HH

Dear Mr. Fiedler:

You don't know me from Adam, but you saved my life once. I don't even know if you meant to, but you did and I owe you forever. In this envelope, you will find three winning tickets from yesterday's race at Santa Clarita. This is a start to paying back my lifelong debt to you.

I have found a way to beat the system at parimutuel racetracks. My method is technically within the law but I work at the track and if they know what I am doing, they will fire me and that will kill the golden goose.

You can cash the tickets at the track on your way home anytime within one week of the date on the tickets. Mr. Fiedler, I propose to share the results of my system with you and ask only as the gentleman of honor that I know you to be that you will set aside half the winnings for me. I will make myself known to you at the end of the year. This is not a con game and I will never, EVER ask you to spend a single penny of your own money or to be involved in any way except to cash in these legal winnings and hold the money. If, when I make myself known to you, you refuse to share, that will simply be my misjudgment, and I will consider my debt to you fully paid. I know that no one will ever question your winnings because everyone knows you are a winner. Each day I will provide you with winning tickets, all purchased legitimately at the track. I will make no direct physical contact with you. To learn each day where the winning tickets have been left for you, all I ask is that you wait for my call at 8:30 a.m. in the phone booth in your lobby. If the line is busy, I will try again in ten-minute intervals. I will never write to you again. Thank you for saving my life, even if you were never aware that you did.

From a friend who cannot lose to a man who always
wins,
   Amigo

I folded the letter and tucked it in its envelope, on which I'd already typed the name and work address of Merrill Fiedler with the words <u>PERSONAL AND CONFIDENTIAL</u>. Finally, I enclosed a black-and-white photograph of a very attractive young woman near an unknown wooded area, plucked from the photo album of the aforementioned Ottawan, Mr. Theodore Stevens, about whom I knew absolutely nothing.

In a full-day seminar whimsically called "Deadlier than the Mail," I had been advised that nothing arouses interest in an unopened letter more than the feel of a snapshot within, especially if the envelope bears a single handwritten word such as "Personal" or "Confidential." The fact that the snapshot would mean nothing to Fiedler would only add to the intrigue. I knew that no one working for Fiedler would dare open a letter to him marked CONFIDENTIAL, lest they incur his wrath, something Meg Keegan feared more than her curiosity craved enlightenment. A postage stamp finished my work. The afternoon was pleasantly breezy, and I strolled to the mailbox on Cypress Street so that the letter would be on Fiedler's desk tomorrow.

I knew it was unlikely he'd depart Woltan during his workday to visit the racetrack, but the course is conveniently along his route home.

Tomorrow, dear X, I'll continue reconstructing the W-10 blueprints, but once I get to the hour when Fiedler's own workday is done, I'll again don my red-framed sunglasses and tropical shirt, head to the racetrack, and purchase another round of tickets (from which will come the next round of winning receipts to offer Fiedler). Then I'll loiter around the Santa Clarita payout windows to see if the shark has been lured by the first round of chum bait I've tossed his way. I feel pretty confident he's bitten. He's always liked to make an easy killing.

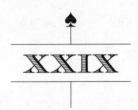

XXIX

Gemma donned her biking trousers, advised her mum she'd volunteered to work the Saturday night shift at the hospital's admission desk, and pedaled into town via the back lanes. Within an oilcloth sack in her bicycle's basket was a manila envelope on which was written "To be opened only in the event of my unexpected demise" in an expertly forged rendition of Adele's block lettering. The detestable Miss Underton may have left the ominous manila envelope in plain sight on her desk solely to flaunt the threat it represented, but Adele had been too clever by half, for it had given Gemma ample time to memorize the layout of the outer envelope (although matching the pattern of the sealing wax would be better achieved once she had the original before her). The forgery had been a cinch, since Gemma had been encouraged to write comments and marginal notes in her supervisor's hand, making it appear it was Adele doing the work and not Gemma. The envelope she hoped to switch with the one in the solicitor's safe would certainly pass muster with Riggins, who likely hadn't given it a glance since placing it there nearly a year ago.

Trees on either side of the lane interlocked their branches above her head, reminding her of the night she and Cliff had taken the bus back from the Labs. He'd appealed to her the first moment she'd seen him in the woods, and at any other college, studying any other subject than murder, surely she'd have let her interest be known to him.

And now she would never see him again. "Dammit, Cliff," she lamented to the night, which hadn't been listening. A sudden chill drizzle ended her reverie. Work to be done.

Gemma knew how to get into the mews behind Riggins and Son without taking the High Street, approaching it from a residential row two blocks north. The passageway, lined with delivery entrances and private garages, was deserted as she set her bicycle in a rack at the far end. She took the oilcloth bag from the bicycle's basket and approached the wooden steps up to Riggins's back door. Logic told her that Kaye was too short to have reached unassisted above the door for a key, and she would have made more noise than she had if she'd been rummaging around the steps. Although there was a doormat, surely even Old Riggins was not fool enough to hide it there. It only took her a moment to find the brick in the back wall that wasn't flush with the others. It rasped as she pulled it out, using her half-finished Delft-embroidered handkerchief to avoid leaving an unlikely fingerprint.

The murky office was lit only by whatever glimmer seeped through the back window from a streetlamp in the mews. She groped her way to Riggins's inner sanctum, where the blinds were down and the curtains drawn. Covering a small table lamp with her damp handkerchief, she switched on its bulb and puzzled over the safe.

Its dial went from zero to eighty, which from her studies made it fairly certain it would be a three-number combination, each number one or two digits, that being the industry norm of its time. She'd also learned that the purchaser of a safe of this vintage would not have been able to request a specific combination that was easy to remember or which had some permanent personal association. This would have created an epidemic of combinations like 10-20-30 or, given the safe's age, 11-11-18, commemorating the end of the First World War. Each unique combination was logged along with the safe's serial number (but not its location or purchaser) at the manufacturer's main office. One copy of the combination was given to the buyer, and they were encouraged to memorize it and store it in a hiding place away from the premises, which never prevented most owners from pasting it on the inside of their right-hand desk drawer.

Some were particularly clever and pasted it inside the *left*-hand drawer.

She now sat at his desk but didn't bother to check the drawers because Kaye had said Old Riggins never looked there; he'd simply walk to the safe and by the time he reached it, he knew the combination. Had it been hidden somewhere in clear view, like Poe's purloined letter? Dean Harrow had told her of a merchant who kept a 1934 appointment calendar on his desk perennially open to December 8 because the combination that he'd been given was 12-8-34. As the 1940s ticked by, this drew some attention.

She stood, walked to the safe as Riggins might have done, and found herself near eye level with the periodic table above it. What had Kaye said? That Riggins attributed his recall of the combination to "an element of luck." As if he'd made a joke . . .

Dean Harrow had once advised her class, "Forget *vino*! It's *in risu veritas* . . . in *laughter* there is truth. If someone says, 'I'm joking, of course,' most likely they are not."

Gemma's dad used to call it "truth in jest." But what *was* Old Riggins's joke? It seemed to center around luck, or rather, an element of luck—

"Oh, for pity's sake," Gemma declared as she realized she was staring directly at the periodic table of the elements.

It wasn't all that strange that words could be formed from the letters on the periodic table (the fourth-form boys had once repeatedly chanted "fluorine, uranium, carbon, potassium!" as an irreproachable obscenity in class). *An element of luck.* Could "luck" be spelled with the abbreviated names of elements on the periodic table, with the corresponding number for each element providing the safe's combination? She certainly knew the last letter in "luck" was on the chart, because of Kaye's school nickname ("Potassium," number 19). Working backward, she remembered from her studies—in fourth-form science, not McMasters—that C was the symbol for . . . calcium? No, there it was, carbon, of course. Number 6 on the chart. Was there a U and an L? (Perhaps the safe had a four-number combination.) There, at the very end! Uranium. All she needed now was the letter L.

But there was none. She *could* find an Li, an Lv, an La— Wait. Forget about uranium. There it was, number 71: Lu for "lutetium."

71-6-19. So it *was* a three-number combination after all, she thought. It would be impressively fortuitous if Riggins's mnemonic was also in the right order . . . but, if not, there were only six variations to work through. Of course, there was also the issue of the number of times to turn the lock between each number. At the conservatory, they'd said that old safes invariably went two turns to the right, then the first number, one turn left, and left again to the second number, then right again to the last. She set to her task, and although the Lu-C-K order didn't work, she wasn't disheartened and had the great satisfaction of opening the safe on only her third try.

Adele's envelope was toward the back atop some "Last Will and Testament" files. Comparing it with her own substitute, she had matched the lettering so closely that if it weren't for the sealing wax on the original, she might not have known which was which. From her trouser pockets she withdrew her own stick of scarlet wax (identical to Adele's, this being the only one sold at the local stationer's) and a box of matches. She lit the stick and used the wax pattern on the original envelope as a guide for sealing her own. Once done, she put the substitute envelope in the safe and shut its door, resetting the dial to zero, with the gratification of knowing she had now defused the threat of Adele's accusations as effectively as a bomb squad from the unexploded ordnance unit. The insurance policy it represented to Adele had lapsed.

Her substitute envelope contained three standard-sized envelopes with the typewritten addresses "To my aunt, with love," "To my uncle, with love," and "To Gemma." Each envelope contained a clipping from a discarded hospital Bible that she'd then placed on a bottom shelf in Adele's office. Adele's parents were both deceased, but she had twice mentioned an aunt and uncle in Croydon with whom she stayed whenever she wished to make merry in London at no expense to herself.

The quotes themselves offered nothing more provocative than gentle biblical succor. The one addressed to herself was intended to reinforce how close she and Adele were and came from Matthew: *Blessed are those who mourn, for they will be comforted.* The two for Adele's aunt and uncle were from Psalms: *The Lord is close to the brokenhearted and saves those who are crushed in spirit* and *He heals the brokenhearted and binds up their wounds.*

If her thesis went well, Adele's aunt and uncle would soon be receiving these comforting if useless bits of solace, sent to them with a regretful cover letter from the firm of Riggins and Son.

From the Second Journal of Cliff Iverson

Dear X: Shortly after my return from McMasters, I went to visit Jack Horvath's widow. Hoping she hadn't moved from their cherished home in Taneytown, I drove to Rifles Lane, where stood their Second Empire Victorian, humble in scale for such an elegant design, with what Jack had called a mansard atop a third story, although this highest floor was attic space rather than servants' quarters.

I walked up the steps to its hooded front doors and was glad to find Lilliana Horvath still at home. With warm recognition, she led me to the front parlor, which looked out on a porch and some well-spaced butternut trees along the sidewalk.

"Our years in this house were contented," she said, setting down a tray of iced tea garnished with fresh-picked mint from the back garden. Jack Horvath's name had actually been Jacek; he and Lilliana had immigrated to the United States after the war, where his mastery of propulsion won him several invites from companies like Woltan. They were both considerably older than me, and I didn't need a Viennese psychiatrist to deduce that Jack and Lilliana had gracefully supplanted my late aunt and uncle who'd raised me. While Jack worked under me at Woltan, I still revered him as an ally and what they used to call a Dutch uncle.

Lilliana's voice still bore an elegant accent and she gave an extra duration to odd words and syllables she deemed important. "In time I suppose I must sell it, but I am not yet pre-pared to surrender it to strangers. That would be unfaithful to Jacek. He wants me here, I know that."

Her hair was still as much auburn as gray, and her eyes were as penetrating as ever. Before I had a chance to ask her what she had been doing with her time, she asked the same of me, adding a pinch of guilt for seasoning. "I saw you at the funeral but not after that, not <u>once</u>. You know he <u>thought</u> of you as a son."

I dutifully recounted my Canadian employment story and swore to her that Jack meant the world to me. I reminded her that when I'd lost Cora, it was Jack who'd persuaded me to pour myself into work instead of a bottle, and the design of the W-10 had been both my salvation and our finest collaboration, until Fiedler had deformed our creation.

I wondered what her response would be to Fiedler's name. "Fiedler, *piszkos gazember*," she muttered under her breath without a shred of elegance. "After Jacek's death, the bastard"—I had never heard her curse before, X, at least not in English—"he sends me a <u>check</u>. No letter, no card, just fifty dollars from his personal account made out to cash . . . as if I would even deposit it! I keep it here, hoping each month he looks for it in his bank statement and its <u>absence</u> speaks my contempt." She indicated the check, impaled on the tip of a poker leaning against the fireplace.

I tentatively asked, "Lilliana, could I offer you fifty dollars for that check? I could make good use of it while I'm here."

She studied me carefully. "I won't take money for it, but you may have it, if you want it. But when you spend it, remember: It is <u>blood</u> money."

"I don't intend to cash it."

"Then consider it a gift from Jacek," she pronounced, giving me her approval if not her blessing. I pocketed the check all the same, because Lilliana had just saved me and my unholy thesis several tedious steps.

I desperately wanted to assure her I hadn't been thoughtless or idle where Jack was concerned. It was maddening, X, being unable to share with her that I'd already attempted to avenge Jack in Manhattan (even if incompetently) and that, thanks to your generosity, I'd been studying hard since then to find a shred of justice for Jack and Cora, and that my sole purpose in returning to the area was to end the regime of Merrill Fiedler. I'm sure I'd dropped by today subconsciously longing to tell her this. And yet once in her home, I knew I couldn't. In Principles of Deletion, we were taught that while "open confession is good for the soul," one's confession should only be opened posthumously. I'll have to keep my mission a secret from Lilliana until I've either succeeded or can speak no more.

I asked if I could see my mentor's old den again, a cozy room in which we'd calculated the W-10's aerodynamics over small triangular glasses of Zwack Unicum, Horvath's favorite liqueur from his homeland. The desk still bore neat stacks of his notes and diagrams, as if he might any moment reenter the room and continue his work. It was both heartbreaking and eerie.

One of the study's walls hosted black-and-white photographs of family and friends from both sides of the Atlantic, picnics, graduations . . . the kind of array you see on doily-draped pianos in homes where no one plays the piano. I noticed a lone color addition to the display that I'd never seen in my previous visits to this house: a framed section of a street map of Baltimore, matted in black-on-white-on-black. Unwittingly, I peered at it and noted that someone had glued a tiny ceramic heart onto a green rectangle labeled "Ellwood Park" in the center of the map. Frost formed around my heart.

I tried to turn away, but Lilliana had been watching from the doorway. "That is <u>where</u> he was murdered," she said, as if I wouldn't remember where and how he'd died for the rest of my life. I could hear her larynx tighten as she continued, ". . . where they <u>found</u> him."

What could have induced a man Jack's age to visit that unholy park—after midnight for God's sake—in the most dangerous ward in Baltimore? He surely must have been meeting someone, but was that the same person who'd murdered him? I'd be crazy not to wonder if Fiedler had something to do with it. Admittedly, I'd accepted that any attempt at whistleblowing on our part about the aircraft's flaws would have been soundly ignored by the establishment and both refuted and covered up by Fiedler. Our careers had been discredited beyond retrieval. But maybe Jack hadn't seen it that way. Maybe he'd tried to make peace with Fiedler or, even more dangerously, threatened to expose him.

When I'd first heard about Jack's body being found in Ellwood Park, I expected Lilliana would tell me it was suicide. Jack was not what I'd ever call self-destructive, but he'd been in a terrible state after being banished from Woltan. I at least was young enough to contemplate a new life and career. But Jack had been closing in on retirement. He knew there'd be no "back to the drawing board" for him, figuratively or literally.

There was a part of me—this is going to sound cold-blooded, X—that was almost relieved when the police immediately identified his death as murder. A verdict of suicide would have been unbearably hard on Lilliana. "How did I fail him? What might I have said differently?" she would think. But there was no need for that, because he'd been killed by a gunshot wound to the heart, death had been instantaneous, and there was no weapon at the scene. A few residents sitting on the adjacent stoops of Jefferson and Orleans Streets had heard a shot and seen a group of kids, possibly a street gang, racing out of the park and scattering. Such sounds and sights were a normal occurrence of an evening in that neighborhood. And Jack was missing his wallet and a watch that had been in his family for years. His wedding ring, a plain pewter band purchased in the couple's struggling years, had clearly not been worth the killer's time to remove.

What troubles me most about Jack's tragedy is not so much the identity of his killer, for I'm pretty sure Jack didn't know him (or her) personally. My guess—and I gathered from Lilliana that the police agreed—was that it had been a mugging gone awry, and at McMasters I'd learned that the .22 caliber bullet that pierced his heart was the type a zip gun might fire. But, as I've said, what's baffled and haunted me since his death has been why Jack would have been drawn to such a place, nowhere near his cozy home in Taneytown, and at such an hour. I cautiously asked her if she had any thoughts about what had happened that night, anything he had said . . .

"He was *részeg*. Drunk, a man from the police said. From his blood they could tell. They <u>performed</u>, you know, the . . ." She clearly didn't want to say "autopsy."

I told her in all honesty I had never seen Jack inebriated in my life. He loved his single glass of Unicum, sometimes after dinner or when we'd ended our late-night skull sessions in this same study. But drunk? Never.

"The level of alcohol in his blood, it was point-two-nine they <u>told</u> me. I don't know what he was drinking, for they swore there was no bottle near his body, but it was not his usual drink—the Unicum—because they do not have that here, he always had to purchase it specially from New York. I think . . . I <u>think</u> being unemployed for the first time, not knowing how he would support us, I think he wanted to lose himself in drink but was ashamed for me to see. Maybe that is why he went where he knew no one . . ." Her eyes went to the framed map, and again she cursed Fiedler under her breath.

I asked Lilliana if there was anything I could do for her. She said no, I was very kind, but her Jacek had always worried he might predecease her and had made sure her simple needs were provided for. "We owned this house so I have no mortgage, you see, and I require very little. But what about you"—her face showed concern—". . . this employment you tell me you took in Canada, you still have something to live on from that? This check from Fiedler, I'm thinking you need that for yourself? You must not act too proud; you were like a son to my Jacek. Another fifty dollars, would it help . . . ?" I saw her glance at her handbag and I rushed to reassure her that I had ample funds for my current needs (as I certainly do, thanks to you, X).

I told her that I would accept from her a bottle of his favorite liqueur, so I might toast him on the anniversary of his death and, as she had said, it was hard to find outside New York City. She smiled and took a key from the blotter on his desk and unlocked its right drawer, where Jack used to stash all the "contraband" items in the house, and whose contents I'd seen whenever we'd shared a drink: his uniquely medicinal-tasting Zwack Unicum, his grandfather's meerschaum pipe and ornate revolver from another era, a privately printed pocket-sized edition of the Song of Solomon with "sophisticated" illustrations, and an enamel snuffbox that apparently had belonged to his mother. Lilliana offered me the erotic volume, the pipe, and the snuffbox, which now were the sole occupants of an open shoebox on his desk, and I responded lightly that I was trying to quit. This caused her to smile for the first time since she'd greeted me.

The drawer was empty now save for two bottles of the liqueur, one of which was sealed. She handed it to me as if transferring a child to a godparent at a christening. "I'm so glad you asked me for it. He loved his little drink with you at the end of your workday. I know my Jacek would want you to have this more than anyone."

I thought to myself, dear X, that what Jacek would probably want me to have is vengeance for what had been done to him, to his wife, to Cora, and to all Fiedler's other victims, past and still to come. "Is this murder necessary?" asks the First Enquiry. For me, the answer has never been more clear.

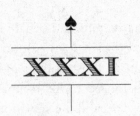

XXXI

Having gotten her bungalow back from Leonid Kosta—an essential first step in her thesis—Doria managed to follow and then bump into Laddie Graham.

"Hullo, Laddie," she said gamely, instantly looking as if she were suppressing tears. Portraying victimized women who wear a stiff upper lip gloss was among her special skills.

His look of pity might as well have said, *Soldier, I can pull the bayonet out of your chest but it's the only thing keeping you alive right now.* But Laddie was a decent man who could muster a jaunty bedside manner when needed. "Well, how's my favorite actress on this lot?"

"Wishing this was not my lot in life," she sulked.

"Better here than Monogram or Republic," he offered, citing the steerage class studios. "Poverty Row."

"Yes, but this studio is *death* row for me now. If you're walking to your car, may I tag along? I'm heading for my bungalow and having you for company might make others think I still have a film career."

"Why, of course," said Laddie, always the gentleman, and so they walked out through the streets of Laredo. She noted his open satchel, undoubtedly filled with scripts that might give voice to contemporary issues and not pigs. "Some light reading for the evening?"

"At least one or two projects I wish I could attach you to," he said sincerely.

She made a wistful pout and quoted Judy Garland. "I don't think there's anything in that black bag for me." This confused Laddie because his briefcase was brown.

He plucked a script from the satchel's leather jaws and waved it at her as if offering Exhibit A to the court. "Doria, I swear I had you in mind for this comedy-thriller I'm doing with Danny Kaye, but when I mentioned your name, Kosta said—"

"Oh I *love* Danny," exclaimed Doria, "what's it called?"

"'—Not on your life!'"

"Fun title."

"No, the title is *Shiver Me Timbers.* 'Not on your life!' is what Kosta said."

As they left Laredo and moseyed into Bavaria, Doria knew it was important to her plan that she seemed to accept her exile in a gritty, resigned manner. "Well, if I must make a hog of myself for this studio, I'm determined to be as memorable as Mel Blanc doing Porky Pig. As for my on-screen career, I'm announcing '*That's all folks!*' minus the stammer. What the Leon giveth, he taketh away."

"Doria, if I were running this studio," Laddie assured her with regret, "I'd be feeding you one plum role after another. Substantive parts that would put you in contention for an . . . I mean . . ." His voice drifted off, knowing that, for Doria, the love that dare not speak its name was Oscar.

As Bavaria became Paris, Doria reminded herself it would be dangerous to express any eagerness for Kosta's abdication or Laddie's ascension, which most of Hollywood assumed would occur either with the mogul's retirement or his death, yum.

"By the time you take over the studio, I'll be old enough to play Aunt Polly in *Tom Sawyer Goes to Congress.* But I suppose I've had a fair run for my money." Stoic acceptance was the tone she needed to strike before she finally struck. "Kosta made me a star and has every legal right to pluck me from his firmament. All I'm asking is to be allowed to exit as if it were my own idea."

His meaningful silence confirmed the bleakness of her future unless she took measures to change it. They turned the final corner of a midwestern street and Doria's bungalow came into view, just barely within the studio gates. She ventured, "It's very good of you to accompany me all this way, but it might not have been an entirely worthless stroll. I've come across a remarkable script I'd like to share with you."

He demurred with regret, "But as I've said, Kosta won't—"

"Oh, trust me, there's no part in it for me. I just thought it might be up your alley, if you have an alley these days. Should it appeal to you, I suppose you could offer me a finder's fee. I'm having to think about dollars and cents now, I fear."

It seemed to Laddie a relatively easy favor to grant and so they entered her once and present but not very future bungalow.

The convenient hideaway had begun its existence as a modest residence fronting a lime orchard in the then-empty expanses of Rancho La Ballona. Although it now lay behind the studio's high whitewashed walls, it was situated a bit closer to Jacaranda Drive than the main gate itself, so it had not been uncommon in the past for guard Finton Flood, stationed at his post, to see Doria arriving at her back patio, turning in for the night. They often exchanged an affable wave. Finton would then, at the direction of Leonid Kosta, make a not-so-affable note of her comings and goings, with particular focus on who might be coming or going there with her.

Two years earlier, Kosta decided he'd elevated Doria Maye to stardom of enough fame and allure that she now merited a weekend sleepover (and under) with him at his rustic Torrey Pines retreat, where he hoped to assist her down from the pedestal he'd built for her. To his astonishment, she evaded all overtures like a theatergoer who loves Hammerstein but hates Rodgers.

Enraged, Kosta instructed Finton Flood to note any romantic peccadilloes involving Miss Maye. At the time, Finny was uncertain if "peccadilloes" related to bullfighting, stuffed olives, or small leathery mammals, but after looking up the word at home, he better understood Kosta's wishes.

The thought of Doria having escapades on the lot hardly raised Finny's conjoined eyebrows, not in a realm where a tryst between two stars, one or both of whom might be married to others, was delicately referenced as "they're blocking tomorrow's love scene." (Finny's understanding was that, as a rule, Miss Ingrid Bergman tended to sleep with her romantic lead until completion of photography, which wrought havoc with both her schedule and stamina whenever she portrayed a woman torn between two men.)

But the same survival instincts that had gotten Finny through the war were still functioning on the Hollywood lot. He'd quickly realized that the contract players, while glamorous, were employees of the studio just like himself. Knowing who buttered his bread and who might overnight become toast, he loyally cast his lot with the executive branch, not the talent. And so it was he who'd reported Doria's continuing dalliance with Marc Danner, and had been rewarded so well for his undercover work that Finny dearly hoped Miss Maye would misbehave again.

She'd only been back at the studio a short while when it seemed his wish had been granted, for he noted that Doria Maye had not only successfully repossessed her old lair but was now entering it with the studio's head of production in tow. Finny was startled when she waved directly at him in his guard booth, her chartreuse blouse glistening like Christmas wrapping above a severe, dark gray ankle-length skirt. As for Laddie Graham, he knew him only from a few pleasantries they'd exchanged as he drove onto and off the lot, but word had it that he was street savvy and extremely firm-handed.

She'll eat him for dinner and have nettles for dessert, thought Finny.

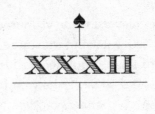

XXXII

Fiedler stepped to the racetrack claim window, his blue and white seersucker suit unwilted despite the heat of the late afternoon. "Read 'em and weep, pal," he said with a smirk. He'd used this phrase each of his past four visits, but he felt it bore repeating, "bore" being the operative word. For this alone Fiedler deserved to die, thought Cliff, who was listening nearby.

"You again," observed the teller sourly, despite track policy that all winning tickets be greeted in cheerful and congratulatory fashion. But Fiedler's preening over his equine expertise was insufferable, especially as it was so richly unearned. From his now-regular observation post at the track's fresh orange drink stand, Cliff noted that Fiedler always cashed in with the same teller, as if the pleasure of gloating meant as much as the spoils of winning.

Fiedler had made a very easy peace with himself over his recurring windfalls. He couldn't recall which of his actions or inactions might have resulted in the debt of gratitude (undoubtedly well-deserved) felt so profoundly by "Amigo," but the tickets were legal and the racetrack could afford the losses since the parimutuel system clearly prevented the house from ever losing its shirt. It was no skin off his nose to drop by the track on the way home, maybe even have a quick one at the Winner's Bar, where he could swagger further when the bartender echoed the phrase, "You again." He was liking the sound of that.

♠

From the Second Journal of Cliff Iverson

I'd given Fiedler five winning tickets this time. Five! I admit that betting every horse in five races did mean I'd lose some money (my apologies, X) but it was the investment I'd planned to make from the outset, making him feel and act like a man who is onto a sure thing.

I turned away as Fiedler, whistling to himself, casually brushed past me in my garish garb, shouldering me aside as if adjusting his own path would be too much trouble. His was as tuneless a melody as one would expect from someone so tone-deaf to others, but Fiedler's false optimism was a hallelujah chorus to my ears.

You'll be pleased to know, X, I've been conservative today and only picked four heavy favorites who will be running tomorrow at poor odds with tepid payoffs. There are sure to be one or two ho-hum winners for Fiedler among the four, but nothing spectacular.

It's as if I'm living in two different frames of time right now: placing bets on a Monday, giving what winners I choose to Fiedler on a Tuesday, which he redeems that evening while I've placed bets to give him on Wednesday. Next I'm going to buy bets on only one horse in each race . . . and only the longest shots. Yes, one or two might actually win, and if they do, I'll be happy to keep those winnings to defray the few losses I've (we've) suffered by design. But I also know that among these dark horses, there will be some big losers, the biggest of which I hope will soon be Merrill Fiedler.

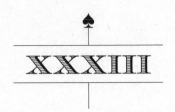

XXXIII

In the bungalow, Laddie was still waiting on the settee, studying the carbonation in a ginger ale for lack of anything better to do, while Doria retrieved the script from her bedroom about which she was so excited. Five minutes turned into ten and Laddie called out, "How you coming along there?"

"I've found the box where I kept it," she called back. A few minutes more and Doria stepped from her bedroom, wearing the same glossy chartreuse top, but now fully unbuttoned and minus her long gray skirt. Laddie spilled some ginger ale at the sight of her bare legs but realized she wasn't quite as naked as she initially seemed, for she had changed into a black one-piece swimsuit with a satiny finish, cut in the current stylish but daring fashion, with the open blouse now serving as an abbreviated caftan. "Don't be alarmed, Laddie!" she calmed him with a laugh. "Your virtue is intact. I'm going to sun myself on the patio after you leave, now that I can tan without worrying I'll suddenly be cast as Marie Antoinette." She quickly buttoned up the blouse. "I need to wear this, though, because my shoulders burn very easily. And . . . here's the script."

She gave him a brad-bound copy of *Happy with the Truth*, an earnest "message picture" that reeked of social relevance which, if produced, would undoubtedly leave the audience vigorously debating in the aisles whose bright idea it had been to see the damn movie. The script meant nothing to Doria beyond an excuse to keep Laddie in her bungalow . . . but she described the story as if she were delivering him the new *Rashomon*. "There's this speech for an old woman that—oh, I can't do it for you unless you loosen your tie and relax, silly thing," she said, adjusting the knot on his tie and unbuttoning his collar button.

"Now listen like a moviegoer and not a genius!" she scolded with a wink, tousling his hair playfully.

The speech could have come off pious, but she milked it like an arthritic dairymaid, carefully underplaying its more sanctimonious moments. When done, they'd been inside the bungalow nearly twenty minutes, which was more than enough for her purposes. "Anyway, see what you think, and thank you for your valuable time," she said, walking him to the patio doors.

As she followed him out, she'd quickly buttoned up her blouse to the neck. It made for a startling sight to the eyes of Finny Flood, who had no way of knowing, as Laddie did, that Doria was wearing a swimsuit under the long-tailed shirt. To the guard's naked eye, her naked legs led to a few flashes of the gleaming V of the black satin swimsuit, which might as well have been panties. The clear impression was that while the two had been inside, she had lost her skirt for some "unimaginable" reason. Laddie looked a bit disheveled as well.

As she bid him goodbye, Doria confided, "By the way, I've been meaning to tell you I loved that documentary you did for Metro, *Children of the Tundra*. It was wonderful."

"Nice to know someone saw it," said the departing Laddie over his shoulder as Doria cast a glance toward the studio gate and observed that Finton was taking in everything. Using her best stage projection, she called after Laddie, "Loved every minute. It was wuuunderful!" Seemingly on impulse, she took a few quick steps after him and touched his arm, which made him turn around. His cheek received the quick brush of a kiss as she tousled his hair again. "You're a brilliant talent and a kind man. I love who . . . you are."

Doria Maye had never expected McMasters to teach her anything about love scenes. But Professor Kalifa Taleb, in her fascinating seminar "Loose Lips," had endowed her with the simple skill of saying "who" with the mouth formation of "you." To any lip reader, the difference between "I love who" and "I love you" is indiscernible, and the "you are" that followed simply seemed to be a second emphatic "you."

As Laddie smiled with embarrassment and turned away again, she giggled, "Oh dear, Laddie, I think your fly may be open!"

Reflexively, he looked down hastily and gave his zipper a quick tug.

It was a small brushstroke in the tableau she was painting, but a telling one. Laddie scurried off with a last uneasy glance, momentarily catching the eye of Finton, who quickly looked away.

Three minutes later, Finny was hardly surprised to see Doria walking quickly across her small backyard toward him, having donned slippers and a robe. "Finny!" she said with a presentational laugh of chagrin. "I've only just realized how things might have looked just now. I was simply giving Laddie a script I discovered. Took me forever to find it."

"Certainly no business of mine, Miss," soothed Finny while thinking, *Yes, but Leonid Kosta certainly considers it his business!* More than once when the studio head had been driving off the lot, Finny respectfully touched the brim of his cap and discreetly handed him a folded slip of paper, saying, "Just a note concerning a little matter I thought you'd want to know, sir." Each time, Kosta had taken the note without comment and driven off, leaving Finny with a ten-dollar bill in his hand. Doria's latest peccadillo might merit a twenty.

Doria curled up on her settee and reviewed the day. She had the bungalow, if only for a short while, and a tryst between herself and Laddie Graham had certainly been surmised by Finton, the same fellow who'd alerted Leonid Kosta to the late-night assignations she'd had with Marc Danner. He'd certainly snitch on her to Kosta once again. Of course, Laddie knew that nothing happened and at this point Leonid Kosta might not care if anything had. But none of that mattered where her thesis was concerned, for the entire scene had been staged solely for an audience of one.

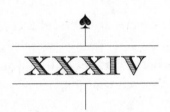

XXXIV

Fiedler was displeased to see a young woman occupying his apartment building's public phone booth at the usual appointed half-hour that morning. While waiting, he made small talk with Ricky the doorman, whose name he never remembered without reading his name tag, and tried to explain why he'd been taking calls in the lobby at eight-thirty so many mornings. "Got an aunt who'd call me all night long if she had my home number," he grumbled. "I let her check in with me every day like clockwork on the pay phone."

"Very caring of you," said Ricky, who'd decided he didn't like Fiedler's face. The young woman finished her call and Fiedler hoped his benefactor, Amigo, was good to his word about calling at ten-minute intervals. He didn't want to wait around all morning for his money.

At 8:40, the pay phone rang. "Look, we gotta find another way to communicate," griped Fiedler without preamble. "I feel like a lovesick teenager waiting each morning for your call."

"This is the only way I can do it right now," said Cliff in his "Amigo" voice. "We have a bonanza coming to us in a few days and then we can give it a break for a while." He gave instructions for a seven-thirty ticket pickup that were so detailed Fiedler was obliged to get pencil and paper from what's-his-name the doorman and write them down. It involved dropping a local newspaper in a trash bin as a cover to withdrawing a container with the next winning tickets, and Amigo stressed that the directions needed to be followed to the letter.

Fiedler pocketed the instructions and returned the pencil to Ricky. "Have to do some shopping for the little lady," he explained.

"What's your aunt's name again?" said Ricky, who was starting to doubt his story.

Fiedler didn't like being questioned by anyone's employee, even if he wasn't their boss. "Just do your job, okay?" he advised and left for work.

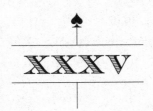

XXXV

"Bob Warrant is coming up from London tomorrow to begin his review of St. Ann's for the NHS," Adele told Gemma. "It would be awfully helpful if you had intercourse with him."

Gemma looked up from her notes. This had to be a joke. She laughed aloud to make it one, but Adele reassured her, "Oh, nothing sordid, you'd have a proper date, he's promised. Supper at the Golden Hind, a spot of dancing at the Mecca, then back to his hotel. The manager of the Red Lion is very open-minded about young couples, even mixed young couples."

"Are you out of your mind?" Gemma asked, the answer already apparent.

"There's no need to carry on so! Bob might even want to take you out again if all goes well. He's here every month or two and he's interested in women who are a bit . . . exotic."

"You discussed this with him already? Like some sort of madam?"

"Well, Bob was actually making a play for me—I wasn't going to mention that, as I thought it might hurt your feelings—but I told him I was already in a relationship, which I hope is true where Peter Ellisden is concerned. Then he said how lonely it gets on the road and his wife not being very interested in S-E-X and asked me if I could fix him up with someone who'd be . . . fun. I told him I thought you're a friendly girl, game for anything as it were, and he couldn't have been more delighted. Really, it's just a matter of showing an influential associate a pleasant evening. All right, a *very* pleasant evening. It will be such a help for this year's budget."

"Not on your bloody life!"

"Oh, but it's not *my* life that's at stake, Gem, is it? And which would be worse for your mum to hear: that you killed Bob with kindness or killed your father with pentobarbitone?"

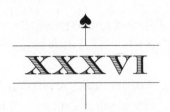

XXXVI

After Cliff had given Fiedler detailed directions for a seven-thirty drop-off and pickup at the arboretum, Cliff called Eddie Alderman at AirCorp, Woltan Industries' fiercest competitor. Of course, Alderman had no idea to whom he was speaking and Cliff wanted it that way.

In the region of Maryland's Chalk Flats known as Aircraft Alley, Woltan had persistently competed for government and commercial airline contracts with the smaller but successful AirCorp, which stood for Aerodynamic Innovation and Research (so named primarily to create its acronym). The "Corp" was pronounced "core" so that the company's sales crew could deploy official-sounding phrases with a faux military spin, such as "We could convene with you at fifteen hundred hours in the briefing room at AirCorp headquarters."

In the hierarchy of both companies, the astute Eddie Alderman was on the same tier as Woltan's much less knowledgeable Merrill Fiedler. And despite Eddie's boyish face, crowned by salt-and-pepper hair with a matching mustache, he was every bit Fiedler's match when fighting for AirCorp's victories or Woltan's defeats. His contentious nature, however, was balanced by a strain of empathy he'd acquired raising two children with health problems, and the accompanying realization that some of his employees had children, too.

After he hung up with (the anonymous) Cliff, Alderman buzzed Wes Trachter, head of AirCorp's security force, and asked him to come by his office instantly, or sooner. Almost that quickly, a man who carried himself taller than his five feet seven inches presented himself, cardboard coffee cup in hand. He felt secure enough in his job and tough frame to wear a polo shirt and khaki pants to work. It had been Wes Trachter who had repeatedly told the AirCorp board that Eddie

Alderman was the man best suited to move the company forward, and Wes was now pleased to take all his marching orders from his former army friend.

"Damnedest thing," Eddie began. "Just received an anonymous call from some guy, clearly disguising his voice, says he has schematics for a new Woltan design to share with me. Wants to show me page one as a sample to prove they're real. Any harm in my looking?"

"I'm no lawyer," said Trachter, who certainly could have been had he wished. He slid into one of the twisted plywood chairs facing Eddie's Danish modern desk. "But I'd say you're okay. After all, you have to verify whether they're real. Only then can you decide what you want to do about it. It could be a prank, a con, or the real McCoy from someone at Woltan doing a little profiteering or maybe even some whistleblowing. No way to know until you see."

"Well, if he's talking about designs or specs for, say, the W-10, just one page could be incredibly informative. The guy specified a pickup location, the whole cloak-and-dagger bit, you know: '*Trash can in the park at precisely six forty-five today, no earlier, no later, bring no one.*'"

"He said that verbatim?" asked Wes.

Eddie Alderman tore a page from his memo pad that already bore his scrawl and offered it to Trachter. "The arboretum's parking lot. He says there's a trash can that has the letter T peeled off, and that the page will be tucked inside a week-old copy of the *Kansas City Courier*, buried a bit down in the trash."

Trachter considered. "Well, that's a good way to both hide it and identify it. You can't get a Kansas City paper around this neck of the woods except at a newsstand with an out-of-town section, so there's not much chance of there being any other Kansas City newspaper in the trash can." He downed the last of his coffee. "The tight window of the timing is interesting. Could be he's not sure when the trash gets picked up, or he's worried someone might dump a milk shake on the plans. My guess is if he says not a minute before six forty-five, he's going to drop the plans in the trash very close to that time."

"You suppose there's any risk for me? Thinking about my kids . . ."

Wes had cared for Eddie Alderman since Korea, although he'd never expressed how he felt. Their friendship meant more to him than risking it for something that clearly was never going to be in the cards. Alderman wasn't so inclined; he loved his wife, and that was just how things worked out. Nothing to be done, lifetime of dull pain. Wes stood and tossed away the cardboard cup. "No worries. I'd never let you go there alone."

On most surveillance jobs, Wes drove a permanently dirty used DeSoto, as nondescript a vehicle as Detroit was manufacturing, and he'd been scrunched up in its back seat since almost six in the evening, the earliest he could get to the arboretum from AirCorp headquarters. He was covered by a dark green picnic tablecloth while sitting between two green canvas beach chairs he'd wedged around himself, an effective duck blind he'd employed in the past. The camera in his lap had a telephoto lens, which was effective whether aimed through the windshield or focused on the rearview mirror.

A lustrous red Buick Roadmaster with four slash portholes pulled into the half-empty arboretum parking lot at 6:28 by Trachter's watch. A man with a blond-and-steel-gray crew cut exited the Buick carrying a folded newspaper and, quickly checking around him, walked it directly to a trash can marked RASH. As he'd been directed by "Amigo," the man thrust the local edition of the day's paper into the can and, his actions masked by the newspaper, removed a Good & Plenty candy box sitting atop the trash and slipped it in his pocket. The man then returned to his Buick and drove away, Trachter noting the license plate number and photographing car and driver, whom he suspected he'd seen before . . . perhaps at an industry convention?

From his vantage point, Wes had only been able to see the depositing of the newspaper, but it certainly matched the timetable and agenda of their mysterious caller. After all, how many people park in an arboretum solely to throw away a newspaper?

He would have preferred to tail the Buick, but his first concern, professionally and personally, was Eddie Alderman's welfare. So he stayed put, awaiting Eddie's Crestline station wagon, which arrived as instructed at six forty-five precisely. Eddie opened the Ford's birch-trimmed door, looked about wondering where Wes Trachter was hiding, walked to the garbage can, and rummaged through it until he found a tightly folded copy of last week's *Kansas City Courier*. He riffled through the paper and discovered to his satisfaction the folded page of an airplane design plan tucked within. Giving a slight nod for Trachter's benefit, he took the newspaper to his station wagon and drove from the park.

While this brief tableau transpired, an old man and a considerably younger one were speaking in familiar fashion on a bench not too far from the RASH can. An open lunch pail sat between the duo, from which the younger man produced a sandwich enveloped in wax paper. He'd dutifully handed it to his senior as if from a caring grandson to a venerated grandfather, and the elderly man accepted it without a break in their conversation. It appeared to be a pleasant ritual for both, but appearances were deceiving, as the two were in no way related and had met less than a half hour before. It had not been hard for Cliff to find an old man alone on a bench well before sunset in the busy park and to strike up a low-key conversation with him. It merely took sitting and asking if the town outside the arboretum had changed much over the years. In this instance, a VFW pin in the gentleman's lapel further prompted Cliff to ask where he'd served, and that was that. (Had Cliff only found an elderly female sitting alone, a pocket-sized crossword magazine and pencil stub in his lunch pail might have required consultation with her; the park had many passersby at that hour and most women of a certain age were happy to share a few pleasant public words with such a charming young man.)

Thus Cliff had been able to monitor the activity around the RASH can while listening attentively to his elder, the daylight winnowing away behind them as they each ate an American cheese sandwich swiped with mayonnaise, capped off with a large oatmeal cookie. The gentleman did not question Cliff's overpacking of his lunch box when he'd said, "Geez, Warren, what was I thinking? There's no way I'll eat this second sandwich. Do me a favor and share it, huh?" Simply hearing the word "share" had lifted the elderly gentleman's spirits, and he acknowledged it would be a shame to see good food go to waste. The seemingly impromptu picnic had not only made Cliff's sentry post innocuous but the repeated small bites he took of his own sandwich, cookie, and now banana, coupled with his low-brimmed baseball cap, obscured a clear view of his face, should an observer have wished one. McMasters teaches that although someone can mask their identity by covering the area around their eyes, the same anonymity can be achieved by hiding one's mouth and chin. Merely holding a sandwich or coffee cup with two hands while eating is a natural-looking way of concealing one's lower facial features. Of course, neither Alderman nor Trachter knew Cliff by sight, but it is a McMasters axiom that if you throw caution to the wind, the wind is likely to blow it back in your face.

Cliff enjoyed the impromptu picnic. He'd been hungry, and now he was doubly satiated, for he observed a man extricating himself from the back of a dirty DeSoto, getting into the driver's seat, and leaving the arboretum in the wake of the station wagon driven by Eddie Alderman. Cliff was hardly surprised at this, for he'd expected Alderman to have a witness to the seeming transaction between Eddie and Fiedler. The sentry would have clearly seen Fiedler drive into the parking lot, deposit a newspaper into the trash can, and leave, after which Alderman had removed the *Kansas City Courier* Cliff had deposited there just after he'd called Alderman with the tip. It certainly would have looked as if an exchange had taken place, with the trash can being both the drop-off and pickup site. Even the most mediocre spy would have had time to note Fiedler's license plate in the minute he was out of the car. Even better, they'd likely have taken pictures of both the Buick Roadmaster and Fielder himself.

Cliff allowed his conversation with the veteran of a foreign war to wind down, warmly bidding him a good evening. Much had been accomplished this day, yet it had literally been a walk in the park.

At the racetrack, Fiedler had extracted two betting stubs from the Good & Plenty box that he'd fished from the trash can a half hour earlier and presented them to his favorite teller for redemption, who gave them a quick look. "Only two winners this time, huh?" the teller said, making no effort to disguise his amusement. "Gee, for you that's almost like losing. And they were both favorites." Having grown accustomed to big wins, Fiedler hadn't even bothered to look at the payout on the tickets; the bets were small amounts and his winnings hardly worth the visit.

Fiedler was by nature a sore winner. "Losing is for losers," he said, being on fairly safe ground with this insight. Scooping up his extremely modest takings, he quickly walked away, intent on having a word with Amigo when they next spoke. After all, his time was money.

Eddie Alderman had returned to his office and quickly trained all three bulbs of a hydra-like gooseneck lamp on the schematic diagram he'd retrieved in the park, as if it were the subject of a police interrogation. A half hour later, Wes entered the office and without looking up, Eddie asked, "Any luck with those license plates?"

Wes walked behind the desk to view the plans for himself. "I made the calls but it's late, I won't have an answer till morning. We're not actually the police, you know, and it's a little tricky. You find anything interesting?"

Alderman waved him to sit. "Well, just at a glance, I'd say the design of the W-10 is innovative, cost-cutting, a big step forward for Woltan, and potentially lethal."

Wes, always a company man, gave a small groan. "Lethal to Air-Corp?"

Alderman grimaced and nearly whispered, "No, I mean lethal to every soul on board a W-10 the first time the cabin crew thinks they've sealed the hatch and discover too late they haven't." He couldn't keep out of his mind the crash site he'd once visited in an advisory capacity and how, after that, he'd insisted he and his wife fly separately for the kids' sake. "It's only implied on the first page, but if the next few pages indicate what I suspect, someone at Woltan decided to save some money at a very steep price where human lives are concerned. Of course . . ." He didn't continue.

". . . our knowing this could be very good for AirCorp," said Trachter, voicing what Alderman hesitated to relish. "So . . . you think our informer is a good guy?"

Alderman frowned. "Not for certain. *I* was able to spot the flaw in this design, but I know something about these things—"

"You know as much as anyone."

"—well, I was looking for trouble. It's possible whoever drafted this page may have blundered and included more information than Woltan would ever want known. Our anonymous source may not realize its significance. He may simply think he's offering us an advance look at our competition's innovations, for a price."

"So he might not be a whistleblower at all? Just doing it for the money?"

"Well, yeah, he's pretty specific about the money." Eddie offered an odd smile. "Three thousand, three hundred, and thirty-three dollars . . . the last three dollars to be silver ones."

"Ohhh-kay," Trachter drawled. "Three-three-three-three. Explanation?"

Alderman could only offer an apologetic shrug. "Got none for you. Our informer called a few minutes ago and would only say that's what he wants for the rest of the designs. Do you have a professional opinion on what the number means?"

Trachter considered for a moment. "Well . . . I've known people in a tight corner—gambling debt, a family member needs an operation—who are desperate for cash but will only ask for the exact amount they need and not one penny more. In their minds, this puts them on a higher moral plane. *Or* the three-three-three-three number might have some personal significance. It's really odd they want the last three dollars to be silver. Could be something superstitious."

"He doesn't want as much as I expected. It's worth a helluva lot more than that to us."

"So do we bite?"

Alderman didn't hesitate. "Absolutely. Three thousand and change is no skin off my budget, as long as we call it 'data gathering relating to safety issues in a competitor's new design.' After all, their planes cohabit the same sky as ours. We deserve to know if they're putting dangerous aircraft up there around us." He continued with feigned fervor: "Senator, we needed to know if Woltan—owing to safety concerns we discovered at our own expense—would be unable to deliver their W-10s as scheduled. That's why we stepped up production on our own designs, to ensure this great country will never fall behind in the race to fill the sky. And that is why, upon detecting these grave design flaws, we immediately shared our knowledge with the Civil Aeronautics Board. It was our moral duty!"

Wes added appreciatively, "Yes, and if in the course of our patriotic investigation we justifiably tarnished the reputation of a major competitor and learned more about their design innovations, that was the furthest thing from our mind."

Eddie rolled up the single blueprint with a knowing smile. "Until proven otherwise, our informant is a noble martyr, risking his career in order to alert the world to his company's dangerous designs, and we've advanced him a modest sum as our grateful contribution to his legal defense fund."

Wes felt obliged to return to the seamier possibilities, since he would be responsible for the success of such a transaction. "Hate to hammer the obvious, but we *do* want to know who he is, don't we? If only as insurance on our end of the deal? I mean, he could turn out to be nothing better than a not-so-petty crook . . . or a Russian spy."

Alderman concurred and told Wes to enlist additional operatives to stake out the drop, tracking whoever picked up the money. Then there was that moment's silence when two people have something on their minds but neither is looking forward to saying or hearing it.

Wes at last tiptoed out the thought. "You know . . . *some* executives might allow Woltan to build these flawed planes and . . . you know. Wait until there's some kind of an, uh, incident or two. Woltan would have to ground its entire fleet, refund orders . . . they could go under."

"You mean we should keep what we know to ourselves and allow the W-10 to fly, so a few humanitarian disasters send our competitor tail-spinning into extinction? Listen, Wes, I'm no Pollyanna, and I'll play any dirty trick I can get away with where it comes to AirCorp winning out, but we can't be accomplices to Woltan's cost cutting where it's deadly, understand? We are not going to help someone commit murder."

XXXVII

Leon Kosta accepted the script from his protégé, a word he often used interchangeably with "prodigy," unaware of the difference. Laddie Graham advised him, "It's the latest revision of *Ember Morgan Comes Home*, which, by the way, I think should just be *Ember Morgan*, leaving room for more than one star's name on the marquee." Kosta's only reply was to reach toward a pewter pillbox on his desk and remove two blue tablets. "The stomach acting up again?"

"It's this chair," Kosta said.

"Well, let's get you a new chair," Laddie offered.

"Place this chair in any Mykonos café with a view of the Aegean and my stomach will be fine. It's this chair being in this office of this studio. Uneasy lies the gut that wears the crown." He downed the tablets with a glass of water. "So does the script need any more flushing out?" He also tended to transpose the words "fleshing" and "flushing."

"I'm afraid so. It's shorter but feels longer. I'll try to restore what the rewrite team lost over the weekend and have it delivered to you at Ledge House, if you'll be there on Sunday."

Kosta confirmed he would and Laddie started to leave, then acted as if a thought had just occurred to him. "Oh, and Doria Maye asked me to stop by her bungalow yesterday," he said casually. "Had a script she wanted to give me."

"And she gave it to you for twenty minutes," stated Kosta.

Damn, thought Laddie, who'd hoped to inoculate himself by raising the topic voluntarily. Clearly Kosta had flies on every wall. "Well, I only bring it up because I didn't want you to get the wrong idea."

Kosta's eyes narrowed. "Maybe you noticed the guard saw you and now you don't want me to get the *right* idea." Even Kosta found his own jealousy a bit strange, but he'd been so stung in previous years by Doria's rejections at his weekend retreat that he still could not bear the idea of any other man besting him. "You have always admired Miss Maye, right?"

"She gave me a peck on the cheek in a town where schtupping is a handshake agreement. Leonid, I know she's off the table, I'd never endanger my relationship with you."

Kostas grimaced. "I'll be keeping tabs on her, trust me, so next time don't let there be a next time. It's you who's going to be behind this desk if you don't mess things up, maybe sooner than later." He reached for his pewter pillbox. "Then your gut can be lousy, too."

During the war, Finton Flood had done reconnaissance for the 2nd Armored Division in North Africa, thus he took the title of security guard to mean more than slipping studio passes under the windshields of vehicles as they entered. He was supposed to notice things.

One of the first things Finny noticed about the woman wearing the peach turtleneck sweater was that it was ninety-two degrees and she was wearing a peach turtleneck sweater. This was not a completely inexplicable sight in Hollywood, where a turtleneck in hot weather was a certain indication of a turkey neck. An actress in a coil of expensive scarves or a leading man with an ascot fooled no one regarding the sin they'd committed of foolishly allowing themselves to grow older.

The face of the peach turtleneck woman was hidden in the shadow of the extremely broad brim of her straw gardening hat. She was pretending to read a newspaper as if waiting for a bus on the lot, but there was no bus stop where she stood and she cast more glances toward Doria Maye's bungalow than at the newspaper. Finny left his station and walked over to greet her. "Morning. You're on studio property. Can I help you?"

"I'm waiting for a friend," she said in a raspy whisper, adjusting her handbag straps with big, white-gloved hands.

"Who's the friend?"

"Could be you," she answered in a gravelly hiss. As Finny's eyes adjusted to the shadows beneath the straw hat's brim, he realized there was a second reason for someone to wear a peach turtleneck in desert heat: to hide a prominent Adam's apple. It protruded within the turtleneck's collar like the padded bra of an aspiring sweater girl. That, combined with the beard stubble discernible beneath too-thick pancake makeup, garish lipstick applied inexpertly, eyelashes resembling twin tarantulas, the stocky frame beneath sweater and skirt, orthopedic stockings with flats, hands too big for their white gloves, and the forced rasp of a hoarse contralto, helped Finny to realize he was talking to a guy.

"So what's the story, buddy?" asked Finny.

The man lowered his face and spoke in a soft baritone. "Keep it down. I'm handling a surveillance for Mr. Kosta."

"Private detective?"

"Not private enough if you don't lower your voice."

With a gloved hand, he clumsily opened his voluminous bag and nodded toward some legal documents nestled alongside a pack of Old Golds, some green paper rosettes, a pocket comb, and a few condoms. He handed Finny a single notarized page and whispered, "My authorization. Recognize the signatures?"

The authorization, identifying the bearer as Lou Bryce of Bryce Investigations, not only bore Kosta's recognizable signature but those of two of the studio's attorneys, whose John Hancocks Finny knew from his daily sign-in and sign-out sheets.

"Yeah, but why the women's clothing?" asked Finny, who couldn't resist adding, "Or do you just like working this way?"

Bryce seemed indifferent to such humor. He took back the authorization, handing Finton an envelope in exchange. "Read the letter inside. We shouldn't be seen talking together this long. There's money in this, if you like money. Go back to your post, I'll wait here."

With understandable curiosity, Flood returned to his station with the stapled pages from the envelope. Clipped to them was a business card that he pocketed; then he began reading the cover letter bannered "Bryce Investigations" with an address on Bromistas Street and yesterday's date. Its heading gave Flood a pleasing ripple of importance:

For the eyes of Mr. Finton Flood only:

    I am Lou Bryce, senior operative of Bryce
Investigations, acting on behalf of a client
highly placed at this studio. There are indica-
tions that a contract player may be entertaining
another employee at NINE P.M. TOMORROW in
violation of the standard morals clause found
in their contract. While such behavior is often
overlooked, it has been decided in this instance
that an example must be made.
    As you may know, a waiver in every artist's
contract grants studio security full access to
all dressing rooms, changing rooms, offices,
and studio housing. Please see attached photostatic copies of said artist's contract for
verification.

Finny was not surprised to see that the marked-up photostatic
copies, with arrows in red ink indicating appropriate paragraphs, were
of Doria Maye's studio contract. So his word in the ear of Leon Kosta
had not gone unnoticed! Very nice, even if it meant Laddie Graham
was probably in a tub of hot water. He liked Laddie, but when you're
Security (he thought importantly), you can't play favorites. The letter
continued, much to Finny's pleasure:

Owing to your loyalty and discretion in the
past, Mr. Leonid Kosta has authorized me to
pay you the honorarium of five hundred dollars
cash for your assistance in collecting evidence
of said violation of the artist's contract.
This will involve a covert mission using reconnaissance photographic methods so the subject
remains unaware of the investigation. No special
knowledge of night photography is required.

    You will be issued a standard camera already
    outfitted with infrared lens and film.

The word "reconnaissance" stirred Finny's pulse. Yes, he'd always had a flair for espionage during the war, even if it had largely been about contraband bourbon smuggled into the officers' mess. And now, when Mr. Kosta needed undercover action, he'd turned to him. Despite his frequent fawning exchanges with Doria Mayes, Finny knew who paid his salary and where his allegiance lay. And of course, there were also the pulse-stirring magic words: "covert mission."

    If you accept the assignment, write a phone
    number on the outer flap where my secretary can
    reach you at noon tomorrow with further instruc-
    tions. If you refuse the assignment, do not
    write a phone number on the flap. Either way,
    please return this letter and all documents to
    the envelope, bring it back to me, and hand me
    any coin you wish. I will pin a paper rosette
    on your lapel as if you have made a donation.
    The rosette contains a one-hundred-dollar bill
    as either an advance if you agree to this
    assignment or as a final "thank you" for your
    time.

Flood tucked the pages back into the envelope, carefully inscribed his home telephone number on its flap, and walked back to the detective, who was keeping his head bowed beneath his gardener's bonnet. Excited by the element of espionage, Finny made a show of reaching deep for a coin in his pants pocket and offering Lou a quarter. In return, the detective reached into his flowery bag, produced a sham-rock rosette, and pinned it to Finny's lapel. The guard was pleased to notice there was a single bill wrapped tightly around its wire stem, hopefully the first hundred of five. This was serious money, and back-ing it up was ample documentation that could only have come from the studio. Still, Finny felt obliged to ask, "But why me? Why not a crony of your own?"

Lou's voice was again a raspy whisper as he inexpertly shifted his handbag. "Kosta wants this information for himself, not the newspapers. He trusts your loyalty to the studio over a third party. And as a senior security guard, you have every right to photograph evidence of misconduct on studio property."

These words all made good sense to Flood, just as Doria had intended them to.

The most challenging part of her impersonation of a man impersonating a woman had been creating believable stubble, which was uncharted terrain, even for McMasters. Months earlier, in the lab at Wump, she'd tried spackling it on with the edge of a brush, but it had lacked texture. Iron filings proved too fine and flew from her face when the magnet in a telephone receiver sucked them into the mouthpiece.

In the end, souvenir sand from (surprise) Black Sands Beach in Shelter Cove, California, had done the trick, pressed into a Vaseline "beard" on her face, then coated with a flesh-colored clay mask to hold it in place, cracks and all, then heavily dusted with pancake makeup. Luckily, the goal was to intentionally look as garish as any movie actor portraying Charley's aunt might appear if seen in tight close-up. The Adam's apple under her turtleneck had been an easy "falsie" to strap around her throat, likewise oversized gloves over further layers of gloves. The hoarse whisper, which nullifies gender, had been a breeze for an actress who'd had to "stage whisper" without a microphone in amphitheaters. She'd also kept her speaking part to a minimum to avoid extensive scrutiny; the majority of her explanation she'd intentionally left to the typed letter that Finton had read at some distance from her.

As for the signatures of both Kosta and the studio attorneys that "Lou" had shown to Flood, they were expertly forged (thanks to Penmanship at McM) by Doria from her own studio contract, from which she also had detached the very real morals clause Flood had glimpsed.

Her seeming afternoon assignation with Laddie, staged only for Finton Flood's benefit, had been to add credibility to Kosta's supposed surveillance of Doria's love life at the bungalow, so that she could then entice Flood to become part of the "stakeout." So while Finny may have thought this sordid situation involved Miss Maye, Laddie Graham, Leonid Kosta, private detective Lou Bryce, and himself, it was really a pas de deux choreographed solely by Doria to equip herself with what Captain Dobson had called "that most coveted of McMasters accessories": an ironclad alibi for the evening of Leonid Kosta's deletion.

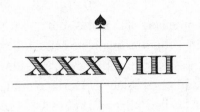

XXXVIII

Wes Trachter dealt a promotional brochure onto Alderman's desk, one which featured the face of a self-satisfied man staring forward in cock-sure fashion. The man was clearly not a hired model but posed as if he clearly thought he could be, and a headline above him proclaimed: *Airlines that fly Woltan's winning W-10 will see their profits soar!*

"Who's this puffed-up peacock?" Eddie asked.

"The guy who dropped the schematics in the trash can," said Trachter with a certainty that Alderman knew he could rely on. "I saw him, I photographed him, and we've traced his license plates. Maybe you'll be surprised by who he is, but then again, maybe not. Merrill Fiedler, your counterpart, you'll pardon the comparison."

Alderman nodded. "Fiedler, yeah, I know the name from conferences. All politics, no expertise." He skimmed the brochure, in which Fiedler predicted the earning power of the W-10 had a ceiling unlimited. "But this three thousand dollars he's asking? He makes more than that in a year. Why the sudden betrayal of Woltan for spare change?"

Wes offered uncertainly, "I mean, people can have their reasons, they're being let go or passed over for an expected promotion . . ." He hated playing analyst and shifted to the pragmatic. "So how do you want to play this? Obviously, we *could* contact the police . . ." He let it dangle, feeling a responsibility to at least offer that option, but Eddie answered as Wes hoped he would.

"And place this sterling fellow in jeopardy?" he said with mock alarm. "Merrill Fiedler is a hero, going against his own company and appealing for help from the enemy while risking his career, purely out of concern for the public's safety!" He smiled and continued conspiratorially, "And if we called the police at this stage, we'd never see the rest of the plans and learn what's with the W-10." He looked down at Fiedler's smugly confident face in the flyer. "But let's be sure to track what he does with the money while we're finding out what the son-ovabitch is up to."

♠

FROM THE SECOND JOURNAL OF CLIFF IVERSON

After living fenced in at McMasters for such an extended period of time (admittedly, dear X, the fence surrounded an expansive, often idyllic campus), I took true pleasure in the smooth drive south toward the drop-off location I'd specified to Eddie Alderman. It was my third trip to Nags Head that week and I enjoyed the ragged coastline, edged by countless dunes topped with beach grass and sea oats, and the countless shacks purveying pan-fried fish, or bait to catch fish for frying, or tackle ready for baiting. Every half mile or so, a cluster of these slatted crackerboxes would seem to huddle for safety near a dock or boatyard overlooking the Brunswick Islands, the Outer Banks, or the Graveyard of the Atlantic just beyond.

Several hours earlier (Dare County being quite a drive from AirCorp) I'd phoned Eddie Alderman and instructed him to leave the specified cash in an attaché case alongside the iron bench near Rudgum Pier's lone fishing and diving rental shop. The drop-off time would be precisely at three, which I knew would send Eddie scrambling to his car along with whatever security he'd enlisted. I'd already sent Alderman a very small, slim attaché case by parcel post specifically for the drop-off and directed him to load it with thirty-three one-hundred-dollar bills, a twenty, a ten, and three silver dollars. I had no concern about whether the money was marked. Frankly, it would serve my purposes better if it were.

I'd also told Eddie to make a discreet identifying mark on the inside of the case with a laundry pen. The case, one of two I'd purchased, was too small and flimsy to conceal any of the bulky homing devices that AirCorp might have wished to use, but its cheap, shiny buttons and catches perfectly served my purposes.

Crossing Croatan and Roanoke Sounds, I parked on a side street in Nags Head and casually wandered in the direction of the scuba gear shop at the end of Rudgum Pier. I'd visited it three days before, surveying their rental diving equipment, then purchased the identical gear from a supply store an hour's drive south. I was now toting a large waterproof carrier bag designed to contain a diver's regulator, but which held other items useful to my mission. Once I set foot on the pier, I produced a cowl-like rubber hood from the carrier, pulled it down over my head, and slipped on my swimming mask, obscuring a clear view of my face. There were already a number of diving enthusiasts on the pier, many fully suited and carrying similar equipment bags. I entered Rudgum Rental, paid two dollars for use of a locker and the men's changing room at the back of the store, and completed my transition from street clothes to diving gear.

I'd improved my swimming skills at McMasters but had never done any kind of deep-sea diving before, nor was I planning to today. It is a McMasters adage that if your first move in a game of chess is White King's Pawn to e4, it is still too early for others to discern whether you're a Grand Master or a greenhorn. (As a piano player, I prefer the analogy that a single middle C played on a grand piano sounds very much the same whether you're a concert pianist or a toddler in your great-aunt's front parlor.) Creating the illusion of expertise is often simply a matter of knowing when to quit, and there was no way to determine, as I donned my scuba suit (having at least practiced donning it), if I were an accomplished diver or an absolute belly flop.

At two minutes to three, Eddie Alderman, cheap attaché case in hand, was sitting as directed on the bench just outside the door to Rudgum Rental. He was keeping his eye on his watch as Wes Trachter kept his eyes trained on him from an iced tea stand across the way. At the appointed hour, Alderman stood and joined Trachter at the stand, leaving the black attaché on the bench.

Cliff, now in full scuba gear minus a compressed air tank, stepped

out of Rudgum Rental, took the attaché case, left in its place a large envelope which Trachter and Alderman hoped contained the remaining
W-10 diagrams, and stepped back into the store.

"Okay, we get the plans first, that's what matters most," Trachter
advised Eddie. He then turned to two men who'd been fishing near
the drink stand. "Check behind the rental store and make sure no one
sneaks out that way. Make it a loose tail if they do. We just want to
identify him, we don't want to confront him just yet. Eddie and I will
cover the front."

Alderman had retrieved the envelope from the bench and trotted
back to Wes's side when eight men and several women stepped out of
the store in standard black underwater suits and gear. A few already
had their face masks in place and one such diver, now sporting an oxygen cylinder, was holding the black attaché case.

Wes said, "We'll follow him from a distance. He can't make much
of a run for it wearing those fins."

"You think that's Fiedler?" asked Alderman as the diver walked to
the end of the pier.

"Could be. Seems a tad short compared to the arboretum, but then
again, swimming fins don't have heels."

They watched the diver descend a wooden ladder from the pier
down to a floating platform almost flush with the water. Still holding
the attaché case, he sat on the platform's edge alongside others in similar diving togs while Eddie and Wes watched from above, unsure what
to do next. Wes turned to a young woman with a clipboard who'd been
checking names off a list while further divers descended the rungs to
the platform below. He asked, "Excuse me, what's going on? What are
all these divers doing?"

"Coastal Cleanup Day," she explained. "Each month amateur scuba
divers collect debris that's been tossed off the pier. Some wear snorkels,
but you need breathing tanks for the bottom. It's amazing what they
find: wedding dresses, TV sets, switchblades, even bodies."

As if part of an aquacade, the divers on the floating platform each
leaned backward to tumble gently into the water. Trachter was stunned
to see the man whom they suspected was Merrill Fiedler drop into the
bay with the attaché case still in his hand.

"If that case he sent us isn't watertight," Eddie said, "he's going to lose all our money!"

"No. As long as the serial numbers are decipherable, it's fine," soothed Wes. The two stared down at the now-still surface.

Minutes went by until Eddie finally commented, "If this water was a watched pot, it would be boiling by now."

"He has to come up sometime. Remember, when you follow him, don't worry about being spotted or losing him, you're the decoy. My boys and I will be tailing him separate from you."

"For all we know, he might just be a go-between, not Fiedler himself." Eddie flexed his arches where he stood. "Jesus, I want to look at these schematics and figure out what he's up to." He snuck a peek at the contents of the envelope he'd swapped for the attaché case. "They look real enough, at least at first glance. Maybe he's been good to his word."

Trachter suddenly straightened with a groan. "What am I thinking?! He could be swimming below the surface along the shoreline and come up on another part of the beach or a different pier! You stay and watch for him here, I'll get my team to scan the shore."

As Trachter raced to the two-way radio in his car, Eddie realized he was now the lone sentry . . . and that scuba divers often keep folding knives to cut their way out of entanglements or fend off barracuda. Eddie's job description did not include disarming knife-wielding frogmen informers. But that disquieting consideration was dispelled as the diver they'd followed popped out of the water, the attaché case in his hand open and empty except for the water dripping out of it.

The diver removed his rubber cowl and looked around expectantly. His face did not resemble any photograph of Fiedler. It was that of an increasingly angry young man in his twenties who was now climbing the ladder up to the pier.

"Hey, buddy, you always take a briefcase with you when you dive?" Eddie asked, pretending to be amused. "What's *that* about?"

The fellow complained, "You tell me. Guy paid me a hundred dollars to suit up and take a case full of his company's waterproof wristwatches down to the seabed, open the case where they were all secured, leave it open for five minutes, and bring them back up to demonstrate they all kept perfect time. I get to the bottom, maybe fifty, sixty feet, open the case, and there's nothing but a little sand for ballast." He looked around again, first expectantly, then just ticked off. "He said he'd have cameras filming me coming out of the water."

"He may have scammed me, too," lied Alderman. "Let me see." He examined the case for the identifying mark he'd inscribed as instructed, but there was none. He could only assume Fiedler switched the case inside the rental store for a duplicate before handing it off to this diver. "What did he look like?"

The diver gestured helplessly. "This is the first time we met and he was in full scuba head gear. We did the deal over the phone, got my name and number from a bulletin board in Rudgum Rental. I teach diving to amateurs. We didn't talk today, he just handed me this." He looked at the dripping attaché case in his hand and discovered a waterproof pouch stapled to its otherwise empty interior. Ripping it open, he brightened considerably. "Left me three hundred dollars, though, so I guess I can't complain."

♠

From the Second Journal of Cliff Iverson

Once I had handed my unwitting frogman accomplice the attaché case (identical to the money-filled one Alderman had left on the bench), I quickly shed my costume in Rudgum's changing room. The suit and my oversized carrier bag being the same makes as Rudgum's inventory, they would undoubtedly be collected and put on the rental rack from which they hadn't come.

While the cleanup campaign divers had paraded to the end of the pier with Eddie Alderman following, I'd walked out the front door of the shop in hiking shorts, a sweatshirt emblazoned with "University of Edinburgh," an olive bucket hat, and bearing an oversized rucksack, previously stowed in my carrier bag, which now contained the small attaché case of AirCorp's money, all the while chatting with a very nice couple on vacation from Utah—the "Beehive State" they'd informed me—until I reached the pier's parking lot. I drove north nice and slow, savoring the strong possibility that, if my thesis was going as I'd mapped it out at McMasters, Merrill Fiedler was not too far away, lacking an alibi, and might soon be laying his hands (and fingerprints) on this very same attaché case himself.

♠

First-time visitors to Franky's Lanes just outside of Nags Head sometimes mistakenly believed the bowling alley was named for the popular song stylist, only to learn that Franky was the sullen owner at the register who held your street shoes hostage until you paid in full for your frames. Fiedler entered hearing rhythm and blues on a jukebox and the baby chimes of a pinball machine, which made the place sound lively enough, and he was immediately assaulted by the trademark bowling alley odor of french fries and wood varnish, as if the potatoes were being cooked in it. But the establishment proved to be relatively empty, save for a few pimply pinspotters; only three lanes were lit, and the alley's proprietor and barkeep (the aforementioned Franky) was running the joint from the register.

Fiedler called the big man over. "Hey, a friend of mine named Amigo checked his bowling bag with you so I could use it. My name's Smith." Fiedler wasn't pleased with the choice of name but that was what Amigo had instructed him to use on that morning's call. He had to suppress asking Franky what Amigo looked like, as it might arouse suspicion and he had no idea what part the burly man played in Amigo's racket, if any.

"Smith, yeah," acknowledged the bartender, "the guy just dropped it off a few minutes ago." Franky felt in his pocket for the crinkled ten-dollar bill he'd been given by an unrecognizable man who'd been dressed as though for Halloween in a wigged and whiskered costume. The disguised man might have been anybody, including the present Mr. Smith himself. "He told me you gotta give it back to me when you're done . . . said the bag belonged to his father." That was fine with Fiedler, who was only interested in what was stashed in the lone bowling shoe he'd been advised would be waiting for him in the bag.

"*This is it*," Amigo had told Fiedler on the lobby pay phone. "*I know last time was no great shakes, but that was the setup for the big one. I bet heavy and all you have to do is cash in our winnings."* He then gave instructions regarding the bowling alley, concluding, *". . . and then we take a little break. Down the line, we can start the whole thing up again."*

Fiedler hadn't yet decided where he was going to land on this notion of a "fifty-fifty" split. *He* clearly was doing nothing illegal, merely cashing in legitimate betting receipts at their point of origin. If Amigo was doing something dishonest, there was no way Fiedler could know, and if Fiedler decided to make the split more advantageous to himself, Amigo might not be able to go to the police. There was already a sizeable amount accumulated and Fiedler had grown fond of pocketing (and sometimes spending) the money.

A lane at Franky's cost fifty cents a game. Fiedler coughed up two quarters; the owner slid back a scoring sheet and pulled a roomy antique Brunswick bag down from a high shelf. "Your friend said to tell you your bowling shoes are in the bag, but I'll still take yours as security, that's how it works." Fiedler, annoyed, gave him his loafers, which Franky put alongside some other street shoes, then returned to slicing limes at the bar. It was surprising that no one at Franky's Lanes had ever gotten athlete's foot from drinking a gin and tonic.

Fiedler unzipped the bowling bag and discovered a cheap attaché case inside. *Stupid Chinese boxes*, he thought, irritated by Amigo's melodramatic cloak-and-dagger games. Despite all the childishness, Fiedler wondered if he should have been wearing gloves for the pickups . . . but that would have looked suspicious. After all, the tickets were legitimate, and he was more than content to remain ignorant as to Amigo's method of picking the winners. They were simply a "thank you" for some past good deed on his part. He wasn't doing anything more illegal than opening some birthday presents.

The cheap case, which although new had already needed repair to its fake leather surface via a swatch of black tape, had two shiny sliders that needed to be pushed outward before unlocking a center catch. Opening the case, he half expected to find another container, but was relieved to discover a small Endicott Johnson bowling shoe, beneath whose lolling tongue was a folded envelope. A quick glance inside revealed six betting receipts from yesterday, which he quickly pocketed.

He returned the shoe to the case, the case to the Brunswick bag, and the bag to Franky, informing him that he didn't feel like bowling after all and the fifty cents was his to keep. Hiding his jubilance at this unexpected windfall, Franky slid back Fiedler's shoes and put the Brunswick bag back on the high shelf.

Now in his red Roadmaster, Fiedler looked more closely at the betting stubs to confirm that the long drive down from Woltan Industries into Dare County had been worth it. He'd acquired a sweet tooth for his winnings; the most recent take had been nothing to crow about, and Fiedler was craving both his guaranteed gloat and the heft of a completely unearned bankroll in his pocket.

When he saw the numbers printed on the stubs, something akin to a sexual thrill raced through him. The stubs represented a massive payout, *six* picks this time, all at long-shot odds: 35–1, 42–2, 45–1, 30–1, 18–1, and, lo and behold, an almost absurd 65–1 . . . and they were all wagers considerably larger than any of Amigo's prior bets! Fiedler had not excelled at trigonometry, but he was a whiz at numbers when a dollar sign was placed in front of them. His take today could pay for a world cruise, if he could tear himself away from the golden goose of the racetrack that long. The only troublesome cloud in Fiedler's blue heaven was the thought of divvying up the money. This fifty-fifty thing with Amigo would need to be renegotiated.

♠

From the Second Journal of Cliff Iverson

Across the street from the bowling alley, I slouched low in my car wearing the same intentionally ham-fisted disguise I'd used when checking the Brunswick bag with Franky, and you can imagine, dear X, my elation when I spotted Fiedler departing Franky's Lanes shortly after I'd told him to arrive there (leaving me enough time for the quick hop from nearby Rudgum Pier to deposit the bag at the bowling alley).

Clearly, the hook is now deep in his lip. The bowling alley is miles out of his usual loop ("Do you often drive for hours to visit a rundown bowling alley and then decide you're not in the mood to bowl, Mr. Fiedler?"). But it is only a short drive from Rudgum Pier, where a cowled frogman had evaporated an hour earlier with an attaché case bearing Eddie Alderman's identifying mark and, by the way, Eddie's "ransom money." I'd divested the attaché case of its cash and replaced it with a bowling shoe containing six racing bets I'd made yesterday at the track. Fiedler was indisputably in Dare County. Minimally, the bowling alley manager at Franky's Lanes had gotten a good look at the suspiciously-behaving Mr. "Smith" . . . and there was an additional way I've linked Franky and Fiedler that I'll explain in another moment, friend X.

So: The marked attaché case now bore Fiedler's fingerprints on its glossy surfaces and snaps. To any investigators—such as Air-Corp's or the police—the only question would be whether: 1.) Fiedler had a confederate pick up the money at the pier who then, donning an absurd disguise, left the attaché case at the bowling alley for Fiedler to retrieve, or 2.) Fiedler did it all, including dropping off the money for himself at the bowling alley while garbed in this obvious costume . . . which of course, dear X, was actually worn by me . . . and which I was still wearing as I watched Fiedler drive away from Franky's Lanes.

Now it was time for me, in the same ludicrous disguise, to get back the Brunswick bowling bag I'd checked with Franky (containing the now-empty attaché case that Fiedler handled) and give him the fifty-dollar bonus I'd promised . . . in the form of a check made out to cash signed by one Merrill Fiedler! (When Franky groused about it being a check, I nodded and handed him another fifty in cash; for holding on to a bowling bag for an hour, he'd done pretty damn well.)

The check, from Fiedler's account and bearing his real signature, had been an additional "prop" I'd been given unwittingly by Lilliana Horvath. At McMasters, dear X, we are taught never to count on fortuitous circumstances, and I do wonder now if Dean Harrow would have advised me not to use it. I just have to hope the education I received, thanks to your generosity, dear X, is helping me make the right decisions. I'm out here in the field alone, with no one to confide in but you. I'm also hoping you still wish me well.

While stopping at a service station to have his tank filled on the drive back to Baltimore, Fiedler used its pay phone to call Shari Dougan in Accounting to tell her she should drop whatever she was doing and dress up for a special night out. She was not yet one of his Woltan conquests, but he didn't think it would take much to change that. He appraised Shari as a smart cookie who not only knew the score but understood how the game is played.

If he were going to cash in these breathtaking winnings tonight, he sure as hell wasn't going to do it without a witness to his achievement, and he'd decided Shari should be the anointed one. (The mental image of Shari being anointed in oil made him dial the phone faster.) First, he'd impress her at the racetrack as if he'd broken the bank at Monte Carlo, then a late supper and bottomless glasses of champagne at the Versailles Room at the Lord Baltimore, and a quick ascent to a room with a 360-degree view of her. He felt the hotel suite would impress her, while ensuring that if things went sour between them, she wouldn't know where he lived.

He picked Shari up on the way to the track. Her taut ice-blue top, navy blue pencil skirt, and metallic gold belt cinching her waist more than met with his approval. She'd also done something to her hair and makeup that she didn't do at work, and he was pleased at the message all her efforts implied.

Shari said little to Fiedler except where a few polite assents were expected. Her goal was to get through the apparently required evening without losing her job. She hated being in this position, but perhaps she could butter his ego enough to gain a pay raise or extra vacation time. She figured she'd put a toll booth on that bridge when she came to it.

He kept Shari at his side at the racetrack's payout window, wanting his "regular" teller to see the grade of company he kept when he wasn't cashing in his uncanny wins.

"Read 'em and weep," he said. "In small bills, nothing bigger than tens." He wanted the payout to be of maximum duration and he winked at Shari, making sure she was noting every nuance of the transaction.

His "regular" teller frowned, studied the tickets, and said thoughtfully, "I, uh, I better check this if you don't mind." He stepped back from the window and went to speak with an older man at a desk inside the payout room, showing him the tickets. The older man consulted a large ring binder, compared the tickets with its pages, and nodded affirmation to the teller who returned to his window. "Sorry for the delay," said the teller. "With amounts of money that are bet on odds like these, we have to double-check. State rules, not ours."

"Sure," said Fiedler, flashing a smile at Shari, who smiled back reflexively.

The teller reached for the display handkerchief of his blazer, which he slid under the window's bars. "You may be needing this," he said.

Fiedler was puzzled. "I don't understand."

The teller pushed the betting receipts back to Fiedler with a cheery expression. "Read 'em and weep. All these bets are losers. One didn't even finish the race."

Fiedler said, "But . . . I was guaranteed these were wins. Something's very wrong here."

The teller rummaged in a drawer and handed him a sheet of paper. "Wednesday's results. Have a seat and check for yourself. Look, you can't win 'em all. Sometimes you're just a loser."

In the lobby of his apartment building the next morning, Fiedler waited for his usual call from Amigo. The remainder of the previous evening had gone as badly as it had started. His outrage made him a poor dinner companion for Shari, he'd drunk too much at the Versailles Room, and when she left mid-meal to fix her makeup, instead of giving her a quarter for the powder room maid, he'd tucked a twenty into the palm of her hand with a wink. Frightened to have him drive her home in his present state (he hadn't yet explained to her that she was spending the night there with him), Shari slipped out of both the powder room and the restaurant, asked the hotel doorman to hail her a taxi, and never returned for her flaming cherries jubilee. Fiedler was forced to spend the night with a woman at the hotel bar who was almost his age.

He'd checked out the next morning without breakfast, wanting to be in his apartment lobby to spew his wrath at "Amigo." Cliff phoned five minutes late, which brought Fiedler to a rolling boil. He growled, "Some system, pal. I had nothing but losers!"

"*There was a mistake*," said Amigo. "*At least you didn't lose your own money.*"

"I lost plenty!" He caught the doorman looking in every direction but his and lowered his voice. "I lost an afternoon driving to a stupid bowling alley and you made me look like an idiot in front of someone I've had my eyes on for some time. Spent a fortune on dinner and a hotel room." He omitted mentioning that the pickup in the hotel had cost him as well, being a professional who worked the bar there.

Amigo sounded contrite. "*It was very unfortunate. The next receipts will compensate—*"

"No, I've had enough of all this 'say the secret password' spy crap! The last two times haven't been worth the effort. You'll meet me in person from now on, and I'm checking the tickets against the racing results before I ever show up at the track again."

There was a pause on the other end of the line. "*I can give you half of what you would have collected last night. We could meet at eight tonight at a roadstand near—*"

"You'll bring the money to my office, in person."

Amigo was silent for a moment. "*Very well. But please bring my share of the money you've already won.*"

"You'll get your money, pal," said Fiedler nastily, who now had no intention of splitting his accumulated winnings with his "amigo."

"*What did you say? The connection is weak . . .*"

"I SAID, YOU'LL GET YOUR *MONEY*!" he bellowed, then noticed doorman Ricky averting his eyes again. "My office is—oh, right, of course, you already know, you sent me a letter there. Meet me at eight tonight and come alone. Sign in at the desk, they'll ring me, and I'll have them send you up. Just be sure you bring me my goddamned money!"

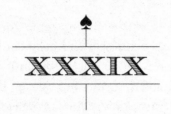

XXXIX

Leonid Kosta was a creature of habit. (One might call him a man of habit, but somehow "creature" seems more appropriate.) Whenever his studio held a Friday night test screening—a standard industry practice that Kosta loathed, since the results might challenge his opinions and decisions—he would leave his office no later than 6 p.m., take dinner at Bel Cañon, a moneyed country club for non-Jewish-but-not-quite-WASP power brokers, and drive directly to Ledge House, his Torrey Pines retreat overlooking the Pacific, thereby ignoring the screening, its audience reaction, and the inevitable panic from underlings as to how to "fix" this film of which they'd all been so proud only hours before. Kosta preferred to hear reports on Monday when the initial hysteria had died down. In any case, he tended to simply go with his instincts.

Thus he traditionally spent Friday preview nights ascetically alone, taking nothing more exciting to bed than a script, stockpiling his reserves for the weekend. Saturday he would entertain a desirable newcomer to his life, who would usually be escorted there by a pair of charming young male contract actors whose interests lay in each other.

What happened Sunday often depended on how Saturday night had evolved.

He also owned a tidy three-bedroom structure (which Kosta called "The Shack") on a small patch of private beach directly below Ledge House. This was maintained by his housekeeper, Freja, and her husband, Aksel, who lived there gratis in return for working as needed up at the cliff dwelling. The couple would discreetly evaporate after dessert on Saturday night and materialize Sunday midmorning to prepare brunch, saying little and seeing even less.

Prior to her enrollment at McMasters, Doria had twice been a guest at Ledge House when Kosta had been courting her professionally and carnally (she refused to call it "romantically"). On both visits, she'd just barely managed to sustain her weekend chastity. On her first Saturday there, she'd driven down with fair-haired Tally Farrell and the turbulent Bolt Lawson, but after dinner, when she went to the east terrace overlooking Los Peñasquitos Lagoon where she'd left them only moments before, she was alarmed to discover Kosta had dispatched both actors to The Shack along with Aksel and Freja, and that she was now alone with him for the remainder of the night. Doria managed to fall back on "that difficult time of the month" and retreated to Ledge House's lone guest room, propping a chair under the doorknob . . . and, yes, she saw the knob turn tentatively at least once after she went to bed.

On her second Saturday, she was brought down from LA by Aksel and learned upon arrival that this time there would be no other guests or servants. She was instantly clobbered by a horrendous migraine, requiring Aksel to chauffeur her home so she could apply the customized ice pack that had been made from a cast of her face, this being the only remedy she'd found for the excruciating pain, had such an ice pack existed and had she ever suffered from migraines.

Now with a McMasters education under her belt, she would make a third but this time unexpected visit to Ledge House. One way or another, it would surely be her last.

It was common knowledge on the lot that a test screening of *Dark Alley* with Cornel Wilde and Jane Greer would take place at Shea's Arabian in Oxnard early that Friday evening. At 10 a.m. on what augured to be the most fateful day of both their lives, Doria placed a call from her bungalow's kitchen phone to Kosta: *Leon, the only purpose of my call is to determine if you'll be driving to dear old Ledge House this evening, as you invariably do to evade the postmortem after a screening, and whether you'll be alone there. But since I can't ask you about this evening without raising suspicion, I'm going to ask you about early tomorrow morning, even though my hope is that you won't live to see it.*

But of course, she couldn't say that, so instead she said, "Leon, it's Doria, this is not about me, tell me: What do you know about the Dalai

Lama? Oh, you must have. This wonderful heroic boy who's ruling Tibet in defiance of Red China? You see, I met him during my travels . . ."

It seemed that the Dalai Lama's emissaries hoped to subsidize a major motion picture about his young life—with thrilling action scenes surrounding his ascension in 1950 and the battles that have raged since—in order to drum up US support for their valiant resistance against Red China. And according to Doria's complete crock of malarkey, she had agreed to act as a conduit for their effort, in return for a modest finder's fee. No, she said, there was no role in it for her, and it would be completely underwritten by Tibet, they just wanted the studio's imprimatur and distribution. Sheer profit with no risk. "Would you be willing to have a quick chat with His Holiness's representatives at Ledge House late tomorrow morning and beat Jack Warner to the punch? Just you and them. My role in this will end with this phone call."

Leonid, a businessman first, assented. But Doria quickly got to the true purpose of her fictitious story. "Grand, but one small thing: You won't have any of your sordid little companions romping around the house or terrace, will you? The emissaries don't approve of licentious behavior. No company coming? Not until Saturday afternoon? Yes, I remember, that's the usual arrival time for your female guests, isn't it? Wonderful, I'll let them know, and come Monday, Jack Warner will feel like a brotherless child. Remember, mum's the word until the ink is dry."

Of course, no representatives of the Dalai Lama would meet with Kosta late Saturday morning because they were entirely her invention. She had only wanted to know 1.) if Costa would be alone that night, and 2.) when he *did* expect guests on Saturday, for she wished him to inform her how long it might be before his body was discovered.

XL

At McMasters, Gemma (and all students majoring in the deletion of their employer) had been strenuously advised not to perform their thesis at their place of work. But now, almost a month back on the job, she feared there might be no other way, as she could find no viable excuse to accompany Adele anywhere outside of St. Ann's. The hospital didn't hold many picnics or outings (curious patients might notice if all the staff took off for the day), nor was Adele any kind of a friend . . . they'd never met for lunch or had a G and T at the local on a Friday. All they had in common was the labor that Gemma did in Adele's name.

Her plan to use the River Strid—the lethal chasm masquerading as a frolicsome country stream, one that sucks down anyone unlucky enough to slip into its warren of underwater tombs—had begun on her very first weekend home. Gemma had found a B&B near Bolton Abbey catering primarily to Pakistani guests. Although the management had no objection to non-Pakistani customers, the woman running the small establishment spoke only enough English to register guests, supply towels, and serve breakfast. Knowing the proprietress would be unlikely to warn them of the perils of the Strid, Gemma intended to book a double there for Adele and herself. They would go for a stroll around sunset. She'd found a relatively safe place to cross ahead of Adele, whom she'd momentarily distract by showing her a brochure for a restaurant where they might dine. Fifteen steps farther along was a location where it looked as if one simple step would bring Adele to the other side. She'd beckon and extend a hand to help her across.

She'd also made a habit of carrying a tube of Softasilk hand lotion with her at all times, applying it frequently while commenting on how she detested having dry hands, so that the act became commonplace and eventually unnoticeable. She planned to liberally apply the lotion just before she crossed the Strid so that when Adele grabbed for her offered help, a quick squeeze from Gemma would cause Adele's hand to squirt from her grip like a wet bar of soap in the tub. At McMasters, she'd practiced offering her left hand reaching across to the right, so that Adele would either have to grasp with her weaker left hand, or use her right, which would turn her at an odd angle on the rock. Adele, who always put fashion over practicality, would likely be in stylish shoes with smooth soles, whereas Gemma had practiced in cleats. She'd considered using a walking staff, and Coach Tarcott showed her how to offer the end of it and flip Adele into the water like Robin Hood with Little John, but they'd ultimately decided it might be too overt if witnessed by another hiker. The "helping hand gone wrong" via a jiujitsu move had seemed the best plan she could muster.

There was only one flaw. Adele would not go hiking with her.

Gemma didn't think this was because Adele was overly suspicious, since her nemesis had no reason to believe her "insurance policy" wasn't still securely locked up in Old Riggins' safe. And since returning, Gemma had done everything in her power to convince Adele she was completely resigned to their loathsome arrangement. She'd gone so far as to rent an Austin Sports convertible from the Newcastle firm that serviced the hospital's fleet of vehicles, hoping it would pave the way for a future holiday jaunt. Adele had gladly availed herself of a lift home to her doorstep each night, rather than waiting in the rain for the bus from Morpeth, but she always insisted on driving the car herself, Adele preferring (for her own protection) to be behind the wheel in all matters.

But where the question of taking the convertible farther afield was concerned, whether over hill and dale or to the deadly Strid, Gemma's blackmailer had no interest in anything involving the great outdoors beyond assuring herself a *Town & Country* future. At the moment, a young doctor named Peter Ellisden was the full focus of all extracurricular activities, and her only concern was whether "Mrs. Adele Ellisden" was dreamily mellifluous or a regrettable tongue-twister. Thus, at even the slightest mention of a country ramble, Adele ceased to listen or respond. Short of forcing her at gunpoint to board a train for West

Burton and dragging her hogtied across the Yorkshire Dales, there was no way for Gemma to execute her McMasters-sanctioned deletion.

It was well-known on campus that Dean Harrow and Assistant Dean Erma Daimler were at crossed daggers about the correct approach to a McMasters education. Daimler had many proponents among the student body and faculty alike for her strongly held belief that an applicant need only be taught how to achieve their specific thesis, whereas Dean Harrow just as strenuously believed that only the well-rounded executor should be returned to "the battlefield"—as he referred to civilian life.

Gemma prayed that Harrow's philosophy was the correct approach because, heaven help her (although no principled deity would), she was going to have to improvise.

XLI

The San Francisco Opera was presenting their production of *Parsifal* at the Shrine Auditorium in Los Angeles that evening, and nearby restaurants like Lucca always saw an increase in early dinner reservations owing to the production's 7 p.m. curtain. As it happened, Harv Wexler and his wife were not seeing *Parsifal*, but Bev had been letting Harv know for over a week that she was in the mood for veal piccata, and a friend of Harv's had suggested both the restaurant and the wisdom of booking a table in advance because of the anticipated opera crowd.

Harv stopped the couple's olive Ford coupe alongside the restaurant and said to his wife, "I don't see a spot on this block. You go in so we don't lose the reservation and I'll join you when I've parked." Bev volunteered that she wasn't comfortable claiming a reservation on her own, as her Midwest upbringing held that women should not enter foreign-named restaurants unescorted. But suddenly the issue of parking was made moot.

"Dining with us tonight, sir?" asked the perky brunette at the driver's-side window, very fetching in her valet outfit, a cut-down tuxedo jacket with a Lucca badge pinned to it and snappy bow tie, white gloves, cummerbund, and trim trousers, all topped by a shiny-brimmed chauffeur's cap worn at a jaunty angle. Harv confirmed their gastronomic intent, amused that Los Angeles never lacked for good-looking valets and carhops, all of whom were aspiring actors hoping to be discovered, this valet no exception. She sprinted to the back of the car, hastily scrawled the last four numbers of its license plate and the words "Green Ford" on a printed card directly below the restaurant's logo. She handed the card to Harv, hurriedly reciting what was clearly an oft-repeated litany: "Please give this card to your waiter when you're finishing your meal, and I'll have your car waiting for you when you leave. Do you have to catch a curtain? No? Then *buon appetito*!" She dashed around the front of the car to open the door for Bev, who disapproved of the female valet's snug pants but appreciated the courtesy. Another car pulled up behind the Wexlers' and after she had closed Bev's door, the valet ran back to this newest-arrived driver, asking breathlessly, "Dining with us tonight, sir? I'll be right with you, please keep your motor running." She then ran back to Harv, who was stepping out of the car.

He asked the valet, "Do you have change of a twenty?" Harv's wife looked away, embarrassed by her husband's familiar ploy.

"Sorry, no," said the valet regretfully. "But I will have change by the *end* of your dinner and I'm here till eleven. So again, *buon appetito*!"

As Harv ushered Bev into the restaurant, she scoffed, "'Change of a twenty!' I know full well you have change because you paid three twenty-five out of a five at the Gulf station."

"I'm told the veal is really good here," said Harv, circumnavigating his wife's disdain. He looked around at the restaurant's romantic decor. "Nice place."

"Try to order something other than lasagna for once," said Bev, while Doria Maye was already four blocks from the restaurant, driving the Wexlers' green Ford at a healthy clip. She unpinned her handmade Lucca valet badge from her jacket, set the chauffeur's cap on the passenger seat, and wheeled the Wexlers' car onto South Figueroa, leaving Harv and Bev far behind, out of her life and never to be thought of again.

Business was always feast or famine at the Royal Street parking garage, depending on whether there was a big event at the adjacent Shrine Auditorium. This particular evening the feast was near-saturnalian, as the 6,300-seat theater threatened to be sold out due to *Parsifal*'s pairing of Kirsten Flagstad with Chilean tenor Ramón Vinay in the title role. On such evenings when the Trojans held a big sports event, both entrances and exits to the Royal Street Garage would be overwhelmed, and a battalion of part-time parking attendants would be hired for the event, usually students from USC who were housed nearby.

The garage's drop-off area was currently a melee in monochrome as silver-haired gentlemen in evening wear and ladies in frosted argent gowns arrived in black limousines swarmed over by college students in ill-fitting black jackets, clip-on bow ties, and white shirts that could have benefited from a good bleaching.

Doria pulled the Wexlers' Ford into the garage and swerved away from a phalanx of broughams and sedans toward the employee parking area by metal stairs that led to the garage's upper levels. Hopping out, she peeled off her white gloves and placed them in her chauffeur's cap, which she rested on a fire extinguisher. A gangly valet with arms too long for his jacket came speeding down the stairs three steps at a time. She ably backed into him as he reached the bottom step and allowed herself to fall on the floor with a cry of pain, as if the collegiate type had bowled her over, a move she'd "McMastered" in Twisted Kinesiology.

Joe College was aghast. "Gosh, I'm sorry, that's my fault, can I help you?" He might have been all of twenty, his clip-on tie dangling from one side of his collar, and if he wasn't a social science major at USC, you could have knocked Doria for a loop, and by the way, she'd just made him think he had knocked her for a loop.

"If you want to help me," she said from the garage floor while rubbing a shin, "you could be a pal and park my dad's car ahead of all those fat cats in monkey suits over there." As he helped her to her feet, she gestured to her own uniform. "I work the lobby bar at the Shrine, and I have to be there before the doors open or they'll send me packing."

Over the years, whenever for some ungodly reason she'd found herself out in the civilian world, her identity was usually camouflaged by context. "The" Doria Maye could not possibly be parking cars, tending bar, or getting a quart of milk at the farmers market in dungarees and a babushka. Lacking makeup, she could stand at the checkout counter and be forced to wait like any other human being. "You know, you look like a young Doria Maye," the woman behind her might offer. "Only she's a lot taller, of course."

Thus, Joe College did not recognize her as the celebrity he'd surely seen before at the movies but simply as a young woman he'd sure like to see again. "Do you make out good at the Shrine?" he asked.

She laughed conspiratorially. "Tonight's Wagner, they're taking four intermissions, and by the last one, the hubbies will be tipping in paper money like sailors on leave. Please be a pal, I've got to check my dad's car now or I'll lose out. The proletariat has to stand together, right?"

"Damn straight," he agreed in solidarity (she knew she'd read him correctly), and produced a claim check labeled "Royal Street Garage East Entrance Level 2." He tore along its perforation and handed her the stub. "Any chance of a date?"

"Gee, I'm engaged. If I weren't, that would sure be another story." She saw him glance at her barren fingers and explained, "I get better tips if I don't wear my ring. Thanks for being my hero!" Pleased to be one, he hopped into the Wexlers' Ford and screeched it up a ramp.

Doria reclaimed her chauffeur's cap and gloves from the extinguisher and strode purposefully beyond the entrance to the garage where impatient drivers were anxious to be admitted. One white-maned banker-type, accompanied by his wife and another couple, was leaning out the driver's window, honking for special treatment despite the line. He showed relief as she gestured the foursome out of the car, which was a nondescript black Packard Patrician, perfectly suited to her purpose. She asked in butler-like fashion, "Seeing *Parsifal* tonight, are we, sir?"

He grumbled assent and she handed him the parking receipt she'd just received from Joe College for the Wexlers' Ford. White Mane could have tipped her for letting him jump the line, but on seeing he had no plans to do so, she hopped into his car with a pleasant, "Enjoy the show!"

"It's not a show, it's an opera," scowled the banker.

She gunned the Packard up to the second, then third level, keeping her head low lest she pass Joe College. At the opposite end of Level 3, she drove down two ramps to the less used Thirty-Second Street exit she'd scouted a week earlier. Removing her cap, Doria shook her hair out and eased the car smoothly along Jefferson, then cruised onto the Harbor Freeway toward Long Beach and points south.

She felt like a college kid with full use of the family car while her parents were away on a cruise. She had free use of this wonderfully uninteresting vehicle for at least six or seven hours (*Parsifal* plus the time it took for White Mane to discover his loss at the garage). It would take but a few hours for her and Kosta to face their conjoined destiny.

At Lucca, the Wexlers would be unlikely to realize their car had been stolen until they handed the fake claim check to their bewildered waiter. Even if they had caught on merely minutes after she'd driven off, the green Ford had already been squirreled away on the second level of the Royal Street Garage with nothing in the car to link it to Doria. Meanwhile, the owner of the Packard had not even begun to see the first curtain rise on *Parsifal*. Much, much later this evening, White Mane would dutifully turn in the completely genuine Royal Street Garage receipt she'd handed him, they'd wait a good long time while scores of cars were brought down, and finally there would arrive . . . the Wexlers' green Ford.

What's this? "Your car, sir," a disinterested attendant would reply. *This is not my car! You've made a mistake, you idiot! My car is a Packard, a black Packard!* Repeated attempts to find it would be made to no avail. *You've lost my car! You gave it to someone else!* "I'm sorry, sir, we're closing in ten minutes, if you want to come back in the morning . . . ?"

Did Doria feel guilty about inconveniencing strangers this way? Perhaps. But then again, she would only be putting them out a little, whereas she would soon be putting Kosta to death. By comparison, the tightfisted Wexler and White Mane were doing extremely well indeed. And maybe next time they'd offer a tip to a poor working girl.

She was well on schedule. The day's bold sun was gradually descending toward its nightly rendezvous with the Pacific, causing steam clouds of magenta to rise from the ocean, or so it seemed. Doria could almost hear the opening strains of *Parsifal* as underscore to the nebula-like display.

She took the exit to the airport, parked in the metered lot there, and headed for the arrivals gate. Near it was a locker for which she already had the key and from which she removed a small striped travel bag she'd stored earlier that morning. Soon she was back on the 110, en route to the Balboa Peninsula in Newport Beach.

Now for the dicey part.

XLII

Endiro Giansante, owner of Fawn Street Florists, descended from the store's attic where he was drying pink larkspur to find his new deliveryman, Ludis Lanka, standing near the register holding two ten-dollar bills upright in his hand.

"A man came in, you were upstairs, so I took the order," he beamed proudly.

"Ludis, you're a nice fellow but you're never to deal with a customer. Unless they're Latvian," he added with a smile, "in which case I'd ask you to translate."

By way of confession, Ludis added, "He gave me a two-dollar tip," and reached to his pocket as if he might have to split it with Endiro.

"No, keep the two dollars, but you're a delivery boy, not a salesman. Delivery *man*," he corrected himself, for Ludis was surely in his twenties or early thirties. He'd only been working there a few days, answering a sign in the window. God knows how the sweet fellow would survive on what he paid him, thought Endiro. He must surely live with relatives.

"*Es biju citur*," said Ludis, which means "I was elsewhere." Not quite apropos but it was the first Latvian phrase Cliff had learned at McMasters and he'd been told he'd pronounced it well.

That evening, as he conscientiously ironed the ill-fitting boilersuit he'd purchased for himself, he idly recalled the first time Dean Harrow spoke of the power of uniforms. The assembly had been called in the Ōideion, a small, covered amphitheater identical to one nestled in the purlieus of Marseille. The resemblance to the original was uncanny, unless, of course, McMasters was actually located in the purlieus of Marseille.

"'Your uniform should not only become you, but you should become your uniform!'" the dean had begun that late afternoon, the sky behind him cobblestoned with oval, amethyst clouds. "Guy McMaster said those words on many an occasion, and they remain true to this day."

He peered about at individual faces amid the students, scrutinizing and appraising their comprehension as he recounted a favorite incident. "One of the most highly regarded if shamelessly flagrant deletions in the annals of McMasters was performed by the brothers Fadi and Armen Haskell, who pulled up to their target's hotel in a rented ambulance from which they emerged wearing spotless white orderly uniforms, tunics buttoned across the collarbone, Fadi with a stethoscope at his neck, which universally brands one as a medical practitioner (although rarely does anyone consider you might instead be a safecracker). The Brothers Haskell raced through the lobby bearing a stretcher and, with quiet urgency, instructed those who'd just entered a waiting elevator to vacate and take the next free lift. Compliance was instantaneous. Achieving the eighth floor, they bore their empty stretcher down the long hallway and pounded on their target's door. When the bewildered occupant greeted them, Fadi brushed past him as if seeking an afflicted party. As the target followed Fadi back into the room, protesting that there was clearly some mistake, Armen set him straight by clubbing him from behind, rendering him unconscious. Placing the newly afflicted on the stretcher, they rushed him back to the elevator, which the operator had thoughtfully held for them, bearing them swiftly downward, ignoring all other floors. There, the doorman held wide the lobby doors, sharply warning hotel guests, 'Stand clear, thank *you*!', which greatly assisted the egress of Fadi, Armen, and their unconscious quarry. Over his shoulder, Armen advised the doorman, 'Have the front desk look at the registration for 814 for any possible family contacts. He'll be at Mercy Hospital!'

"They loaded their 'patient' into the back, Armen joining the nearly departed while Fadi took the driver's seat . . . and off they roared, waiting until they'd rounded a corner two blocks away to turn off their siren and rotating beacon. Fadi cruised in city traffic while Armen completed the deletion in the privacy of the ambulance. It was a moving experience for all, quite literally. Later that evening, they gave their deletee an informal burial at sea, dumping him in a reservoir several counties away."

Harrow beamed. "A starched white tunic, white pants, white bucks, and a sportily worn stethoscope will triumph every time. And when asked for a description, bystanders will tend to describe the uniform rather than the individual, even to the extent that they describe what they *think* a person in that particular uniform should look like. Depending on one's presumptions and prejudices, a construction worker will be described as gritty, a nurse caring, a soldier honorable."

Cliff could have sworn the dean was looking directly at him, although most of the assembled shared the same feeling. "This does not mean that your uniform ends with apparel. Accessories are invaluable. Anyone can wear a badge marked 'Press,' but if you also have a tripod with mounted camera and flashgun, the crowd will clear a path for you. A clerical gown will cover a multitude of sins including telltale stains, but if you must return to the scene of the crime, for God's sake bring a rosary so you may administer last rites to your victim while the police look on sympathetically!"

The man's face was concealed by an unfashionable fedora with its long brim pulled low, a wig of straggly gray hair, a false beard of a nearly matching color, and a pair of MacArthur-style sunglasses. Under an oversized trench coat, his frame was obviously padded. Any fool could see that he was trying to conceal his identity, but only Cliff could properly appreciate the poetry of the outfit he was wearing, since it was nearly identical to the disguise he had chosen for his inept murder attempt on the New York subway platform. If only Captain Dobson and Sergeant Stedge could see him now! And unlike all the techniques of impersonation that Doria had shared with him in exchange for pitching for her batting practice, McMasters' Wump labs had taught him that the easiest impersonation is when you don't mind people knowing you are in disguise, while still concealing who you really are.

Perhaps he had not been so wrong on the subway platform after all; he'd had the right idea but had lacked the education to apply it to the correct situation.

He was carrying the small attaché case in a large shopping bag with string handles, so as not to smear any of Fiedler's fingerprints on it. It was unlatched and slightly open within the bag so its contents could be easily accessed. He stepped up to the window of a female teller and counted out thirty-three hundred-dollar bills, a twenty, a ten, and three silver dollars, then pushed the money toward her, along with a completed deposit slip indicating the amount, the name of its intended recipient, and their account number. "There. I wish to deposit this."

The teller said, "Uh, one moment . . . Mr. Harding?" She stepped away and consulted with a bank officer, who rose from his desk and sidled up to the silly man.

"Good day, sir. Three thousand dollars is a great deal of money for a cash transaction," said the bank manager.

"Three thousand, three hundred, and thirty-three dollars, and it is not a transaction, it is a deposit," said the man in the foreign accent of a diplomat in a Marx Brothers movie. "I wish the money to be placed in the account of a Mr. Merrill Fiedler. You don't accept cash at this bank?"

"Well, we prefer not to accept cash sums over five hundred dollars without proper identification and some record of the money's source," explained Harding. "We wouldn't want to be complicit in money laundering or tax evasion, for example."

"Merrill Fiedler has no account at this branch?"

"I don't know the gentleman personally, sir, but . . ."

Harding had a word with the teller, who'd rummaged through a filing cabinet drawer and handed him a card. "What we *could* do is open an account for *you*, sir. All we'd need would be some pertinent information . . . name, identification, residence. Then you could write a *check* to this, um"—he consulted the card—"Mr. Fiedler."

"This is infuriating!" announced the costumed man, who was drawing the attention of customers and staff alike, so much so that the bank's guard worried his rage might be diversion for a robbery. The irate man rammed the rejected cash into his oversized pockets. "If you don't want Mr. Fiedler to have his money—a man who has banked with you for years!—I will find some other bank to assist me!" He turned on his heels, almost losing his fright wig in the process.

As Harding offered his apologies to the bank's customers, he noticed the costumed man had, in his anger, left the shopping bag with the empty attaché case in it. A swatch of tape had peeled away from its edge, revealing the monogram "M.F." which had been embossed on the case at Cliff's request at a jewelry store in Washington, D.C., just down the block from where he'd purchased it.

Harding handed the shopping bag to a young trainee. "Put this in our safe-deposit vault and don't touch the case itself. There's something suspicious about that . . . *man* wanting to make all that cash accessible to this Merrill Fiedler. If he returns for the case, tell him we'll need to see identification." He inspected the card bearing Fiedler's signature and pertinent information more closely. "If I have to contact the authorities, I'll lay you odds whose fingerprints they'll find on that case."

At 4 p.m. the pay phone in the lobby of Fiedler's apartment building rang long enough for Ricky the doorman to decide that answering it was preferable to hearing it for the rest of his shift.

"Hello?"

"*Who is this?*" came a menacing voice.

"I'm the doorman in an apartment building. This is a pay phone. I think someone gave you the wrong number."

"*No, someone gave me a wrong check. Let me tell you where you work. You're speaking from the lobby of the Monumental City Terraced Apartments in Guilford. Am I right?*"

There was no reason Ricky could think of to lie. "Yes."

"*Okay, so you tell Mr. Merrill Fiedler that his bookie not only knows where to call him each morning but also where he sleeps. And let him know if he doesn't pay me the three Gs he owes me by tomorrow, I'll help him touch his right elbow with his right hand. He's into more than that with some of my associates and I'll give them his address as well. You got that?*"

Ricky stammered, "Uh, not exactly. How much money . . . ?"

"*Where I'm concerned, it's three thousand, three hundred, and thirty-three dollars. That so hard to remember? Three is his lucky number,*" *except not this time. Either I'm paid tomorrow or his lucky nose will get broke in three lucky places. You let him know. Three thousand—"*

"Three-three-three-three dollars, yes sir." There was a click on the line. Ricky hung up the phone and returned to his station. Remembering that messengers who deliver bad news often get their heads handed to them, he decided to pretend it was the night doorman who'd answered the phone. He'd never liked Fiedler anyway.

Cliff, who'd portrayed the nonexistent bookie on the phone, knew that if he were successful that evening, the doorman would never be able to deliver the message to Fiedler, but Ricky would certainly remember the gist of what had been said, and that this amount was only a portion of Fiedler's outstanding gambling debts, should the authorities ever inquire. Who knew to how many nonexistent bookies Fiedler owed the same . . . or more?

♠

From the Second Journal of Cliff Iverson

Within days of my return to the area, I'd tested the shallow waters of Woltan's delivery entrance and marveled at how easily I could access their service elevator employing little more than a shabby overall apron with self-inflicted marinara stains, a dingy white garrison cap, and a flat box of hot pizza I'd purchased just before donning my uniform and upon whose receipt I'd simply scrawled the building's address, along with the name and floor of Fiedler's receptionist. Gesturing to the receipt was all the proof I needed to gain admission with no ID beyond the box's admirable reek of garlic and oregano. The guard, who'd seen me once or twice in the days when I was employed there, looked right through me. I was an unshaven pizza delivery guy, what was there to know about me? My limited test having succeeded, I got off on a low floor and left the pizza in a common room for all to enjoy. Piece of cake, or rather, slice of pie.

Two mornings ago, having already secured the highly coveted position of delivery boy at Fawn Street Florists, I ordered a COD bouquet from my home to be delivered that morning to Fiedler's secretary, Meg Keegan, at her desk. I then took my now raggedy-bearded self to Woltan, dropping off the modest bouquet "from an admirer" before Meg or Fiedler started their day. This last dry run confirmed that the office's layout and displays were as I'd last experienced them before McMasters, and that the spare key to Fiedler's office was still hidden in Meg's desk. I, of course, handed over the COD payment for the flowers from my pocket upon my return to work.

My thesis is tomorrow, dear X. Should all go badly, this will be my last entry in this journal. It's that sort of a thesis, the stakes being life-or-death for myself as well as for Fiedler. I have no bail-out plan. This goes against McMasters principles, and Dean Harrow did his best to persuade me from this approach, but this is the only way that will work for me, and that I can live with, should I be so lucky. So while this is not a suicide mission, it certainly is do-or-die.

The one thing I'm serene about is that, pass or fail, I've already set in motion the discovery of flaws in the W-10. Being a disgruntled former Woltan employee, my death under suspicious circumstances could only accelerate AirCorp's interest in the potentially lethal modifications made under Fiedler's regime. Surviving my thesis is a best-case scenario that I'm genuinely hoping for, but no matter the outcome, this last confrontation with Fiedler could spare many innocent souls. I can't bring back Cora or Jack. But I can try my best to protect others, people I'll never meet whose lives are easily as worthwhile as my own.

In any event, I want to reiterate, perhaps for the last time, my gratitude at the second chance you provided me, along with the invaluable gift of a McMasters education. Tomorrow, I will at last cross the line between the conceivable and the irreversible. Wish me luck, X, for I'll need it. And again, many thanks, no matter what the outcome.

XLIII

The nice young man might have been an antiques salesman or art appraiser. Nervous and withdrawn, his uneasiness as he entered Dolly Winslow's, a lounge secreted off Balboa Boulevard, made it seem as if he'd never been to this sort of bar before. Yet there was a well-bred, refined assurance beneath his willowy manner, as if he felt no need to apologize for his delicate features, slim frame, and aristocratic bearing. He was attractive, to be sure, dressed in a well-tailored gabardine suit. He set his matching homburg on the bar, revealing a smooth-sheened, almond-colored mane swept into a proud pompadour. He clearly sought anonymity, for he continued to wear his sunglasses even though Dolly Winslow's was as dark as a tunnel of love (for much the same purpose). In the corner, the club's lone woman was playing "My Foolish Heart" at an upright piano.

The bartender was a cheery fellow in his fifties who resembled a Santa who'd just shaved off his beard that morning. His long apron with an intricate flower pattern gave him the appearance of a den mother. He dealt a cardboard coaster onto the bar. "Evening, young man. What's your pleasure?"

"Perfect Manhattan?" The young man made most of his sentences end as questions.

The bartender would sooner have heard "rye on the rocks," for the bar was beginning to fill up, but he set about the task. One of his many roles was to make first-timers more comfortable in what likely was a much-debated visit on their part. "New to the area?" he asked over his shoulder as he measured precisely equal amounts of sweet and dry vermouth into a shaker.

"My first time here. Meaning Los Angeles, don't you know?" There was a certain lilt to his voice that was charming in this setting but which at a younger age in the schoolyard might have gotten him into trouble.

"Oh, don't let the natives hear you call this Los Angeles. This is Newport Beach. To us, LA's a million light-years away."

Someone lightly tossed an arm around the young man's shoulders, and he saw it was attached to a well-tanned gent in his forties wearing white trousers, an open navy blue shirt, and a white neckerchief. "We're over there," said the breezy fellow, gesturing toward a table near the piano. "I've made some new friends and the next round is on them. Join us? My name's Keith."

"Damon," said the young man. "Perhaps a bit later?"

Two men at the other end of the bar were making no secret of eyeing him. One was in his fifties while the younger one no longer looked quite as much younger as the older one would have liked. A sotto voce comment from the junior partner to his companion drew a short laugh. Damon returned their glances with curiosity, neither side averting their eyes, although the older man's laugh retreated into a knowing smile.

The bartender placed the drink in front of Damon, for which he quoted an exorbitant price. Seeing Damon's raised eyebrows, he counseled, "No one's trying to take advantage of you, son. It costs a bundle to make sure the local police give us the blind eye, the state liquor board takes their cut, and we have a few genteel bouncers mixed in with the crowd who intervene if there's any kind of trouble. Plus, we like to keep the premises in pristine condition. You know?" He cast a glance in the direction of the restrooms.

Damon reached into his pocket and laid down a ten.

"Thanks so much," said the bartender, not offering any change. "Now let me toss a little wisdom your way. I'd be just a mite careful who you go home with, should you decide to. Friday nights, we sometimes get a few rough-edged guests along with the regular crowd, and a nice, soft-spoken lad like yourself might have problems if things got, you know . . . a little crazy?"

Damon said, "But I enjoy it when things get, you know . . . a little crazy?" He took the smallest sip from his drink and slid gracefully off the stool. "Mm, that *is* a perfect Manhattan. Would you mind it for me, please?"

Past the piano was a loosely curtained doorway leading to a surprisingly long hall lined with framed eight-by-ten stills of Mary Martin performing a tasteful striptease, each image displaying an increasingly diminished costume. The hallway ended in restroom doors. Damon chose the one marked MEN.

The room was hospital spotless. Damon seemed to be the only occupant for the moment. That would soon change, of course, by the nature of things. The sterile setting and germicidal odors of pine and grape jarred "Damon" out of her adopted, languid manner, as she focused on the task "at hand."

No matter how often she'd rehearsed it in Eroticide, using props supplied by Vesta Thripper, it was a kind of assignation about which she'd had no knowledge before McMasters. She removed her sunglasses and studied her reflection in the mirror above the restroom's sinks.

It took a moment to find her face, so skillful was the wig and so effective the disguise, but after a few seconds she located Doria Maye looking back at her. *Sans* lipstick, powder, or pencil, she'd made the loveliest of young men.

Was she really going to proceed? She had to remind herself that this was hardly different from a doctor or nurse who deals with all aspects of the human body, its organs, fluids, and functions, in order to save the lives of total strangers. Her actions would be swift and presumably not painful for the as-yet-unknown other party, who of course was seeking and fully complicit in the anonymous transaction. *I'm not trying to do anything immoral or decadent*, she told herself. *I'm just trying to commit a murder.*

She'd researched the room on a previous visit, entering as a breathless woman in need of a restroom. She'd made a quick "mistaken" dash through the door marked MEN and swiftly verified that it was indeed ideally suited to the needs of her thesis.

There were four stalls. Doria now entered the one farthest from the door. As she'd confirmed on her earlier visit, there was a thigh-high circular aperture in the wall between this stall and the third, similar to what she'd been shown by Vesta Thripper at McMasters.

Precisely how Vesta had come by this enlightenment herself was anyone's intriguing guess. But here now was Doria Maye, star of stage and screen, standing in a men's room stall, about to lend a helping hand to an unknown patron of the lounge . . . all thanks to her having received a higher education.

She reached into her pants pocket and withdrew a luxuriant masseuse's glove, one side ermine, the flip suede, along with a vial of dark oil.

From her inner breast pocket she removed a shallow jar whose lid she unscrewed.

She heard the screech of the men's room door opening and closing. Was this an applicant? she wondered, feeling simultaneously apprehensive, foolish, and nervous. Yet she was no babe in the woods of Hollywood; she'd given assorted "back rubs" to the right casting directors, leading men, and even one leading lady—and certainly there was no victim here, except hopefully Leon Kosta. But what if this were an undercover policeman from the vice squad? How on earth would she then be able to explain all that was outrageously wrong with *this* picture? The Legion of Decency alone would see to it that she never made another movie again!

And then she remembered that was already her certain future if she didn't succeed here . . . and in all the dark hours ahead.

Only minutes later, her mission accomplished, she hastily departed both the restroom and Dolly Winslow's, aware of the many eyes that followed her, walked around the corner to where she'd parked her purloined Packard, and resumed her southerly drive to Torrey Pines. Leon Kosta would just now be finishing dinner at his country club more than an hour's drive to the north. She had a good jump on him.

Once his dead body lay on the floor, perhaps she would have another.

XLIV

Enquiry #2: *Have you given your target every*
last chance to redeem themselves?

Above her slit skirt, the blonde wore a yellow basque shirt whose black stripes struggled to remain parallel despite the swell of her figure, transforming her into a human YIELD sign for all male drivers who believed that owning their own vehicle made them an object of desire. While she waited to cross the busy highway near the entrance of the Surf Crest Motor Lodge, a passing truck demonstrated the effectiveness of its air brakes by juddering to a halt just two hundred yards beyond her. The driver idled his engine, anticipating the blonde's grateful dash to his cab under the darkening sky. She didn't budge. The driver grudgingly backed up until he was alongside her.

"I'm heading down to Ensenada in Mexico," shouted the driver. "Where you going?"

"Vermont," she said without looking at him.

He shrugged and the truck lurched on. She shifted her shiny bag from one wide shoulder to the other as a Pontiac skidded to a stop so that its driver could share his musings on the subject of headlights, to which she suggested a use for his dipstick he might never have considered. All this in less than a minute, indicating she had clearly dressed for success.

A momentary break in the traffic finally allowed her to cross all four lanes and reach the narrow uphill road that branched off the coastal highway to her quarry's home. If Kosta didn't arrive within the next hour, she'd have to trek up the hill to his retreat and feign a broken-down car on the main road, but she really hoped—

A sports car with a distinctive prow was approaching. She stuck out her thumb and pulled in a plum: Leonid Kosta, sitting short in the driver's seat. "You are in need of a ride?"

The blonde looked appraisingly from the shoulder of the road. "I'm in need of a lot of things. You got some?"

Leonid Kosta certainly saw his quota of aspiring starlets on a daily basis, and it was not unusual for the loathsome man to eye a fetching carhop with a sense of déjà vu, only to discover she'd auditioned for him the week before. In some instances, she might have even read some lines. Despite its notoriety, Hollywood is a relatively small town, and he often encountered a vaguely familiar face at a casting call, or among the extras while viewing rushes, or simply in a stack of eight-by-ten headshots on his desk.

"I am asking if you need a lift," he stated.

She cast her eyes knowingly down to her vibrant blouse. "What do you think?"

Kosta smiled. "How far do you want to go?"

"How far can you take me?" was her prompt response. Kosta thought: *Not Dorothy Parker or even Dorothy Kilgallen . . .* but there was something pleasingly familiar about her cheap banter, the kind his writers loved to swerve around the censors. In fact, her manner was reminiscent of the title character of *Ember Morgan Comes Home*, as was her appearance: the French streetwalker skirt and tight striped top were virtually identical to the novel's cover, except the top had been kelly green instead of this woman's canary yellow. Her blond hair had also delayed him from immediately noting the similiarity because Ember's was flaming red. But if Lucille Ball could go from brunette to blond to redhead, this woman was already halfway there. She looked a bit younger than he'd imagined Ember, and it would take time to train her, build up publicity—what was he thinking!? He didn't even know if she could read a line convincingly or, for that matter, read.

"I make movies," he was pleased to confess. "Have you ever acted?"

"Only on my impulses and honeymoons."

Who needs screenwriters when she can write her own dialogue?
Kosta noted.

She patted her open mouth, feigning a yawn. "Anyone can say
they're a producer. You could be a salesman who put a year's salary
into a car like that, just to impress a girl like me. Where do you live?
Where are your Oscars?"

Kosta opened the passenger door. "Get in and you'll see both," he
said. She did, and he sped them up Appian Way, the long dead-end
road that terminated at Ledge House.

His living room was suspended above the Pacific like the lounge
of a zeppelin on a windless day. Kosta ushered in his possible Ember
and made no move to turn on the lights. From his wraparound couch,
there was no sight through the wide-screen windows of the coastal
hills beneath them, only dim ocean to the horizon. But from below that
black edging at the seeming end of the sea, the sunken sun was still
defiantly trying to light the lowest band of the sky, and the resultant
glow was doubled in the broad mirror of water below it. Kosta let this
be the room's only illumination, not only fostering a romantic mood,
but veiling his less-than-dashing features in the merciful dusk. He was
an old hand at staging an evening at his home.

As she took in the increasingly poignant view, the little man
stepped to the stylish bar that had once graced the set of *Mad Abandon.* He was pleased to see Freja had left fresh ice before departing for
the day. He had not yet asked his guest for her name (it mattered little
because, should he grant her stardom, *he* would choose her name for
her) nor did he ask her what she'd like to drink, but simply began to
mix a pitcher of stingers, which he found worked well. As he plucked
cognac and white crème de menthe from a shelf below the bar, he
commented, "You asked where I lived. The answer is Holmby Hills...
this is merely my retreat. Still, does it seem like the residence of a
salesman?"

"I wouldn't know," she said, "I never go home with salesmen. How
many bedrooms?"

"More than enough for our purposes. Which particular one depends on what color sheets you prefer."

"Clean," she said. "Ironed and starched white cotton, providing maximum contrast for dark deeds." She flounced into a plush lounge chair. "You make some pretty big assumptions."

He swirled the pitcher's contents with a long glass wand. "How you negotiate the next hour may profoundly affect the course of your life."

"Oh, I never took that course," she said. "My mother couldn't afford me an education, except about men like you." She extended her legs, resting her heels on an ottoman. As his eyes followed the curves of her calves, he was surprised to note her oversized sandals.

"Not very feminine footwear you're wearing," he commented.

"They're not mine. A guy who picked me up on the road decided to throw a bottle party for me at an auto court near where you found me. A free drink's a free drink, but he started loving me beyond his means, so I hightailed it while he was in the can. Unfortunately, so were my shoes, these are his sandals. It at least guaranteed that if he tried chasing me, he'd have to do it barefoot or in stilettos." She dangled a sandal from her right toe. "That's why I was about to walk up the hill in hopes of being rescued by a knight in shining sports car."

Kosta escorted two pale bronze cocktails across the room and offered her the drink with the same solemnity as offering a contract, which to some extent he was, pending his approval of her performance tonight and, later, for the studio's cameras. She took the cocktail half-resigned, half-protesting her fate. "You know, some people are born with plain faces and lumpy bodies and no one assumes anything about them. God decided to give me a face that looks like I'm bound for trouble and a figure like I know what to do when I get there. After a while, it gets so you decide, okay, that's what everybody thinks I am, I'll try not to disappoint them." Her tone was more wistful than bitter, and it played nicely in the room. "I was a nice girl. I attended Baptist Sunday school, the pastor flirted with me and kept asking when I'd turn sixteen. In desperation, I converted to Catholicism and, stupid me, made my confession to the one heterosexual priest in the diocese. I have an okay brain, I've read a bunch of books and given them thought. I try to see the good in all people, but what people see in me is a good time who's been had by all. It's not very fair."

For all his libido, Kosta never fully left work behind him. He mused that if she could transmit this kind of tough vulnerability on the screen, he had his Ember. How would he launch her? In a B movie to see if people took to her? A single effective scene in a major picture? He lifted his glass. "Well, here's to you . . . what's your name, my dear?"

"Toby," she said. "And thanks for asking. Toby Jones."

That would never do. "Toby, you are at what they call a fork in the road."

"I don't think you mean *fork*," she said pointedly, and took a quick sip of her drink as if it were well-chilled hemlock.

"I'm saying I have a film part in mind for you. You could become a star overnight."

"Yeah, I guess 'overnight' is the operative word. Okay, so you have a fancy car and a fancy retreat. You may even have a mansion—still, that doesn't mean you're in the movie business. Every third man I meet says he can put me in pictures, and so far the most legit guy drew comic books."

"Come with me to my bedroom," he said, picking up both their cocktails and leading the way without looking back.

"Refreshing approach," she acknowledged. "I bet you say that to all the fallen women." She closed her eyes for a moment so as not to betray her rage. He'd not asked her where she was from, what she did for a living, why she was having to hitchhike . . . she clearly held no interest for him as a human being, beyond the ways he could personally, and perhaps professionally, exploit her. She was actually relieved by this. It made the next step easier.

She followed him up a short flight of stairs to a plush aerie with a wraparound ocean view; this one featuring dark cliffs to one side, the sun having closed shop for the day. A snug fireplace carved from mottled tan marble sported twin Academy Awards on its mantel.

"Those are just my spares," he said with a careless wave of his hand, thus calling attention to them. "Best Short Subject and Best Cartoon. The more significant Oscars are in Holmby Hills and my office."

"These are *real*?" she reacted, displaying what she hoped was appropriate awe.

"If they were counterfeit, do you think I would have had one made for *Catnip Catnap*?"

Toby approached the trophy on the mantel's left with reverence. "Jesus H. Christ. Can I hold it?"

"I suppose, but be careful in doing so. And if you were thinking of running off with it, I should be mentioning I did not leave the keys in the car, I have a loaded gun close at hand, and Academy Awards are only gold-plated."

Toby rolled her eyes across the heavens. "You think I'd be so stupefyingly dumb to steal something from you when you're offering me a *screen test*, for the love of Mike? Just . . ." She sat on the far side of the bed with the gleaming trophy in her hand and set it on the night table closest to her, staring at it as if it would give her resolve. ". . . just tell me what you want."

He tossed his blazer onto a lounge chair near the bed and began unbuttoning his shirt. It seemed the seduction phase of the evening had ended, and she hadn't even finished her drink. "Tonight will be the first of several tests you'll take for a specific part I have in mind, and you should try your very best. You already have a certain look and manner that fits the role of what we call a 'tough cookie.'" He placed his shirt atop his blazer. It took her a moment to learn that Kosta wore no undershirt because his chest and back were thickly stippled with snow white fur. "I need to know you also have warmth and a . . ."—he searched his mind—"a tender side as well. I don't care if it's real or not, I just need to know you can *present* that. It's not enough to let me have you, you understand? I need you to make me *like* you, to care for you as much as *desire* you. It is a tall order. Can you deliver? Do you think you can offer me that?"

Her features softened and her lower lip came forward a little as she murmured, in a voice less coarse, "I can try. Growing up, I had a lot of hard knocks, had to steel myself, you know? Maybe that reads as if I'm hard. But all I've ever looked for is a man who'd take the trouble to know me. For a guy like that, I'd do anything." She lowered her glance, half-embarrassed. "I mean that."

He liked her response immensely and cared not a whit if it was an act. If that were the case, she was already a more than capable actress. If not, she was a natural.

"Good," said Kosta with several nods of satisfaction, "this is good."

Her brusque manner reasserted itself. "Yeah, but before we start, book that screen test for me."

He snorted. "It's almost nine."

"If you're the head of a studio, they'll take your call."

Kosta groaned but reached for the phone on the matching night table on his side of the bed. His engagement secretary would likely be in at this hour, as she cared for her mother and had no life of her own, this being a key reason he had hired her. There were still no rotary dials in this part of Torrey Pines, and he instructed the operator, "Get me Stanley five-three-one-three in Hollywood."

As he waited, Toby continued to barter. "You'll have to let me hear whoever's on the other end. So I know it's a real call."

Kosta gave her a look but didn't protest as she sat on the bed next to him. He tilted the earpiece, allowing her to hear Martha's responses. "Martha, Kosta. I want to shoot a test on Monday at four. Book it for Toby . . . ?" He gave her an inquiring look.

"Jones," she reminded him. She'd only told him three minutes earlier but it was a hard name to remember.

". . . Jones. Have Whelan shoot it. I'll attend. Put it in my calendar."

He tilted the phone so Toby could hear: "*Yes, sir, Toby Jones, sir, Monday at four, have a good evening . . . I'm sure.*" The last was said in a knowing voice. This was not the first time Kosta had booked a screen test late at night. Many a time by Saturday afternoon there'd been another call to cancel it.

He hung up the phone. "Satisfied?" And she clearly was, for the call had accomplished all she'd wished. He stood and unfastened his belt buckle. "Then let's see if you have an award-winning performance in you."

"Can I give you my acceptance speech before I debut?" she asked with a playful moue.

At least the woman had a sense of humor, thought Kosta, and Doria Maye most certainly did . . . because as a private joke to herself regarding the diminutive studio chief, she had specifically removed from the mantel the award for Best Short Subject. She now cradled it lovingly to her bosom and spoke to an imagined throng. "I have but one person to thank for this incredible opportunity, a man who made me into the woman who stands before you now."

If she ever wished for verification that she was a fine actress, her ability in this moment to hide the trembling of her hands and racing of her heart was all the proof she'd ever need as she gave her target one last chance to reprieve himself.

Kosta hurriedly shook off his trousers, eager not to extinguish her compliant mood with the sight of his simian form. He almost knocked the bedside phone, a water carafe, and a pewter pillbox off the night table in his haste.

She rested the award at the foot of the bed and unbuttoned the back of her striped sweater. Off it came, along with much of her shoulders, revealing a dual-strapped bullet bra whose cantilevered construction was a triumph of engineering. With a proud smile, she unclasped its eight hooks and shrugged it down her arms. Kosta was first horrified, then angered as her sponge-like breasts fell from her chest to the floor. With another sweep of her hand, the blond wig was torn from her head, and although her painted features still obscured her real face, there was no mistaking the voice and carriage of the woman before him.

"*Now* will you admit I should portray Ember?" entreated Doria. She could not have been more open or vulnerable, especially with her oft-complimented real breasts bare for him to see. She'd proven she could inhabit Ember Morgan so convincingly that he was considering offering the role to a hardened hitchhiker with no acting experience. All he had to say was yes. It would be the right answer, in so many ways, for both of them.

His casting genius tarnished and lust diminished, Kosta regarded her with all the warmth of an X-ray machine.

"Oink," he said, this being the biggest and last miscalculation of his life.

It would have been aesthetically satisfying to Doria had this been his epitaph. But instead, he turned his torso away from her to reach for the phone, saying, "I'm calling for a tax–," which was not much of an exit line or acceptance speech. He was dead on arrival of the trophy's base to his cranium. Even at the last, when she was prepared to spare him, his behavior had made him irredeemable. Truly, Kosta had deserved his Oscar.

XLV

Enquiry #1: *Is this murder necessary?*

In the course of your existence, you may have once or twice awakened with the dawning sense that the day ahead might be life-changing. On this particular morning, Cliff Iverson woke with the certainty that the day would be life-ending . . . although whether it was Fiedler's life or his own that would cease this day was as yet undetermined. Unlike most McMasters students, he'd already failed once, and his thesis made no provision for a third try. As in a shoot-out on a Western street, only he or Fiedler would walk away from the showdown . . . unless each achieved the end of the other.

In the late afternoon he'd departed Fawn Street Florists for the last time, still in the guise of Ludis Lanka, while the owner was plying his craft in the back room. Cliff helped himself to a tall flower arrangement in the refrigerated display shelves, leaving cash that covered its cost on the register. His car was parked three blocks away, and walking there, women smiled at him and the flowers he was carrying, likely speculating if they were for a birthday, his mother, or a marriage proposal. Cliff doubted they were thinking *I bet they're for someone he's going to murder!*

In the back seat was an open cardboard tote box containing the bottle of liqueur he'd been given by Lilliana Horvath and a small wooden case the size of a portable record player. He placed the vase of flowers alongside them and drove to Woltan headquarters.

His face, already unrecognizable behind his beard now grown wild, was additionally obscured by the flower display in the box as he greeted the receiving guard at Woltan's deliveries entrance. He had confirmed during his recent trial run that the entrance still closed promptly at six, and it was now 5:49 on a Friday. Using hand gestures and uncertain English, he conveyed to the guard he would have to position the flowers by the office window, spray them, and treat them with plant food since the flowers would go untended over the weekend. At this late hour, he knew the receiving guard, eager to leave for the weekend, would advise him to exit the building via the main lobby. This was in accordance with Cliff's plan, for it insured no one would notice how long he was over-staying his delivery to the fourteenth floor . . . and when he did finally leave the tower, it would certainly not be in the guise of Ludis Lanka.

If he left the tower, that is.

Cliff reached the fourteenth floor via the service elevator, circum-navigated several corridors to arrive at the double glass doors marked WOLTAN INDUSTRIES – ADMINISTRATION. Unless Fiedler had de-cided to stay in his office until their 8 p.m. appointment, Cliff might have the place entirely to himself, knowing from his many late-night work sessions when he was an employee that the night watchman didn't look in until ten.

As he'd confirmed when reconnoitering a few weeks earlier, a small hutch was still located in the duplication room along with neatly stacked coffee cups and an electric percolator. He fiddled with its elec-tronic Ditto machine for a moment, filched a coffee cup, and pulled from a bulletin board Fiedler's weekly inspirational memo bearing his signature in bright aniline purple. He added these to his open tote box and headed directly to Fiedler's office suite, knowing from his recent dress rehearsal that Meg Keegan still kept a spare key to it in her desk. (Fiedler had once been locked out of his office by a female cost ac-countant whom he'd addressed in an amorous moment by the name of her predecessor.) But when Cliff gently tested the doorknob to see if it were locked from the inside, he happily discovered it was not.

Of course, if anyone remained in the office, his flower delivery would have explained his presence, and fussing with the arrangement—its positioning, watering, feeding—could have kept him there past any straggler's departure on a Friday evening. Fiedler would certainly want to keep private any transaction between himself and "Amigo" and could be counted on to instruct any late-working Woltan employee to de-camp for the weekend. And had Fiedler himself been unexpectedly present when Cliff walked in his office, it would simply mean their showdown would commence earlier than scheduled. But Cliff's calcu-lations had been correct, and he had the floor entirely to himself. The Woltan cleaning staff was always off Friday and Saturday evenings, not returning until Sunday night to ready the offices for the new workweek.

Cliff had known full well that by proposing to delete Fiedler at his place of employment, he was flying in the face of a McMasters precept. But Fiedler's private office was also his de facto bachelor's quarters, and Cliff had convinced the dean to let him hit his ex-boss "right where he lived."

He shed his work suit, beneath which he wore a black shirt and slacks, then removed in one motion Ludis Lanka's unkempt mane, tou-pee tape and all. He'd decided upon returning from McMasters that that a bare scalp would be his most effective disguise, at least where Fiedler was concerned, since he'd had a full mane while working at Woltan and few young men go completely bald in only a year or two. His shaved head also enabled a better fit for the several hairpieces he'd worn in recent weeks and should any of them have slipped, it would have been clear to any observer why he was wearing a wig: because he was *bald*, of course!

The black outfit topped by his wild beard, black-framed sunglasses, and sleek skull definitely skewed his appearance toward "menacing," the last word Fiedler would have ever applied to Cliff Iverson. But he wouldn't need to fool his target very long, for he wanted Fiedler to know exactly who he was before the thesis reached its conclusion.

It gave him genuine pleasure to occupy the chair behind Fiedler's desk, but he could only savor the feeling for a moment. There was immense risk ahead, to such an extent that Dean Harrow had been reluctant to approve the final step of his plan. Cliff understood his advisor's reservations but had explained that he'd mapped the only endgame that would allow him the chance to reclaim his old life free of self-reproach . . . should he be successful. It would require danger-ously blind faith in his appraisal of Fiedler's character. Both men's fates would rest in how accurate his assessment was.

From his cardboard tote box, Cliff produced a large roll of surgical gauze. He could credibly bandage both hands in under six minutes, and it was not even six-thirty, but he felt it best to do so, lest his target arrive ahead of schedule.

Merrill Fiedler returned to Woltan Tower after capping a supper of London broil and potatoes Lyonnaise with a double shot of rye to ratchet up his swagger when confronting Amigo. He was not bringing a penny of his horse race winnings to the meeting. If Amigo had been dumb enough to type *If you refuse to share, that will simply be my misjudgment*, then Fiedler was fine with letting that be the dumb sucker's blunder. The fiasco of those losing bets had cost him time, pride, and possibly Shari Dougan, so there'd be no apologies for his decision. He would merge "possession is nine-tenths of the law" with "winner takes all" and leave it at that.

Fiedler asked the guard in the main lobby if any unfamiliar faces had entered in the last fifteen minutes and been told a respectful "No, Mr. Fiedler, sir." Thus, he was genuinely startled to discover in his dimly lit office a smooth-scalped man garbed in black down to the canvas shoes he was—damn him!—resting on Fiedler's desk as if he owned the place.

The intruder's agile frame, shaved head, and wild beard gave him the appearance of an exhibition wrestler who cheats whenever the referee is distracted. Although the intruder's hands were swathed in gauze to his wrists, he held an office coffee cup like a tumbler and set it down on the surface of Fiedler's desk, ignoring a leather coaster placed there. He beckoned in a friendly drawl, "Well, now pull up a chair, my friend, and make yourself at home."

Fiedler was surprised to see a tall floral display on his desk alongside a squat bottle of liqueur bearing the curious label Zwack Unicum and a small wood case with a Bakelite handle. Fiedler was entirely confused and riled. If he'd ever saved *this* man's life, he'd certainly done so unwittingly and now regretfully, considering his high-handed appropriation of Fiedler's desk.

But Fiedler was prudent: first collect the money, *then* boot the bum out the door. He took what usually was the visitor's seat across his own desk from this stranger.

"'Amigo,' I assume?" he inquired none too pleasantly. Cliff gave a modest nod, pleased that Fiedler hadn't instantly recognized who he really was. It helped that only a single standing lamp in the corner was lit. Fiedler nodded toward Amigo's hands. "What's with the bandages?"

Amigo forced a contorted smile as he offered, in a refined legato that owed something to Doc Pinckney at McMasters, "Some freelance employees of the racetrack had a heated discussion with my hands regarding what temperature the outside of a furnace can achieve. It was either that or have my knuckles broken. I appreciate that the gentlemen offered me the choice."

"So should I assume your method for picking winners is *kaput*?" asked Fiedler, viewing Amigo's injury only through the prism of his self-interest.

"For a while, regrettably, at least until my hands get themselves healed."

"Well, while we wait for that day, how about you get out from behind my desk and give me my money as promised." In Fiedler's mind, the windfalls he'd been receiving were owed him by virtue of his existence and he now required recompense for his recent losses, even though he had neither bet nor lost a penny of his own.

"Why certainly, that's precisely why I'm here," responded Amigo affably. "If you'll be kind enough to type up a receipt, the amount will be yours in but a jiffy." He took his feet off the desk and removed the lid from the wooden case, revealing a Remington portable typewriter, barely half a foot tall, with a sheet of paper tucked neatly in place.

"What do you mean, 'receipt'?" asked Fiedler warily.

Amigo inquired, as if addressing a senior officer, "If I may be candid, sir? My wife is about to initiate divorce proceedings against me, and I'd sooner go broke than see her get what I've worked so hard for. That's why I've been settling all my outstanding debts, both financial and, in your case, personal, owing to your having saved my life."

"Yeah, and *when* was that exactly?" asked Fiedler, who was perfectly willing to accept the man's winnings without justification but who had become mildly curious about his noble deed.

"I'll prod your memory in a moment," came the reply. He lowered his voice and confided, "Truth is, if my spouse caught wind of my winnings at the track, she could try to claim it as community property. I'd sooner *you* have it, and I'm banking on your honor as a gentleman to share the winnings with me after the divorce is settled. That's why I need the receipt, just type: *Received as payment in full for gambling debt, the amount equal to . . ."*

The five-figure sum he named instantly tenderized the executive's resistance. "Fair enough," understated Fiedler. "So we're going to call my payoff a gambling debt?"

\ "Yes, and that will be true enough if you'd be kind enough"—he produced an oversized coin and slid it across the desk to him—"to flip it and call heads or tails."

Fiedler looked dubious, but then, money was money. He took the coin and flipped it. "Heads," he pronounced. The coin landed on the desk with an eagle facing up.

"Best two out of three shall we make it, then?" asked Amigo slyly. Fiedler again called heads and this time Lady Liberty showed her face, twice in a row. Amigo slid the coin back to his side of the desk with one of his bandaged hands. "Took a few tries but you beat me fair and square in a game of chance, and you could take a polygraph test to that effect. So now, if you'll just type up the receipt—"

"I don't type. I have employees for that," said Fiedler.

"You can hunt-and-peck, can't you?" Amigo held up his wrapped hands. "Clearly I can't."

It was Fiedler's nature not only to look a gift horse in the mouth but to count its teeth while he was in there. "But why typed instead of written . . . and why with a typewriter you lugged here when there are better ones all over this office?"

"Because I can throw this portable typewriter into the Chesapeake Bay, which I can't do with one of Woltan's typewriters, not without your staff noticing its absence. As for why it has to be typed, the receipt is to protect us both and if it's handwritten, it can't do that—" Amigo's patience was fast eddying away. "Look, I've made you some real money already, type the receipt and I'll explain how it works. If you don't like my plan, you don't have to sign it, right?"

"True enough, I suppose," Fiedler conceded. He hadn't looked at the layout of a typewriter in over a decade and it took him a while but eventually the undignified deed was done.

Amigo then produced the memo he'd removed from the bulletin board. "Now then: This note bearing your signature is posted all around the building. Anyone could have a copy. So instead of signing the receipt freehand, put the receipt on top of the memo and carefully trace your own signature."

Fiedler was genuinely curious. "The point being?"

Amigo smiled. "You know the truism that no one writes their signature the same way twice? Well, if you ever wish to prove that this receipt is a phony, all you have to do is ask any expert to compare the signature on this receipt to this memo. They'll match too perfectly, and the police *always* take that to mean it's a forgery. So if my wife ever goes after my winnings, I have this receipt that proves I lost the money to you. But if I ever use this receipt in a way you don't like, you can prove it's a forgery by showing the police or anyone you like that your signature was traced from this memo. Nice, huh? One document, two purposes. That's why we had to type it. Won't work if you wrote the receipt freehand."

Fiedler grasped the logic, but his inborn wariness kicked in. "Nah, I don't like it," he said flatly. "I'm thinking you want this receipt for the boys who burned your hands. You'll show it to them and then they'll come after *me* for the money. No dice." He removed the receipt from the typewriter, crumpled it into a ball, and tossed it into the wastebasket next to his desk. "And now I think I'd like to know exactly when it was I saved your life."

Looking defeated, Amigo put the typewriter back in its case. "You saved my life on the day you were shoved on that New York subway platform and almost fell into the path of a train."

Fiedler was instantly stunned and disoriented, Amigo's words felt as flat yet scorching as an electric iron . . . how the hell could he know about that incident? This race track slush fund for a rainy day he'd been anticipating was taking a bizarre turn. "And what . . . did I do that saved your life?"

Amigo shut the typewriter case. "You didn't die. Because if you had, I might have gone to the electric chair."

Fiedler didn't know whether to attack the stranger or run for the elevators. "*You're* the guy who pushed me?"

Cliff remembered his words from that strange morning in New York because he'd chosen them carefully, and he abandoned the dripping magnolia accent to quote himself. "Someday I hope it gets knocked into you—*knocked*, hear me?—how you made decent people dread going to work. You'd be as happy running a prison or a hospital, you wouldn't care. You just need to be The Boss."

And now, thought Cliff, *he knows who he's dealing with.*

Except, of course, he didn't.

"You better tell me who the hell you are," demanded Fiedler.

Cliff was stunned to be so unacknowledged. "It's *me*, Fiedler. Cliff Iverson," he said wearily, removing his dark glasses. "I worked here for a number of years, remember?"

Fiedler relaxed. He'd thought he might be dealing with a deranged intruder, but Iverson didn't alarm him one bit. "It was *you* who shoved me on that platform? I'll have you arrested."

"You'd have to prove that first and my tracks were expertly covered, no thanks to me."

"And this 'Amigo' thing is . . . if it's a prank, it's gonna be an expensive one, 'cause you're not getting a penny of what I collected and I want every dime you promised me for my wasted time. That's the only reason I'm here. To get that money."

Cliff begged to differ. "No, you're here to answer for what you did to Cora and Jack, if you even remember them. To make sure you remember, we're going to toast them." He reached for the peculiar liqueur bottle resting on Fiedler's desk and pulled its stopper, which emitted a pleasing pop. "Zwack Unicum was the professor's ritual drink to celebrate the conclusion of a project, so it's very appropriate today. I'll warn you, it's an acquired taste."

"I'm not drinking anything *you* pour for me, pal," Fiedler scoffed. "Not if you tried to kill me once already. For all I know, it's drugged or poisoned."

"Oh, don't be stupid, the stuff is harmless. Although a lot of people think it tastes pretty weird." He splashed a decent slug into his coffee cup and knocked back the liqueur in one swallow. "There, see? Why would I murder you before your misery has even started? Now pick out two manly glasses from that bar of yours. There's no money for you until we both drink to them."

The money was a matter of both profit and principle now for Fiedler. He grabbed the bottle and asserted, "I'll just keep this with me to make sure you don't slip something in it."

"Sure thing," said Cliff. "You pick the glasses, you do the pouring, it's all in your hands."

Fiedler selected two opaque green Kings Crown wineglasses from behind his office bar, brought them to the desk, and spilled the rusty gold liquid into them, pushing one toward Cliff while eyeing him warily.

Cliff accepted the offered glass. "That's all I ask, Merrill. One toast, one acknowledgment of the spirits you've crushed or degraded, the lives you've ruined or impaired . . . not to mention the souls on board the W-10 whose lives you'd risk solely to curry favor with the Woltan board." He paused and looked Fiedler in his eyes. "And Cora."

"She killed herself. That was her call."

Cliff fought to control his feelings. "Is suicide always a choice . . . or can a person be made to feel so alone and ashamed that there seems no alternative? You made Cora believe that ending her life was the least painful option she had . . ." He contrived a smile, continuing conversationally, "And I'm hoping you'll soon feel the same way. You see, I've been trying to make things so bad for you that you'll consider suicide yourself this evening."

He rummaged in a pocket and produced an opaque medicine bottle bearing a skull and crossbones. Patiently he explained, "So this is delphinine, a toxic alkaloid derived from the genus *Delphinium* in the Buttercup family. I'm told it offers a smooth transition from this plane to the next: a quick drop in blood pressure, slowed heart rate, and you're on your way. Euphoria leads quickly to unconsciousness with no pain. All in all, a very kind-hearted exit indeed." He helpfully slid the small cork-stoppered bottle to a position between their glasses. "I offer it in the same supportive spirit as a British officer handing a disgraced soldier a key to the study while advising him there's a revolver in the right desk drawer."

Fiedler looked as if he'd love nothing more than to hurl himself at

Cliff, but like a seasoned heavyweight in Round 1, he just bobbed his head slightly as he took the measure of his opponent.

Cliff was pretty sure he could hold his own with Fiedler, especially after his training at McMasters. All the same, it seemed a propitious time to set his adversary back on his heels a step or two. "Here's what's going to be a problem for you, Merrill," he explained. "Tomorrow, I send a report to Deterich Woltan in New York revealing that you sold secret design plans to Eddie Alderman of AirCorp in order to cover your gambling debts."

Fiedler blurted a laugh at this absurdity. "What plans would those be?"

"The duplicate diagrams of the W-10 you had me draft for you when I worked here."

Fiedler extended his reach to the cigarette case on his desk. "I asked you no such thing and I've never possessed any duplicate plans."

"An associate of Eddie Alderman's at AirCorp saw you park your car in the arboretum just to place a newspaper in a trash can several miles from your home."

"A Good and Plenty box. I took it, *from* the trash can . . . the betting slips."

"He didn't see the candy box, it was too small, but it's for certain he saw your license plate number and took photographs of it, and your car, and of you putting the newspaper in the trash."

"To cover taking the candy box. As per *your* instructions."

"Over the phone. There's no record I said that. Right after you put the paper in the trash can, Alderman removed an out-of-town news-paper containing airplane design plans unique to this office. And when the rest of those plans were left for Alderman on Rudgum Pier, you were spotted nearby less than an hour later at a bowling alley near Nags Head, hundreds of miles off your beaten track. You didn't play a single frame. You just reached into a bowling ball bag that had been checked at the alley by a man in a clumsy disguise—let's call him Mr. Obvious—who'd promised the bartender fifty dollars to hang on to it for a while. Mr. Obvious leaves and then, after just the amount of time it might take you to remove that heavy-handed disguise, you appear asking for the same bag. You check for something inside it, and shortly after, Mr. Obvious returns to claim the bag, paying the bartender with a fifty-dollar check made out to cash from your personal account, signed by you."

"You *forged* my signature?"

His pious outrage amused Cliff. "No, it was a personal check from your account, bearing your real signature, all nice and proper." He let that sink in and could almost hear the gears in Fiedler's brain rasping into motion—*What check would that have been? When . . . ?*—but Cliff continued smoothly, "Mr. Obvious is next seen at your bank the day before yesterday, trying to deposit three thousand, three hundred, and thirty-three dollars in your account, the precise amount you demanded from Eddie Alderman. Mr. Obvious ends up taking the money with him in a huff. Sadly for him, he left behind the case, the one you found in the bowling bag, which, underneath some tape, bears the monogram M.F. and has your fingerprints all over its latches and handle. I'm sure the bank assumes you or your accomplice were trying to deposit the cash into your own account while in disguise. Oh, and while it's difficult to raise fingerprints on printed money, your thumb and index-finger prints are on this silver dollar you were flipping just now, one of three you demanded from AirCorp." He gestured to the 1935 Peace silver dollar on the desk. "When I put it back with the remaining three thousand, three hundred, and thirty-*two* dollars, it will helpfully link the cash and W-10 plans to you, along with the prints on the attaché case, the testimony of Franky at the bowling alley, the personal check you gave him, and whatever surveillance evidence Alderman has from the arboretum."

Fiedler recalled that Iverson's strengths as a designer had thrived in the planning stages of a project, and this all sounded methodically devised. Still, their roles hadn't changed. He was Iverson's superior, and it was the employee's responsibility to convince the employer. "And tell me why a well-paid senior executive would do all this."

Cliff leaned across the desk and confided, "Because you have the fever. You play the horses and thought you had a system that couldn't lose, you crowed over your victories, you came to be a regular, disliked face at the payout window. Then you started losing big. Shari Dougan and a teller at the track will gladly recount the day you were so deluded in your invincibility that you tried to cash in six long shots, convinced they were winners."

"That happened one time only!" shouted Fiedler.

"Can you *prove* how many times you lost, Merrill? The grandstands of racetracks are carpeted with losing bets. The only reason we know of those particular losses was because you delusionally believed you had winning tickets. How do we know you haven't been losing all along, and only gloating over your few winners? There are roulette addicts who bet on both red and black with each spin because they need to win every time . . . until the ball lands on zero."

Fiedler nodded at Cliff's bandages with a snort. "You're the one who got his hands burned trying to cheat the racetrack." *So Fiedler hasn't yet realized the bandages are simply to avoid leaving fingerprints,* thought Cliff, his confidence bolstered. "Gambling is for losers like you."

"You don't gamble?" asked Cliff in mock bewilderment. "Your doorman, Ricky, sees you at your lobby pay phone every morning at half-past eight taking calls so your bookie doesn't learn your home phone and address. That same doorman heard you scream on the phone, 'I had nothing but losers. I lost plenty! I said you'll get your money!' And your bookie told Ricky you owed him three thousand, three hundred, and thirty-three dollars and threatened to break your arm."

Fielder rose menacingly. "I'll have you put in jail."

"For what, Merrill? Gifting you with my winnings from legally placed bets? Using my skill as a draftsman to call attention to the deadly flaws in the W-10 that you overlooked?"

"You took money from AirCorp."

Cliff clumsily removed a wallet from his pocket and displayed its plush lining of hundred-dollar bills. "I've yet to spend a cent of it. Alderman told me they'd say the money was advanced to me for my legal defense as a whistleblower."

"You impersonated me."

"I've never told anyone I was you, Scout's honor," Cliff assured him. "And by the way, I've been in Canada all this time. I'm there even now.

Since you last saw me, I acquired a new superior, the kind who'll go to bat for me. I'm nowhere to be found in the mess you're in, boss."

Fiedler was beginning to feel like a yearling steer being systematically isolated from the herd by a cutting horse. Seated on the wrong side of his own desk at the subservient level of the guest's chair, he noted the night sky wallpapered with clouds and the tall windows behind Iverson looking like onyx. His office was mutating into a luxurious prison. But Fiedler had not achieved his station in life by accident and he possessed as much cunning as others had compassion.

"All right, I've let you talk," he said, as if he were concluding a job interview and resuming control once again. "Do you want me to rehire you?"

Cliff's laugh was a reflex of genuine amusement, not even remotely bitter. "Oh my gosh, you be my boss again? How funny you are." He searched his mind for the right words. "Uh, no, you don't have to do a single thing for me. Just . . . go home." Fiedler looked at him uncomprehendingly. "Really. Or go wherever you like. It won't be in my hands, but just a question of whether Deterich Woltan and the board want you arrested or merely fired. The good news for you is that they may not want to publicize how close Woltan came to selling a deadly aircraft. They might let you resign without pension. But word will get out—I'll see to that—and nobody in this industry will hire you again."

Cliff stood as if their business was completed. "But if they press charges, I'm afraid you're looking at grand theft, and since some of the W-10s were slated for government use, maybe federal charges, too. Your best hope may be foreman in the license plate shop, although in prison, your underlings may have a different way of telling you they hate you."

Fiedler had always been slow to gauge new data, and all this had been a great deal to process in a few minutes, but Cliff was surprised to see him slowly smiling, almost serenely.

"That fifty-dollar check made out to cash . . . the one you say has my real signature? I think you made a mistake there." Fiedler could detect a cloud of uneasiness pass across Cliff's features. He continued, "I avoid like the plague writing checks for cash that any Tom, Dick, or Harry can use. There's only one such check I've written for fifty dollars in recent years. It went to Horvath's widow—Lulu or something—I couldn't recall her name, that's why I made it to cash."

Instead of being a monarch butterfly pinioned to a spreading board, Fiedler idly stretched his arms in alarmingly relaxed fashion. His predatory skills could spot an Achilles' heel at ten paces, and he was pleased to have found a breach in Cliff's armor. "I could drag her into this as your accomplice. She's old and alone. The accusation, the questioning, the fear could kill her."

Fiedler greatly enjoyed the view he was witnessing, that of Cliff attempting to mask his frustration as months of meticulous planning were being made meaningless.

"I'll always be at a disadvantage dueling with you, won't I?" responded Cliff, staring out the dark window as he considered the sheer pointlessness of his endeavor. "Because you don't care who gets hurt. Weeks of work and one stupid mistake . . ." The heel of his right bandaged hand struck the desktop. "So when you write a personal check to cash, you keep a record of who it's for?"

"My secretary does," Fiedler was pleased to inform him. "So tell me, what happens when the police ask Horvath's widow why she gave my piddling check to you . . . unless you were both trying to frame me?"

Cliff swore a single quiet curse, and all his bravado suddenly seemed no more than backed-up water vacating an unclogged drain. But as an aircraft designer, he had never dawdled when an unpalatable choice was the only option. "Well, I can't let Lilliana suffer more than she already has," he said.

"No, she's suffered enough," Fiedler humanely agreed, "though there's heaps more suffering in store for you."

Inexplicably, Cliff's mood seemed to brighten. "But then, it's not as if I didn't anticipate this. That's the advantage of a higher education." He removed a manila envelope he'd taped to the inside of the typewriter case and extracted two legal-sized pages.

"What's that?" asked Fiedler.

Cliff held the pages to his chest like a stern schoolmaster giving a last-chance makeup exam to an untrustworthy student. "This? This is your way out."

"You'll be the one who's lucky to get out of here when I'm done with you," said Fiedler.

"Oh, we'll both leave this building," Cliff assured him. "The only question is which one of us leaves vertically and which horizontally." He handed him the pages with a bland smile. "I'm very eager to learn your position on this."

XLVI

Dobson's Rule #3: *Create Ignominy*

Debased by Kosta yet again with his porcine epitaph of "Oink," all the detachment and coolheadedness that McMasters had infused in Doria had vanished as she swung the Oscar at the back of his head with a defiant cry, dispatching the loathsome ape to oblivion and all points south. It was harsh comportment by McMasters standards, a lapse into mindlessness that the conservatory could never officially endorse, yet it had undoubtedly bolstered the lethality of her swing.

Doria could also attribute her emphatically successful deletion to her daily regimen in the batting cage, a battle she won on the playing fields of McMasters, honing her swing into a short but powerful one, for the necessity from the outset had been to achieve her objective with one blow. The thought of merely stunning him, then having to club him repeatedly as he scrambled about like a half-dead spider was repugnant to her, although the aptness of him playing arachnid to her avenging swine did not evade her. Luckily, the Academy Award she employed was not from the war years when, owing to a shortage of metal, the statuette had been made from gold-painted plaster. This Oscar weighed in at a healthy ten pounds and with her grip on the trophy being tightly wrapped around Oscar's torso, its base made for a truly distinguished blunt instrument, an honor second only to being bludgeoned to death by the Nobel Peace Prize.

Having at last performed the deletion for which she'd prepared as earnestly as Nora in *A Doll's House*, she went back to the living room and withdraw from her bag a pair of rubber gloves, a vial of 91 percent rubbing alcohol (the preferred McMasters solvent for its additional uses in treating cuts, erasing ink, and starting fires, although one of the school's least favorite poisons, being painful and yielding uncertain results). She'd kept scrupulous track of what she'd allowed herself to touch, "Keep your hands to yourself!" being a McMasters adage. Obviously, the Oscar and her cocktail glass needed to be wiped. Fingerprints were near impossible to lift from fabric, so the items of clothing she would be intentionally leaving behind needed no care, including the multiple hooks on the back of her well-padded brassiere, which were too small to retain an individual print.

She quickly slipped into a normal bra and a deep gray blouse she'd produced from her bag, then withdrew what looked like a pair of black satin panties (although they were not precisely that) and the sealed specimen jar, now wrapped in the warmth of a protective hand towel, whose contents she had acquired in the restroom of Dolly Winslow's.

The next task was the most difficult for her, but luckily it would only take a moment, in which she would be putting matters not only behind her but Kosta as well.

A private security patrol car eased up the long curve of Appian Way and stopped six blocks above the coast highway. "You okay, Miss?" asked the man in the passenger seat, aiming a flashlight on an attractive woman with short-cropped hair in a deep gray blouse and black skirt.

She looked up from the leash she held, her just barely visible dog stirring behind a favorite tree. "Sure, but thanks for your vigilance." She gestured to her dog. "His name's Spunky, but mother says we should have called him Spongy 'cause he holds so much damn water." The leash wriggled in her hand as the patrolman laughed and drove on.

Doria gave the leash two hard yanks and the realistic Steiff mohair terrier landed at her feet. Parisian ladies of the night had long ago learned that walking a dog answers the question of what they're doing out alone late at night. The problem had always been what one does with the dog when a client expects undivided attention. The stuffed doll on a stiff leash had been her bailout should she be seen by a patrol car, and her preparation had proven wise.

She returned the Steiff dog to her bag and continued downhill another four minutes back to the Surf Crest Motor Lodge, where she'd parked her "loan-out" Packard and rented a cabin two hours earlier—"cash in advance, *sir*," the disinterested owner had said, giving the 'sir' a little something extra as he'd surveyed the prim man who'd registered as "Toby Jones." She drove the car to the Torrey Pines racetrack outside the abandoned Camp Callan, parked it by some shabby barracks, and left the keys in the ignition. Some teenagers with time on their hands were bound to take it for a drive and ditch it elsewhere, while she would take the ten-fifteen Los Angeles bus from the Camp's gates to Union Station. From there, she'd call the police from a pay phone with a husky-voiced tip about a body at 805 Appian Way in Torrey Pine (using the singular of "Pines" because she'd been taught that a hard *s* can betray gender), check her bag in a locker and throw away the key, don her "Doria" wig and makeup in the ladies' room, take a taxi to Palermo's Ristorante across the street from the studio, have the hardest-earned and most-deserved martini of her lifetime (maybe two), and reenter her bungalow on the studio lot as if she'd stepped out for a quick one across the street, momentarily unnoticed.

She looked at her watch. It was nine fifty-five. Kosta's phone call to his engagement secretary, Martha, established him as being alive shortly before nine. She didn't think she'd need an alibi, but a conscientious McMasters student makes sure to have one all the same. Doria had the comfort of knowing that, if all had gone as her thesis anticipated, she had just been miraculously photographed in various seminude poses in her bungalow on the studio's back lot, some two hours away.

Captain Dobson might have inquired: But how could that be? If she'd managed it right, it would be a question the LA police would never ask.

Lieutenant Congreve took in the Ledge House crime scene and popped a stick of gum to cover the bad taste in his mouth from the sight of it. Having to wait for a second-string coroner's permission to proceed didn't make him any happier, and he took it out on the fledgling detective he'd been saddled with for the last week. "Well? Come on. What do you make of it?" he asked.

"Robbery gone wrong, sir?" offered Timmons much too quickly. He gestured toward the blond wig, oversized bra, and what appeared to be black satin panties. "Lady cat burglar breaks into movie producer's home, he discovers her, wham?"

"So I should issue an all-points bulletin for an amply endowed naked lady?" suggested Congreve. "That should bring out most of the force. Why'd she undress?"

"He ripped the clothes off her?" asked Timmons.

Congreve swore at the man and said with false patience, "Look around you. Very peaceable crime scene except for the poor dope's skull. No sign of struggle or burglary in progress. The guy was already naked under the sheets, his guest was undressing at the foot of the bed. Look. Think."

"All yours, gentlemen," said the prim-lipped coroner, rising from the body with a swab that he placed in a glassine envelope. "I'm going to let Downtown handle the autopsy. Victim would seem to be a Hollywood bigwig and they usually slip on the kid gloves for that sort of thing. Especially under *these* circumstances."

"Sordid story?" asked Congreve.

The coroner affirmed this with a quick, distasteful bob of his head.

The lieutenant turned to his assistant. "Want to try again?"

The aspiring detective looked around the room in quiet despair. "Safe to say we're looking for a woman?"

"Really. Blond wig, oversized bra but padding on the floor, size twelve sandals, and a gaff?"

"What's a gaff?" asked the detective-in-training.

"Oh, poor baby. A *gaff*. A *cache-sexe*. Panties with panels. Male entertainers who impersonate female celebrities use them to hide their private parts." Congreve bent down and asked the police photographer, "You got a picture of this?" indicating the black undergarment. The photographer said he had, and Congreve lifted it off the floor with the eraser of a pencil and dutifully peered within. "Stain on the inside panel. I'm betting it's semen." He offered it to the coroner, who was removing his gloves. "Semen?"

"We'll have to wait for tests, of course, but it would hardly surprise me," said the coroner with an air of disdain.

The lieutenant turned to Timmons. "Semen. So turns out we're not looking for a woman after all, are we? Motel says there was a soft-spoken man of interest registered this evening, room's been abandoned without being slept in." Timmons stared dimly. "Think! Padded bra, oversized panties, traces of semen?"

"I found it *elsewhere* on the deceased's person as well," added the coroner.

"Elsewhere . . . ?" Congreve ventured.

"Quite sordid," pronounced the coroner gravely.

XLVII

"Even with your lack of interest in aircraft design," Cliff explained to Fiedler as he handed the two pages to him, "you know that when I create planes for the government with top secret systems onboard, I'm required to include a self-destruct mechanism so that the system can't fall into enemy hands. And the first rule of self-destruct mechanisms is that there damn well better be a way of turning it off should it be accidentally tripped. If there isn't, the Pentagon, the pilot, and the crew will be peeved as all hell with me." Cliff turned the pages toward Fiedler. "For you, this letter is the equivalent of that 'undo' switch."

Fiedler reviewed the succinct page.

To Whom It May Concern:

Cliff Iverson is responsible for the difficult circumstances I find myself in, circumstances that might destroy my name and reputation and place me at risk of losing my freedom. I here stipulate that no other person is responsible for the problems I face, and I wish to ensure no blame falls on any "innocent bystanders," with particular emphasis on the late Jacek Horvath's widow, Mrs. Lilliana Horvath. As stated above, there is only one malefactor in this sorry situation, and I blame no others.

Signed this day of _____.

Below the blank date was another line for a signature.

Fiedler's puzzled expression prompted a quick response from Cliff. "Within an hour of my giving the fifty-dollar check you sent to Lilliana Horvath to the owner of the bowling alley, I feared I might have made a mistake. And regrettably, my first obligation is not to your downfall but to Lilliana's welfare. It was childish overreach on my part, and it's turned out to be my undoing. The check was unexpected ammunition I hadn't needed, and I realized too late that you or your secretary might recall who it was intended for, dragging poor Lilliana, who had absolutely nothing to do with this, into my scheme. I casually mentioned the check just now as a test, hoping it would fly below your radar, but no such luck. You're sharper than I took you for."

"Damn right," agreed Fiedler.

"I was taught a good plan never allows any room for sentimentality, but I suppose even my advanced training can't completely change me being the person I am. So I came here this evening prepared for this. Absolve Lilliana and I'll get you out of this mess I got you into."

Fiedler held the piece of paper as if it might be infected. "But why *my* signature on this?" he asked warily. "You're the one who framed me, shouldn't it be *your* signature?"

"I'm the one who framed you, so my absolving Lilliana carries no weight. But if you, the victim, say it was all me and no one else, that'll hold water. I want Lilliana to have this as her insurance against you, no matter what happens to me."

Fiedler shook his head. "I won't even consider signing anything until you explain how you're going to clear *my* name."

"With this," Cliff replied. He handed him another page from the manila envelope. "It's my total admission to having set you up."

The document outlined all of Cliff's actions in detail. Fiedler took his sweet time reading it, so much so that at one point Cliff looked at the clock on the desk, adding, "That's the deal. You sign the disclaimer for Lilliana, I sign the confession for you. It's my best offer and if you don't take it, I'd encourage you to try this as your next best recourse." He stared at the bottle of poison biding its time between the two untouched glasses of liqueur that Fiedler had poured. "No matter what you choose, though, we're drinking that toast to acknowledge the wrong you did to Jack and Cora. That's part of the deal I'm offering."

Fiedler again eyed the Lilliana Horvath "exoneration" and countered, "Fine, but you sign your confession first."

Cliff rolled his eyes. "Don't insult me. I wouldn't put it past you to grab my signed confession, race out of here, and leave me up the creek with no paddle for Lilliana."

"And what's to stop you from doing the same?" Fiedler countered, not without cause.

Cliff shook his head as if Fiedler were a child. "Don't be stupid, Merrill. My confession gets *you* off the hook, what I'm demanding *you* sign only gets Lilliana off the hook. I'm in deep trouble either way." Cliff again glanced at the clock. "If memory serves me, the cleaning crew should be starting their rounds pretty soon." Fiedler started to comment but thought better of it. With bandaged hands, Cliff managed to extract a pen from Fiedler's desk set and rolled it toward him. "Sign it, roll the pen back to me, and I'll do the same with my confession. Then we can swap them."

Fiedler sat motionless, which Cliff knew was his most dangerous mode. At meetings, he might appear to be pensive, weighing opinions voiced around the conference table, but he was actually as inert as a spider on a freshly spun web, patiently waiting for someone to blunder and become his next casualty. Now Fiedler was calculating the odds, a branch of math at which he truly excelled.

"Fine," he said at last, and, without further hesitation, signed the document exonerating Lilliana, then folded his arms across it.

"Hang on. Let me see that you signed your real name," instructed Cliff. Fiedler shrugged, held up the document for inspection, then pushed the pen and Cliff's as-of-yet unsigned confession to his side of the desk.

Cliff reached with his bandaged hand for the pen, his eyes shifting to the desk clock as he grumbled, "Fine. I'll sign this, and then we'll exchange documents like we're trading spies in the middle of the bridge between East and West Ber—"

There was a sudden noise outside the office. "Damn," said Cliff, standing. "I didn't think they started cleaning *this* early . . ." He strode from the office, leaving the confession on the desk.

The noise was coming from the duplication room toward the back of the office. He opened the door and stepped to where an electric Ditto machine had started a printing cycle even though there was no paper loaded in it. He quickly flipped a switch and the machine ceased its rhythmic grind.

He had only left Fiedler's private office for a moment and when he returned his former employer was seated exactly where he'd left him, very still, and Cliff's confession was just where he'd left it, as was the pen. "False alarm," Cliff explained. "The Ditto machine decided to start up on its own. So where were we?"

"You were about to sign that confession," Fiedler reminded him in an unusually even voice. "Then you were going to exchange it for this, uh"—he looked down at the page—"this Get Out of Jail card for the Horvath woman."

Cliff managed to wedge the pen in his bandaged hand, wrote *Clifford*, and paused. "This is not an easy decision for me, you know. You'll have even more power over me than when I worked here. And for deviating from my plan, allowing my concern for Lilliana to steer me off course, my final grade is sure to be a Fail."

These last words had no meaning to Fiedler, of course. But oddly, he responded, "I suppose you could always say I forced you to sign it, at gunpoint or something, and claim I'm trying to make you the fall guy for things I've really done."

"Oh, you've thought that through already, have you?" said Cliff, his pulse rate doubling even as he struggled to keep his face sullen. God, it would be *such* a good sign if he was reading Fiedler's mind correctly! "Yeah, it would be a case of your word against mine."

"He who laughs last," said Fiedler reflexively. It seemed an odd response unless Cliff was correctly aboard Fiedler's train of thought, as he fervently hoped he was.

Cliff sighed, added *Iverson* to his first name at the bottom of the confession, and inscribed the date below it. He wondered if Fiedler would pounce for the document but, no, he just nodded like a high school principal who's gratified a student has *finally* done the right thing.

"So now we swap them, right? On three," said Fiedler, and began to count aloud as if they were playing rock-paper-scissors.

Cliff dutifully chimed in on "two" with this man he despised and on "three," he pushed the confession across the desk as Fiedler responded in kind and the exchange was made.

Cliff broke the momentary silence. "I still want to drink that toast," he insisted, folding up the Lilliana exoneration.

His ex-employer made a face that resembled annoyance. "It seems sloppy-sentimental to me, but if it's what you want, I won't let you say I didn't live up to my word. We can toast both of them and I'll throw in two choruses of 'Auld Lang Syne' for nothing." Fiedler took the green glass closest to him and raised it. "Here's to Jack and Cora: Time cuts down all, both Great"—he indicated himself—"and Small." He winked at Cliff. "Bottoms up."

They downed their drinks. Cliff's throat reflexively tightened as his tongue detected an odd, vile flavor so unlike the glasses of Unicum he and Jack Horvath had shared of an evening. But his intellect overrode his impulses and he swallowed.

Fiedler looked at the bottle. "Strong stuff," he commented. "Not like anything I've had before. Maybe anisette?"

Cliff had always considered Zwack Unicum to have a medicinal, cherry cough syrup flavor with nods to licorice and burnt plum pudding. This acrid glass of the liqueur, however, tasted nothing like that. "So, I think we're finished?"

Fiedler was unable to resist. "If you're using the royal *we*."

The two men appraised each other.

"Now what?" asked Fiedler.

"We wait."

"For what?"

"For the poison to take effect," offered Cliff.

Fiedler did not seem alarmed but acted mock wounded. "Oh, now you've hurt my feelings! You're thinking I put the poison in your glass while you stepped out of the room? To be rid of you and your knowledge of the W-10 completely? To pocket the money you showed me in your wallet, to tear up my exoneration of the Horvath woman and leave your confession by your body so it looks like you committed suicide? How suspicious you are, Cliff! Did you even consider that I've done nothing and that the liquor isn't poisoned?"

Cliff shook his head a bit sadly. "No, I can assure you there's poison in both glasses."

Fiedler took his time in replying because time, he felt, was currently working to his advantage. "I give my word I didn't pour the poison in that bottle into both glasses."

Cliff smiled. "Oh, well, here's the thing: The poison bottle doesn't contain poison. It contains potassium permanganate, known as Condy's crystals, which, when interacting with delphinine, instantly renders it harmless. It's not exactly an antidote, it simply changes the poison into a nontoxic but awful-tasting liquid, as I can attest. But for simplicity's sake, let's call it the antidote."

"So this was another stunt? There was no delphinine?"

"Oh no, it's real. It's already in the liqueur, enough to kill both of us. I added it to the bottle today. It was in both our glasses."

Not easily suckered, Fiedler shook his head. "No, the poison can't be in the bottle, because you already drank the liqueur that you poured straight out of the bottle."

"Yes, I poured it into my coffee cup, but my coffee cup contained the same potassium permanganate that neutralizes the poison. I put it in my cup before you arrived."

Fiedler's smile dissolved, replaced by deep-seated terror. To Cliff, it was just the loveliest sight. "You're saying you've poisoned us both?" he choked.

"Well, if you *didn't* try to poison my drink, and we both drank the Zwack in its current state, then yes, we are both poisoned. But no need to worry! You have *just* enough time to take the antidote right now. It should still be in the poison bottle. I'm afraid there's only enough for one person, but I'll let you have it. Here, let me pour it for you—" He pulled the stopper out of the stoneware bottle and tried to empty its contents into Fiedler's glass but, of course, the bottle was empty.

"Oh dear," said Cliff, all vexed to high heaven. "It seems you *did* put what you thought was poison in my drink. So now the antidote is gone.

I was sort of gambling on that. Get it? My very last bet, where you're concerned."

He offered a friendly smile as Fiedler's look of snowballing horror changed to one of intense pain as he clutched his midsection. "You're dying, you understand, yes? If you'd done nothing with the supposed poison, then we'd both be dying . . . but I would have let *you* have the antidote, honest. I'd have deserved a"—he searched for the phrase—"a taste of my own medicine." Fiedler was now hearing Cliff's voice as if through a speaking tube from a very great distance. "Oh, and by the way, I guess you're also learning I kind of exaggerated the part about it being painless."

The room began to divide for the dying man, who felt as if he were simultaneously sliding down a steep slope and up a precipice. He divined a flavor within himself he'd never before encountered, and he heard his body advising him internally, *I have no way to override this, I can spasm with every muscle I possess but I must yield to it and my heart must stop.* He sensed there was something greater in existence than himself, but knew at his core he could never achieve the higher plane where it resided. Fiedler was fast severing all connections with a world that would continue perfectly well without his presence or memory.

Say what one might about the pain associated with delphinine, it was at least swift. It took only another minute for Fiedler to become the boss of no one. If there were an inferno in hell reserved for damnable employers, Fiedler was now well and truly fired, unto eternity.

Looking at the vehicle of Fiedler's body now divested of its driver, Cliff could only wish more Woltan employees had stood up to the man and said, *Who are you to pour your poisonous self into the only life we have?* Maybe then the monster might have been nullified in some other way. But Cliff had no illusions about his own culpability. His entire thesis had banked on Fiedler's susceptibility to killing him, with Cliff becoming a lion tamer whose act consisted of lying down in the center of the ring precisely at feeding hour. Had Fiedler done anything other than try to murder him, Cliff would have ingested the poison himself. And had that been the case, yes, he truly would have given Fiedler the antidote in the stoneware bottle. Cliff had convinced the dean that he was sincere in this aspect of his thesis . . .

. . . but of course, not being suicidal, Cliff *did* happen to have an additional bottle of the antidote in his pocket. Once Fiedler tried to poison him, however, he felt no responsibility to inform his target of this fact.

Cliff knew he was just as responsible for this deletion as any Mc-Masters graduate had ever been. But it was a death he could live with.

Removing his clumsy gauze bandages, he put on a pair of surgical gloves from his pocket. From the desk, he picked up the legal-length page Fiedler had signed to exonerate Lilliana and withdrew another typed sheet of the same length from the manila envelope—one he had not shown Fiedler—and brought both to the paper guillotine located at the back of the outer office.

As a draftsman, he was no stranger to straight lines and, placing the two sheets precisely three inches past the cutter's edge, he cleanly sliced the top of both pages away. In the case of the page that Fiedler had signed, this neatly removed its "To Whom It May Concern" heading, which Cliff had intentionally typed above that demarcation point. He had already typed another "To Whom It May Concern" *below* that point on what was this new first page.

He then took a large metal stapler from Meg Keegan's desk and brought it into Fiedler's office, put Fiedler's right fingers on its handle, and used his lifeless hand to staple the two pages together. He then moved the portable typewriter to where Fiedler might have used it before drinking the poison and set the pages and stapler alongside it.

The new first page (the one Fiedler had never seen) read:

```
To Whom It May Concern:
    I, Merrill John Fiedler, am alone responsible
for the misfortunes that have befallen me. That
is why I have chosen to end my life.
    I took to gambling and after a string of
victories which I now attribute to beginner's
luck, I suffered some extremely serious losses
both at the track and with illegal betting
parlors and bookies.
    Needing a large sum of cash in a hurry, I
```

made a very bad decision. I decided to sell
an advance look at the designs for the W-10
aircraft being manufactured by Woltan
Industries to a competitor. I absolve the
competitor, who will go unnamed here, of all
blame. Their interest in the drawings, created
by former employee Cliff Iverson for my personal
use, concerned a deadly flaw in the design.
    I am also singly and totally responsible
for the decision that created that flaw.
I wish for the record to assert that no one
I've worked with at Woltan, especially Jacek
Horvath and the aforementioned designer named

This was the end of the first page. The second, also now minus its
top three inches as well as the heading "To Whom It May Concern,"
continued:

Cliff Iverson is responsible for the difficult
circumstances I find myself in, circumstances
that might destroy my name and reputation and
place me at risk of losing my freedom. I here
stipulate that no other person is responsible
for the problems I face, and I wish to ensure no
blame falls on any "innocent bystanders," with
particular emphasis on the late Jacek Horvath's
widow, Mrs. Lilliana Horvath. As stated above,
there is only one malefactor in this sorry
situation, and I blame no others.

It ended, of course, with the day's date and Fiedler's typed name
below the signature his freshly deceased employer had inked with the
pen that Cliff now placed atop the two newly trimmed letter-sized pages.
    Yesterday, before he'd typed this confession for an unwitting
Fiedler, he'd taken a pocketknife and scored a few nicks into several
letters on the typewriter's typebars, guaranteeing that anything typed

on it could be matched to the pawnshop-purchased machine. Then, wearing surgical gloves, he had put a virgin ribbon in the machine, advanced it ten revolutions, and typed the two-page "suicide note," the second page of which had, on its own, seemed to simply be an exoneration of Lilliana.

When finished, he'd wound the ribbon back to its unused beginning, upon which Fiedler had, just this last hour, typed the "paid in full" receipt he'd decided not to sign.

Cliff couldn't have cared less whether Fiedler had signed the receipt. Its sole purpose was to get Fiedler's fingerprints on the typewriter keys.

Now, still wearing the surgical gloves, he carefully eyeballed the ribbon, until it came to within a few letters of where he'd begun typing the complete note yesterday. He then advanced the ribbon to just past the last words typed on it. In the unlikely circumstance that the police bothered to examine the ribbon, it would look like Fiedler had previously typed a receipt for his bookie to sign, with the initial intent of paying his gambling debt, the page now crumpled in the wastebasket and bearing Fiedler's fingerprints, but later, realizing that AirCorp and Eddie Alderman were likely going to expose his cover-up regarding the W-10's fatal flaws, had typed the suicide letter instead. The unsigned receipt, if retrieved, would merely enhance the recounting of a desperate man's final hour.

Cliff took his own glass, rinsed it in the sink of Fiedler's wet bar to make sure there was no residue of the liquid he'd drunk (although it bore no trace of poison, thanks to Fiedler having neutralized it), and replaced it on the shelf. It gave him pleasure to ignite his own confession with the big lighter on Fiedler's coffee table, let it burn until it was nothing but ash, then rinse it down the drain, letting the water run long and hard.

He, of course, left on the desk the poisoned bottle of Zwack Unicum that, happily, bore Fiedler's fingerprints, but pocketed the protective bandages he'd worn and the empty poison bottle. He would remove his surgical gloves just before exiting the elevator, and dispose of them, the gauze, and the empty poison bottle once he'd left the building via the main lobby, where there was no record of his arrival. He would just be an employee who had worked late. The generic delivery uniform he'd worn over his black outfit would be found folded in the broom closet, with nothing to link it to the flower shop, where no more was known about Ludis Lanka other than his willingness to work for a meager salary and tips.

He locked the dead man's office with the spare key in Meg Keegan's desk and returned the key. The night watchman knew better than to disturb Fiedler's infamous lair when it was locked. No one would find his employer's body until well into Monday morning.

In the duplication room, he turned off the timer he'd set on the electronic Ditto printer that had been responsible for the momentary distraction, one that had permitted Cliff to leave his glass unattended, which he'd done to give Fiedler the opportunity to poison him, if he so chose.

The police would certainly deem Fiedler's death a suicide. But Cliff knew better.

Merrill Fiedler had murdered himself.

XLVIII

Enquiry #3: *What innocent person might suffer by your actions?*

Although unmoored from her McMasters-sanctioned game plan and now acting entirely on her own recognizance, Gemma feared the conservatory still expected her to attempt her deletion. She knew the penalty for failure (or failure to act) was dire, and yet her approved stratagem was clearly inoperative. While McMasters would never so crudely articulate her current state as "kill or be killed," the thought was uppermost in Gemma's mind.

If she hadn't found a way to deal with Adele far away from the workplace—as the conservatory's curriculum had sternly counseled—she'd at least found a setting outside the main hospital: a pediatric center under construction at the rear of an expansive staff parking lot.

Gemma felt comfortable, even cozy, at construction sites. They'd been a part of her childhood, for she'd often played near her dad while he was on a job. In retrospect, she was alarmed how freely she'd been allowed to roam the ever-evolving playgrounds of new rooms, stairways, and hidden passages. At least her dad had always kept a close eye on her, even pirating a child-sized protective helmet and inscribing it with her name. She particularly loved taking rides with him in the caged elevator.

So the dank scent of newly mixed cement and the curious odor of the arc welding torch were like the aromas of popcorn and candy floss for her, and she hoped committing her newly conceived deletion in such an evocative setting might transform the dark deed into an homage to her father. And the more she mapped out her plan, the more it seemed an improvement over the lethal Strid.

She'd chosen the timing of her thesis via the intersection of Adele's courtship schedule with concepts gleaned at Signe Childs's lecture series on lunar phases and nocturnal ventures. At McMasters' underground planetarium, she'd seen a moonless sky give birth to the waxing crescent moon, a sliver of light wanly illuminated by the reflected glow from the Earth ("the old moon in the new moon's arms" her father used to call it), which would offer just enough illumination to make ready the scene of her crime without a telltale flashlight. Her complexion would make matters easier (for once in her life!), camouflaging her in the shadow-dappled dusk.

It was 8:03 p.m. as she breached the future pediatric center's concrete and steel framework, three of a projected five stories currently standing like ragged ramparts. Even this precise time had not been chosen haphazardly. In her happier days at McMasters, she'd offered her former classmate Cliff the bribe of lunch at Jade Flower Spring (whose decor changed to reflect China's seasons) in return for a tutoring session . . . this having nothing whatsoever to do with having been attracted to him the moment he'd stared at her in the forest his first day on campus.

"Put simply, Sasaki's principle involves state vectors that evolve in time while the operators remain constant," explained Cliff, who realized he was not putting things simply at all as Gemma paused in ladling out steaming subgum chow mein. "The idea is that there are moments in the day when people collectively unfocus and time becomes elastic. The Lull of the Null, he calls it," added Cliff with a boyish grin. "Claims that four-fourteen is an insentient time, that it doesn't really exist."

She took a sip of jasmine tea. "So if I want to go unnoticed some evening . . . ?"

He crunched down on a water chestnut. "He says the ideal time would be between 8:11 and 9:03. It all sounds pretty looney tunes to me."

She could have used Cliff now, not only as a sounding board but . . .

Useless thinking. Work to be done.

McMasters taught that when a skilled deletist discovers that their best-laid plans have gone awry and a new path through the maze to their target must be carved, it is helpful to review any dependable routine in their target's schedule as an alternative corridor to their vulnerability. "Show me an advertising executive who religiously takes a martini in the Plaza's Oak Bar after work and I will show you where to take your poisoned olives" is a campus adage with many variations, although Guy McMaster expressed it first and best in four simple words: "Old habits die hard."

Gemma believed she had found just such a habit with Adele, who frequently departed work early whenever she had dinner with her increasingly steady beau, the promising Dr. Peter Ellisden. His were the grueling hours of an intern, and many nights he took dinner in the hospital canteen during back-to-back shifts. Adele, who'd decided Gemma's rental Austin convertible was hers to use as she required, frequently found herself instructing Gemma to continue working alone in their office, and to meet her when she and Peter had finished supper. Adele would then drive herself and Gemma to Adele's home before she relinquished the wheel to Gemma, who lived sixteen miles in the opposite direction. This strange routine was because Adele worried a desperate Gemma might one day play roundabout roulette, aiming the convertible at an oncoming truck and putting an end to her servitude, either taking Adele with her or (even better for Gemma) surviving where Adele did not.

It was the certainty of Adele being in the driver's seat while on the road in order to ensure Gemma didn't intentionally cause an accident that made Gemma consider if she might cause an accident with Adele in the driver's seat while they were *not* on the road. So yesterday, when Adele said she'd once again be supping with Peter Ellisden the following evening (the first night of a waxing crescent moon!) and that she'd expect Gemma to meet her in the employee parking area around eight-thirty, she knew the hour, place, and lunar phase heralded that the time to strike was *now*. Or rather, tomorrow.

Once Adele went to supper, Gemma was alone and could leave St. Ann's unmonitored. It was easy to pick her way through the thicket of woods that bordered the rear of the hospital's construction site, far from the shack of the lone (and frequently napping) parking lot attendant. His primary responsibility was shooing away cars from the employees' lot and redirecting them to Visitors' Parking, often accompanying his gestures with the unfathomable, "If I went t'ospital, would I park where *you* work?"

The builders of the pediatric center always left their ladders and scaffolding ready for the next day's work, so it was easy for Gemma to scale the construction site. She'd always been limber, and her sessions with Coach Tarcott had only increased her agility. Wearing the calf-skin driving gloves she'd purchased when she'd rented the convertible and carrying the jack handle from the car's trunk, she quickly mounted a metal staircase on locked wheels to the scaffold's second level, then up a ladder to the third story where construction had ceased for the day. From several dozen cinder blocks stacked there, she carried one up another movable staircase to a floor of wood planks serving as a temporary landing for a fourth story-to-be. Soon she'd stacked four cinder blocks atop the partially completed fourth-story wall and aligned the hollow spaces within each to form a well, into which she inserted the jack handle so that it stood upright, its bent end protruding from the top. As a test, she toggled the handle a fraction of an inch to confirm that all four blocks tipped slightly with it.

Her studies in Nodology, perfected while fishing on campus in the Mere, came into play now as she shed her gloves and quickly tied an expert Palomar knot around the jack handle's lug wrench hole, using clear nylon fishing line attached to a fifteen-meter roll in her pocket. She dropped the roll from the uncompleted wall until its spool hit the ground four stories below . . . then retrieved a fifth cinder block and dropped it, too. When it hit the dirt below, it broke into three large pieces along with smaller shards and cement dust. She waited to see if the dull thud of the impact had disturbed the parking attendant, but it failed to prompt his attention.

Putting on her driving gloves once again as she returned to the ground floor, she nabbed a black safety helmet from a stack of them beside the time clock. (She'd made sure to wear a helmet only a few days earlier on a staff tour of the construction site; her hair was unique enough among the populace of Little Bavington that, if a strand were ever found in the helmet, she needed to have an explanation for its presence.) She placed a second helmet atop it to maximize her protection, then walked to where she had parked her Austin Sport that morning, after Adele had driven herself to the hospital's main entrance and she'd reclaimed the wheel. There it was, trim and game for anything, its pristine windshield soon to be ruined. She might as well have parked a guillotine in its place, considering its impending function.

She'd parked the car close to the construction site and left its canvas top down and windows lowered. There was no one to be seen in the lot (the morning hours being primarily for surgeries, the afternoon for doctors' rounds, and the evening for matrons' bed check once visiting hours ended at seven). Turning on the Austin's ignition (though not its headlights), she put the car in neutral and released the parking brake, pushed it at a walking pace, then sprang over the driver's-side door, smoothly releasing the clutch and shifting into first. Having almost silently jump-started the convertible, she now slowly drove it to where its front grille was flush with the newly constructed wall, below where she'd balanced the cinder blocks four stories up. This was actually the most dangerous part of her plan, because at this moment she was precisely where the cinder blocks would land should a sudden powerful wind propel them from their perch above . . . thus the twin safety helmets and a watchful glance upward as she shut off the motor.

Now she stepped from the car, raised its canvas hood while leaving the windows lowered, and retrieved the nearly empty spool of clear nylon line from the ground. Exchanging her driving gloves for a chamois cloth in her pocket, she pretended to clean some bird droppings from the windshield, using this task as cover (in case any eyes were watching) for tying the nylon line to the metal latch on the frame of the convertible's hood. She gently slipped the knot until the line to the stacked cinder blocks above was straight and taut. Then, donning her driving gloves again, she found the remainders of the block she'd intentionally dropped. Of its three broken pieces, the heaviest was particularly ragged, and she tucked it just under the rear of the driver's seat. She then returned the helmets to where she'd borrowed them and reviewed the results of her handiwork. In the dark, it was impossible to see the transparent, high-gauge thread running upward from the convertible's roof. From the driver's seat, the line's steep angle took it out of the driver's field of vision unless they had reason to look straight up, and Adele at the steering wheel would either be looking over her shoulder prior to backing out (since she couldn't move any farther forward without hitting the base of the wall), or talking to Gemma, who would certainly try to keep her distracted.

She'd arranged to meet Adele near the entrance by the parking attendant's shack, and Gemma would be sure to greet the attendant to ensure that she and Adele were seen together. Gemma would open the car door for Adele, who preferred to have the top down at night unless it was raining, and Gemma would quickly move to the passenger side and slide the canvas roof back toward the rear seat squab, whether Adele asked her to or not. This would pull the jack handle, tipping the four cinder blocks so they would land on the car below. At least one or two should strike the windshield and the now roofless driver's seat. Gemma, knowing what was to come and still outside the car, would leap away before Adele could understand what was happening. There would be the very loud noise of cinder blocks striking metal and glass, and the very good chance Adele would be deleted in that moment, never knowing what had hit her. No matter what happened, Gemma would scream repeatedly to the parking attendant, who might already be stepping out to see what had caused the ominous noise of four cinder blocks shattering. He'd certainly take note of a distraught Gemma standing by the smashed car. There would be no way she could have dropped anything on the car from four stories up and run to where she now stood amid the rubble, not in the few seconds between the sound of the hopefully fatal impact and the attendant witnessing the screaming Gemma right by the car. He would then see her race around the car to Adele's side, who at that moment would either be dead, unconscious, or simply shaken. Gemma would scream to the attendant to phone the hospital directly for an ambulance. The attendant would run back to his shack to make the call and, if Adele were regretfully still alive, Gemma's gloved hands would grab the jagged piece of block she'd hidden under the driver's seat. "What's that?" she'd scream, pointing to Adele's left, and when Adele turned to look, she'd smite her as needed and toss the fatal cinder block on the ground where it would seem to have ricocheted after doing its damage. Then she'd toss her gloves in the car, undo the slipknots of the nylon thread from both the fallen jack handle and the convertible's latch, toss the handle in the boot of the car where it rightfully belonged, and stuff the loose thread in a box of fishing gear alongside a first aid kit she'd already placed there. If the attendant returned to see her rummaging in the trunk, the illusion would be that she was finding the first aid kit for bandages to stanch Adele's bleeding.

Gemma prayed (yet again wondering just what kind of God would entertain such a prayer) that she wouldn't need to use the broken cinder block as the coup de grâce for Adele. She hoped at least one of the four cinder blocks would score a direct hit so that she wouldn't have to do the bloody deed with her own (albeit gloved) hands. She uttered a quiet curse as self-indictment, knowing this had been her Achilles' heel all along: She had wanted the River Strid to do the dirty work for her, just as she now hoped the cinder blocks would enact her deletion, with gravity their mute accomplice.

She ached to postpone the deed but had no idea how long McMasters would wait for her to act before they ruled that she'd developed cold feet and should be permanently put on ice. Circumnavigating the rear of the construction site and the spinney of trees behind it, she hastily circled back alongside the paved road leading to the parking lot's entrance. It was 8:25 and the reliably tardy Adele had agreed to meet her on the half hour.

At 8:47, an approaching Adele announced, "Here we are!" and for a moment Gemma feared she had brought her intern boyfriend with her. But peering into the gloom, she saw that Adele was referring only to herself. She made no mention of her tardiness. Adele apologized for nothing. It was very good to be Adele, except possibly this particular evening and, following that, for the rest of eternity.

"Ta-ta, Mr. Paulding!" Gemma called out to the attendant, who was always glad to set down his copy of *John Bull* to speak to an attractive woman. "We're both calling it a night."

"'Night then, Gemma. And you, Miss Underton," he said, revealing how he viewed the two women's status at the hospital. He offered his invaluable counsel, "Mind how you go."

"Will do, Mr. Paulding!" said Gemma with forced cheeriness. She fell in step with Adele and asked, "Did you enjoy dinner?"

Adele made a face. "Prawn curry and chips was the best available option."

"What did Peter have?"

"Oh, he eats breakfast three times a day when he's doing double shifts. Eggs, chips, beans, and what the canteen calls coffee. I'll cure him of those habits once we've tied the knot."

Adele had alluded to the entrapment of Peter Ellisden on a few occasions, but this sounded decidedly more confident. If marriage was looming, Gemma wondered, should she consider staying her hand, in case her problems might vanish of their own accord? . . . Still, where would that leave her with McMasters?

"If you got married, d'you think you'd quit work?" she asked in a casual tone, though it was an imminent matter of life-and-death if Adele did but know it.

"Not bloody likely, in case you're thinking that would let you off the hook," Adele warbled in rebuff. "Though I might take time off for a proper honeymoon and setting up a nice home. But a doctor needs a wife to support him while he's establishing his practice. That's why doctors' divorces are always so generous to the wife, for the long hours she put in during their struggling years. Thank God I have *you* to take care of that."

If Adele had possessed prescient hearing, she might have heard a last nail being driven into her coffin by the sledgehammer of her words.

They were now nearly at the end of the expansive lot. "Why'd you park so far away?" questioned Adele, a tinge of suspicion in her voice. "Trying to get me alone? I hope you aren't forgetting the letters I gave Old Riggins. It would be a terrible miscalculation on your part."

"Oh, you never fail to remind me of those letters," Gemma acknowledged. "And as much as I wouldn't want anyone at St. Ann's to read it, I'm much more terrified of my mum learning what I did. As long as she's alive, you're safer than safe."

This seemed to placate Adele, for whom Gemma opened the driver's-side door. Circling to the other side of the car, she watched Adele take her place behind the wheel.

"Has Peter proposed to you yet?" Gemma asked as casually as she could, considering that her brain was screaming, *Am I really going to kill her now???* as she reached for the latch of the convertible's top, her heart clocking at something over two hundred beats per minute.

"He's getting close to popping the question," Adele said, looking for the keys, which were still in Gemma's purse. "I certainly plan to raise the topic when we next meet."

She unlocked the latch. "You sound confident."

Adele plucked a lipstick from her pocketbook and removed its cap. "He'll have to marry me. And *you'll* be busy as all hell for the many months when I take my leave." Gemma pulled back the roof and the sound of rasping concrete could be heard high above. It took all her will not to look up, as that might tip her hand a second too soon. As Gemma braced to hurl herself away from the car, Adele continued proudly, "Peter got me in the family way. I'm pregnant."

"Look out!" screamed Gemma, reflexively throwing herself over Adele as the cinder blocks rained down, smashing the windshield and Gemma.

I'm no good at this, were her last thoughts as Adele's piercing scream rocketed away from all Gemma's awareness, leaving her in a void without light or sound.

XLIX

Very late the morning after Doria's deletion of Leonid Kosta, she awoke as most of us do—passing into mindfulness while still cocooned in ignorance and innocence, until it gradually dawns on us where we are, what we've done, and what we may be facing in the day ahead. For a prisoner gradually recalling that he now resides on death row, it is the dream that awakens to a nightmare.

Outside her window, the sun was stapled to a baby blue sky, and as she stirred beneath satin sheets, Doria slowly remembered that she was Doria Maye (oh good), that she was back in her well-appointed bedroom on the studio lot (very nice), that she had deleted another human being (oh dear) named Leonid Kosta (oh *good*), and that, so far, she had not been accused of same.

There was a no-nonsense knock on her bungalow door. Despite the confidence instilled by her studies at McMasters, she was only human, and her mouth went dry as alum while the proverbial chill slithered down her spine and eeled its way into her stomach. She draped a lounge robe over satin pajamas that matched her sheets, stepped from the bedroom into a short hall and down six carpeted mezzanine steps to the bungalow's foyer. The knock repeated itself, and through lace curtains on the patio doors, she was alarmed to see a trooper-like uniform . . . then realized with relief it was Finton Flood, security guard from the Jacaranda Gate.

Opening the doors, she responded to his grim countenance by cooing in a caring tone, "Finny, cherub, you look terrible, come in, whatever is the matter?"

Finny stepped into the bungalow, a bit dazed to have gained entry there for the first time in his life. She gestured him toward her overstuffed morning room, where he lowered himself onto a divan, holding a large gray envelope in his hands, which shook just slightly. "I've done something I'm not sure was right, Miss Maye."

She walked to the drinks table. "Can I get you something, dear boy?"

He allowed as how he could use a quick something at that. Doria poured him a slug of rye and he downed it, after which the guard plunged headfirst into a breathless account of private detective Bryce, disguised as a woman, and in the employ of Mr. Kosta, and how Mr. Kosta had wanted surveillance of you, Miss Maye, as per the morals clause in your contract permitting the monitoring of your behavior on the lot including this bungalow, which is studio property after all, and how Mr. Kosta suggested the detective should enlist the aid of his own loyal self because of his discretion. And after all the kindnesses Mr. Kosta has shown him, taking him into the fold right after the war and all, he felt he should do as Mr. Kosta requested, forgive me Miss Maye, so he'd taken photographs as instructed last night at 9 p.m. at her open kitchen window with a camera the detective had supplied that takes pictures in the dark. He couldn't tell what he was photographing through her window, as it was dark inside and he'd been told to keep his head down, but he did as instructed and rested the camera on the center of the windowsill and squeezed the remote shutter cord eight times and he heard the camera click and saw it glow dimly from something like a flash attachment, except it was barely bright enough to see what it illuminated because the light was a kind called "infrared." This morning, he started having second thoughts about what he'd done. So instead of taking the camera to the photo lab recommended by the detective, he'd taken it to a friend of his, Roy Kilfoyle, who'd served in his battalion and joined the studio's film processing department after the war. He'd asked Roy if he could develop the images double-quick for him, so he'd know if he'd done something wrong. Finny made him promise not to look more than it took to develop the pictures nor to breathe a word, and you can barely tell it's you, Miss Maye, unless you know who you're looking for. But the pictures, I'm ashamed to say . . . He left the sentence unfinished.

Doria mused, "Well, let's see, last night at nine p.m., I'd showered and was probably walking around in nothing more than my birthday suit."

Without comment, Finny shamefacedly opened the manila envelope and spilled out a dozen enlargements, avoiding looking at them. "A vision of loveliness, to be sure, Miss Maye."

Appraising the photographs objectively, Doria was inclined to agree. The oddly hued infrared light softened the images as if through a diffusion disk, and her poses, supposedly taken unaware and lacking self-consciousness, offered her graceful form in a flattering manner. The calisthenics and physical activities at McMasters had only sculpted her body into the most supple shape of her life. Oink, indeed!

Of course, she *had* been posing deliberately and knowingly for the camera, the photographs having been taken the night *before* Finny Flood believed he'd taken them himself. Last night, while she was awarding Kosta his much-deserved statuette, the roll of film was already exposed and tightly wound on the take-up spool in the camera whose shutter Finny was pointlessly clicking eight times. The night before that, she'd perched the camera on the sill of the same open window and allowed its self-timer to capture eight clandestine snaps of her naked self, posed with seeming ignorance by the oversized monthly calendar she'd been keeping on her refrigerator, where the box for the following day had already been X'd out along with all prior days of the month, while the wall clock displayed a little after nine. It all added verisimilitude to the account of a security guard photographing her while Kosta was being murdered two hours away. She'd already done three trial runs the previous week, albeit clothed and with her back to the camera, and had the film developed at three different overnight camera labs in the downtown area. (Her Camera Obscura course at McM had helped her determine what pose, exposure length, and aperture best served her purpose.)

In all modesty, she thought posing so immodestly had been a commendable idea, one the dean had heartily endorsed for its cunning and pluck. After all, what actress of any stature would intentionally allow naked photographs of herself to be taken? Surely that would be suicidal to one's career! (Although a nude calendar photograph didn't seem to be damaging Miss Monroe's current rise to stardom . . . Doria wondered if it would be all that terrible if one of her more artful poses slipped into the pages of an art magazine, fomenting a *scandale* and attendant publicity.)

Her plan now stood at a juncture in the road, and in requisite Mc-Masters fashion, she was prepared to deal with either fork. But she believed she'd appraised Finny's character correctly and that her analysis of how he would respond would make her alma mater proud. "May I inquire how much you were going to be paid for taking these pictures, dear Finny?"

Finny set down his drink. "It's not important. I'm returning the money."

"But . . . surely you shouldn't be penalized for doing the right thing."

He waved the question away. "I only took the money because I work for Mr. Kosta and that's how it should be. But these pictures . . . there's no harm in them. Beautiful they are."

The doting look he cast toward the glossies made Doria wonder if he'd kept copies for himself. What was she thinking? Of course he had. "You still have the negatives?"

He shrugged helplessly. "I should have burned them, I know, but the pictures are so lovely, I didn't have the heart."

But you didn't bring them with you, did you? was Doria's discerning thought. "Finny, here's what I propose. I'm going to give you a thousand dollars"—the guard started to protest but Doria overrode him—"for your honesty, for your financial loss, and for the negatives, of course. They'd be worth a pretty penny in the wrong hands."

"If you insist, Miss Maye," he said compliantly. "Our little secret. I'll tell Mr. Kosta I couldn't get the camera to work and threw the film away in disgust."

Doria knew he wouldn't be telling Mr. Kosta anything, not ever again, but there was no need to share that particular news bulletin with Finny or anyone else right now. "I'll write you a check this moment," she said, moving toward a writing desk in the corner.

But Finny stood abruptly and shook his head with surprising resistance. "No. No, then never mind, ma'am. If I were to accept your kindness—and I'm thinking now I shouldn't—I could never take a *check*, you see? Then there'd be a record of it and somehow it would catch up with me, I know it would."

Doria offered, "All right, then give me until tonight, when you go off duty, and I'll have the reward for you in cash. Say around nine? Only this time I won't be naked." She laughed, so he laughed as well. "No one will know about it, not the studio, not the IRS, not anyone. It's the very least I can do under the circumstances."

Finny reluctantly succumbed. "As you wish then, miss."

— ♠ —

As a guard whose primary job was minding everyone else's times of arrival and departure, punctuality came second nature to Finton Flood. He had arrived a minute early for his engagement but would have never considered knocking on her patio door until precisely 9 p.m., whereupon he rapped lightly and, on being let in, immediately handed her an envelope.

"The negatives, ma'am."

She held the ghostly images to the light and asked, "Just to be sure, these are the pictures you took last night? You've never taken any other on another day or at another time?"

Finny looked stricken. "You make me feel like a Peeping Tom with those kinds of questions, Miss Maye! Check the clock on the wall and your own calendar in the photographs. I only got the camera yesterday morning, and there was only the one roll of film in it, may I be struck dead."

She went to the kitchen and returned with a well-stuffed white envelope. "I can't thank you enough, Finny. One can't put a price on gratitude, but a thousand dollars isn't too shabby, I suppose."

He raised the palms of his hands. "A thousand dollars is just not right, Miss Maye."

"Oh, there's no need to be noble. So many people in your shoes would have tried to take advantage of the situation. I insist."

He corrected her patiently. "No, you misunderstand, ma'am. A thousand is not enough."

Doria stared at him for a moment, then put the negatives back in the envelope and walked to the small gas fire flickering beneath ceramic logs. "Negatives burn so easily," she commented.

Finny smiled at her foolishness. "I never understand why people in crime stories make so much about the negatives. It's not hard to make another set of negatives. These aren't the originals, to be sure. Those are still safe with me. You said a thousand was the very least you could do, and I said, 'I suppose you're right.' Because it really *is* the very least you can do, ma'am, and a bit more won't put a dent in your purse. I'm thinking five thousand. Fair enough?"

"Five thousand dollars for all the negatives? The originals?"

He started to speak, then stopped to consider, as if he hadn't given the matter any prior thought. "Well now, there are two I really should save for a rainy day. You see, it's a bit of a speculative investment for me, all related to how your career goes from here. The more you have to lose in terms of your image and your bank account, the more I ought to gain, don't you think? And should it be announced that you're starring as Joan of Arc or our sainted Mother Mary—"

"Okay, that gives us all we'll need, Miss Maye," came a sharp voice from the kitchen. A man in a dark blue suit entered the parlor, followed by a uniformed cop. The blue suit displayed a badge. "Finton Flood, I'm Lieutenant Garnett, this is Detective Cortez. You're under arrest for extortion in violation of Penal Code five-one-eight, attempted blackmail of Miss Maye, to which we are witnesses. You'll also be charged with loitering outside these premises for the purpose of peeking in violation of California Penal Code six-four-seven-i, a Class A misdemeanor."

Being a professional security guard, Flood knew the legal boundaries of his work. "I had a lawful purpose being on the property. I was following the instructions of my employer."

"Whose instructions?"

"Leonid Kosta."

Garnett smiled a very strange smile. "I'm afraid Mr. Kosta won't be able to verify that, owing to the fact that he's been murdered."

Doria gasped in shock and sat down hard on the couch. "When . . . how . . . ?"

The lieutenant was often called on by his division to interact with the film studios because of his diplomatic skills. This slip-up was atypically insensitive, and he looked angry with himself. "I'm very sorry I broke it to you that way, Miss Maye, it was thoughtless of me." He turned back to Flood. "Was anyone else with you when Mr. Kosta supposedly gave you these instructions?"

"He didn't give me the instructions. They were from a private detective in his employ."

"Can you tell me the detective's name or address?"

Flood fumbled and handed him the Bryce Investigations business card, which Garnett examined with a dubious expression. "I never heard of any Bromistas Street. You, Cortez?" he asked.

His uniformed companion said, "Nah. For what it's worth, *Bromistas* means jokers."

"Anyone can have business cards printed, including you, Mr. Flood," pointed out Garnett, and Doria knew this to be true because she'd had them printed. She felt bad for Finny, but then again, he *had* shunned her generous reward and tried to blackmail her. It had been easy to get starstruck Lieutenant Garnett to listen in, for he'd been technical advisor on her heist flick *Hard Eight in Reno*. Had Finton not attempted blackmail, their exchange still would have established her alibi, not that she felt she'd be needing one. And had Finny instead behaved honestly and turned over the photos to her "private eye Bryce" character, she simply would have blackmailed herself by anonymous mail, called in Garnett to investigate, and anonymously sent him the envelope Finton had signed when he accepted the mission, again establishing her whereabouts for that evening.

But she'd suspected all along that Finton would bring the photos directly to her and attempt to up the ante via extortion, as he'd always seemed to her like a corrupt concierge with a palm ever eager to be greased. She was grateful to him for saving her several tedious steps.

As cuffs were snapped on Finny, Lieutenant Garnett explained that he'd have to retain the revealing photographs as evidence, but that he would keep them under lock and key, to which Doria thought, *Yes, in the strongbox in your garage where you hide magazines from your wife.*

As Finton was being taken away by Detective Cortez, Lieutenant Garnett consoled him. "Hey, look on the bright side, pal. After Mr. Kosta's murder, the Homicide boys will be looking at everyone on this lot who's done anything suspicious. But these pictures give you an iron-clad alibi for where you were when he was killed. You too, Miss Maye."

"Well that's the *naked* truth, I'm afraid," she joked with a touch of embarrassment. "I certainly do seem to have exposed myself last night . . . though not to suspicion, I trust."

"No, Miss, that would be against the laws of nature. You see, we know for a fact that Mr. Kosta's killer is a male. One with specific . . . interests."

She made her face grow grave. "I don't understand."

The detective liked to tell his friends he was sort of in the movie business and he confided, "Well, since I'm a lifelong fan . . . it would seem your Mr. Kosta was killed by a man who takes pleasure in dressing as a woman."

Doria sputtered, "But, but . . . Leon was *renowned* for his amorous appetites!"

It pleased Garnett to play man of the world with a movie star. "The most public womanizer often hopes to prove to others, or to himself, that he's not 'that way.' Or Mr. Kosta may have been fooled and thought he was with a real woman. I'm told some sort of striptease took place in his bedroom that would have eventually revealed the truth. The big question for us is sorting out, if we ever can, whether he had relations with his killer voluntarily."

"'Relations'? I don't—"

"There's physical evidence this male killer had sex with Kosta. Question is, was your boss a consensual participant? We also don't know if sex took place before, during, or *after* his death. There's limits to forensics, even nowadays."

"Oh, the ignominy of it all!" sobbed Doria. The detective didn't know that particular word, but the ones that followed were familiar. "The disgrace! The sordid, shameful end to him!"

"Well, we're trying to keep it under wraps as best we can for the good of the studio."

"But this is Hollywood!" despaired Doria, inwardly exulting as much as outwardly exclaiming, "It will be in every gossip column, scandal sheet, and muckraking book for years!" to which she silently appended the thought *If I have anything to say about it.* How sad she couldn't share with the industry trade papers that she, Doria Maye, had been the ferryman who'd steered Kosta down the river of Hades to counter the shell game he'd played with her career.

STYX FIX NIXES PRICK'S TRICKS, she headlined in the *Daily Variety* of her mind.

Enquiry #4: *Will this deletion improve the life of others?*

Perhaps that afternoon seemed particularly dreamy to Cliff because Fiedler no longer had the option of enjoying it, but those he passed walking to Lilliana Horvath's home seemed to sense the despot's absence as well. More than one passing person in their Sunday finery intoned a sincere if ritual, "Lovely day, isn't it?"

Lilliana had him sit on the porch for lemonade and Hungarian honey cake. He was wearing a wig today, for his current if temporary bald state might require too far-fetched an explanation. He *had* gotten rid of his unkempt beard, much to his own relief. He'd missed the rite of lathering, shaving, and rinsing each morning, along with aftershave's fortifying slap and sting.

When he'd drained his first glass of lemonade and gratefully accepted a refill, Cliff lowered his voice and said, "Merrill Fiedler is dead."

Lilliana nodded slowly and allowed herself a moment with this information. "How *did* he die?" she eventually inquired.

Cliff stepped out his next words carefully. "If I were possessed of unusual mental powers, I'd envision him poisoning himself with a glass of your husband's favorite liqueur. I would also imagine that, as he died, he knew his death was in part because of how he treated our Jacek."

Again, she processed this with little response. At last, she asked, "Painful?"

He responded, "It was not without pain. There was, additionally, fear and despair."

She took a small sip of her lemonade, and it must have needed more sweetening, because her lips compressed tightly. "That is good," she reflected. "Thank you."

They sat as if each had taken a communion wafer and were waiting for the wine. Then the gentle woman said, with her habit of emphasizing an unlikely syllable now and then, "If only the person who killed my Jacek *could* be punished as well."

"That person is dead," Cliff responded.

She drew in a quick breath, her first real sign of emotion. "Fiedler? It was *him*? I always suspected—"

"No. The person who shot your husband is dead as well."

"But . . . how did you find him? We *assumed* it was a stranger."

"I'm certain whoever Jack encountered in Ellwood Park that night was not someone he knew," answered Cliff, who continued with precision, ". . . and the person who shot your husband has died because of what he did there. That's all I can tell you, but you may take my word on this."

Lilliana took his hand. "I can, I do, I don't want you to *risk* any further harm to yourself."

"And I don't want you to be hurt any more than you already have been," he answered in kind.

"Will you stay for Sunday dinner? I rarely get to cook for someone *other* than myself these days."

"I'm so sorry, I have some serious paperwork to deal with today," he answered truthfully.

"Another time, I hope." She reached for his glass, as if the temptation of further lemonade might keep him there longer. "Are you planning to stay in the area? I'm thinking this may not be the best place for you now."

"I'll probably be moving along one way or another," he responded. "You shouldn't expect to see me for some time to come. I assume you're okay, financially. Comfortable. I know Jack was dedicated to providing for you, in case . . ."

". . . he were to pass first, my being the younger. Yes, the insurance took care of everything. Too much really. But I was grateful for the money," she said with no air of apology. "I needed it for my own purposes."

Cliff patted her hand reflexively. "Well, I'm glad the insurance money went to you, and I just hope someday you'll spend it on something you'd really enjoy . . . maybe a trip to Hungary."

She looked at him as if he were her son, and a young and naive son at that. "I have very simple needs, and the house is paid for. Most of the insurance money is gone now." Her expression turned to amusement. "Do you not understand, little bear?"

"No, Lilliana. What are you saying? Where did it go?"

"It went toward your education. Very expensive, but it is what I wanted."

He blinked slowly, twice, trying to see things as they were. "*You*, Lilliana? You're my sponsor?"

"From things you say to me, at the funeral, in the days that followed, and this not so long after the young woman you *cared* for dies, I could see your good mind growing dark. I knew you would try something foolish that would not succeed, and you would end like Jacek and Cora, gone too soon. I wanted to punish our Mr. Fiedler, but I am too old. It had to be you who found us our *bosszú* . . . our revenge."

"But how would you know of McMas—"

"Shush!" she scolded. "We do not say the name of this fine school of yours. After the funeral, I speak with my cousin Patrik from New York. Back in Hungary, he is the hired ruffian"—she lowered her voice—"in New York he performs services for the Italians they do not wish to do themselves. He is *knowing* of dark things, and he told me that if you were to punish Fiedler, there was only one path you *should* take, but that it would be costly. I told him I had the money, because I did."

"But how did Patrik know about the school?"

"He was a student there, *five* years ago." Now her voice receded to an absolute whisper. "He was sent to be tutored for a dangerous assignment, what they call 'the contracting,' to be rid of the man who was their boss, *his* boss, what they called the *capo dei capi* . . . the boss of all bosses. Like you, Clifford, he had to murder his employer."

Student ID I-23597
Address withheld as per instructions
Date withheld as per instructions

McM Ltd.
Post Office Box 303
Tórshavn, Faroe Islands

Kindly forward the enclosed letter to

Office of the Dean
Slippery Elms
The McMasters Conservatory for the Applied Arts
Address unknown

For the eyes of Dean Harbinger Harrow only

Dear Dean Harrow:

I am writing this letter separate from the journal in which I have already made my final entry, now that my thesis is complete and my Pass or Fail lies in the hands of the board of McMasters. I do not wish to share this last page with my benefactor (farewell, dear mysterious X) having at last learned their identity. After you read the following, I think you will understand why.

My thesis was hopefully rendered according to the teachings of McMasters, and I have attempted to be mindful of the Four Enquiries and the principles of deletion you have tried to instill in me during my time at the school. However, in performing my thesis, upon which you will soon be passing judgment, I intentionally gave my sponsor the impression that I further avenged the death of Jacek Horvath by ending the life of his killer. (The word "deletist" would be inappropriate in this context.)

Since my sponsor may have further contact with you independent of me, I'm concerned she may give you, Dean, the impression that I extended the approved boundaries of my thesis to include another human being without the sanctioning (and against the principles) of the conservatory. You have treated me in what I consider to be a thoughtful and patient manner, and on both a personal and academic level, I would hate it if you thought me that arrogant and unappreciative a student. Yes, you have taught me that sometimes a McMasters deletist must revise plans on the fly (which is the primary reason we need pilots even as aviation becomes more instrument assisted), but I wouldn't want you to think I had been such a wretched apprentice that I'd kill another person or two along the way, like some trigger-happy gunslinger.

The impression I knowingly tried to give my sponsor was that Jack Horvath's killer is dead and has been punished for his murder. This is true, because Jack's killer was himself, and the punishment for any successful suicide can only be the death penalty, beyond the reach of any human intervention.

He went about committing suicide with admirable skill and courage, so much so that you might think _he_ had been the one with a McMasters education. I know from our discussions in those last awful weeks that he felt his life and work were at an end. While I might have been able to start a new career (and shortly will have to, although God knows doing what), Jack was already near retirement age, suddenly robbed of all work benefits after being discharged in disgrace, with very little he could do to sustain the comfortable life he and his wife had led. Although I viewed them both as an extension of the aunt and uncle who'd raised me, Lilliana was considerably younger than Jack, and he'd scrimped and sacrificed to make sure she would be well taken care of should he predecease her. And now, his life in ruin, he was left with only one asset, a blue-ribbon insurance policy. But, of course, committing suicide would render all benefits null and void.

My own thesis called for making my target's deletion appear a suicide. Jack's tragic personal mission was to make his suicide look like a murder.

I visited Ellwood Park and began working my way around the perimeter of the sordid rectangle, visiting the many pawnshops that alternated with bail bonds outfits as if they were seated boy-girl-boy-girl along the neighborhood streets.

I tried the same routine at each pawnshop and got lucky on my sixth try.

"I'm in the market for a twenty-two," I said to the owner who looked as if he'd been born with a toothpick in his mouth. "I don't care if it works."

"You will if someone comes through your window," he said smoothly. "But we don't get much call for twenty-twos in this part of town. They don't exactly stop people in their tracks."

"A twenty-two. Something foreign, maybe a mother-of-pearl handle? It's for a movie."

He didn't believe this for a second, but he didn't care in the least. "Hold on." He went in the back and returned with a large box. "This one's a twenty-two, Hungarian make, antique but working condition, takes standard ammo. Quite a piece."

He placed a small gun with a mother-of-pearl handle and gold filigree on a velvet pad in front of him. Its patina reminded me of the tiger snake in McMasters' deadly menagerie, and both were things of beauty except for their deadly capabilities. I had first seen the gun in the right-hand drawer of Jack Horvath's study desk, but it had been absent when I visited his wife on my return, and that had prompted my mind to consider a possible scenario for his death.

"How much?"

He sized up my worth. "Three hundred, cash."

"Six hundred," I countered to his advantage.

"No way," he snapped out of habit, then realized what I'd actually said and smiled. "Hm. I like the way you negotiate, my friend. You trying to be funny?"

I shook my head. "The extra three hundred is for you to forget I bought it and not fill out the state forms for the sale."

He tried his best. I mean, he was a pawnbroker. "Why don't we say seven hundred?"

I shook my head. "No can do. I'm already having to pay myself three hundred dollars to forget about you."

The existence of Jack's family's pistol in a pawnshop in godforsaken Ellwood Park was all the proof I needed of his plan. If Jack had wanted to pawn his pistol, there were better-paying antique stores and gun dealers than this fleapit in the worst part of the city. And he certainly hadn't pawned the pistol after he'd died. And it's definitely not as if whoever shot him had stolen the pistol from Jack's home for the poetic gesture of killing its owner with it at a later date in a desolate park, and *then* pawned it.

No, Jack had made himself an easy target for the rampant muggers and gangs of Ellwood Park. He'd probably gotten drunk in a nearby bar, to make himself seem an easy target and to fuel himself for the ordeal ahead. Likely he showed the gun off in the bar and bragged about its value as an antique, then wandered into Ellwood Park, to be the voluntary prey of its muggers and gangs, or even more likely, of someone who followed him directly from the bar. He'd forced a struggle with them and, with all the rabid strength of a drunken, fearless creature who wants to die, he'd pressed the small gun into their hands and shot himself in the chest.

Jack was diabolically clever: If his assailant left the gun with Jack, it would likely have their fingerprints on it and might even lead the police to said "assailant." If the mugger wiped the gun clean, Jack couldn't have done that after dying instantaneously, particularly since he didn't have anything like a handkerchief or gloves on his person. And if the mugger took the gun (as he clearly did, pawning it later or having another party do so), then obviously Jack didn't kill himself, because if he did, where was the gun? So, no matter what his involuntary accomplice did, Jack's death could only be pronounced a murder.

I've withheld this scenario from Jack's widow, as I wish her to enjoy the remainder of the bequest that Jack intended her to receive without the guilt that can afflict those who've survived a loved one's suicide.

Dean Harrow, clearly my valuable time at McMasters was intended to help me achieve a successful deletion and not a mystery's solution. How Jacek Horvath met his end is only my personal theory (although the presence of his .22 pistol so near to the place of his death is all the proof I'll ever need), but I'm convinced it's correct. As I said at the outset of this letter, I am relaying this to you in case my sponsor mentions to anyone at McMasters my assurance to them that Jacek's killer has been punished, lest that be misconstrued as a breach on my part of McM's strict ethical code.

My thesis now completed and awaiting the school's review, I thank you for your time in reading this, Dean Harrow, and wish you a pleasant new semester at a place I shall always remember with the greatest fondness.

Yours truly,

Student ID I-23597

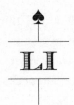

LI

Cliff posted the letter to the accommodation address he'd been given. The night was admirable but he felt . . . what *did* he feel? For months, his life had held meaning only as it related to Fiedler's end. Now he was beyond that, but where did that leave him? He'd avenged Cora, but she was no more alive than the day after her funeral. He'd learned the identity of his benefactor, which was meaningful but also meant he wouldn't spend another penny of his trust on himself. He'd conveniently envisioned a noble patron in the library of their chateau . . . but that illusion had certainly evaporated now.

He'd made murder his sole vocation. His work in aeronautics had served as only a small component of his plan and it was, sadly, no longer a profession he wished to pursue; he'd just find himself in the same power structure, accountable to someone whose authority over him had more to do with their foxlike cunning than their love of flight. He could barely remember when he chose aeronautic design as a career. He'd had an aptitude for certain subjects and the right schools had admitted him. He'd survived his showdown primarily to ensure that Fiedler did not, but now was it time to fold his cards and cash in his chips, and if so, what chips did he have?

"There he is," said Captain Dobson.

"Look at that face," said Sergeant Stedge. They were parked in a wood-paneled station wagon across from Cliff's home. "From his expression, you'd think he'd failed."

"Happens all too often," said the captain, who'd disguised himself for this stakeout by taking off his hat. "It's like training a marine to be an effective killing machine and then peace gets declared and you instruct them to forget what they've learned. Now's when a graduate poses the greatest threat to the school. He might seek professional help and tell some headshrinker too much."

Stedge appraised Cliff's aimless, slouching gait. "Poor guy looks like he no longer has a reason to live," he observed.

Dobson nodded in agreement. "Someone should put him out of his misery."

Sergeant Stedge reached into his breast pocket. "Me or you?"

Master's Thesis

Student: Gemma Lindley
Location: Intensive Care, St. Ann's Hospital
Date: July 1, 195–

Final Report by Dean Harbinger Harrow

We found our failed student in a private room at the hospital of her employment. We'd been informed her vital signs were now closer to normal. Both her shoulders had been broken, but her cranium had providentially sustained nothing worse than a fracture, albeit with severe bleeding. Luckily, she'd been only a minute from St. Ann's emergency room, and the surgeons there worked with particular intensity, knowing that Gemma was not only a much-liked member of the St. Ann's family but had heroically protected Adele Underton from injury. Having identified myself as her great-uncle, I was allowed a few moments alone with her, with Father Pugh at my side should there be a sudden need for last rites to be administered.

She was sipping Lucozade through a straw as she saw me enter. A look of bleak resignation came over her face, and she swallowed with difficulty. Nurse Pynn, seeing this was an emotional visit, kindly left the three of us alone.

"Hello, Miss Lindley," I said as the padre added his own gentle greeting. The slight tremble in Gemma's lower lip betrayed her fear, but she gave as much of a nod as her casts and head bandage would allow. I inquired solicitously, "Do you know why we're here?"

Her look of grim acceptance could not be mistaken for cowardice. "I imagine you're here to . . ." Gemma sought the right word. ". . . *fail* me?"

As she was still recovering from her injuries, I tried to calm her nerves with a small smile, although the reality of the situation was inescapable. "You do understand the position in which your lack of success places the school and your fellow classmates?"

"I botched it," she said, trying to moisten her dry mouth with another sip of the Lucozade. "I had Adele precisely where I wanted and still I failed." Without a hint of self-pity, she added, "So now I'm back in the world while knowing of the school's existence, its purpose, and its students, many by sight. I didn't complete my thesis and I represent a danger to all of you. Anyway, I'm assuming it's only a matter of time before the police arrest me. I obviously didn't have the chance to detach the nylon thread from the jack handle."

Father Pugh, his tousled hair the shades of a Black and Tan, drew closer as if to give unction. "I took care of that, Gem. I was first on the scene, dressed as an orderly. Helped you into the ambulance myself, then walked away as if returning to the hospital. No one was any the wiser. Your plan wasn't half bad, all in all."

"You . . . how long have you been . . . *here*?"

"I was very concerned about your thesis when you departed the conservatory, and I have an aunt in Beamish I've wanted to visit for some time," the padre explained.

"And if he didn't have an aunt, he'd have invented one," I added knowingly. "We frequently keep a faculty advisor or local graduate close at hand for high-risk deletions, just in case chestnuts need to be pulled from the fire. In your case, should the police suspect foul play, a second such dangerous 'prank' will be staged while you're still in the hospital, with a note threatening more such incidents if St. Ann's doesn't provide free meals for impoverished children, giving you some cover . . . but thus far, it seems the authorities and Adele Underton have taken this to be an accident in which you comported yourself heroically."

"You did, you know," said the padre, with admiration. "Saving mother and child."

Gemma was stunned. "How on earth did you know that Adele is pregnant?"

"Oh, she told the sister at the receiving room in case her baby was injured. I'd exchanged my orderly outfit for my usual uniform and overheard her when I made myself available at the ER for anyone wanting a clergy visit. Clerical collars open many doors. Adele also said she'd just told you her happy news and you'd sacrificed yourself to protect her."

I tried to convey to Gemma the importance of my next proposal, which was, truly, a matter of life and death. "Miss Lindley, although the challenge would be great, we *could* grant you the chance to re-take your final exam. Meaning your thesis."

Gemma replied helplessly but without a moment's hesitation. "End Adele's life *now*? Impossible. Maybe she's a blackmailer, but she's also a mother-to-be. Can't." She looked squarely into my eyes with admirable courage. "You'll have to flunk me."

The padre spoke as if in her defense. "You were prepared to sac-rifice your own life to save two others."

"Pure reflex," she said with noteworthy candor.

"Of a good heart," the priest countered antiphonally.

"I suppose." She sounded as if she wished she hadn't been so cursed. "I always felt I wasn't McMasters material, trying to stay arm's length from my dark deed. Dulcie had the right idea. I used to watch her whacking away at baseballs. She knew it was best to take a grip on her thesis with her own two hands." She pictured Cliff's limber arm hurling fastballs at her classmate as the spring sun had warmed the baize-like lawn of the baseball and cricket pitch. "Well, there's poetry enough to it," she added philosophically as she glanced around the room. "I ended the life of my father on this very same floor. Now I'll die here as well, perhaps the way he did, via this IV tube. I was warned McMasters is effective and quick in such matters, but this was quicker than I anticipated. Do I not get to see my mother a last time?"

Padre Pugh cleared his throat. "Gem my child, perhaps you mis-understand. An act of mercy is not automatically viewed as a flaw at McMasters. You had literally two seconds to answer Enquiry Three: 'What innocent person might suffer by your actions?' You saved a blameless child."

"Further affirmed by Enquiry Four," I reminded them both as the senior-most living authority on our code. "'Will this deletion improve the life of others?' From that we extrapolate that where *not* causing this death greatly improves the life of others, a deletion should be nullified. We may jettison certain humans from this life . . . but we are not without humanity."

Gemma looked as if she were trying not to assume a miracle was in the offing, which would undermine her resolve to accept her fate with dignity. I decided to spare her any further anguish. "My dear, compassion toward an innocent bystander, in this case the guiltless child of your loathsome target, overrides our standards and practices. I am in a position to offer you one alternative to expulsion: you could become a member of our staff."

Gemma, honest to a fault, reacted to what seemed an absurdity. "Let me understand: I'd teach others to follow in my footsteps where I stumbled and fell on my face?"

"No, you'd tutor in McMasters morality, with your own experience as a glowing example, and report directly to the padre here."

Father Pugh eagerly added, "Unlike God, I can't be everywhere, nor are some of our female students at ease opening up to me. Nor I with them sometimes. You could provide a middle ground between myself and the worldly Vesta Thripper. In addition to which, Coach Tarcott is in desperate need of an agile assistant trainer and has always spoken highly of your athleticism and balance."

Gemma tried to comprehend. "This isn't some kind of setup or test?"

I'm sure I looked disappointed, perhaps even wounded. "Miss Lindley, you've presented us with a dilemma, and this is the best solution I can proffer. There are, to be sure, drawbacks to what I'm proposing. The position you'd be innovating would be unsalaried, save for a modest honorarium for pocket money. And it would be a lifetime commitment, unless you discredited McMasters or yourself in some way, in which case you'd be summarily deprived of your tenure in the most irreversible way, with no recourse for appeal. I'm afraid this is your first, last, and only chance."

"But would I ever be able to see my mum again?"

The padre brushed aside a gold-and-brown cowlick and lowered his voice as if making a confession. "As it happens, Gem, I've popped in on your splendid mum several times recently, representing myself as a St. Ann's chaplain and your friend. Oh, such memorable black currant roll! After cautiously tiptoeing into the topic, I broached the possibility that you might have spared your cherished dad from extended suffering. Hosanna on high, what a response from her! She said she's been thanking her savior each day for lifting your father from his pain, but now she can be thanking you instead. And she's utterly *stricken* you've had to bear this burden alone. Emboldened, I brought up your employment offer from the conservatory, and she declared you're her whole world. And while she doesn't lack for acquaintances, she'd only be happy being wherever your work might take you. I'd wager Girard Tissier could use an experienced cook from an ICI cafeteria, well accustomed to the pressures of feeding the assembled masses, to serve as an extra pair of knowing hands around the baking ovens."

In the delirium of this utterly unexpected rescue from the brink, it was surely easy for Gemma to determine that living life on the handsome campus was a superior option to death in every imaginable way. Under such circumstances, our luxuriant surroundings have enabled us to forge unique relationships which permit us to maintain minimal-salaried staff at a time when other colleges struggle for survival. When we can facilitate a reversal of fortune in this way, no one cherishes the moment more than I.

"Curfew shall not ring tonight, Gemma! If you and your commendable mother vanish without the proverbial trace, Adele Underton can hardly blackmail you further. She will have to acclimate herself to a healthy child, a successful marriage, and pulling her own weight at work. Rest, recuperate, and we'll arrange for your return to school in time for the new semester."

"Dean Harrow," she asked as I started toward the door, "if I'd messed up my thesis without knowing Adele was pregnant, strictly from ineptitude, would you really have . . . flunked me?"

From the folds of his cassock, Father Pugh withdrew a small black case and gave Gemma a momentary glimpse of its contents: a hypodermic needle, tip glistening. The padre snapped the case shut and tucked it away.

"If you'd been a different sort of failure, you'd have already been gently but permanently dismissed," I soberly affirmed, then offered her my most benevolent smile. "We look forward to seeing you next term, Gemma."

Master's Thesis

Student: Dulcie Mown (Doria Maye)
Location: Rome, Italy
Date: July 6, 195–

Final Report by Dean Harbinger Harrow

Cinecittà, the sprawling Italian film studio, had been built by Mussolini. "Cinema is the most powerful weapon!" he'd proclaimed while standing on the balcony of his palace. Later he reversed his position, being hung upside down in the Piazzale Loreto after Italy's surrender.

In the early postwar years, the studio had served as a center for displaced persons, and it was apparently still doing so where Doria Maye was concerned. I visited her on the set of *Peleus and the Empress of Death* (*Peleus Combatte La Regina della Morte*). She took small sips of Franciacorta from the bottle so as not to disturb the layers of makeup that transformed her into Caesonia, last wife of Caligula and nemesis of the strapping argonaut Peleus, whose death she sought even though, according to Homer, he'd lived and died thirteen centuries prior to her reign.

I found her seated in a canvas chair that bore the printed legend: MISS MAYE (and also bore the film legend, Miss Maye). Garbed in Roman regalia, she regaled me with a progress report that closely matched one I'd received from our field agent. A few days after Leonid Kosta's demise, she'd been summoned to his office, half expecting Laddie Graham to already be ensconced there. She was instead greeted by Claude Revenson, financial head of the studio, who genially explained that the era of movie studios being operated as a film czar's fiefdom had ended. She was delighted when he said that her absence from the screen for purely vindictive reasons had been an outrage to her as an actress and a squandering of a valuable asset to the studio and its shareholders.

Drinking this in like cognac and feeling a similar resultant warm glow, she asked who would be the new head of production. Revenson said that while his murder was unexpected, the board of directors had secretly been planning for months to replace Kosta with himself. He explained that the studio's physician, who reported directly to the company's insurance provider, had discreetly apprised them that Kosta's days were numbered in double digits.

Doria now recalled the pewter pillbox on Kosta's desk and a similar one on his Ledge House nightstand. With quiet despair, she began, "So there was no need for me . . ." then hastily continued, "to grieve his murder? He would have died *anyway*?" The "anyway" was much too revealing but understandable, as she realized months of study, meticulous planning, and the grueling enactment of her thesis had instantly been made unnecessary.

Luckily, Revenson was tone-deaf and lacked insight beyond the margins of a balance sheet. "Financially, Kosta's departure was best for the studio's survival. Television is decimating our business, but there are lots of proven ways for us to harvest income. We're selling off most of the back lot for real estate development, dumping our cartoons and old features for TV syndication, and loaning out our contract players to other studios at a distinct profit."

Doria could feign regret as well as anyone. "Well, I'll loathe working for anyone other than you, Claude—" she started.

"Oh, we would never let you go. Your name is still an international commodity!" he declared, much to her liking. "We're very much holding you to your contract. And we're pursuing the production of inexpensive movies overseas, paid for by the foreign box-office profits of our Hollywood features, money that would otherwise be frozen in Europe and Britain. In return for all the overseas jobs we're providing, we're getting some sweet tax breaks and permission to cast one American—someone who may have perhaps seen better years—so that the movie resembles a Hollywood product. With that name attached—yours, for example—we can shop the picture around the world or use it to fill out the lower half of a drive-in double feature, or even sell it directly to local TV markets. You're going to be busy as anything, Doria."

"So you want me to make films in England?" she asked, thinking England wasn't so bad.

"Rome. They have all these open-air *Quo Vadis* sets standing empty. We'll make sword-and-sandal oaters with hundreds of extras in togas working for a tin of sardines . . . but we'll call them 'epics,' and of course we'll have *you* as the queen of Crete, the empress of Sheba—"

"And who would be my leading man?"

"Bodybuilders."

"But . . . can they act?"

"They don't have to. The movies are entirely dubbed since the cast all speak different languages. That means we never have to reshoot if someone forgets their lines. You can recite the alphabet if you like. And your part gets dubbed while you go on to film the next feature."

The good news was getting worse with each update. "And who supplies the voices?"

"American expatriate actors in Rome who dub movies every day, grinding them out. We've got a woman who does a very good impression of you. She's honored to replace you."

"So I've gone from being a cartoon pig with my voice coming from its mouth to a close-up of me with some swine's voice coming out of *my* mouth?" She clutched at last straws. "What about *Ember Morgan Comes Home*?"

"I've sold the rights to Universal. Laddie Graham is directing it as a vehicle for Susan Hayward." He stood and walked her toward Kosta's tall doors, opening them so that she could exit that portal for the last time. "Well, *arrivederci* Tinseltown," he bid her as Doria considered that she'd deleted the wrong man. "You speak any foreign languages yourself?"

She gave Revenson a withering glance. "*Et tu, Brute* is the only ancient Italian I know."

Doria Maye told me she'd been living in quarters near the Borghese gardens in a charming, studio-provided villa of cool marble surrounded by parasol pines. "It's lovely, I suppose, but July is a grisly time to be filming in Rome, especially in this ridiculous garb. The Italian sun can be unrelenting." She gave me a look of reproach. "I might as well be in hell."

She was clearly experiencing what we at McMasters call posthumous depression. This is not the only syndrome that can afflict successful deletists. There is post-traumatic confess disorder, a most serious condition considering that an errant tongue could sink our entire enterprise.

I pulled my chair closer and elicited her response. "Was this murder necessary?"

She paused to consider, then emitted a single sob from deep within. "For my own survival as an actress, yes."

"Yes. And did you give Leonid Kosta every chance to redeem himself?"

"Oh, God knows I did! I pleaded, cajoled, proved I could do the part, but one last time he made it clear that he would make a sow's ear out of the silk purse of my career. What I did was virtually self-defense!"

"Very well," I said. "Then next I ask: Who will mourn him?"

"No one," she said without hesitation.

"And is this world a better place without him?"

"Oh dear God, yes, except for the starlets to whom he'd promised parts, the ones who hoped going to bed with him would be a headboard for their career. It's just that . . . at night, I take off all this makeup, layer after layer, until it's all stripped away, and I'm left with the face God gave me: pale mismatched lips, albeit fascinating in their way, barely any eyebrows, a splotch of freckles . . . I look at this endearing person and think, *Murderer*."

"This is not an abnormal reaction."

She sighed. "I've murdered more than a few times in movies. But now I look and think, 'This was *real*. You ended the life of another human being.'"

"And what did you feel?"

"Well, uh . . ." She sought the right word. "Pride, for starters."

"A job well done," I offered.

"Yes, like learning a special skill for a role. Sword fighting or horse jumping." She stood self-righteously. "I thought this would be transformative, but it feels as if it's all been for nothing. I'm stuck in a situation not much better than when I arrived at the school: working this pointless grind, devaluing my career filming these *Iliad*s for the illiterate. I feel as if I signed my soul over to the devil and my reward is that I get a discount on my next hairdo. The deletion, planning and performing it, was as thrilling as any role I've ever played. But the result of my killing seems to simply be that I'm making a living."

At that moment, the assistant director advised her they were ready to shoot the master shot of her scene with Peleus on the portico of the Temple of Saturn, which two weeks ago had been her palace in Crete, and two weeks before that the Roman Forum. She glanced quickly at a translation of the Italian responses Eduardo Politano ("Ed Powers" in the American release) would be giving her English lines and a translation of the German lines written for her movie daughter, played by Austrian ingenue Heike Richter. I tiptoed out of camera range and watched the three of them arguing in character with each other, looking quite dramatic but sounding like the Three Stooges at the Tower of Babel. Doria was all arched eyebrows and venomous scowls and I doubt there was the slightest bit of acting involved in her portrayal.

As the crew set up for a new angle, Doria wandered over to me like a lost soul. "Please, Dean. Please . . ." she implored. "May I come back to McMasters? I was happy being Dulcie. Life was fun as a campus coed, I had purpose and someone's death to live for." She saw the regret in my face and pleaded, "I could be a dialect coach, teach disguise—"

I pointed out, "When one has specialized gifts as you do, it is appropriate to make them a part of your deletion. Our long-standing concept of becoming one's own accomplice was exemplified by you as woman as man as woman. And tempting Kosta in a reversal of the Pygmalion myth by transforming yourself into a living role he'd already sculpted in his mind was a deletion I doubt could be taught to anyone who lacks your gifts."

"This is all Claude Revenson's fault!" she railed. "At least Leon wanted to make great pictures. All Revenson wants is 'product.'

He's fiddling away my career while Rome burns at high noon and Gary Cooper makes *High Noon* without me." Her eyes flashed with the same icy fire seen in *Samson and Calpurnia*, her previous release for Revenson. "I could just kill him . . ."

NOTE TO REVIEW BOARD: As the graduate spoke this last sentence, I noticed her eyes narrow and, while I can't be sure, I thought instead of her saying "I could just *kill* him," I may have heard her say the far more speculative "I *could* just kill him . . ."

It's not hard to imagine Miss Maye using her McMasters-honed skills to restore her place in the Hollywood firmament. I pity Claude Revenson should he visit Rome on studio business. We should have our Los Angeles field agent monitor his travel plans.

Incidentally, despite my seeming rejection of Miss Maye's request to return to our campus, I do have a thought about how a thespian of her caliber might help our students avoid getting "caught in the act."

(To be discussed next term.)

LII

The absolute lack of a single cloud, not even a few stray wisps of vapor loitering at the horizon, might have been disturbing had the day not been so resolutely pure and bright. The sky gleamed clear, verging on transparency. It was surely as exuberant a morning as McMasters had seen in many a term. The birds of its unheard-of woods called to each other, warbling and cackling at the sheer joy of the day, as they soared and spired higher than they'd thought themselves capable, while a silvery sun presided approvingly over the handsome, idyllic, murderous academy.

Parallel to the quadrangle's main boulevard, a black, windowless van pressed along the paved access road, skirted the campus bookshop, and veered onto the long loop that rings the broad village green, its spacious pond, and its attendant village of quaint shops, puzzling alleys, and snug but atmospheric restaurants.

"That's the Black Maria," the dean explained to Hedge House's resident advisor and the adjunct science professor. "Newly purchased for the transport of students from a central rendezvous point to Slippery Elms. Come, I have some new arrivals to personally greet."

As they followed the Black Maria's route, it had already eased to a stop by the Market Hall. Sergeant Stedge exited from the driver's side, unlocked its rear doors as a short gangway was rolled into place by two uniformed attendants, and a covey of new students descended, shielding their eyes from the sudden sunlight, wearing identical expressions of expectation, discovery, and delight while, by way of greeting, McMasters' small wind ensemble launched into a sprightly march from the Mere's Victorian Gothic bandstand, loosely patterned after the Albert Memorial.

The last passengers to disembark were Gemma, who had changed into a black-and-crimson gym instructor's uniform provided at their last rest stop, and her mother, Isabel, who had worn her best frock. For Gemma, seeing the campus again was as if she'd managed to rejoin an enchanting dream precisely where she'd left it after awakening, but now she could enjoy McMasters free from the burdens of guilt and revenge. For Isabel, McMasters reminded her of an exquisite 1930s model village at Bourton-on-the-Water that she and her husband had once taken Gemma to see, except here everything was of human scale, including a thriving populace.

Gemma began pointing out the sights to her mother. "That's our local, the Skulking Wolf, its guv'nor is Wilfred Mussel, he also runs the Tuck Shop in that little chalet there. You'll love the cheeses, Mum. And that's the Hillendale Shop, they do ready-to-wear and millinery." She took her mother's arm. "And this small lake is Mead Mere, I row and fish here just like I did with our Da— oh my gosh, it's Connie!" She'd spied Constance Beddoes, who she'd thought would by now be deleting her much younger gigolo husband. Constance was close to Isabel's age and Gemma introduced them while explaining her own new status and rank at the school.

Isabel's eyes wandered in wonderment about the teeming diorama that surrounded her, from the flower beds along the Mere banks to the jewel-box Rialto Dance Hall, from which recorded music blared in pleasant cacophony with sinister folk ballads sung by choristers in the village square. Her savvy culinary nose was teased by a fluttering of beckoning scents from the bustling stalls and smoky braziers of the Market Hall. Isa was also pleased to see so many students and faculty her own age. It was encouraging to know that even in one's senior years, the desire to do in another can still beat strongly in the human heart. It seemed a most civilized community.

"And who's that handsome man?" Isabel asked, indicating a teacher sprawled on the grass in a cable-knit sweater already engaging some students in a spirited discussion.

"That's Matías Graves," pronounced Dean Harrow, who'd just arrived on foot. "He makes the case that Don Quixote was a cunning murderer and Cervantes was the inventor of the insanity defense." He offered his hand to Isabel. "Mrs. Lindley, a very warm welcome to you. And Gemma, sublime to have you back in our fold! Vesta Thripper and Father Pugh look forward to meeting you after lunch to discuss your new counseling position. And you might like to greet our Hedge House resident advisor and newest science instructor . . ."

Gemma looked for the always welcoming face of Champo Nanda. But where she expected to see two men, there was only one. He had his back to her and was chatting with Coach Alwyn Tarcott. "Where's Champo Nanda?" she asked.

"Oh, he's moved up to our newly created Automaton Department. No, our new Hedge House RA is also our new adjunct science professor, holding down two posts just as you'll be doing. Our first practical physics professor ever, cunning as the devil but a good sort!" He tapped the man on the shoulder. "My dear fellow, ignore Tarcott for one blessed moment and turn around if you have any idea what's good for you."

The man did as requested, and it would be impossible to say which of the two new faculty members was the more surprised or overjoyed.

"Cliff!!!" Gemma was never happier to shout a name, and she gripped his arms to confirm his existence. "Can it be true? I . . . I thought you died!"

"Yes, but I'm much better now," he assured her. "And you, Gemma, I'd have thought you'd have been long gone—"

"*Ach-y-fi!*" snapped Coach Tarcott. "You can't be standing around, Gem, you're leading PE in ten minutes. Come along now!" He trotted off, indicating Gemma should follow.

"One of my new bosses," said Gemma under her breath. "I'm sure there'll be days when I'll want to just kill him."

Cliff registered horror. "Perish the thought!"

The dean cleared his throat. "With Miss Lindley due on the playing field, I suggest Constance and I escort Isabel to her new digs to settle in." With a happy wave to Gemma, Isabel strolled off with Dean Harrow and Constance down the scenic path to Bramble Cottage.

A voice bellowed Cliff's name and he saw Cubby Terhune trotting toward him. "Cubby's *still* here?" groaned Cliff. "God help me, I suppose I'm his advisor now!" He took Gemma's hands. "Listen, lunch at Jade Flower Spring, *my* treat this time . . . say, noon? So much to talk about." She nodded, brushed his cheek with a graze of a kiss, and sprinted off to catch up with Tarcott.

Cliff watched, as men have watched for centuries, to see if Gemma would give him a backward glance. She did, a long look over her shoulder, before she fell in stride with the coach.

Behind Cubby, he saw that an impromptu greeting committee was forming across the village green and heading his way: Father Pugh in white clerical garb and matching panama hat accompanying Vesta Thripper in a haute couture business suit that meant serious business for someone, and Champo Nanda walking his way while simultaneously using his feet to prevent a Burmese chinlone ball from touching the ground. June Felsblock and Doc Pinckney were a startling sight in bone-white tennis togs so capacious the two could be a twin-masted sailboat, joined by a welcoming (for once) Simeon Sampson, jaunty as ever and linked in arms with Audrey Jäeger, radiant and no longer mournful in the slightest. They were all his fellow staff now . . . as were, he considered, the reflective Matías Graves, Girard Tissier with his memorable last meals, the always-game Coach Tarcott . . . not to overlook his supportive mentor, Dean Harbinger Harrow.

And Gemma, of course.

A tap on his shoulder turned him round to see Sergeant Stedge and Captain Dobson (the latter in his usual hat but wearing a grin he may not have tried on before), a duo who'd won him a second chance to rid the world of Fiedler, conveyed the dean's offer of a permanent post (with opportunities for advancement), and brought him back to McMasters a second time.

From his first day on campus, he'd longed to know the location of the conservatory, if not a county or country, then at least a latitude or continent.

Now, at last, Cliff knew precisely where he was.

He was home.

Postscript

From the Desk of Dean Harbinger Harrow

While this volume was still in its earliest stages of development, I was delighted to receive confirmation that a vaunted publishing house had agreed to make it available in the form before you now, for a readership extending well beyond the confines of our exclusive conservatory. I am hopeful that, in traveling through this tome, you have become fluent enough with McMasters methodology and philosophy to assist you in your own crucial if independent efforts. And while this volume has focused primarily on deletions related to one's employer, I'm confident the principles of McMasters will now better inform your own endevour, that being an undertaking which will hopefully result in . . . undertaking.

The commonalities in the case histories contained herein are surely as useful to note as the divergences.

It will hardly surprise you, dear aspirant, that some of my associates on the board are not as pleased as I am that our clandestine conservatory has at long last "gone public," if only within the pages of this volume. And though I think I've ably camouflaged the location of McMasters, there are those—such as Assistant Dean Erma Daimler—who have maintained that, merely by admitting of the school's existence, I have gone too far and placed graduates, past and future, in jeopardy. Unfortunately, the die (pun intended) is cast. The publishing contract was signed well before this day and the manuscript has been delivered, lacking only this postscript, which my trustworthy associate Dilys Enwright will shortly dispatch to my editor.

However: I am gratified to say that these naysayers have recently come to accept my decision. As it happens, I will be laying down my pen momentarily to descend from my office, with Sergeant Stedge,

Coach Tarcott, and the aforementioned Erma Daimler as my honour guard, to view a bust created in my honour and likeness, which will take its place in the boardroom alongside the busts of past deans, including the man who began it all, founder and chancellor Guy McMaster. Oddly, the ceremony is to be held in Mr. Koniec's kiln room, the simple explanation for this being that the artist will be ceremonially removing the bust from the powerful oven, where I'm told its many layers of glaze will have now been baked to a perfect sheen. Since the bust was created solely from a photograph, I look forward to meeting the sculptor of my likeness, or as Mr. Koniec so amusingly put it in his inexpert English, "We wish you to meet your maker."

I shall return to this desk after the ceremony to commence work this very evening on one of the next volumes in this series, perhaps related to mates, relatives, attorneys, former fast friends, or the oft-requested *Murder Those Cruel to You in Adolescence*, no matter what initial objections were voiced from the board. I give full marks to my associate Erma Daimler for reversing her objections with a gracious and charming paraphrase of Shakespeare's eighteenth sonnet, saying, "Harrow, these volumes of yours will continue so long as you can breathe and your eyes can see!" For what more generous a turnabout could I ask?

Ah, and here is my honour guard now! I shall conclude this postscript after I've been "handed my head" (ha-ha!). However, let me say to *you*, faithful reader whose patience I've so deeply appreciated across these pages, that if I have accomplished nothing more than to have introduced you to the bas

[*The text ends here. —Ed.*]

♠

Rupert Holmes has received two Edgar Awards from the Mystery Writers of America and multiple Tony® and Drama Desk Awards for his Broadway mystery musicals, including the book of *Curtains* and his sole creation, the Tony® Award–winning Best Musical *The Mystery of Edwin Drood*. His first novel, *Where the Truth Lies*, was nominated for a Nero Wolfe Award for Best American Mystery Novel, was a *Booklist* Top Ten Debut Novel, and became a motion picture starring Colin Firth and Kevin Bacon. His second novel, *Swing*, was the first novel with its own original, clue-bearing musical score. He has adapted Agatha Christie, John Grisham, and R.L. Stine for the Broadway and international stage. His short stories have been anthologized in such collections as *Best American Mystery Stories, Christmas at the Mysterious Bookshop, A Merry Band of Murderers*, and *On a Raven's Wing*. Some of Holmes's earliest story-songs were published in *Ellery Queen's Mystery Magazine*, and he is also the writer of several *Billboard* Top 10 hits, including his #1 multi-platinum classic with a memorable twist ending: "Escape (The Pina Colada Song)."

Anna Louizos has designed eighteen Broadway productions and received three nominations for the Tony Award in scenic design, which include *In the Heights, Rodgers and Hammerstein's Cinderella, Avenue Q, School of Rock, White Christmas, Curtains*, and *The Mystery of Edwin Drood*, the latter two having been written by Rupert Holmes. Rendering this new world created by Rupert has been an extraordinary gift for this stage designer who loves to draw.

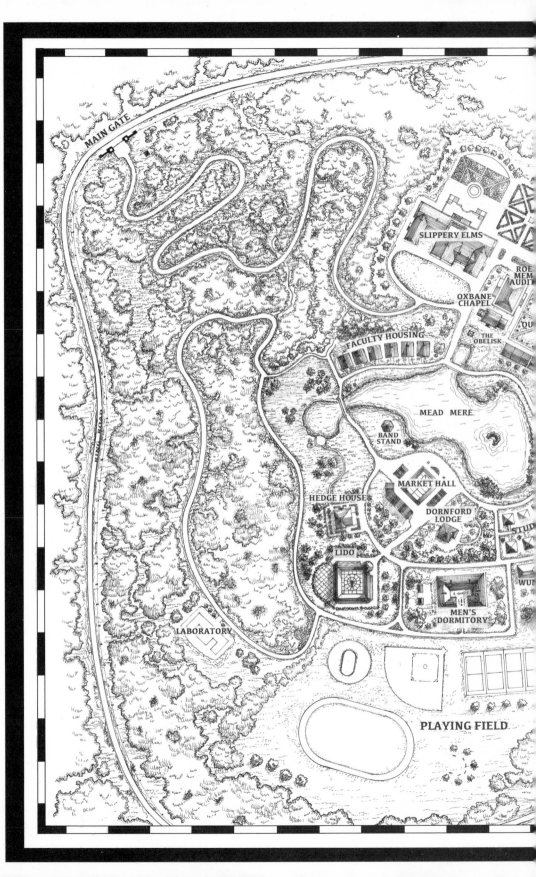